SAVING PAULO

Saving Paulo

David J. Walker

FIVE STAR
A part of Gale, Cengage Learning

GALE
CENGAGE Learning™

Detroit • New York • San Francisco • New Haven, Conn • Waterville, Maine • London

GALE
CENGAGE Learning™

Set in 11 pt. Plantin.
Printed on permanent paper.

LIBRARY OF CONGRESS CATALOGING-IN-PUBLICATION DATA

Walker, David J., 1939–
    Saving Paulo / David J. Walker. — 1st ed.
        p. cm.
    ISBN-13: 978-1-59414-655-8 (hardcover : alk. paper)
    ISBN-10: 1-59414-655-1 (hardcover : alk. paper)
    1. Guardian and ward—Fiction. 2. Chicago (Ill.)—Fiction. I. Title.
PS3573.A4253313S28 2008
813'.54—dc22   2008003286

First Edition. First Printing: June 2008.

Published in 2008 in conjunction with Tekno Books and Ed Gorman.

Printed in the United States of America
1 2 3 4 5 6 7 12 11 10 09 08

To Ellen

ACKNOWLEDGMENTS

This is a work of fiction, and the persons, places, and organizations it depicts are imaginary or are used fictitiously. On the other hand, what *is* real is the author's gratitude to the following actual persons: Carol Padron, RN, for a bit of pharmacological advice; Jim Jackson, for some telecommunications info; Stacy Sheard, for generously sharing her experience and expertise as an ex-military Blackhawk pilot; John Robert Schmitz and Fernanda Farinha for help with Portuguese; Dave Case, for gun stuff; Danielle Egan-Miller and her staff, for constant encouragement and assistance; and the Red Herrings, for chocolate-coated criticism.

★ ★ ★ ★ ★

PART I
CROSSING OVER

★ ★ ★ ★ ★

Lieutenant Colonel Bill Grayson, United States Army, Special Operations Forces, woke up in near-total darkness and, like always, drenched in sweat.

You'd think, growing up poor and black in a red clay town in Alabama, he'd be used to heat. But not this. By noon it would feel like a hundred degrees. And humid. The wood and mud walls of the hut so slick the goddamn two-inch roaches would be having trouble getting traction. They'd climb up, then slip and fall on their backs on the floor, waving their legs in a panic till they could flip themselves over. Then try again. Persistent little bastards, although why they wanted to climb the walls was beyond him. Nothing up there but those huge spiders . . . just hanging there . . . waiting.

Beautiful Brazil. A tropical paradise. Well, maybe so, if you were on leave in Rio and slept until noon in an air-conditioned hotel room and spent the rest of the day surrounded by brown-skinned, high-assed ladies, strutting the beaches in their thongs. The ones who went topless, he'd heard, were the best bet to be whores, and the whores were plentiful in Rio and—like everyone else in Brazil—they were never, ever, in a hurry. That's what he'd heard, and . . .

But dammit, he was two thousand miles from Rio, up in the Amazon jungle. He had to stay focused, stay smart, keep his mind on how to get out of here, away from the suffocating heat and the bugs and the stink of shit that never went away. And on how to get these three scared DEA guys out with him.

Himself, he was more frustrated than scared. He'd volunteered for this gig, willingly crossed over the border from Colombia into Brazil, when he could have turned thumbs down. Hell, this many years in, he could be somewhere stateside, pushing papers, kissing ass, and playing . . . what? Golf? Tennis? Some damn way to pass the time till he died.

Down among the slash pine and wire grass where he came from the mindless occupations of choice were drinking, gambling, and lying to your mama—and later, your woman—about looking for a job, when there never were any jobs. And then you got old and sat all day on a bench under the scrub oak by the gas station, drinking wine and playing chess.

Grayson, though, was Special Op. Always go where the action—

"Silencio!" The door swung open and sunlight poured in so bright it hurt his eyes. It was that short skinny prick of a guard, with the gold front tooth. The guy loved to holler out commands and wave his ancient little Ingram M11 around.

Grayson stood up. His Portuguese was pretty bad, so mostly he didn't even know what the little shit was saying.

"Silencio!" Gold Tooth yelled again. Like there'd been anyone talking.

The DEA guys' Portuguese was even worse than Grayson's. The three of them sat wide-eyed on the floor with their backs against the wall. Gold Tooth spat on the floor and spoke again, gesturing with the assault rifle. Grayson knew he'd been ordered to sit down with them.

This seemed as good a time as any, though, to test the boundaries, to look for an opening, a weakness. Or maybe the fucking heat had softened his brain. Anyway, Grayson stayed on his feet, crossing his arms and leaning back against the wall. Gold Tooth grinned, then turned and called out through the open door. When he looked back at Grayson he shook his head, as though to say: "Not a good time, asshole."

Gold Tooth stepped to the side and another man appeared in the doorway, a man Grayson had seen just once before, the day they were brought here. He was fiftyish, tall, overweight, and too handsome—almost pretty. Jet black hair fell down to his collar under a wide-brimmed cowboy hat. His skin was almost as brown as Grayson's and his light-blue uniform shirt was tight on him. In a holster near his right hand hung a .45 automatic, and he had a police baton as long and thick as a baseball bat clutched in his huge fist. He was smiling.

Grayson spread his hands, palms facing out in surrender, and slid down the wall onto his haunches. The man kept coming, though, his eyes bright with amusement and cruelty combined. Grayson sat with his hands clasped around his shins. He lowered his head and closed his eyes.

The baton struck just once . . . whop! *. . . on the side of his left knee, and he heard, and felt, a snap inside the joint. He managed to stay absolutely silent through the searing pain, but wondered if he'd ever walk a straight line again.*

Worse than the physical pain, though, was the knowledge that he'd been so stupid, that he'd brought this on himself.

"I will return," the man said, "and we will have another talk."

ONE

On the Friday after Labor Day, Charlie Long gave away his last pack of Marlboros, half full, to the shy mail clerk with the long blonde hair and the big boobs, gave up his bullshit job with the city of Chicago's legal department, and walked out into the sunshine at high noon.

Okay, so maybe "gave up" his job wasn't it, exactly. He got booted. But it was time, anyway. Three months of running errands for low-end city lawyers and taking crap from a supervisor who divided his time between picking on people too scared to speak up and talking on the phone to his bookie, was two and a half months too long. "Attitude," Cronin said when he pink-slipped him. "Oh, and false time cards, too," he added.

The time cards part was bogus. But the attitude part? What happened was Charlie had raised hell with Cronin about the guy constantly asking the mail clerk if her boobs were implants. It made her cry. Cronin was a bully, and Charlie had a thing about bullies. He told the guy to stop being such an ignorant asshole . . . and maybe said a few too many other things.

So out on the street he loosened his tie, unbuttoned his collar, and headed for the Billy Goat Tavern . . . and lunch with Sal, the one person he didn't want to talk to right now. But get it over with. Face-to-face. Man-to-man. Then he'd feel better.

The Loop was crowded, the temperature in the seventies. Too warm, really, for a corduroy sport coat, but it was the only sport coat he owned. He reached for his smokes and remembered

13

he'd just given them up. For good this time. His old man dead nineteen years—no, twenty next week—from lung cancer.

Inside the Billy Goat it smelled like beer and cigarette smoke—so much for keeping his lungs clean—and it was noisy as hell. The lunch crowd was lined up along the right wall of the big open room to order their burgers or whatever from the grill in the back. The jukebox blasting out something by one of those old-time sixties black groups: *DOO-wah, doowah, doowah . . . DOO-wah, doowah, doowah . . .* Great lyrics. The TV above the bar along the left wall was on, but nobody watching and the sound down too low to hear.

The line moved fast and the tables were filling up. A hundred people, maybe. Young crowd. Guys outnumbering chicks, like five to one. Loading up on beer to jumpstart their weekend. Some in those colored jackets that said they worked at one of the markets—commodities or whatever. Cocky and thinking it was cool, playing with other people's money. Plenty of tradesmen, too, with all that new construction going up all over. Most of the pinstriped crowd stayed away from here.

Charlie picked up his two jumbo dogs and his fries and went over to the table by the wall where Sal was, right next to the hall back to the washrooms. Sal was his cousin, and his real name was Eugenio Salvatore Pacelli. Fourth generation from the old neighborhood, six years older than Charlie.

"What?" Sal said. "You forget your Pepsi?"

"Fuck, no." Charlie set his lunch on the table and went to the bar for a couple of Bud Lights.

"Hey!" Sal called. "You nuts, or what?"

Charlie didn't answer. He'd called and asked Sal to meet him here for lunch, even if it was Friday. They came here once a week, but always on Tuesday. Sal was always here ahead of him, always at the same table. Tall, dark, thick black hair. Suit and tie, of course. People said him and Sal looked a lot alike, except

Sal was, like, six-one, and Charlie an inch or two taller. Thing is, Sal had a way about him. Smooth. Like a connected guy on the way up. Which he could've been, since his family was in the business. But he wasn't. Not really. Otherwise he wouldn't be practicing law. Or at least getting started with it. He'd spent a few years defending tort cases for the CTA—people falling down in front of a bus or tripping on the L steps—and now he was out on his own. Nothing big yet. Getting started.

Anyway, heading back with two cool, slippery Bud Lights, Charlie thought again how his cousin had the look, for sure, even if he wasn't in the life. Hardly at all. And way less since he got married.

"I said are you crazy or what?" Sal said. "I get you a friggin' job with the city and—" He stopped and Charlie could tell he was trying to calm down. "They smell brew on your breath, Charlie, you're outta there. Only hanging on by a thread, anyway, what I hear."

"Yeah, well, they cut the fucking thread." This was the bad part, which is why he did it right off. Sal was way more than just a cousin. Your old man checks out when you're six years old, you need a man to look up to, and for him the man was Sal. "Told me to leave at noon. Said they'd mail my check."

"Shit." That's all Sal said. Charlie knew he wanted to say a lot more, but they both just ate in silence, Charlie not even tasting the dogs. Finally, halfway through his second cheeseburger, Sal looked up at him. "How you gonna pay for those college courses, then, so you can get into law school? You got potential, man. You promised me . . . this time you'd follow through."

"Hey, I said I'd go and I'm going, you know? Anyway, the fall semester's already paid for." They were night classes and it was Sal who'd paid, and now Charlie wished to God he hadn't.

"But no tuition help from the city? How you gonna *keep* paying?"

"I'll just have to . . . you know . . . get a job."

Sal leaned across toward him. "You *had* a job, Charlie. You *had* a goddamn job." Then, without another word, he stood up and walked to the front door of the Billy Goat, and out.

So that was it. Charlie'd gotten it over with. Face-to-face. Man-to-man. And now he felt worse.

He was thinking he should go after Sal. Apologize or something. Instead, he went for a third Bud Light and tipped it up and let the cool liquid slide down his throat. He'd let Sal down. But Jesus, three months of Bates-stamping bullshit pieces of paper in the lower right hand corner with *000 001, 000 002,* up to God knows—

Hey, what's this?

What got his attention was this black guy—nice enough look-ing, in a suit and tie—pulling a little boy along by the hand, weaving among the crowded tables, coming his way. Like in a hurry. It just seemed strange. He'd never seen a kid in this place before. And then the look on the boy's face. Charlie thought first maybe he just needed to go to the bathroom real bad. But no way. This kid was scared.

Then they were right beside him, pausing at the entrance to the hall, the man turning and scanning the noisy, crowded room. The boy, though, staring straight at Charlie. Looked like a mix of different races. Brown skin. Black hair more curly than kinky. Thin black jacket, ragged and dirty. Small kid. Maybe six years old? Seven? Charlie was no judge. But it was the eyes that held him. Big brown eyes with flecks of green—and full of tears. Then the man moved on, pulling the boy down the hall.

What he'd seen in the kid's eyes was fear, all right. But worse than that. Like he knew there was no way out. Like a dog's eyes when it scrunches down and looks up and knows it's gonna be whipped.

It wasn't the black guy who scared the kid, because he went with him easily down the hall. Charlie drained the last of his third beer and leaned out sideways to watch. They went past the door to the kitchen on the right, toward a rear exit at the end. But the black guy stopped short and pushed open the door to one of the two restrooms on the left. The first one. The women's, for chrissake. He shoved the boy inside and then ran for the exit. He was pushing through to the outside, and—

"Move!" Some guy slammed into Charlie's arm from behind and the Bud Light bottle went flying as the guy ran past.

"Hey!" Charlie said. *"Asshole."*

The guy glanced back. A big flat-faced ugly mope in a leather jacket, short black hair combed forward, looked like one of those immigrants. A thug. A Russian gangster. Charlie'd bet his life on it.

The mope turned away and kept going, not yelling like some honest guy would if he wanted someone to stop. But no question, either, that he was after the black guy and the boy. He disappeared out the exit.

Charlie got up and followed. He didn't know why, really. None of his business. But that look in the kid's eyes, he just couldn't stop himself from going to see what was happening. Just as he reached the exit, though, the door flew open and a different man came backing in, pulling a hand truck stacked high with boxes of hamburger buns. Charlie let the man through, then went out into the alley. The rear end of the bread truck was right there, the truck facing east, to the left. Charlie turned that way, too.

The mope in the leather jacket had caught up with the black guy. Except there were two thugs now. One must have already been in the alley. Charlie shrank back inside, peeking out just enough to see.

They had the black guy up against the wall, maybe ten yards

ahead of the truck. The leather jacket working him over with a goddamn sap. *Whap* to one side of his head. *Whap* to the other. Fucking professional. The second thug, older, leaning in talking to the guy. Nothing Charlie could do, and why should he? *Whap* again, and the guy finally crumples and sags to the concrete. He's like sitting against the wall. *Shit.* Charlie stepped out to do . . . *something.*

The man who'd been talking suddenly had a gun in his hand, with an extra long barrel. He leaned down and shot the black guy, once. Right down through the top of his skull, and the shot not very loud. Charlie stood there, paralyzed, and then—Christ almighty—the two thugs were looking right at him!

He spun around and ran back inside and down the hall. And there was the boy. Not stopping, Charlie lifted the kid up off his feet and kept going with him.

Two

In the Billy Goat nothing was changed. Jukebox still blaring, Springsteen now, making it hard to hear. TV still on and nobody watching. Charlie started toward the front entrance, the kid in his arms, then stopped and looked around. *Jesus, what am I doing?* He stood there surrounded by people, and no one paying any attention. The kid wasn't saying anything, wasn't struggling. Charlie put him down and right away the kid grabbed hold of his hand. Just then the mope in the leather jacket appeared in the doorway to the hall. He stopped right there, though, obviously looking past Charlie at something, and not sure himself what to do.

Charlie turned again toward the front entrance and spotted two uniformed cops on their way out the door with coffee. "Hey," he called, but no way could they hear. He started after them, but the kid yanked hard on his hand and he looked down. The kid stared up at him and opened his mouth to say something, but clamped it back shut. He struggled to pull Charlie away from the door, his eyes wide with fear again. He seemed as scared of the cops as he was of the bad guys.

Charlie looked around, expecting to see the goon coming across the crowded room toward him. But he was gone. Must have thought Charlie was heading for the cops—which he should be, for chrissake. He turned back and, damn, the cops were gone, too. He pulled the kid toward the entrance, and through the window saw the cops already getting into a squad car.

"You win, kid," he said, and pointed out the window. The kid looked out as the car pulled away, then looked back toward the hallway, and finally pulled on Charlie again, this time *toward* the front door. "Uh-uh," Charlie said, "that's the way the bad guys think we'll go. So we'll go the way they *don't* think."

When they got to the hall the bread man was hustling out the rear exit with two empty hand trucks, pushing one, pulling the other. Charlie looked down and saw the kid looking back at him again, still not saying anything, but asking questions with his eyes: *Am I safe now? Is everything gonna be okay?*

Charlie couldn't help nodding and squeezing the kid's hand, like saying he was safe and everything was gonna be okay, and all the time wondering what the hell he was doing, anyway.

At the end of the hall, he held the kid behind him and looked out into the alley in time to see the bread man, in a big hurry, yank down the overhead door of his truck with one of those straps, then run around and climb into the cab. The door hit the bottom, then bounced back again and ended up halfway open. The guy was running late, or in a rush because it was Friday. The truck's engine roared to life, the driver revving it up and honking the damn horn right away. But he couldn't go anywhere in that narrow alley, not till that silver BMW in front of him got out of the way.

The Beemer hadn't been there before. Or had it? And Jesus, the black guy's body. Where was it? The trunk of the Beemer?

To the right the alley was empty clear to Wacker Drive, but that was a pretty long way for the truck to back up. Charlie squinted. There was a man down there by Wacker. He was a big man and Charlie didn't like the way he just stood there with his arms crossed . . . facing this way. The back exit seemed a bad choice after all.

The truck driver kept goosing the engine and hitting the horn, and Charlie suddenly thought maybe there was a phone in the kitchen he could use to call 911. He turned to try that . . . just in time to see the thug in the leather jacket step into the space at the far end of the hall. Charlie grabbed the kid up and carried him into the alley, where the Beemer was just now pulling away. The bread truck ground into gear and lurched after it, and Charlie ran and caught up with the truck and heaved the kid up and inside it.

Still running, he glanced back and saw the leather jacket burst out the door and pause for a second to yell at the guy way down the alley. Charlie turned back to jump in the truck himself, but it had picked up speed and was pulling away. *Damn!* He ran, but there was no way he'd catch it. He almost gave up then, except there was the kid, on his knees between the bread tray racks, stretching two hands out to him. Charlie ran faster, but was still losing ground.

At the end of the alley, though, the truck had to stop for traffic. Charlie caught it in time, scrambling and flinging himself just inside. It lurched forward again and turned sharply into traffic and almost threw him back out onto the concrete, but he grabbed hold of one of the metal racks and pulled himself farther in. When he got his balance he pulled the overhead door farther down, leaving it open just enough so if he got down low he could still see out. He did that, and saw the son of a bitch in the leather coat come out of the alley and stare at the truck as it pulled away.

They went north on Franklin across Washington, then turned left at Randolph. All the while the kid kept grabbing at him like he was hysterical or something, but not saying one damn word.

"It's okay," Charlie said. "Everything's gonna be fine, all right?" Wishing he believed that.

★ ★ ★ ★ ★

The truck smelled like bread and exhaust fumes, and was lined with racks for bread trays. The body was closed off from the cab so they couldn't get to or even see the driver—and he couldn't see them. They went a few blocks west, Charlie and the kid hanging on as the truck bounced along, stopping and starting, weaving through traffic. The boy was still silent and that surprised Charlie because he'd have been screaming and crying like hell if it had been him. They turned left—south—going too fast, and then suddenly screeched to a stop. Charlie raised the door. They were on the street in front of a little lunch place on a busy stretch of Halsted that was slowly recovering from years and years of poverty and sleaze.

Charlie was out and lifting the boy down by the time the driver got to the back of the truck. "Hey," the driver said, "what—"

"Sorry. This kid *loves* to climb into stuff." He grabbed the kid's hand and pulled him away without looking back, and before the bread man could say anything else.

They headed south on Halsted toward Greektown, the kid holding his hand and having to run to keep up and still not saying anything. When they were almost to the end of the next block Charlie looked back. *Damn!*

The silver Beemer was pulling up alongside the bread truck and the guy in the leather coat jumped out and ran into the diner, where the delivery guy was. Charlie yanked the kid into the nearest doorway, set in a few feet from the sidewalk. There were two doors, side by side, and he pushed open the one on the right and pulled the kid in.

"Hey, get outta here!" It was a fat lady with frizzy blonde hair, behind a high counter to the right just inside the door. "Get the goddamn kid outta here, creepo."

Charlie looked around. Damn, an adult bookstore. "Oh," he

said. "Sorry."

"Yeah, I bet you are," the fat lady said, and he pulled the kid back outside and then pushed him in through the other door.

THREE

Charlie stood with the kid in a plain little room with a couple of chairs and a table with a lamp. No one else there. It looked like a waiting room for a dentist or something, except the place reeked of sweet incense like he hadn't smelled since his old man's funeral. Three huge spider plants, like one his ma used to have in the kitchen, hung in the storefront window and covered up a lot of it. Heavy purple drapes blocked off the rear of the place. There was no sign painted on the window, but there was a square piece of cardboard hanging by a string from one of those little suction cup hook things stuck to the inside of the glass door they'd come in by. Printed in big letters on the cardboard, on the side facing in, was the word *CLOSED*.

The bread guy had seen which direction he and the kid went and he'd tell the goon, for sure, and the fucking Beemer would come creeping along any minute. He turned the sign around, and locked the door with the turn bolt under the knob. The side of the card that faced in now said *READER & ADVISER*.

"Okay, little guy, let's . . ." He spun around. Where the hell did he go?

Charlie pushed through the purple drapes and found the kid standing, wide-eyed, in another small room, this one lit only by some sort of dim blue lamp that made the stars and the weird-looking shapes and figures stuck to the side walls and the draperies glow in the near-darkness. Two wooden chairs faced each other across a little round table. The table was covered with a white cloth that hung almost to the floor, and in the center—on a base that looked like the bottom half of a human skull—was a goddamn crystal ball, for chrissake.

The kid stretched out his hand toward the glass ball, but Charlie yanked him back. "Don't touch anything," he said. "We don't—"

He heard a noise. A second set of purple drapes blocked off the area beyond where they stood, and the sound came from there. "Hey," Charlie called, "anyone here?" The kid grabbed his hand again.

There was silence for a few seconds, and then a woman's voice said, "One moment, please."

She had just enough of an accent to make *please* sound almost like *police*. The kid must have heard *police*, too, because right away he started pulling away, like when he saw the cops at the Billy Goat. Charlie looked down and saw the fear back in the kid's eyes and without even thinking he lifted the little guy off his feet and hoisted him up on his shoulders. He seemed small for whatever age he was, but was still pretty big to ride on someone's shoulders. But then, Charlie was big, too. He'd been recruited as a defensive end at Michigan State, but got off on the wrong foot . . . like a run-in with one of the coaches and then downhill from there.

He was just about to call out again when the woman slipped through the curtains from the rear of the place. She was short and a little stooped over, and wore a long blue dress that almost hit the floor and had stars and figures on it like the ones that glowed on the walls. With her hands hidden somewhere inside the dress and her hair tucked up under a matching blue scarf thing, about all you could see of her was her face. It was a round face—but not chubby—with a kind of flat nose, tanned like she'd been out in the sun all her life. With lines and wrinkles around her eyes and mouth, she looked serious, but not mean or angry.

She stood and stared at the kid. She was old, maybe even old enough to be Charlie's grandmother—and something about her made him nervous. "Didn't you hear us come in?" he asked, his voice louder than he meant it to be.

She turned then, and looked right at him, and that's when he first noticed her eyes. The pupils were dark blue, and the whites were very white, not like most old people he knew. She kept staring right at him, making him feel like . . . well, like he should button his collar and straighten up his tie. "I heard you," she said.

"Yeah, well, y' know . . . how come you didn't come out? We coulda been robbing the place."

"I saw the boy," she said, "and you. A frightened child, and a man helping him. I saw nothing to make me—"

Bam, bam, bam, bam! Someone banged on the front door like a maniac, and Charlie didn't need to look. He knew who it was.

Bam, bam, bam!

"There a back door here?" he asked. "We gotta—"

"Remain where you are." The old woman was looking up toward the ceiling and Charlie looked up too. There were mirrors up there and one of them showed the guy in the leather jacket hammering on the door. "You are safe here," she said.

"Yeah, right." Charlie pulled the kid toward the curtains to look for a back door, but the woman moved in front of him faster than he thought she could. She laid a small hand on his arm and he stopped. The pounding on the door got even louder and now the guy was yelling something, too.

"The boy is in danger," the woman said, "and he may be safer here for now than in the alley." She pointed upward. "You see in the mirror, but the man does not see you. I will make him go away."

"Okay," he said. He had a sense, somehow, that she might really get rid of the guy. Besides, she was right. Someone could be out there in the alley, too.

The pounding never stopped. There was a wooden cane hanging over the back of one of the chairs and she took it and then, bent way over and limping like she could barely make it, she went through the curtains to the front door.

"I am coming," she called. "I am coming."

FOUR

Charlie stood behind the kid with his hands on the kid's shoulders and they both looked up in the mirror and watched the old lady talking through the locked door. The goon trying to act friendly and telling her—with a goddamn Russian accent—to open the door. Her saying no, she was sick and he should come back next week if he wanted a reading.

"I am looking for little boy," he said. "Is emergency."

He said the boy had been kidnapped by a man in brown pants and a sport coat. She said yes, of course, she'd been watering her lovely spider plants and saw the two of them pass by her window. She pointed in the direction Charlie and the boy had been going and Charlie knew if she'd have pointed the other way the goon would have known she was lying.

"I would help you," she said, "but I am a sick old woman, and—" She stopped. "Ah, but *here.*" To Charlie's surprise, she hung the cane over her wrist and pulled a cell phone out of her dress. "I will call nine-one-one. The police will help you." She poised a crooked forefinger over the phone and the bastard said to forget it . . . and left.

When she came back through the curtains the kid ran over and wrapped his arms around her waist and hugged her. He didn't say a word, but he was thanking her, that much was clear.

"No, no, no," she said, prying the kid's arms loose. "You will break these poor bones." She frowned at the kid, trying to look mad when Charlie—and probably the kid, too—knew better. Then, looking at Charlie, "Come with me. This boy is hungry. And tired. He must eat, and rest."

Charlie followed her through the curtains into a room which was mostly a kitchen, because there was a stove and a sink and a refrigerator and cabinets. Plus a table and four chairs. Everything looked like the damn 1950s or something, except for a little portable TV and a reclining chair that were maybe only twenty years old. If everything hadn't been so ancient, it would have looked like a furniture showroom. So clean, and no stuff lying around. One faded-out picture in a cardboard frame on top of the TV, of a little boy, like a first-grade school picture. No other pictures anywhere, and no little statue things like his ma had all over the house.

"You live here?" Charlie said, thinking it was none of his business.

"For now," she said. She pointed to the right. "Through there is the door to the alley. And over there," she pointed to two doors on the other side of the room, by the TV, "the sleeping closet and the bathroom. It is enough."

The kid gave a little cough. He was shifting his weight from side to side.

"Peepee?" the old lady said.

The kid nodded and she pointed to the bathroom and he ran over and opened the door and went in. Charlie heard the toilet seat slam up. He went over and closed the bathroom door and came back.

"You may sit down," she said, and Charlie did. "You have already eaten, but I will make the boy some lunch." She turned the fire on under a teakettle on the stove. "He does not speak?"

"Not so far. I think maybe something's wrong with him. How do you know I already ate lunch?"

"Because you did not have the look of hunger when I spoke

of feeding the boy."

"And that other stuff. Like, how'd you know the kid was scared, and in danger? And which way we were headed on the sidewalk? And how do you know I didn't kidnap the kid like the guy said?"

"What is your name?" she said.

"Charlie. Charlie Long. But—"

"My name is Zorina. I have the gift of seeing. Not entirely magical, but a gift nevertheless. That the boy is frightened anyone could see. That you were frightened for him, and helping him, were clear at least to me." She was slicing bread beside the sink and twisted around to look at him. "A frightened child and his angel seek refuge behind a locked door, and a man bangs wildly on that door. Is such a child not in danger?" She opened her refrigerator and reached inside. "The man at the door was not a good man. This I saw. And two more men in a gray car on the street, facing to the right. So they came from the left. So you came from the left. A guess, of course, but . . . was I not correct?"

"You were, but—"

The bathroom door opened and the kid came out. He walked over in silence and showed them his hands, first the palms, then the backs. Charlie realized he was showing them he'd washed his hands.

"Have a seat," Charlie said, pointing to the chair beside him. "Grub time." The kid sat down and immediately laid his head on his arms on the table and closed his eyes.

"Wait, child." The old lady who called herself Zorina lifted the kid's head gently and set his lunch in front of him. Bread, cheese, grapes, a cup of hot tea. Hot tea for Charlie, too. "Eat first, child," she said. "Then you will sleep."

Ten minutes later the kid was out cold under a blanket on the cot in Zorina's "sleeping closet," and Zorina and Charlie sat facing each other across the table. The kid had marked a sign of the cross on himself before he ate, but hadn't said one word. Afterward he was so sleepy that Charlie had had to carry him in and lay him on the cot.

Now he and the old lady were talking. He didn't like tea, really, but drank it to be doing something with his hands. He wasn't exactly comfortable with the direction the conversation was going.

"But you don't really *know*," he said, "that the guy at the door wasn't on the kid's side. You don't really *know* that he's the bad guy and I'm the good guy, that I didn't snatch the kid like he said."

"Forgive me, Charlie Long," she said. "Forgive me, but I know these things. Just as I know that you don't care for tea. And as I know that my calling you an 'angel' a few moments ago disturbed you."

"Yeah. What's that—I mean, why the 'angel' business? And besides, call me just Charlie."

" 'Angel' is merely a word. Is not an angel someone sent to help a person who is in need?"

"I don't know. But I know I wasn't *sent*. I just happened to be having lunch at the Billy Goat when all this started. That's nothing new. I been there every Tuesday for three months."

Zorina leaned forward. "Every Tuesday?"

"Yeah, me and Sal. Sal's my cousin."

"But this is not Tuesday."

"I know, but . . . well . . . something happened and I told Sal to meet me there today." *Jesus, why was he even fucking telling her this?*

"At this Billy Goat place," she said. "On Friday. And that's when you saw the frightened boy?" When he nodded, she said, "So then, where is Sal?"

31

"What? Oh, he left before . . . before I saw the kid. He was pissed off when I told him I just got fired. I mean, it was him got me the job and I wanted him to hear the news from me, so I met him for lunch, and he got mad at me and walked out. Left half a cheeseburger."

"So it happens that today you lose your job in the morning. You arrange to meet with Sal. You are having lunch. But Sal walks out and leaves you there alone. Leaves you at the Billy Goat, today, where you never are on Friday, and the little boy comes in."

"He didn't just 'come in.' He—Wait a minute. I think I know where you're going with this. But no one *sent* me. It was just a coincidence. I mean the kid got my attention and I was curious and I went to see what was going on. That's all."

"And the restaurant, was it crowded at lunchtime?"

"Of course it was. Packed."

"And who else saw all this that was going on? Besides you?"

"I don't think—Look, it was just a coincidence."

The old lady leaned back in her chair. "I understand. A mere coincidence. Such things can happen, perhaps, and this is what you choose to believe." She leaned in toward him again. "What is important is what you are going to do now. Have you thought of that?"

"Not really." There'd been no time to think. So he thought now, or tried to, while she just sat and stared at him. "As soon as the kid wakes up," he finally said, "I'll take him to the nearest police station and . . . and let them handle it. I should have done that when I had the chance. A couple of cops were just leaving the Billy Goat with coffee and I was headed their way with the kid, but . . ." He didn't finish. He could almost feel again the kid's frantic pulling on his arm, see him trembling.

"But what?" she said.

"I just couldn't do it."

"Why?" When he didn't answer, she pressed him. "This boy, he is frightened also of the police, is this true?"

"Yeah."

"Should you not find out why he is frightened of the police before you put him into their hands?"

"It's not up to me, y' know? I'm not his . . . I'm not his 'angel,' or anything else to him."

"Perhaps," she said, "but—"

"Hey, I'm just me, y' know? A guy living in one room, with no job, and about three weeks left on his goddamn rent." Jesus Christ! Why was he so worked up? Stress, maybe, from being chased and all. "Look," he said, "I wasn't *sent* anywhere, by anyone. I'm just this guy who's . . . who's pretty much of a fucking loser." He touched his shirt pocket. "Shit, I need a cigarette."

Zorina looked sad then, and breathed a deep breath. "You are not 'pretty much of a fucking loser,' Charlie Long." She spoke almost in a whisper and stared right at him. "You never will be that."

He didn't understand what the hell she meant, so he lowered his eyes and didn't say anything.

"Charlie Long," she said, "look at me."

He looked at her.

"What do you see?"

He saw a round-faced little old lady. Dark, wrinkled skin; nose too short and stubby; teeth not very white and not very straight; hands with age spots. Shit, he couldn't say any of that, and somehow he was sure she'd know if he lied. But her eyes, though, he could mention them. "I . . . uh . . . I see a person who, you know, sees things maybe other people don't."

She stood for a few seconds just staring at him. "Yes," she finally said, "this is what I see, also."

FIVE

The flight was late and it was past one in the afternoon when Maria McGrady opened her cloth carry-on bag at customs at O'Hare. She waited while the agent, a tight-lipped, fortyish black woman, flipped through her passport and then poked around in the bag. It was about the size of a large purse, and there wasn't much in it: a tiny cosmetics case, a change of underwear in case she'd gotten stuck overnight in Sao Paulo, a wild shirt for her dad which he'd probably never wear, and a blue and yellow sundress which Alicia would "absolutely adore, darling." Otherwise, just two books written in Portuguese, since she was struggling to bring her Portuguese up to the level of her Spanish. Even with heightened security, customs should go pretty quickly.

The agent took her time, though, looking through each book and feeling around the edges of the bag. Was she looking for secret compartments, for God's sake? Maria watched other people pass through around her. Maybe it was a profile thing, because Maria was young—not quite twenty-four—and the carry-on and her leather handbag made up her only luggage.

"How long was your stay in Brazil?"

"Just over a year," Maria said, thinking the woman must have seen that from looking at her passport.

"Where?"

"What? Oh . . . Rio de Janeiro. I work in an orphanage there. I'm here for a home visit." She was surprised at how nervous

34

she suddenly felt. As though she had to prove herself worthy to come back into her own country. She also felt her temper start to rise. "They looked through all my things in Rio," she said, "and again in Sao Paulo." She opened her handbag and took out an envelope. "Here. This will prove—"

"You don't have to prove anything, miss. May I see the contents of your purse, please?" Maria dumped everything out on the counter. Not much there either, of course, and the agent told her to put it all back and zip up her carry-on. "And enjoy your home visit," she said.

Maria scooped everything up. "May I ask," she said, her voice trembling with indignation, "just why you—"

"Because I work here, honey," the agent said, giving Maria a pat on the wrist and a genuine smile. "It's how I pay my bills." Stunned, Maria tried to smile back, but by then the woman had turned to the next person in line. "Step forward, please!"

With the cloth bag slung over her left shoulder and her handbag over her right, Maria joined the throng of people streaming into the noisy, crowded terminal. She recalled Sister Noonie's advice about anger. It mostly disturbed the person who owned it, and seldom accomplished much of value. Sister Noonie—Sister Mary Annunciata, actually, but no one called her that—had lots of opportunities to get angry. Born in Iowa, she'd been in Brazil for over forty years, and running Porto de Deus for twenty-five of them. She saw every day what neglect and abuse had done to the children who came to her. On the other hand, Sister Noonie was a saint, and Maria just a lay volunteer. So maybe she should be patient about her anger. Sister would have agreed with that. Not the part about herself being a saint, but the part about Maria being patient with—

"McGrady? Mary McGrady?"

Maria jumped, suddenly recognizing her own name out of all the shouting and calling and general confusion around her. A man's voice. She stopped walking . . . and someone crashed into her from behind.

"Sorry," Maria said, turning, "I—"

"Jesus! Wake up, would you?" It was a woman in a business suit—with a cell phone to her ear. She hurried by without even looking back.

Welcome to the USA.

"McGrady? Mary McGrady?"

Maria looked around and saw at least a dozen people scanning the arrivals, holding up signs with names printed on them. Finally she saw the one with her name. Or almost hers. She thought of herself as *Maria* now.

She didn't recognize the young man holding the card. Hispanic, certainly. Maybe early twenties. Her father must have sent him. As though she were incapable of getting home on her own, and him too busy to meet her plane himself. She considered simply ignoring the guy and taking a cab. But he looked like the anxious type, so she walked over to him.

"Yo soy Maria," she said. *"Supongo que mi padre le ha mandado a esperarme."*

"What?" Obviously clueless.

"I'm Maria . . . Mary McGrady. You don't speak Spanish?"

"Uh . . . not at all," he said. "Mr. McGrady sent me. I'm one of his paralegals. Let's go." He was already walking. "Mr. McGrady said I should get you downtown to his office right away."

He made no effort to take her bag, which was fine with her. But if he'd been from Rio—a *Carioca*—and educated enough to work in a law office, he'd have introduced himself, welcomed her home, inquired about her flight, insisted on taking her bag. Which wouldn't have made him a better person, necessarily. Just different. Plus, a *Carioca's* eyes would have been all over her, and quite open about it.

She hurried to keep up with him. "You haven't told me your name."

"What? Oh. It's Raymond. Raymond Sanchez." Saying *Sanchez* like an Anglo.

"And how do you know I'm really Maria . . . I mean Mary . . . McGrady?"

"What? Oh. From the picture in Mr. McGrady's office. Looks just like you." He stepped onto an escalator going downward. "This way," he said, speaking as though he were in charge of someone.

She stepped onto the moving stair above and behind him and rode down. "Raymond," she said, "we're headed down to where people pick up their baggage."

"Yeah, I know. I checked ahead to save time. Yours will be coming out right over there." He pointed.

"No, it won't."

"What?" He seemed to say *what* a lot.

"I didn't check any luggage." They'd reached the bottom and she stepped off onto the floor. "This is it," she said, and slapped her carry-on.

"No bags? Why didn't you say so?" He was walking again, this time toward an upward-moving escalator. "We could have saved time and—"

"And you could have gotten me downtown in a hurry, like my father wants." She stopped walking. "Raymond!"

He stopped, too, and turned to face her. "What?"

She pointed to the right. "Out through those doors I can get a taxi."

"But Mr. McGrady sent me to pick you up."

"Tell my father I arrived safely, and I'll be home when he gets there." She turned and started walking.

"Yeah, but I—"

" 'Bye, Raymond," she called, and headed for the cab stand.

Actually, she thought, she *might* be home when her father got there, and she might not. He was too busy to meet her at the airport, and she might be too busy to wait for him at home.

She tried to put aside her petty anger. The fact was, though, that she had lots to do. She'd stuck to her decision not to use e-mail while at Porto de Deus, which meant she had so much catching up to do, with so many people. Donald Fincher, for one, who'd taken to sending her cards almost every week, saying how much he missed her. She thought that by this time she'd have made up her mind about their future together, but . . .

She'd have to deal with that. Right now, though, there was someone who needed her attention more than Donald or anyone else. He was out there somewhere . . . a frightened little boy.

Six

What the old woman, Zorina, had said about him not being a loser, and how she said she could see things, and then pretty much said *he* looked like a person who could see things, too . . . all that really threw Charlie. He didn't know how to answer.

But he couldn't keep the kid either, for chrissake. He shook his head to clear his brain, and then said he was calling the cops. "I have to," he said.

He could tell she was pretty unhappy about that, but finally she asked him if he could at least let the kid sleep a little longer first. "You saw how tired he was," she said, "and once the authorities come for him he will get no sleep for many hours."

"Okay," he said, "maybe a half hour or so. Then I'm calling."

"Very well," she said. "It is your choice. After all, the boy is your responsibility."

"What?" He couldn't believe she said that. "Look, the kid was with this guy, and they were being chased, and the guy got killed, and—" Jesus, he shouldn't have mentioned the killing. "Anyway, I just happened to be there and picked him up. That doesn't make him *my* responsibility."

"So," she said, "can one step into another's life and take that person in a new direction, and then not be responsible for the person?" She had that same disappointed look in her eyes Sal had when he found out Charlie'd been fired. That pissed Charlie off. People always *expecting* things from him, like he was something he knew he wasn't.

"I'd have to be nuts *not* to call the police," he said. "What the hell would you do," he asked, "if you were in my shoes?"

"I could not be in your shoes. I am an old woman. I could not do what you could do."

"Christ almighty. You—" But he dropped it. It was his decision, not hers. He didn't have to explain anything to her. He picked up his cup, and then set it down again.

"Would you like something different to drink?" she asked. "Water, perhaps? Or coffee?"

"How about a Bud Light?" He was just joking, trying to lighten it up a little.

"I do not have beer," she said, taking him seriously. "But I have a bottle of red wine. I seldom drink it, and I keep it cold so that it lasts longer." She was already up and headed for the refrigerator.

"Hey, that's all right. I was just kidding. I don't wanna take your wine."

She turned and looked at him. "I should not have tried to tell you what to do. And I apologize." She was serious, and he nodded his acceptance. "But you did agree to let the boy sleep for awhile at my request," she said, "and so I owe you hospitality in return. Please do me the kindness of accepting."

"Fine." He'd already proven he was a person who made up his own mind on the important things, so he could give in on this to make her happy. "I'll have some wine." Hoping it wasn't too damn sweet.

"Thank you. And oh," she added, "perhaps you would like to check on the boy."

"Good idea." He stood up.

"And . . . you may use the bathroom if you like."

"Okay," he said, wondering if his own need to go was as obvious to her as the boy's had been.

The kid was sound asleep, breathing deep, peaceful breaths.

Funny. Wouldn't most kids have been screaming and crying and asking for their mommy and daddy through all that had just happened? Charlie closed the door softly. He went into the bathroom and took a leak. While he washed up he smiled to himself, remembering the kid holding out his hands to show they were clean.

When he got back to the table there was a glass—like a big water glass—with a little red wine in it, and a small plate of crackers beside it. The old woman was sipping her tea. "I regret that I have no wine glasses," she said.

"No problem," he said. "It's what's inside that counts."

"Yes," she said, "that is always the case."

He wondered if other people she talked to ever noticed how she kept saying things that seemed to mean more than what she said. He sipped the wine and was surprised at how good it tasted. Not that he was much of a wine drinker, but he could tell the cheap crap from the good stuff. He took another drink. "So," he said, lifting the glass toward her, "tell me all about yourself."

"Oh, there is little that would be of interest to you."

She'd taken this little joke seriously, too. He refilled his glass—more than half full this time. "Well," he said, "what about the kid?"

"What?" She looked surprised. "The boy? He is sleep—"

"No," Charlie said, "I mean the one in the picture on top of the TV. He your kid?"

"Yes. My son."

The sudden sadness on her face made him wish he'd kept his mouth shut. But he couldn't just drop it now. "Uh . . . he must be grown by now. How's he doing? I mean, is he—"

"He is dead. He was . . . taken from me. Not long after that photograph was made. I never . . ." She didn't finish, just shook her head. Then she smiled a little, like she didn't want Charlie to be embarrassed for bringing it up. "This is a sign, your coming here today, with the boy. Do you believe in signs?"

"Signs? I don't know. I don't think so."

"No," she said, "perhaps not."

So they talked for awhile.

For an old lady—and sort of eccentric, too—she was easy to talk to, and asked lots of questions. He told her about his ma, who was sick and weak and never really talked much. And his grandma, who used to tell him every day how worthless he was. "She treated my old man the same, always saying he'd never amount to anything. And he didn't, either. He got cancer and died before I got to really know him."

"I am sorry," she said.

"Yeah, well . . ." He shook his head and poured himself some more wine. He told her about his two sisters: Loretta, who was a lot like his grandma; and Gina, the one he liked, who moved to Seattle a few years ago.

"Were you successful in school?" she asked. She was washing dishes and putting things away, but paying attention, too. He could tell.

"I never liked grammar school. Teachers sending home notes like: 'Charles misbehaves to get attention,' or 'Charles is very bright, but doesn't live up to his potential.' Stuff like that."

"You didn't believe them?"

"What'd they know about my potential? High school was better, though. I was good in sports. Football especially, but basketball too. I felt good about that."

"As though you meant something to someone?"

"I guess so. Anyway, I got passing grades so I could play. Otherwise, though, the guys I hung around with were losers. Pretty much the same as now, y' know? Drinking buddies. The only person I ever really talk to is my cousin, Sal. He's older and . . . well . . . with my old man dead and all . . ."

She nodded and said, "Sal is a gift to you."

That sounded weird, but they gabbed on and he told her how he screwed up in college, and how Sal was trying to get him to go back and graduate. She seemed interested in what he was saying, but the wine was sort of strong and pretty soon he couldn't remember just what he'd told her and what he hadn't.

Finally he had enough sense to notice the bottle was almost empty. "Jesus," he said, looking at his watch, "we've been talking almost an hour."

"Really?" She seemed surprised, too. "I don't have a watch."

Good thing he stopped when he did. With all that wine on top of . . . what? . . . three beers? He had a pretty good buzz on. "I better call the cops."

"If you wish."

"Yeah, I wish." Thinking she would try to talk him out of it again, but she didn't. He looked around. "You got a phone?"

"No."

"Oh yes you do," he said, wagging his finger at her, "you naughty girl. Lemme use your cell phone."

"Oh, that." She pulled the phone out from a pocket in her dress. "I found it in the alley. It does not work."

He picked it up. No time on it. "You're a *tricky* girl, too," he said, laughing. "You sure fooled that big bad wolf at the door."

She leaned forward. "Have you had too much to drink?"

"Nah, I'm fine. That dirty bookstore next door. They must have a phone."

"Yes," she said. "But I know they never allow customers to use it."

"Yeah? Well, this is an emergency. I gotta call the cops." When he stood up he felt suddenly dizzy. "I'll go call, and then come back and wait."

★ ★ ★ ★ ★

He went through both sets of drapes, managed to unlock the front door, and went outside. It was way brighter out here and he felt light-headed and even more dizzy than before. The bookstore had a sign he hadn't seen when he was worried about getting the kid off the street: *BEAUX AND EROS*. Cool.

He steadied himself and went inside. The fat lady clerk wasn't there. Now it was a fat man clerk. What's with it with these people? Charlie stepped farther in.

"Deposit," the man said. He had a huge gray beard that looked like steel wool and a baseball cap with a little Confederate flag sewn on it above the bill. "Deposit," the guy said again.

"What?" Charlie said.

"Ya have to pay a deposit. Can't ya read the sign, for chrissake?"

"I gotta use the phone." He felt himself swaying now, a little. "Just lemme use the goddamn phone, asshole."

He could have taken the fat guy easy, but he didn't need trouble. Plus he thought he might throw up, so he left as soon as the guy came around the counter. That bar across the street, they must have a phone.

There was a helluva lot of traffic for this time of day. People honking their horns like maniacs, swerving all over, and him almost buying the farm right there on Halsted Street. But he made it to the other side in one piece. He tripped a little on the curb, and was just getting his balance when another car honked. Loud. Like an air horn.

He turned around and it was a blue and white squad car, stopped right beside him. He wouldn't have to call, after all. He started toward the car and then, just as the cop in the passenger seat opened her door, Charlie finally threw up.

SEVEN

Charlie realized he could've done a lot worse, copwise. A black chick—pretty hot for a cop—and a stubby white guy. They handled him better than he would have himself. They figured him drunk as a goddamn skunk at three in the afternoon, but at the same time listened to what he had to say.

The reason they stopped was to warn him to be careful crossing the street. Then, when he started his story, they put him in the backseat of the squad and let him talk. His brain was a little fogged up and he wasn't sure he should tell them the whole thing started two or three hours ago and he was just now telling the police—police who only happened by and hadn't been called by him. So he just told them how these men had been chasing a kid and he helped him and took him inside Zorina's place. He could tell the rest of it—about the Billy Goat and the dead black guy and the bread truck and everything—once they went and got the kid, and after he'd had a little time to think.

They went back across the street to Zorina's door and the cops pointed out the *CLOSED* sign. Charlie said he was the one who turned it that way. He pushed on the door, but it was locked. He banged on the glass and swore what he said was true, but they said he didn't expect them to break the door down, did he?

They went next door then, into *BEAUX AND EROS,* and the fat guy said, "Yeah, he come in here. Drunk and hollerin' about using the phone." Charlie said he'd been trying to call the police about the kid. "I didn't see no kid," the fat guy said, and Charlie explained how the kid was with Zorina and the fat guy said Zorina's place had been closed since he got here an hour ago. She was away a lot and he had her key to water her plants and put her mail inside so it didn't pile up. He didn't want to give them the key. But he probably figured—the type of business he was in—that it was better to piss off Zorina than the beat cops, so he unlocked her door, for which Charlie was thankful.

Except Zorina's place was as empty as Charlie's bank account. No lights on anywhere. No glasses or cups or teapots on the table. The sink dry. No kid sleeping on a cot. So they locked up and the fat guy took the key and Charlie and the two cops went and sat in the squad car again. Him dizzy and sick as a dog now, and hoping he wouldn't barf up right there in the backseat.

They talked it over and he admitted he'd been drinking. "A few beers at lunch, and then . . . you know . . . some wine." They said they hadn't heard about any kidnapping and maybe he'd like to think this over and, after he slept it off, if he still wanted to pursue it he could come into the station and talk some more—to a detective. Meanwhile, they needed his name and address for an "incident report." For his address he gave his ma's house, where his sister Loretta lived with her. That was the address on his driver's license, and he'd be back living there, anyway, if he didn't get a new job pretty quick.

When they let him go Charlie walked a few blocks, then took a bus. No silver Beemers followed him. His place—where he actually lived—was northwest of the Loop, in a mostly Mexican neighborhood that was just then starting to be grabbed up by people with money. He knew for a fact that his landlady and her son were already getting calls from real estate people. Hell, they'd been living here for years, and didn't want to go anywhere. But pretty soon, not being able to pay the rising property tax, they'd sell and have to go somewhere and start over.

When he got there he climbed the outside stairway up the rear of the old frame building to the second-floor porch, and then another flight up to the platform outside his own door, which you could tell had been a window until someone enlarged it into a door.

The landlady, Mrs. Rivera, lived on the first floor with her two daughters and one of her grandkids. Her son, Juan, and his wife, Carmela, and their two kids lived on the second and used their back-porch landing like a balcony. Charlie rented the third floor. Just an attic, really, but fixed up with drywall. One long room was all, and a tiny bathroom. The floor space was big enough, but those sloping ceilings closed in on you. You couldn't even stand up straight in the shower.

It beat living at home, though, with his ma still smoking and her emphysema so bad she could barely creep around the house with a walker, dragging her oxygen tank along. Plus Loretta firing up one cigarette after another herself, and whining all the time about how "the burden's all on me, takin' care of ma." Charlie couldn't handle it.

The rent at the Riveras' was cheap and he paid cash because it was an illegal apartment, not up to code. Besides the door to the outside stairs, the only other way in or out of his place was through a trapdoor down to the second floor. They left that with no lock on it, so if there was a fire on the back stairs he could get out through Juan and Carmela's apartment. Charlie had put a heavy dresser on top of the trapdoor, because otherwise Juan and Carmela's kids climbed up and played in his place.

This was his third apartment since he came home from

Michigan State, each one cheaper than the one before. The Riveras were nice people, and he was learning Spanish from talking to Juan. But it wasn't a place you could be proud of, or bring a chick to. Mostly he stayed away.

When Sal saw the place he said, "It's a dump, all right. But at least it's pretty quiet. You got no excuse for not studying and passing your college courses. Then you could keep living here while you go to law school." Sal was always bringing up college and law school.

"Y' know," Charlie had said, "I don't think I'm such a great bet for law school. I don't even—"

"Jesus, Charlie." Sal shook his head. "Nobody thinks you're even a good bet for *barber* college. Not now. What I'm saying is you *could* be, asshole. There's not a fucking thing wrong with your brain. It's motivation you need. Which is why I'm gonna throw you off the fucking Sears Tower if you don't pass those courses. Got it?"

So Charlie had promised to study, just to keep Sal off his ass. He'd get to it one of these days, when it was closer to exams. But right now what he needed was sleep. Jesus, what was it? Three beers and a few glasses of wine? Was he getting old or what? He flopped onto his mattress.

He was glad he hadn't insisted on going to the station with those two beat cops and trying to persuade some detective his story was true. One reason he hadn't done that was because he'd been so dizzy and sick, and needed time to get his head together so he could explain why he hadn't told the two cops right off about when and where he'd first seen the kid—and about the black guy getting shot.

And the other reason was because while he was in the backseat of the squad car giving his name and his ma's address—and trying to sit straight and look sober—the silver Beemer had driven by, going the opposite way from the way the squad car was facing. The goon in the leather coat was in the backseat and turned and looked out, straight at Charlie. The son of a bitch's eyes went wide open in surprise. Then he smiled—very scary—and pressed his finger to his lips and then drew it across his own throat and, pointing at Charlie, mouthed a silent message whose meaning couldn't have been clearer: "Shut up, or you're dead."

The whole bit had lasted about a second and the Beemer was gone. Charlie knew the cops hadn't seen a thing, and he should have said something. But just then he almost tossed up what was left of his jumbo dogs and fries. He swallowed hard, and then choked. And by the time he got his breath back and was able to talk, it seemed like it was too late.

Eight

"Is beautiful home you have," the cab driver said. He was in this country only a short time, he'd told her, from Lithuania. He knew where Lake Forest was, but Maria had to guide him street by street once they were off I-94 and closer to Lake Michigan. Now, driving between the stone pillars and under the arch that spelled out *SHOREWOOD POINT* in wrought iron letters, and heading down the long, curving, tree-lined lane that eventually swept past the home's front entrance, he was clearly impressed. "Is very beautiful home. Very big."

"Yes," she said, "both of those." Being away nearly a year made her see it with new eyes. A lovely home on a large parcel of wooded, lakefront property. On the North Shore, a place of wealth and prestige.

A year and a half earlier, with her mom dead from cervical cancer, her brother living down in Asheville, and Maria herself anxious to go off to Brazil, her father had been thinking of selling Shorewood Point, but then his relationship with Alicia Harper had taken a serious turn—like marriage serious—and for Alicia selling was out of the question.

Maria hadn't cared whether he sold or not. Not with her mother gone. Her loss had been devastating. People told Maria she shouldn't go to Brazil, that running off like that wouldn't resolve her continuing grief. But she went, and she'd been more deeply happy with her life during her year at Porto de Deus than she'd been for a long time, even when her mother was alive. Strange to—

"Is very beautiful home," the driver repeated, and Maria realized they weren't moving anymore.

"Oh, sorry," she said, and fumbled in her purse.

The driver made a show of offering to carry her bag, which she declined. She paid the flat-rate fare plus a large tip with the credit card her dad had sent her, the first time she'd used one since she'd canceled her own cards a year ago. She still had her house key, but the door was pulled open by a black woman whom she'd never seen before, and who was obviously the housekeeper.

The woman greeted Maria with a smile. "My name's Annie," she said. "Your daddy's secretary called to say you was coming straight here and could I wait till you got here, 'cause it's a new lock and your key wouldn't work." As she spoke she took a tan cloth coat from the front entrance closet and put it on. "Miz Alicia's out shopping for tomorrow night's party. Your room's done up, and there's food in the kitchen."

Annie left and Maria, alone in the house, carried her bag up to her room. Nothing to unpack, really. She had tons of clothes in her dresser and walk-in closet. She stood there and looked around at the walls covered with posters and photos, the stuffed animals, the frills and pastels and ribbons and lace. All as familiar to her as her own breath, yet strangely uninteresting now—like an old friend you still recognized, but could wave to from across the street and walk on by.

She stuck her return-trip ticket under the edge of her mirror. One month. Sister Noonie said she could decide then whether she still wanted to come back to Porto de Deus for another year. But except for Donald Fincher—and she wasn't sure yet about him—Maria had no reason to change her mind. In fact, she already missed her tiny plain room, the other teachers and staff, and especially the children. Still, the time here would pass quickly, and she did need to touch base with her friends.

But mostly there was little Paulo.

She'd been in charge that day, and by the time she realized the boy had lagged way behind the group, it had been too late. She saw from a distance what happened, and she screamed and screamed and a policeman ran to help. But Paulo was gone. More policemen came, and they interviewed Maria and acted very concerned. Later, though, Sister Noonie made it clear that she thought the police would be no help at all. To them it was just one more unsolvable case of a child being snatched off the streets of Rio, an all-too-common occurrence.

Sister Noonie knew how badly Maria felt about Paulo, but had been surprised later when Maria told her she'd hired a detective agency in Rio to look for him. She'd been even more shocked when Maria told her what the detective said, and that Maria wanted to leave for her home visit three weeks early.

"Your detective is surely mistaken," Sister said. "But even if he's right, and if his agency's office in Chicago is able to find Paulo there—and why would the boy be there?—I fear that they will merely inform the police in Chicago, who will then contact the police here in Rio. And that, I believe, would not help Paulo at all." Sister wouldn't say why that was. She just shook her head, and said it was not Maria's responsibility to concern herself with detectives, or with trying to find Paulo.

But of course Sister Noonie couldn't keep her from going home early. Besides, Sister had been ill for many days, and not up to arguing. The doctor said it was exhaustion, and Maria was sure it was partly from all the worry about Paulo.

"We must leave all things in God's hands," Sister said. "God sent Paulo to us, and if God wants him back with us, he will see to it. And if not, and if we must leave this place, God will provide another *porto* for . . ." She stopped, and once again wouldn't explain what she meant.

So Maria had been frightened for Paulo himself, and now added to that was what Sister Noonie said about having to move the whole orphanage if he didn't come back. Why would that be? And with all the surrounding land being gobbled up by the wealthy for huge amounts of money, where would the children go?

Maria went downstairs and wandered from room to room through the first floor of the huge, empty house, and eventually out onto the patio. With her father wrapped up in his own hectic world, her mother dead, and her brother far away, she felt very alone. Nor did thoughts of Donald Fincher, who wanted to be so much more than a friend, fill the void.

She looked across the lawn that stepped away in wide terraces toward the lake, ending at a steep bluff and the stairs down to the beach. The sun had warmed the stone patio and she sat on the ledge and stared out at Lake Michigan, calm and sparkling in the sunshine, and the loneliness flooded back. She let it come, let it wash over her. It was not so terrifying now that she knew it was just a feeling, and that it would go away, and that she wouldn't float off along with it. Not so terrifying, but still very heavy. She sat on the ledge for a long time and looked out, and let the warm tears flow.

Finally she wiped her cheeks and stood up. She walked across the sloping, terraced lawn, and out onto the broad wooden deck from which the stairway led down to the beach. This had long been her favorite spot at Shorewood Point, high up on the bluff, with the lake spread out before her. She leaned against the railing, gazing at the water and listening to the gentle waves lap up on the sand below.

She looked down then, and saw a man and a woman walking together along the otherwise deserted beach. They were headed north, to her left, and were well past the foot of the steep stairway down from the deck. This stretch of lakefront was private, with the owners of the properties abutting the lake all owning their sections of the shoreline. Signs were posted, and at the far north and south ends of the private stretch there were fences that went out to the water's edge to discourage trespassers. But people from one of the lakefront estates, or people who simply disregarded the signs and evaded the fences—a rather rare occurrence, and never a cause for alarm—could walk unimpeded for over a mile along the beach. And it was a romantic walk, especially on such a beautiful day.

She looked down at the strolling couple. They weren't holding hands, and didn't seem to be talking. Were they friends? Lovers? Maybe future lovers. Then the man must have felt her eyes on them, because he glanced up and over his shoulder at her, then turned away again and kept walking. Maria didn't recognize him. She wished the woman would look up, too, because she seemed somehow familiar. Was it the way she walked? Her clothes? It was certainly something.

The pair rounded a curve in the shoreline and were beyond her view. She turned and went back to the house to make a few phone calls.

NINE

Charlie slept about five hours and woke up to Juan Rivera's kids downstairs yelling about something. His bed was a box spring and mattress right on the plank wood floor, and when the kids were in their bedroom the sound carried up almost like they were in the same room.

He didn't feel too bad. A headache, and a little washed out. He thought about the boy, and . . . what was her name? . . . Zorina, and the thugs who killed the black guy, and tried to convince himself he'd dreamed the whole thing. But that didn't work. He knew he hadn't dreamed getting pink-slipped by the city and going to the Billy Goat to meet Sal. Maybe he should go talk to the cops again. And maybe not. Maybe forget about it, and if it got him in trouble somehow he could always say he tried to report the thing but the cops wouldn't listen.

Christ, it was Friday night. He should go find someone to hang out with. Some bar somewhere. Except maybe he shouldn't drink any more that day. It might make him barf up his guts again. Or worse, get him going on about his whole life story like he did to that Zorina woman. When he thought about it he was surprised at how long they talked. He sure didn't want to get blabbing like that to some chick who'd be bored to death.

He sat up with his back against the wall and aimed the remote at the TV. He flipped through the channels and punched the damn thing off again. He didn't get good reception here and didn't have cable, and didn't think there'd have been anything he wanted to watch if he did. Maybe he should call his sister Loretta. She'd be up till one a.m., glued to the tube. So he called.

"Hello?"

"Yeah, it's me. Charlie."

"Nice of you to call your family every couple months or so," she said.

"I called a week ago." Then he thought. "Well, two weeks. Last weekend was Labor Day and I was busy. How's ma doin'?"

"Same ol', same ol'. Like you cared." There was a pause and he knew she was dragging on a cigarette. "You know, we oughta at least have your address, phone number. Someone comes looking for you, I don't know what to tell 'em. Makes me look stupid. My own brother."

"Nobody ever comes looking for me," he said. "Anyway, say hi to ma. I gotta be—"

"They did today. Two guys. And here's me peeking out the door with the chain on, my thumb up my behind and saying, 'Jeez, I don't know where my own brother lives. I'm just his oldest sister, the one who takes care of his sick mother, but he doesn't tell me shit.' How you think I feel, Charlie?"

He didn't say anything. His mind was spinning too fast.

"Charlie?" she said. "Hey?"

"Were they, you know, cops?"

"Didn't say so. Why? You in trouble or something?"

"Course not. It's just . . . there's some cops I play basketball with and—You say two guys?"

"Yeah, well . . . one stayed out in the car. Guy at the door had like a foreign accent. Said he was a friend of yours. Sort of a creep, if you ask me."

"What kinda car?"

"How do I know? Ain't like I ever go anywhere." She sighed and he could hear the wheeze of her breathing. "A gray car, I guess. Or . . . kinda silverlike. Anyway, I gotta go 'cause the movie's startin' up again."

"Yeah. Okay. Say hi to—" But Loretta hung up.

Shit. Now what? Go to the cops? Only . . . was there any way the two goons could've gotten his address *except* from the cops? Maybe the cashier at the Billy Goat. She might know his name. She knew Sal's name. They could have asked around, found out where he works . . . where he *used* to work. Got his ma's address from someone. Maybe.

And maybe they got it from the cops.

The kids downstairs had quieted down. Probably asleep. Charlie knew if he went to the other side of the room, where his TV was, and sat against the wall and waited long enough, he'd hear the sounds coming up from Juan and Carmela's bedroom just as clear as he could hear the kids' bedroom from this side. He'd hear Juan and Carmela banging their brains out like they did just about every night. Carmela had a loud, husky voice and he'd learned quite a few new Spanish phrases. He wasn't sure what some of them meant, but he wasn't about to ask. Anyway, that had got pretty boring a long time ago.

He took a shower and put on fresh clothes and headed out the door. He knew he shouldn't do what he was going to do. Going back there was stupid. But it was a little like when you were into some chick you knew was trouble, but you couldn't help going back. This was sort of the same, but different. This was about a scared little boy.

Right, and this was way more stupid.

TEN

It was eleven o'clock and the door was still locked and the sign still said *CLOSED*. When no one answered his knock, Charlie went around to the back. The alley was dark and it was hard to tell which back entrance was which, but he managed to find a solid steel door with a small sign that said *BEAUX AND EROS*, so the next one had to be Zorina's.

That door had a little window—maybe a square foot—at about eye level, and . . . Damn! All the glass had been knocked out of the window. The door was closed, but not pushed tight, and there was no light on inside.

His stomach squeezed in on itself and the blood pounded along the left side of his head like it always did when he got scared or excited. He looked both ways in the alley, but saw no one. He knocked on the door.

No answer.

He pushed and the door opened. Reaching in, he found a switch and flipped it up and a dim ceiling light went on. He stepped inside. It was a little back hall with a mop and a broom and cleaning stuff, and then another door. That one was open just a crack, too. Both doors being a little open like that somehow reminded him of his sister Gina's favorite joke when they were real little: "A door's not a door when it's a jar." They had no idea what it meant, but they'd both laugh like hell. Then one day his grandma explained what "ajar" meant, and then they didn't get the joke anymore. He missed Gina.

He didn't bother knocking on the second door, just pushed it open. No one was there. Most of the cabinets and drawers were open. He checked the bathroom and the tiny bedroom and found no one. He went through the draperies to check out the place where Zorina looked into her crystal ball and did her "readings."

There was no one there, but someone had pulled the white cloth off the little table and thrown it on the floor. The crystal ball and the little skull thing it sat on were on the floor, too. The blood was still pounding in his head and all he wanted was to get out of—

Bam, bam, bam, bam!

Jesus! Someone banging on Zorina's front door again, like before. He looked up into the ceiling mirror. Cops, two of them, in uniform.

Bam, bam, bam!

Charlie had the hall light off and was headed through the back door while the cops were still pounding out front. When he got to the end of the alley—walking fast, not running—he looked back, just in time to see a pair of headlights swing in way down at the other end. He turned and went down the sidewalk and didn't look back again.

He used up too much of what cash he had on a taxi ride home. He'd order a pizza delivered from a place he knew that had your phone number on their screen as soon as you called. That'd help prove he stayed home all night. So if the cops saw a guy in the alley it wasn't him.

He started up the stairway to his place, quietly because Mrs. Rivera had a German shepherd who slept in her kitchen and woke up the whole fucking neighborhood if it heard any noise. He got past the first floor and then, almost up to Juan's porch, he stopped.

He'd heard something. Up above.

Or maybe not. He wasn't sure. There was a light over Juan's back door, but higher than that it was mostly shadows. Not pitch black, but the alley lights barely reached there.

No one knew he lived here except the Riveras, who made him swear not to tell anyone they rented out the attic because it would get them in trouble. Plus Sal, who wouldn't tell anyone without checking with Charlie first. And that was it. No one else. Not even his sister Loretta, so she couldn't blab it to some guy in a "kinda silverlike" car with a foreign accent who claimed he was Charlie's friend, and was "sort of a creep."

He stood still, one flight below his porch, again feeling the pulse pounding on the side of his head. There were no more sounds. And the longer he stood there, the more certain he was that he was getting paranoid. Besides, if he turned and left, where the hell would he go? So fuck it. He started up again.

"Is that you, Charlie Long?" The voice was barely audible.

Charlie took the rest of the steps three at a time. "If you're so good at seeing things," he said, "how come you hadda ask?"

Zorina sat on her haunches against the railing on the tiny porch, facing the stairs, with the kid sitting backed up to her. She had her arms around him, holding him close to her, wrapping him in the folds of a coat she wore over the blue dress. The kid seemed to be sleeping, but the old lady's eyes were wide open, somehow shining in the dim light.

Jesus! Those were tears making her eyes so bright, and he suddenly realized how goddamn cold it was. Like in the forties or something. She was shivering, and crying from the cold. He unlocked his door and then had to help the two of them up onto their feet and inside. The woman didn't seem to weigh much more than the boy. She was like all bones.

Or no, not all bones. Bones and eyes.

ELEVEN

Charlie was tied behind a moving subway train that dragged him deeper and deeper into a long, dark tunnel. Running, stumbling, fighting to stay on his feet. And then he stopped moving.

He sat up and opened his eyes. His joints were stiff and his head ached worse than it had the night before. Sunlight leaked in around the shades on the two windows in his apartment—one at each end of the one long room. He had padded the floor with a piece of shag carpeting and slept with his clothes on, under his old down-filled ski jacket.

Zorina and the kid had fallen asleep right away on Charlie's mattress—the kid in one of Charlie's flannel shirts and the old lady in her same blue dress with the stars and all—before he could get out of her what the hell was going on.

"We will discuss these things in the morning," she had said.

Now it was morning and the kid was still asleep on the mattress. But, Jesus, where was the old woman?

Maybe in the bathroom? No, the door was open and he could see into the tiny cubicle that passed for his bathroom. Just a toilet and a shower stall, barely enough room to dress yourself. No sink. To wash your hands or brush your teeth you had to use the kitchen sink. Not that he had a real kitchen. Just a sort of half-refrigerator, like they have in college dorm rooms. And he had a hot plate and a microwave, but no stove.

Anyway, the old woman was gone. Christ, now what?

He went and took a leak and when he came back out the kid was sitting up on the mattress, his back against the wall and the blanket pulled up around him. His eyes were wide open, but he didn't say anything.

"Gotta go to the bathroom?" Charlie asked. The boy just sat there, looking like he didn't understand. "Bathroom?" Charlie repeated. Then, remembering how the old woman had put it the day before, he said, "Peepee?"

The boy nodded solemnly then, but didn't move.

"Over there." Charlie pointed toward the bathroom, and when the kid still didn't move, he went over to the bed. "C'mon," he said. "Up and at 'em." He reached down and tugged at the blanket.

The kid shrank back, struggling to hold the blanket around him, but Charlie gently pulled it away. Up till then he hadn't noticed the smell of urine, but now he did, and realized that the kid had wet the bed.

"Damn," Charlie said, "you should have—"

The kid yelped. He leapt off the bed and scrambled across to the other side of the room. Keeping his eyes on Charlie, he slid to his right along the wall till he bumped into the dresser, then sank to the floor in the corner made by the dresser and the wall. He huddled there with that scared puppy look again, sort of sitting back on his heels with his arms crossed in front of him, hugging the flannel shirt to himself.

There was that same look of helpless terror in the kid's eyes as when that black guy was pulling him into the hallway at the Billy Goat, or when Charlie started taking him toward the two cops. "Jesus," Charlie said, "you think I'm mad at you, don't you?" Actually, he *was* a little pissed off, but not enough to hit a little kid, for chrissake.

The boy stayed perfectly still, until suddenly his whole body started to shake.

"Christ almighty," Charlie said, and what little anger was left drained out of him. He shook his head. "You think I'm gonna beat the shit out of you, don't you?" He stood there a second, and then he couldn't help himself. He started laughing. "Jesus, kid," he said, "if I went through everything you did, I'd have peed in the bed, too."

He didn't think the boy understood, but he kept talking as he pulled the sheet off the mattress and tossed it on the floor. "Me, I'd have crapped in my pants." He didn't see any wet spot on the blanket, and folded it up. Meanwhile, the kid seemed to be calming down, but hadn't come out of his corner.

The mattress wasn't too bad. The kid probably had a small bladder, or maybe he woke up and was able to stop. "I'll just let this dry out and maybe it won't smell." Except it already did. He turned to face the kid and spread his arms, trying to look friendly. "Hey, c'mon," he said, gesturing with his hands, "stand up."

The boy stood. He seemed to understand, finally, that Charlie wasn't going to hit him.

"Bathroom's over there," Charlie said, pointing, "if you have to go again . . . or still, or something." He shooed the kid into the bathroom and closed the door on him. "Take your time," he said. "Maybe you—"

His phone rang and he jumped a foot.

Not that it was loud. It was turned down so low you could hardly hear it, but this was . . . what? Eight thirty Saturday morning? He let the machine answer it, and all his recorded voice said was: "Leave a message if you want."

There was a pause, and then, "It is Zorina."

He grabbed the phone. "Hello?"

"It is Zorina."

"You said that. What the hell's going on? Why aren't you here? And why weren't you there yesterday when I brought the cops back to your place? They thought I was nuts. Who broke into your place? Why'd you bring the kid here? Shit. I gotta call the cops." He was babbling, but who wouldn't be?

"I left this morning to think . . . and to learn what I can. As for yesterday, when you went to get the police the boy woke up and he and I saw you talking to the police in their car. He became terrified. His body was shaking, and I thought he would be ill. I was so frightened for him. I could not allow him to be taken by the police. I just could not do that. And I took him."

"But why's he so scared of cops? Did he say anything?"

"He says nothing. But he knows police when he sees them, and you have seen his reaction. I took him, thinking perhaps you would change your mind and try to find out more before you deliver him to the authorities. This would be a great help to him, to find out where he belongs."

"I don't even know this kid. He's nothing to me. Who chose *me* to help him?"

"How can I answer that? Who is the one who makes such choices?" She paused, then said, "You saw the boy's need and cared about him and—"

"Bullshit! I ran into him and scooped him up. That's all. Why would I care about him? It's not up to me to help him."

"But you *do* want to help him. That is the reason you went back to my studio."

"I just—" He stopped. "You don't know that I went back there."

"I *do* know. You said you saw that someone broke in."

"Yeah . . . well . . . that doesn't mean I'm signing on to help him." Then he remembered the biggest thing. "How did you know where I live, anyway? No one knows that."

"When you shared my wine and talked, you spoke of many things."

"I don't remember saying that."

"You spoke of many things."

"What else did I say?"

"You spoke of yourself and your life, your grandmother and the death of your father. Many things." She paused. "The boy, is he awake?"

"Yeah. He's in the bathroom. He peed in my bed, for God's sake."

"And he would be afraid," she said. "But you did not punish him."

"How do you know?"

"You would not have done that."

"Anyway, you should have seen how scared he was when I found out. I mean, it's gonna stink a little, but I figure he's got enough—"

"So you *do* care for him. You will help him. First, you must—"

"Wait a minute." Who did this woman think she was, for chrissake? His grandmother? "I don't 'must' anything. I'll take him to the goddamn cops is what I'll do."

"Charlie Long, I do not wish to order you. I apologize. I say only that this boy, he is from another country. I can see that. He has endured terrible things. Things which may have been done by police wherever he comes from. I do not know. But he may fear the police here would send him back to whoever did these things. And he may be right."

"Hold on. What are you talking about? What terrible things? If someone's been abusing him he'll be turned over to the state and they'll check it out. They'll put him in foster care or something."

"Or they may return him to whoever hurt him. At least I fear they may, and I believe he fears this also. You must . . . I mean to say . . . will you help him?"

"I don't know that he was ever abused in the first place. I don't know who he is. All I know is—"

"He has a name."

"What?"

"The boy, he has a name. He does not speak, but I have learned that much."

"How did you—"

"His name is Paulo." She pronounced it *Pow-lo,* which sounded like Spanish for Paul, except . . . wasn't *Pablo* Spanish for Paul?

"Paulo." Charlie repeated the name, and suddenly wished she hadn't told him.

"Yes, Paulo," she said. "And he has suffered great abuse."

"Oh? If he won't talk, how do you know that?"

"I have seen." She paused. "You recall that I helped him change into your shirt for pajamas?"

"Yeah?"

"I have seen him." She paused, then said, "We must know more about him. I wish to find someone with knowledge to help us help him, and I have an idea. So please, at least wait for me to try to do this before you give him to the police. I beg you, Charlie Long."

"Look, I don't—"

"Wait at least until noon. Will you promise me that?"

"Jesus, noon wouldn't be so bad, I guess. Let me—"

"Thank you, Charlie Long. Thank you." She hung up before he could say he'd think about it.

He went over and knocked on the bathroom door, and then opened it. The kid was still wearing the flannel shirt, just sitting there on the closed down toilet seat.

"Paulo?" Charlie said.

The boy's eyes widened, but not in fear this time. He nodded his head as though acknowledging his name.

"You wanna take a shower?" Paulo looked confused, so Charlie stepped into the shower stall and mimed taking a shower.

Then he pointed at the boy and said, "You?"

Paulo nodded.

He took the flannel shirt off and Charlie gave him the soap and adjusted the water so it wasn't too hot. The kid seemed to enjoy it and Charlie went and got him a clean towel to dry himself off—the only really fluffy towel he had. He got Paulo's clothes and told him to put them on. And the whole time he tried not to react to the terrible sight he was seeing. He was afraid if he showed on his face what he felt in his gut, it would scare the kid.

He closed the bathroom door while Paulo was putting his clothes on, and ran across and put his arms on the sides of the kitchen sink. He leaned his head down low, toward the drain. His stomach was pretty empty already, so there wasn't much but a thin, sour liquid to dribble out when he heaved.

Twelve

The boy had a name: Paulo. For some reason it made a big difference and Charlie told himself he better be damn careful. Getting attached to this kid would be a major mistake. Just take him to the cops in a hurry. That would end it.

Zorina had begged him not to, though, and if he hadn't quite promised to wait "at least until noon," she obviously *thought* he promised. She sure stepped up and got rid of the Russians when they would have grabbed the boy back—and would have grabbed Charlie, too. He owed her something for that, and it showed she wasn't a flake.

Besides, she had a damn good reason for wanting time. Those scars on the kid's butt, and even around on the front of him, were proof that some sicko had been fucking torturing him. Her idea was to find someone who could help them learn who Paulo was, so they could turn him over to people who'd take care of him properly, and not take a chance with the cops. There had to be a reason Paulo was scared of cops.

Of course he'd been scared of Charlie, too, but only for those few minutes there, after he wet the bed. Most of the time with Charlie he just went along. And he wasn't afraid of Zorina, either. He could probably tell they were both on his side.

Even when you were on a kid's side, though, you probably had to do a lot of things the kid didn't understand. Like Charlie wasn't looking forward to seeing Paulo's face if he had to hand him over to the cops. And pretty soon he'd have to.

He had no love for the goddamn Chicago Police Department, but they wouldn't abuse a lost little kid. The problem was, they might give him right back to the person who hurt him. Stories like that were in the papers all the time. People getting their kids back when anyone in their right mind would know they'd just abuse and beat the shit out of them in the future, same as they had in the past.

But what could Charlie and some weird old lady do about it?

Anyway, right now he and Paulo could use some breakfast.

He held Paulo's hand as the two of them went down the steps from his apartment—and ran smack into a parade of Riveras in the backyard. Jesus! He tried to turn around, but too late.

Juan and Carmela and their two kids and Juan's mother and her daughters and another grandkid. Carrying bags and heading out to the alley to Juan's ancient white Chevy conversion van, with the lions painted on the side. All eight of them, for chrissake. And the German shepherd, too. No one was talking much, which was unusual.

"It's my ma's cousin," Juan said. "Funeral's Monday in Oklahoma City. Be back Tuesday." He shook his head, then suddenly noticed Paulo. "Hey, who's the kid?"

"My . . . uh . . . my nephew," Charlie said. "He's like, you know, real shy. Doesn't talk much." Then, to keep Juan from trying to talk to Paulo—because he would have tried—Charlie said, "Hey, doesn't *'lo siento'* mean 'I'm sorry' in Spanish?"

"What? Oh, to say to my ma? It's not exactly—Yeah, well, she'll get the point."

"Good." Charlie pulled Paulo away from Juan and toward Mrs. Rivera, already up in the van's front passenger seat. *"Lo siento,"* he said. "About your cousin, I mean. *Lo siento.*"

She nodded back, looking pretty sad.

"Well," Charlie called back to Juan, "gotta run." Hustling away, pulling the kid with him.

Charlie thought Zorina was probably right that Paulo came from another country. One of Juan Rivera's kids was named *Pablo*, which is how Charlie knew that was Spanish for Paul. So what language was "Paulo?" And what did kids eat for breakfast wherever he came from?

"You like Burger King?"

But of course Paulo didn't say anything.

"Yeah, man, it's my favorite," Charlie answered for him. Then he looked in his wallet. Damn! This babysitting shit was expensive.

They went to Burger King and got their breakfasts and Charlie carried the coffee and orange juice and Paulo carried the two paper sacks. They walked to a nearby park and sat on a bench and ate. The whole time Charlie tried to get the kid to say something, but it was no use. Somehow he must have told Zorina his name, but otherwise he wouldn't say a goddamn thing.

He didn't seem stupid, and it wasn't just a language thing, either. He usually got the point when you told him to do something, so he must know at least a little English. Plus, he didn't seem like the stubborn kind, keeping his mouth shut to prove you couldn't make him do what he didn't want to.

No, it was something else. Charlie wondered if the kid had taken so much abuse, abuse he couldn't stop no matter what he said, that he turned off the word faucet. And now he couldn't get himself to turn it back on.

Charlie finished his breakfast sandwich and wadded up the bag and tossed it like a basketball into a trash barrel a few yards away. "Two points!" he said, and pumped his fist up into the air.

He wadded up Paulo's bag, too, and gave it to him to throw. Paulo threw, and his bag landed on the ground about halfway to the barrel, but he pumped his fist just like Charlie had. Charlie couldn't help laughing. "That's called an air ball, kid," he said, and then went and picked up the bag and slam-dunked it into the barrel. "Two more!"

Paulo just looked at him.

It was a small park, not even half a block long, but there was some playground equipment and Charlie took Paulo over and they watched a few other kids playing there with their mothers. Paulo, though, didn't want to play. He didn't want to do anything, as far as Charlie could tell. He just took hold of Charlie's hand and walked when he walked and stopped when he stopped. That's it.

Charlie crouched down to put his face even with Paulo's. "Look, kid," he said, "you gotta help me here. I mean, you can't just walk around hanging on to me the rest of your life. You gotta go home."

The boy looked at him with those sad brown eyes of his, and said nothing.

"Come here." Charlie led Paulo off the wide asphalt sidewalk and they sat down in the grass.

Charlie couldn't even remember the last time he sat in any grass. He used to play in a park district softball league and there was lots of grass in the ball fields. But he never sat down in the damn stuff unless he slipped and fell. He ran his fingers over the tops of the soft green blades, and felt just a little bit of dew still clinging to them.

"Here," he said. He took Paulo's hand and rubbed it over the grass. "Nice, huh?"

Paulo just looked at him.

"Okay," Charlie said, "here's the deal. I can't keep you with me. And the old lady, you know, she can't keep you either. So you gotta go home. Got it?"

Paulo went back to rubbing his hand in the grass.

"Home," Charlie repeated. "Mother. Father. Uh . . . *padre?*" Paulo didn't look Mexican, but he could be Cuban or something, so Charlie tried Spanish. *"Donde su padre?"*

Paulo didn't look up from the grass, but his shoulders twitched a little. Charlie leaned and put his first two fingers under the boy's chin and lifted his face. His eyes were full of tears.

"Okay!" Charlie raised his fist in the air in triumph. "So you know what *padre* is, right? And you miss your old man, right? Now we're getting somewhere."

But he tried for another fifteen minutes and got nowhere at all. Paulo just shut down. Period. After he cried when Charlie mentioned his *padre,* he didn't respond to anything else. Not *madre,* not *familia,* not *su casa.* And that pretty much used up Charlie's vocabulary about relatives and home. What he knew of Spanish he'd learned from the Riveras. He should have known the words for brother and sister, but he couldn't think of them. Besides, Paulo could have made *some* kind of response if he wanted to. He just wouldn't, which pissed Charlie off.

"Christ," he said, "if it weren't for that damn Zorina, I'd take you to the cops right now."

THIRTEEN

Maria drove into the city in a car her father had already leased for her, a red Mercedes convertible. They'd talked briefly the night before and he'd given her some cash, but she hadn't seen him that morning. Not surprising. He was more comfortable arranging things—like credit cards and rides from the airport and automobiles and cash—than engaging in personal conversation. She wished she didn't so often accept his help. It only added to the confusion about her feelings toward him.

In fact, it was because of help from him that she was going where she was going right then. Poor little Paulo had been under her care when he was snatched off the street, and she felt responsible. So when the Rio police were no help, she'd called her father and asked how to find a good detective agency in Rio—not saying why, nor that she'd be using her own money. He assigned a lawyer in his firm to find one for her, and she'd hired the agency the lawyer recommended. Called Intertec International, it had offices in cities around the world, including Rio, and its home office was in Chicago.

Saturday morning traffic was light and she easily found Intertec's headquarters, a mile north of the Loop on LaSalle Street. She parked in a nearby lot, slid her handbag over her shoulder, and walked back.

"Erica Donaldson, please," she told the receptionist. "I called yesterday."

"Let's see." The young man had close-cropped hair, a friendly face, and an openly masculine interest in her. He hit some keys and checked his monitor. "Ten o'clock. Um . . . you don't mind waiting a few minutes, do you? There's been . . . well . . . a lot going on this morning already."

"That's fine," Maria said.

She sat in one of four matching upholstered chairs. The magazines on the glass-topped coffee table all concerned travel. She ignored them—and ignored the receptionist, too, who kept looking at her. He seemed to want to start a conversation, and was struggling to find an opener.

He hadn't succeeded by the time his phone rang. He answered it, and then got up and led Maria back to a long hallway. "That's Ms. Donaldson's office, way down at the end. See?" he said. "Right where that man's coming out."

She walked slowly on the soft gray carpet, fighting the feeling that she was in over her head. The worried-looking man who'd come out of Ms. Donaldson's office ducked into another doorway ahead of her. That door was slightly ajar and as she passed she heard him talking to someone else in the room. ". . . about Riggs," he was saying, and the alarm in his voice drew her attention and she stopped walking. ". . . that call at noon from outside the Billy Goat, and then nothing. It's like he dropped off—"

"This way, Ms. McGrady."

Maria jumped. "Oh," she said, "thank you." She walked on, hoping the woman at the end of the hall hadn't caught her eavesdropping.

"I'm Erica Donaldson," the woman said. She seemed preoccupied, and obviously wasn't accusing Maria of anything. "Come in, please."

Maria followed her and they sat facing each other across a cluttered desk. "Thanks for seeing me on such short notice, Ms. Donaldson."

"Please call me Erica. And may I call you Maria?" She paused barely a beat while Maria nodded. "Would you care for coffee? Or a soft drink?"

"Oh, no. No thank you. I'm not—"

"I spoke with Sister Mary Annunciata yesterday. After you called."

"You did? That's—"

"I called her. She seemed somewhat . . . distracted. Or tired. Is she ill?"

"She says it's just fatigue," Maria said. "She has so many responsibilities. And now this. But why did you call *Sister*, when I'm—"

"She *is* the boy's legal guardian, after all. When our Rio office called and said you were the client, I was surprised you weren't a relative."

"Well," Maria said, "what I want—"

"You just got in yesterday, right?"

"Erica, wait a minute. Let me ask you something."

"What is it?"

"Just this: do you constantly interrupt *everyone?* Or just foolish young women who run off to Brazil to do volunteer work?"

"Everyone, I suppose," Erica said, unapologetic and apparently unfazed by the question. "This is a rather hectic business." She frowned. "I'm not aware that you're especially foolish. Maybe impetuous?"

Maria had no answer for that.

"The policy of this agency is to make full reports to our clients."

"And I'm the client, not Sister Noo . . . not Sister Mary Annunciata."

"You can understand, I think, that there are certain precautions we must take when the subject is a minor."

"I wire transferred a very large advance to your office in Rio.

I don't have to be someone's guardian, or relative, to ask you to find him."

"That's true. And I'm reporting to you." The woman folded her hands on the desk and leaned forward. "You already know that our people in Rio are convinced the kidnappers are part of a group of Russians, people engaged in the acquisition of children for use in the sex trade."

"Your detective in Rio told me that. I saw it happen, you know. I saw the man take him, although from too far away to give a description."

"He obtained information that they later took the boy out of Brazil."

"He told me that, too," Maria said. "He also told me that such children generally just vanish completely. But he said he learned that this particular boy was taken to the United States . . . to Chicago. He said he told the Rio police, but they didn't seem to take the idea seriously. The thing is, he wouldn't say who told him that, or—"

"Operatives frequently cultivate informants whom they cannot identify. The police understand that. But I can assure you, to have convinced our man this source must have been proven quite reliable in the past. I say that because the information itself—that kidnappers would transport a boy from Rio to Chicago—is . . . well . . . it's curious."

"But why? Is there no market here for . . . for what they provide?"

"In my experience, Maria, there's a 'market' for anything . . . anywhere." Erica leaned back in her chair. "That's why it's curious. Although there's evidence that this Russian gang has been headquartered in Chicago for some time now, why transport the boy such a great distance? And into this country? They apparently used a private plane they have access to. Still, it seems a high risk . . . not to mention the expense."

"And you're sure that's what happened?"

"Our people in Rio are more than competent, and that was their determination. When I spoke with Sister about it she agreed that it seemed odd. She . . ." Erica paused, as though trying to choose her words. "Sister suggested the kidnappers might have come up with an alternative way to . . . to profit from the boy."

"An alternative? I don't understand."

"Sister did not elaborate. I assume she meant a possible ransom demand."

"But Porto de Deus has no money. How could—"

"At any rate, I put one of my best men here on the case, and word from him indicates that perhaps he did locate the boy here, but—"

"You found Paulo? Where is he?"

"I don't know anything beyond what I've told you. I'm awaiting . . . a further report."

"Awaiting a report? If your man found Paulo, and hasn't called in, they could *both* be in trouble. Injured, or—"

"Our agents work independently, and call in when there's something to report. If I had evidence of a crime, or if I believed I knew where the boy was, I would call the . . . I would notify the authorities."

"But you're working for *me*, and I want Paulo back." Then, recalling Sister Noonie's fear, Maria added, "And I would rather the police not be involved."

Erica shook her head. "First, it's not our policy to physically seize a minor . . . not without parental authority, which you don't have. And, more importantly, you are no longer an Intertec client."

"What are you talking about? I paid. I haven't terminated your services."

"We have withdrawn from the engagement."

"But you can't—"

"The unused portion of your payment will be wired back to your account, and we'll do nothing further on the case. Of course, when I hear from my man, if he reports that he has information regarding the boy in question, we will certainly inform the . . . the proper authorities."

"But you already *did* hear something from him. You said so." Maria hesitated, then decided being considered an eavesdropper was unimportant. "He's the one who called from a place called the Billy Goat, isn't he?" Erica looked startled and Maria added, "I overheard that. It was him, wasn't it?"

"I . . . I'm afraid that's not something I can divulge."

Maria fought to get control of her breathing. "Why . . . why are you doing this? Hiding something, and quitting the case?"

"We've been—That is, it's . . . a policy decision."

"Did you tell Sister you were quitting? I mean, she has parental authority. She could be the client, even though I'm paying."

"As I said, Sister didn't seem to be feeling well." Erica leaned toward Maria. "Look, the reason I told you what Sister said was to encourage you, because if her suspicion is right, and if those men believe they can profit from the boy, then you know he's of more value to them alive and healthy." Erica stood up before Maria could think of a response. "At any rate," she said, coming around from behind her desk, "you were our client, and I've given you as complete a report as possible. And now . . ."

Maria let herself be shown the door. She wouldn't have known what else to say or ask, even if she'd been given the chance.

She stood at the elevator, remembering back to her own conversation with Sister Noonie about Paulo. Sister seemed not to be saying everything she thought, and then said they should leave the matter in God's hands. But if there really was a God—and Maria had lots of problems with *that* whole issue—but if there *was* one, and if he wanted Paulo back at Porto de Deus, then . . . whose hands were God's hands, anyway?

She went back to the reception room. "Hey, welcome back." The young man smiled. Guys were so . . . obvious, sometimes.

"I wonder," Maria said, "did I have a raincoat with me when I came in?" Erica Donaldson wasn't in sight.

"No," the guy said. "I mean, it hasn't rained for a week, so . . ."

"Maybe not," she said. "I'm just so upset." She moved closer and, hating the idea, put her left hand on the desk and leaned toward him. "Ms. Donaldson told me all about the man assigned to my case being missing."

"She told you?"

"Of course," she said. "Mr. Riggs."

"You mean Riggins."

"Oh, right. You must all be frantic. Ms. Donaldson seems to think very highly of him."

"Tell me about it. Came over from the FBI. He was their top African-American agent in Chicago. He's smart and very aggressive. Although I guess he doesn't always . . . you know . . . stick to the rules."

"Really." She leaned a little lower. "Did you talk to him when he called in?"

"No. Uh-uh, not me." The guy was getting a little tongue-tied. "I just heard . . . well . . . that he called in from down in the Loop somewhere."

"Really. Did everything seem . . . okay?"

"Well . . . I guess so." His eyes seemed fixed on her fingers, as she ran them lightly over her skin from her throat down to the top button of her blouse. "I mean, that's all I heard."

She believed him. He'd have given his social security number and his mother's maiden name if she'd asked. "Yes," she said, and straightened up. "That's pretty much what Ms. Donaldson told me." She looked around. "Well, I guess I didn't have a raincoat, after all."

FOURTEEN

It was easier to leave the Mercedes parked where it was, so Maria hailed a cab and the driver actually spoke English. "The Billy Goat?" he said. "In the Loop? Sure, I know the place."

It was a ten-minute ride. The Billy Goat was one large room with a bar along half of one side and square pillars holding up the floor above. It was basically a tavern that served get-it-yourself food from a grill. There were tables and chairs for maybe a hundred, but it was Saturday, and not even noon yet, and there were just a few people scattered around here and there.

The guy at the grill pointed at a woman sitting alone at a table, and said her name was Joanie. Not really having much hope that the woman could remember one particular man out of a Friday crowd, Maria went over and Joanie said yes, she'd been working the register all day yesterday.

"I hate to bother you on your break," Maria said, but sat down across from her anyway. "I'm looking for someone who was here right around noon yesterday. A man."

"Yeah, well, that narrows it down to about two, three hundred guys." Joanie blew two little streams of cigarette smoke out through her nostrils. She was maybe five years older than Maria, with a weary expression, but friendly—maybe even glad to have someone to talk to. "He a regular?" she said. "A few o' them I know their names."

"His name's Riggins. I can't say whether—"

"Don't know the name."

"He's African-American."

"Great. That cuts it down to maybe—" Joanie suddenly frowned and shook her head. "Say, why's everyone so interested in noon yesterday?"

"I'm sorry," Maria said. "I don't know what you mean."

"There was a couple guys in here yesterday afternoon, asking if I knew some guy who was in around lunchtime." She knocked the ash off her cigarette. "But it wasn't a black guy they were asking about."

"Probably just a coincidence."

"Uh-huh. Except I been working here four years and nobody ever asked and now I got two people asking about the same lunchtime."

"But they weren't asking about a black man. Right?"

"Right," Joanie said. "They were looking for the guy who had the little boy in his arms." Maria felt her jaw drop open for an instant, and she lost track of what Joanie was saying. " '. . . a big guy? With a dark complexion?' I ask," Joanie went on. "And they say 'yeah,' and I say—"

"Wait! This guy that had the little boy, he wasn't a black man?"

"Didn't I just *say* that? I said he was—"

"Okay." Maria was confused. "Well, could he have been, like, Russian, maybe?"

"No way. I told you. Italian. I seen him in here before, always with another guy. His cousin. Sal, I think. We talked a couple times. Not Sal, I mean, but me and the guy. Works for the city. Whatcha call it? Corporation counsel. Gonna be a lawyer, he says. Both of 'em great looking. Hot, y' know?" She raised her eyebrows and pursed her lips. "Except they both look more like Mafia guys than lawyers. Sal, especially." She paused to suck on her cigarette. "Guys asking about him, though, *they* could've been Russian or something. Both of 'em real creeps, too. I told them to buzz off, 'cause I'm too busy to notice anyone in particular."

"Two of them? Russian?" Maria was out of breath just trying to keep up.

"Uh-huh. I mean, some kind of accent like that." The woman stubbed out the cigarette in the little foil ashtray. "You know," she said when she looked up at Maria again, "you don't look so good, honey. I mean, if there's something wrong you oughta go to the cops or something."

"No, no, I'm fine. Just tired. Jet lag, maybe. Except I don't think you get jet lag flying up from Brazil." Just talking, not knowing what to say. "Anyway, it's just like, you know . . . it's like a divorce thing. Sort of complicated. Not a police thing, though."

"That's good, 'cause I don't wanna get—"

"No, no, no," Maria interrupted. "Nothing like that. But let's see if I got it right. There was this Italian guy who had a little boy in his arms, and there were these two Russian-like guys asking about him later, and . . ." The woman was nodding along with her. "And no black guy at all?"

"Well, I mean sure, they come in all the time, but—Wait, hold on a minute. I didn't think of it before, but when I first noticed . . . I mean little kids are hardly ever in here. First time I seen him was right here." Joanie stuck out her hand and pointed straight down at the floor next to her. "Walking right past this table, which is where the Italian guy and his cousin always sit. And there was this black guy, and the kid—hadda be the same little boy, y' know?—right beside him, like they were together."

"You mean . . ." Maria's mind was spinning again. The Intertec agent, Riggins, must have somehow gotten Paulo away from the Russians. "Where did they go?"

"I wasn't paying much attention. Never noticed the black guy after that. And not the kid again, either, not till I seen the Italian guy carrying him. Scrawny little kid, but still, kinda old to be carried around. Anyway, that's the last I seen 'em."

"You didn't see them leave?"

"We were pretty busy, y' know? Fridays are the worst."

"Of course." Maria had the same shoulder bag she'd emptied out at customs the day before, and remembered there was a pen in it. "Um . . . do you have something to write on?" Joanie gave her a book of matches and Maria wrote in it and gave it back. "There's my name and number. Would you give this to the Italian guy if you see him again? Ask him to call me? I mean, about the little boy, y' know, we're not . . ."

"I know what you mean and . . . yeah . . ." Joanie looked at the matchbook. "Yeah, Maria, I'll give it to him, but—" She was staring at something behind Maria. "One of 'em's back."

"One of who?"

"One of the guys asking questions yesterday. Russians or whatever. Coming this way. What an asshole. You wanna talk to him?"

"Oh God, no. I don't even want him to see me, or know who I am, or that I'm interested. Where can I—"

"Too late," Joanie said.

Their little table was only big enough for two, but the man grabbed a chair from another table and sat down with them, without asking. His clothes were casual and expensive. Dark pants, brown leather jacket, tan crewneck sweater that looked like cashmere. He was athletic and aggressive looking, and for some reason Maria thought of those European soccer players you see on TV during the Olympics. But there was something else, too. Even though he smiled as he sat down, she couldn't help but shudder. There was something—a sense of meanness, or cruelty—that hung in the air around him like an unpleasant odor.

Joanie glared at the man. "What now?" she said. Maria couldn't have said a word if she'd wanted to.

The man pointed to the pack of Newports lying next to Joanie's empty cup. "Smoking is too bad for you," he said. His accent reminded Maria of the cab driver who'd driven her home from O'Hare the day before. "Is making cancer," he added.

"What's with you?" Joanie said. "You wanna talk, you're outta luck. I don't know nothing now I didn't know yesterday."

"Is fine. Just checking does my friend from yesterday come back today."

"People in here during the week work downtown. They're not here on Saturdays."

"Is okay, honey." It sounded like *hawney*. "I wait."

"Yeah, well, my break's over." Joanie gathered her cigarettes, the matchbook, and her coffee cup and stood up. "And my friend's got somewhere to be." She looked at Maria and gestured toward the door. "You don't wanna be late . . . uh . . . Judy."

"But my name's—" Maria stopped. "Oh, sure." She looked at her watch. "But I have a few minutes yet. You go ahead back to work. And . . . thanks, okay?"

"Yeah, sure." Joanie gave her a look that said she must be crazy, then headed for the cash register.

When Maria turned back the man was staring at her, with that cruel smile on his face. He didn't drop his gaze until finally she looked down and pretended to sweep some crumbs off the table with her hand. She was scared, and had no idea what to say, but she couldn't just walk away from maybe her only chance to learn what happened to Paulo.

"No food?" the man said, waving his hand across the empty table. "No drink?"

"Um, no." She didn't dare even smile. This wasn't a man you'd flirt with to get information. "I just stopped by to talk to my friend."

"Your friend," he said, "gone."

"I know. I just . . . I'm curious about your accent. Is it . . . Lithuanian?"

He made a face, and moved his lips like he was spitting. "Not Litwanian," he said. "Rawssian." Then he leaned toward her. "You want something drink, huh. Beer?" He had an entirely new look on his face.

She leaned back away from him, startled. He must have thought she was coming on to him, for God's sake. "Oh no," she said. She stood up and knew she was blushing. "It's like a habit of mine . . . guessing accents. I have to go now."

"Bye-bye," he called, as she hurried away. "Bye-bye . . . Judy."

She hadn't noticed how many people had come in since she arrived. Most of the stools at the bar were taken, and maybe six or seven tables, and people were lining up to pay and pick up their orders from the grill. Joanie was too busy to look up to return her wave.

As Maria got near the front door, a woman stepped in front of her to go out, too. A small woman in a cloth coat that stopped at her knees to reveal a blue, ankle-length dress. She had a wool scarf on her head, tied under her chin and making a hood that put her face in shadow. A *babushka,* Maria thought. Good Lord, was *she* a Russian, too? She looked pretty harmless, though, and Maria hurried and reached around to push the door open for her.

"Thank you," the woman said, but she didn't raise her head, not until both of them were out on the sidewalk and a few steps away from the door. Then she stopped directly in front of Maria and turned, and did look up at her.

Maria stared back. The woman's face was round and

pleasant-looking, full of lines and wrinkles as though weathered by the sun and wind. She was pretty old, and she had the clearest, deepest blue eyes Maria had ever seen.

"It is not safe here for us to talk," the woman suddenly said.

"What? I don't—"

"You and I might help each other if you come with me, my dear."

FIFTEEN

It was a tough call. They were up off the grass and back on a park bench. Paulo had found an old stick from a Popsicle and fiddled with it like it was something interesting. Charlie was thinking maybe he should go to the cops, and get it over with. What use was it to wait until noon?

He just couldn't make up his mind. He leaned back on the bench and closed his eyes, and right away he saw again all those little puffed-up red circles on Paulo's rear end, and around his crotch. The other scars, too, double-line scars that looked like pinches from a fucking pair of pliers. His stomach churned and bubbled up, and he belched and leaned forward and dropped his head down between his knees and kept his eyes closed tight.

But he didn't throw up, not this time. And now he didn't even see anything. Instead, he heard something.

It started like it came from far away, from the other end of the block or something. It was a little kid, screaming. Howling. Louder and louder, moving closer. Over and over, and Charlie couldn't open his eyes and he couldn't make it stop. And finally it was right there, all around him, filling the whole world with one high-pitched wail of pain and terror after another, in a series that would never end, never—

Snap! Something broke and the screaming broke off with it.

He opened his eyes. Those cries of pain, and worse than pain, had seemed as real as the bench they sat on, as real as Paulo and the Popsicle stick he had broken in two and dropped

in front of them. But they'd existed only in his head. He turned
to Paulo and saw the boy's eyes wide open, staring at something
past Charlie's shoulder. He twisted around and looked. There,
right in the park, a blue and white squad car, headed along the
asphalt path toward them.

He stood up. He hadn't actually promised Zorina he would
wait, and this was the perfect time to stop dicking around and
get it over with. But when he turned back Paulo's eyes were
squeezed shut and he was shaking so hard anyone could have
seen it. Damn! He shouldn't just hand the kid over to a couple
of uniformed cops who wouldn't know what to do . . . and
wouldn't care. He should take him into a station. Explain
everything to, like, a youth officer. A woman, maybe. Someone
who wouldn't scare the shit out of the kid.

Anyway, not here. Not now.

He grabbed Paulo and lifted him up and held him with both
hands way over his head and—where he got the idea from he
didn't know—started spinning around like they were playing
airplane and Paulo was the plane.

"Zooooom, zooooom," Charlie said, hoping the cops would
drive on by. "Zoooom, zooo—"

"Hey you!" It was the one on the passenger side, yelling out
the open window. "Hey! Captain Marvel!"

Charlie slowed down and, still waving Paulo around in the air
a little, looked at the cop. *"Sí, señor?"* He put on his best imita-
tion of Juan Rivera, when Juan was pretending he didn't know
any English.

"You see a black guy run through here?" the cop said. "Blue
pants and a red T-shirt?"

Charlie lowered Paulo from above his head, but kept him in
his arms. He leaned toward the cop as though trying to figure
out what he was saying. *"Por favor?"* he said. *"No hablo Inglés."*

"Aw, shit," the cop said.

Charlie felt Paulo shaking, and he squeezed him a little tighter. *"No hablo Inglés,"* he said again, but like he really wanted to help.

The cop's partner, in the driver's seat, gave it a try. *"Hombre?"* he called. He pronounced the "h," and then gave up on the Spanish. "Tall, skinny black guy. In a red shirt."

Charlie squeezed Paulo tight to him. *"Hombre?"* he said. *"No hombre aquí, señor."* He swept one arm out to include the whole park.

The cop closer to him stared at Paulo, then said to Charlie, "That your kid?"

"Uh . . . no hablo Inglés." He was taking a huge step, and he knew it. But with Paulo trembling like he was? No way Charlie could hand him over.

The cop turned to his partner. "Looks like that Brazilian kid, the one in the picture they showed us at—"

"Fuck that." The driver yanked on the shift lever. "We got a homicide to—" The car roared away and that's all Charlie heard.

The bus was nearly empty and Paulo sat in the window seat. Afraid the cops would come back looking for "that Brazilian kid," Charlie had scooped the boy up in his arms and left the park and caught the first bus he could find. It turned out to be a Grand Avenue bus, headed for downtown, but he didn't care where they were going.

That your kid? The cop had given Charlie the perfect chance to hand the boy over. Instead, here he was, with—

Clang . . . clang . . . clang . . . clang.

A loud, insistent bell sounded a warning outside the bus and Charlie and Paulo both looked out the window. They were crossing the bridge over the Chicago River. Just after they got across, the bus stopped. The bell was still clanging its warning and Charlie turned Paulo's head a little and pointed back to show him where a barrier with flashing red lights had come down to block off the bridge they'd just crossed over. Then, as they watched, the whole bridge started to tilt itself up on end to let a boat pass under.

The silent boy squeezed Charlie's hand, and the bus lurched forward again, and they left the bridge—and the barricade—behind them.

★ ★ ★ ★ ★

PART II
REAL LIFE

★ ★ ★ ★ ★

Lieutenant Colonel Bill Grayson's aching, swollen knee kept him awake all Friday night.

The nights were always bad. During the day the light was poor enough in the windowless hut, but after sundown the four men might have been shut inside a tomb. They had to feel their way to the hole in the floor that served as a toilet and opened into a pit too shallow to keep the stench at a distance.

With the first dim light of morning, Grayson stood up and began his stretching routine. The biggest struggle was the mental one, to keep your bearings, to stay strong. He tried to get the DEA guys to join him, but they were in a sour mood. Last night was the worst so far, for him because of his knee, and for all of them because the woman, Nita, hadn't shown up with supper. They were hungry—and rightfully angry at him for his stupid, useless show of resistance.

On all the other nights Nita had come, always a few hours after sundown. The food she brought was mostly scrapings off other plates. Gnawed chicken or pork bones, cold rice, congealed sauces. All in a big wooden bowl. Still, it was the best—and often the only—meal of the day.

A guard would enter and set a dim lantern on the wooden floor—sending the roaches and the occasional scorpion or centipede scurrying—and Nita would come in behind him. She would set the bowl beside the lantern and divide the food with a wooden scraper onto four metal plates. On the first night the guard spoke to her after she split up the food, obviously telling her to wait outside. She spat something back and they had a sharp exchange, all in Portuguese. Then the guard hung his head and went out and closed the door, and Nita—and the light—stayed.

She was older than Grayson. Sixty, maybe. Her skin was blacker than his, her features more African. She was a tall woman, and wide; with short, tightly curled black hair turning gray. Her large breasts swung freely under the long, shapeless dresses she wore.

On the first night he had wondered why she stayed and watched them eat. Because that's all she did. Stood with her back to the wall and watched them eat with their fingers and suck up every last scrap that wasn't solid bone. Then she gathered up the plates and bowl and knocked on the door. The guard opened it and she was gone, the light gone with her.

On the second night, though, after the guard left and they all had their plates, Nita beckoned to Grayson. Leaving the lantern on the floor in the middle of the room, she drew him over to a corner. "My name is Nita," she said, her voice barely more than a whisper. "Tell me your name." Her accent was like the guards', but more musical. More African, he thought.

Grayson and she talked together each night after that, while he and the men ate. The guards would not interrupt, she explained, because she lied and convinced them the capitão *would be furious if they did. She said she was African, like her parents, but born in the "wild mountains" north of Rio. She must practice her English, she explained, and learn about America, where she and her grand-*

daughter were going soon to live.

He thought at first it was a trick, but soon decided she actually believed her childish dream of going to the US. Except she always talked about her own tragic life more than asking him anything. The DEA guys were pissed off, wondering why she talked only to him. He said she chose him because he was black and she'd never met a white man she trusted—which she hadn't said, but was probably true. He told them it couldn't hurt to cultivate a friend in the enemy's camp.

He learned that Nita was the oldest of five children and her father had worked in a gold mine. She and her sister were sent to a "nuns' school," where they learned English. But when she was twelve her father died in the mine and her mother took the two girls and their three small brothers to Rio de Janeiro. "To make a fine new life," she told them.

They settled in Juramento, one of the favelas*—hopeless shanty towns that rose up on the hills around the city. Her mother worked in a laundry twelve hours a day and died in only a few years, "because of her terrible sadness." By then Nita's sister had been lost to the street life and drugs. Nita had a baby herself, and became a mother also to her brothers. "But for nothing," she said, because none of them lived to see twenty. Two were shot by Rio police for the crime of running the streets and making the merchants' customers nervous. The other sold himself and died of AIDS. Her daughter died giving birth to a child, Rosa, a beautiful girl Nita raised as her own. Then, when Rosa became a teenager and was hired as a maid, Nita got a job as a cook for the same man, Flavio Rabassa—which was how Grayson learned their captor's name.*

"A capitão *in the police," she said. "He lives in a big house in Rio, and when he comes here he brings servants with him."*

"So he's a very rich man, then?" Grayson asked.

"He is a bad policeman. He makes money on the poor people, and those who take the drugs." She spat on the floor. "But me," she said, "I practice the English and I save from the little he pays me, to take

my baby to New York City, USA, where we will make a fine new future."

Dream on, he thought. It sure beats the hell out of real life.

Then last night Nita hadn't come; and this morning, Saturday, still no food.

Finally, about midway through the morning, Flavio Rabassa appeared in the doorway. "Good day, gentlemen. I hope you had good sleeping." His voice was soft and smooth; his English awkward, but understandable. He turned and said something in Portuguese.

"Sim, capitão," someone answered.

Gold Tooth came in with his M11 and a straight-backed wooden chair painted yellow, then stepped aside as the big capitão *carefully lowered himself onto the chair. "I also hope you have learned to obey orders," he said, "and do not all go hungry because of one man's foolishness."*

Amusement and cruelty shone again in the man's eyes, a look Grayson had first seen years ago, in the eyes of a bully he'd known as a kid. One of his friends had found a turtle near Granny Creek and named it Myrtle and carried it with him everywhere. One day the bully, older and bigger and stronger than any of them, grabbed Myrtle and smashed her flat against a slab of rock . . . splat! "Damn," the mean boy said, laughing, "musta been one o' them soft-shelled *turtles." Lucky for Grayson the bully's head was tougher than Myrtle's shell, and didn't cave in when Grayson slammed it against the same rock.*

Those cruel, mocking eyes were back again today, as Rabassa said, "Do I make myself clear?"

"Very clear," Grayson said. "So, what are the charges against us?"

"Ah, but I am not the one here to answer questions." Rabassa smiled and took a small notebook and a pen from his shirt pocket.

Grayson did the answering. They'd been on a drug mis-sion in Colombia and got separated from their guide. If they were in Brazil when they were picked up it was news to them. When he demanded medical attention, Rabassa laughed. Grayson's knee hurt like hell, but to tell the truth—which he didn't—it was functional.

Rabassa seemed more interested in taunting them than in getting answers, and finally Grayson challenged him. "If we'd broken some law your country would want us held publicly accountable. So you're acting on your own. You have no—"

"Please," Rabassa said, shaking his head as though saddened by a child's foolishness. "You are not so stupid as you pretend. We both know your adventure has broken many laws and treaties."

"Then why aren't we charged? Why aren't we taken before a court?"

"Ah, but ask a better question. Why is there no one to rescue you? Are you forgotten by your government? Or are they less interested in you, and more interested in keeping your illegal invasion of my country a secret?"

"But you can't just keep us in this—"

"Look around and see what I can do." Rabassa spread his arms. "Of course, I could also put you on display, make known to the world one more scheme by the Americans to destabilize the countries of Latin America through covert military operations. 'Covert,' that is the word?"

"I told you. It was a drug—"

"Ah, yes . . . and maybe you will go home soon." He sounded suddenly optimistic. "Or maybe," in a nastier tone, "maybe quiet negotiations with your leaders will break down, and you will be taken before a judge, and then rot your lives away in some Brazilian shithouse." He stood up and Gold Tooth grabbed the chair. Rabassa stopped in the doorway and turned back toward them. "That is the word, yes? 'Shithouse'?"

Sixteen

Maria stood outside the Billy Goat Tavern and watched the old woman walk away. *You and I might help each other,* the woman had said.

Why in the world should Maria follow after someone she didn't even know? The woman was obviously eccentric. On a warm spring day like this, to wear a wool scarf over your head and a long black coat? Unusual. Not normal. All Maria had done was push the door open for a stranger.

Except she was certain now that the woman had deliberately stepped in front of her, wanting to go out the door just when Maria did. And she'd spoken with a sort of gentle insistence; first warning her, then inviting her. Or actually . . . more advising than inviting. Which was absurd, of course.

The woman had walked west and was all the way to the end of the block now, waiting for the light to change at Wacker Drive. She'd probably turn around pretty soon now, to see if Maria was following. But no, when the light changed she went across Wacker, a wide four-lane street, and then turned left. That would take her under the tall, stone-pillared portico that ran the whole block along the front of the Civic Opera House. Maria lost sight of her. What a strange—

Bang! The door of the Billy Goat burst open and she jumped a foot. Two men came out, laughing and talking, and Maria suddenly thought about the Russian. She didn't want him coming out and finding her still there. He was obviously part of the group that kidnapped Paulo. So she hurried down the sidewalk, in the same direction the woman had gone.

The Russians were looking for a man with a little boy, so obviously they didn't have Paulo any more. That agent, Riggins—who was only supposed to keep Paulo in sight—must somehow have interfered. He had to be the black man Joanie saw. But he didn't have Paulo now, either. Some Italian guy had him.

The light at Wacker turned green and Maria went across and then turned south, the way the old woman had gone. The Italian guy shouldn't be all that hard to identify. Worked for . . . what was it? The corporation counsel's office. Had a cousin named Sal. The police could find him, for sure. But Sister Noonie had been quite anxious not to involve the police, obviously not trusting them to act in Paulo's best interest. Maria hadn't understood that, and still didn't. If a crime was committed you called the police. But Sister Noonie was no fool and even if Maria had disregarded her advice, she wasn't about to do something Sister thought might be harmful to Paulo. So no police, not yet. Maybe she should tell Erica Donaldson about the Italian guy, and what the Billy Goat cashier had said. Then again, maybe not. Intertec had quit the case, period, and for reasons they didn't even want to explain.

She came to the next corner, Madison Street. Now what? Maybe she shouldn't have let the old woman out of her sight. Was she still around somewhere?

There! Halfway across the bridge over the branch of the river that ran along behind the Opera House. Walking west again. Maria followed her, stepping up her pace a little. Why was she doing this? The woman was probably loony tunes. Except Maria had seen her eyes and they sure didn't look like the eyes of a crazy person. They were unusual eyes, yes, but not crazy. They showed kindness and . . . and what? Intelligence?

As far as her being able to help, all Maria wanted was to find Paulo. How could this woman possibly know anything about Paulo?

She was still up ahead, walking over the bridge, then across Canal Street. Maria gained on her, about half a block back now, but the light at Canal turned red. Maria waited and watched for an opening, then dashed across against the light. She didn't want to lose sight of the woman again.

But . . . where was she? She'd gone straight after crossing Canal, but now there was no black coat in sight. There were cabs parked all along the curb, and Maria realized she'd come to the Ogilvie Transportation Center, a high-rise that on its lower levels housed the Metra commuter train station.

But no black coat. The woman had either flown away, or hopped into a cab, or gone into the train station. The first two seemed about equally unlikely, so Maria went through the revolving door into the station.

Ten minutes later Maria spotted the woman again—black coat, scarf on her head—at a table by herself in the huge ground-floor food court. Maria hurried over and then, when she got there, didn't know what to do or say.

The woman looked up. Not smiling, but again with a calm kindness in her expression. "Please, sit down," she said. "I bought two lunches, from over there." She pointed off to one of the food counters. "They appear to be quite fresh." She had an accent Maria couldn't place.

She found herself sitting down, wondering whether she should. On the table were two salads in clear plastic boxes—both unopened—two dinner rolls with butter, and two soft drinks in paper cups that said Pepsi on the side. She'd had no breakfast and was suddenly very hungry, and those salads looked *soooo* good. "Is one of these," she asked, "for me?"

"I'm sure you prefer diet soda," the woman said, and pushed one salad and one drink closer to Maria. "And a salad for lunch is—"

"Wait," Maria said, finally getting hold of her wits. "Just wait one minute. I don't know you. How do you know what I eat or drink? And what made you so sure I was coming? I didn't even know myself, and you didn't look back. Oh, and why did you say we might help each other?"

"My name is Zorina," the woman said. "I have the gift of seeing." The accent was European. German, maybe? Not like the Russian's. "I know, for example, that your name is not Judy."

"No, it's not. It's Maria." Why did she give her name? "But how do you know this?"

"The name? When the cashier woman called you 'Judy' I saw and heard how you responded." The woman opened her salad. "And the food? Would someone look at you, and buy a cheeseburger or a slice of pizza for your lunch?" She smiled a patient smile. "A gift, but not so magical," she added. "But please, eat first. And then we shall discuss . . . about the boy."

"*What?*" The word came out so loud it turned a few nearby heads. Maria leaned forward and half whispered, "What do you know about—"

"Please," the woman said, "I have not eaten since early yesterday."

"Fine," Maria said. She poked a straw into her drink and opened her salad. "But here." She pulled a twenty-dollar bill from her purse. "This should cover the lunch."

"It was less than that," the woman said. "But I don't have enough money to give you change."

Maria told her to forget the change, and they started to eat. Maria felt a little like Alice after her tumble down the rabbit hole. The woman claimed her knowledge wasn't magical, but . . . "You haven't answered how you knew I'd come after you."

"Let us say I decided. I did not wish to stand and talk where that man might see us. I had watched you in the restaurant. I heard some of what you said to the cashier, and to the man. I decided you were a person who might take the chance." She paused. "Are you going to eat your roll?"

"No, you take it." She did, and Maria asked, "Were you waiting for me at the Billy Goat? What do you know about . . . about a boy?"

"Waiting, yes. For you?" The woman gave a little shrug of her thin shoulders. "Waiting for anyone connected to the boy. Perhaps I most expected the return of that man. He is a dangerous man."

"I know," Maria said. "But I didn't see you."

"People often do not see what is around them." She ate the last of her salad, and reached for her drink. "People often do not look beyond what they expect to see."

"But you do?" Maria felt she should challenge this Zorina person. She seemed to be avoiding talking about Paulo . . . if she knew anything at all about him. "That's your so-called *gift?*"

"Yes." The woman ignored her sarcasm. "That is a part of it." She'd finished her salad and both rolls, and sucked on her straw until the sound said there was nothing left but air and ice. She set the cup down and smiled a shy smile. "I'm so glad," she said, "that you took the diet one."

Maria laughed in spite of herself, and finished her own drink. "I'll get us each another."

"Yes," the woman said, obviously pleased. "Then we will discuss."

Maria got up and took both cups with her. Who was crazier? She? Or this Zorina? What could the woman possibly know about Paulo? There was a line of people ahead of her and when she finally got to the counter the young man told her that refills weren't free. "That's okay," she said, and handed him the two cups. "One diet, one regular."

He threw away the two empty cups and handed her two more, already filled, from rows lined up on the counter.

As she paid she said, "Sort of wasteful, isn't it?" But he clearly had no idea what she was talking about. She turned and headed back to the table. She was halfway there before she noticed Zorina was gone.

She looked around. Less than half the tables in the food court were occupied. Probably because it was Saturday. But no Zorina. There were more tables on the other side of the escalators up to the train departure area, but the woman wasn't there, either. Maybe she went to the ladies' room. Maria started that way, but her handbag kept wanting to slide off her shoulder and made carrying the two cups difficult.

She turned and set the drinks down on a table—and Zorina stepped up and took one of them. "This way," she said. "Hurry." She stepped onto the escalator, walking up the moving stairs.

Maria followed, feeling more like Alice than ever. By now, though, she was also convinced that this Zorina, as weird as she was, had no bad intentions toward her at all. Besides, the middle of the day? In such a public place? She had Alicia's party to go to that night, but nothing until then. Why not see where this was leading?

At the top, without pausing or turning around, Zorina headed out the doors to the train departure area, paused just an instant, then scurried toward a train that several other people were running to catch.

Beside the last car of the train a conductor in a short-sleeved white shirt stood by the door, one hand on the bar to pull himself up. *"All aboard!"* he shouted, just like in the movies. "Up you go, young lady," he said, half lifting poor old Zorina up the steep steps.

Maria stepped up, too, and behind her the train's doors closed.

SEVENTEEN

Charlie and Paulo transferred to a bus that was headed back in the direction of Charlie's place. This one was pretty empty, too, and Charlie led the boy all the way to the backseat.

"So," he said when they were settled in, " 'that Brazilian kid' . . . is that you?" Paulo, of course, didn't respond and Charlie was thinking how Juan Rivera would say it. *"Bra-seal?"* he asked, exaggerating. *"Pow-lo,* from *Bra-seal?"*

The boy blinked and his big eyes went wet with tears again.

"Hey, relax," Charlie said. "Everything's gonna be fine."

So he had learned that Paulo was Brazilian . . . and that the cops were looking for him. Now he had to talk to Zorina. She might have found out something, too. She did have *some* kind of gift. Maybe they could learn enough about Paulo to be able to turn him over to someone besides the cops, someone who didn't make him shake like his joints might tear loose. Zorina must be right. The kid was afraid the cops would give him back to whatever fucking creepo had tortured him. Well, no way Charlie was gonna be part of that.

By the time he and Paulo got off the bus, Charlie had decided that if he got in trouble with the cops he'd remind them he tried to tell those two on Halsted Street, and they weren't interested. And if that didn't work, then fuck it. He wouldn't let Paulo be sent somewhere without at least trying to make sure he didn't go back to being beaten and burned all over again.

They walked past one of those storefront branch public librar-
ies and he had an idea. He took Paulo inside and went up to
the woman at the desk. "They don't speak Spanish in Brazil,
right? They speak . . . what is it again?"

"Portuguese. That's the primary language of Brazil." She
looked at Paulo and smiled.

"Yeah, right," he said. "I knew that, but I couldn't think of
it."

"We have some lovely children's books about Brazil." She
stood up. "I can—"

"No, that's okay."

They went back outside and he bought a *Sun-Times* and they
walked to his place and started up the back stairs. It was still a
while until noon and it was a warm day. The Riveras were gone,
so they sat at a little table on Juan and Carmela's back porch
and Charlie paged through the paper. Paulo found a coloring
book on the porch floor with a picture of some kind of fat purple
animal on the cover, and laid it on the table in front of him.
And every time Charlie turned a page of the *Sun-Times,* the kid
turned a page of the coloring book.

It made Charlie nervous.

There was nothing in the paper about a missing kid. Nothing
about a black guy murdered in a Loop alley, either. The body
was already gone when he went back there with Paulo, so why
tell anyone he saw what happened? No one knew that but him—
and the killers. Telling the cops wouldn't help the dead guy, and
it wouldn't mean anything but trouble for himself. He could see
that Russian again, staring at him in the backseat of the squad
car, then smiling and warning him to keep his mouth shut.

He went through the paper, half reading things he wasn't
even interested in, waiting for Zorina to come back so they
could figure out what to do.

So where was she?

He suddenly remembered his phone. Maybe she left him a message. "C'mon, Paulo, let's go."

His place was all closed up and smelled stuffy. Or was some of it the smell of Paulo's pee? He had a screen door, so he left the inner door open. His answering machine showed two messages.

He hit *Play* and heard Zorina: "I have found someone who will help," she said. "I beg you. Do nothing with the boy until we talk. Please. We are coming there."

She *found* someone?

The machine beeped and went into the second message: "There's some cops on the way to talk to you about something." His cousin Sal. "You must have given them your ma's address and your sister sent them to me. I hadda tell them where you really live."

Damn! How long ago did Sal call? He ran and shut the door and locked it, then went back to the phone to call Sal. But before he could tap out the whole number he hung up because he heard someone on his porch. Then banging on his door. Loud. The door had no window, but he'd bet it was the cops knocking.

Or worse yet—the Russians.

Paulo looked scared, and Charlie scooped him up and ran as far from the door as his one-room apartment allowed. The knocking stopped, then started up again. If he didn't answer maybe they'd go away. But they might leave someone watching and he'd have to go out sometime, for chrissake, and there was only the one way out. Except . . .

He set Paulo down and ran and slid the dresser to the side and pulled up the trapdoor. The knocking didn't let up. "Open the door, please." It was a woman's voice. "It's the police."

Paulo started shaking then, as he and Charlie looked down into a closet in the apartment below. There was a ladder attached to the wall and they could go down there, and then down another flight and out through Mrs. Rivera's front door. But then he realized the cops might be watching the front of the place, too.

"You go down there," he said, pointing and gesturing to spell out what he was saying, "and I'll stay up here and answer the door."

Paulo's eyes widened and he threw his arms around Charlie's waist. Charlie pried him loose and, as the knocking got louder, Paulo gave in and climbed down. Charlie leaned and put his finger to his lips to say be quiet. Then he closed the trapdoor and put the shag rug over it.

The knocking kept up. "What?" Charlie finally yelled. "Who is it?" Taking off his shoes and socks, and his shirt.

"It's the police, Charles," the woman said, using his first name like cops do. *"Open the door!"*

He ran into the bathroom, stuck his head and chest in the shower, and turned on the water. God, it was cold! "I'm coming," he hollered, then grabbed a towel and ran over and opened the door.

"Investigator Swanson," the female cop said, and waved a badge at him. She was short, white, over forty, and wore a gray pants suit. "You're Charles Long?"

Two male uniformed cops were with her. One was the male half of the team he'd talked to on Halsted the day before. "That's him," he said.

How would Sal act, Charlie thought, if something like this happened?

"You're Charles Long?" the woman cop, Swanson, asked again.

He rubbed the towel through his hair with one hand and made a point of locking the screen door hook with the other. Showing he wasn't scared. Which he was. "Yes ma'am," he said.

109

"But I go by Charlie."

"Can we come in?" she said, and reached for the door handle.

"No, ma'am. It's locked." He and Sal had talked about this a hundred times. You don't let cops inside your fucking house without a fucking warrant. Period. You don't know what kinda shit they might find—or might *say* they found.

"We'd like to talk to you," she said.

"You have a warrant?"

"What are you, a *lawyer?*" This from the other male cop—not the one from yesterday—who stepped up beside the woman. Light brown hair, long for a cop, and a sneer like a fucking Nazi in an old-time war flick.

"Not me." Charlie was pissed off now, but controlling himself. "I got a cousin who's a lawyer, though, and he says—"

"Sorry, pal, but your guinea cousin's not here." The cop yanked hard on the door and ripped the hook right out of the wood and stepped inside, brushing past Charlie.

"Get back out here, Harter," Swanson said. "Use your head."

"Maybe he's got the kid here." The cop named Harter took a look around the apartment, which took about five seconds. "No one here," he said, and went back outside. "Place smells like a toilet. You got another cousin who's a plumber, you should call *him.*"

"I call anyone," Charlie said, "it'll be nine-one-one." He was starting to lose it now. "Tell 'em how some cop named Harter pulled the hook outta my door and fucking broke into my place. Tell 'em—"

"Relax, Charlie," Swanson said. "I'd like you to come with me right now to the station." She paused. "Then you can report your door hook in person if you want to."

He calmed down and she said they were there about the boy—"the one you told the officers about yesterday." He knew sooner or later he'd have to go, and with Zorina on her way it was best to get the cops out of here right now. He said he'd be out as soon as he got dressed, and closed the inside door and locked it.

He opened the trapdoor and whispered down to Paulo—with hand signals to help explain—that he had to go somewhere and Paulo should stay there until he got back and everything would be fine. Paulo stared up at him and seemed to understand, and nodded. Eyes wide open like Charlie was God, and he knew Charlie would take care of him and keep him safe.

Yeah, right!

He started to close the trapdoor, then stopped. "And hey," he whispered, "if you gotta take a leak or something, find the bathroom."

Paulo nodded again. Whether he understood, who knew?

Charlie closed the door and covered it with the rug and got dressed in a hurry. He remembered to delete his phone messages, and yelled, "Won't be long now!" and, "I'm coming!" to cover the beeps when he did. He thought of leaving a note for Zorina, but was afraid someone besides her would see it. Then he went outside to go with the cops to the station.

He started down the steps and the asshole, Harter, said, "Forget to lock your door, pal?"

Charlie didn't bother to look at him. "You broke in and looked around. You see anything worth stealing?"

EIGHTEEN

When the doors slid shut behind her and the train started to move, Maria turned and looked out the window. Two stragglers had missed the train: a teenaged boy wearing a Cubs cap, and a tall, attractive woman in tan pants and a blue blazer. The boy walked away, but the woman stood there fumbling with her cell phone, tapping out a number.

"What on earth?" Maria said, to no one in particular, and leaned against the window. But the train moved on and she lost sight of the woman. It couldn't have been the same woman who—

"Come," Zorina said, stepping up to the vestibule platform. Maria followed her up and into the car and they sat together, Zorina in the window seat. She sipped her Pepsi. "Ah," she said, and Maria realized she'd left her own drink behind when they'd made their sudden dash.

"Whatever are we doing on this train?" she asked.

"We will get off at the first stop."

"But why—"

"Tickets, please!"

Maria jumped a foot and looked up and told the conductor they had no tickets and were getting off at whatever the next stop was.

"That's Clybourn," he said. "We'll be there in five minutes."

He said it was two dollars extra each for not buying their tickets in the station. Zorina held out the twenty-dollar bill, but

Maria paid for both of them and the conductor moved on.

"Look here, Miss . . . I mean . . . Zorina." Maria struggled to keep her voice down to a whisper. "You owe me an explanation." She felt like grabbing the woman by the shoulders and shaking her.

Zorina turned to her, and the look on her face was one of surprise. "You are angry?"

"Of course I'm angry!" she whispered. "First you lure me on a wild-goose chase, then promise to explain, then disappear, then drag me onto a train and . . . well . . ." She let her words trail off, because Zorina was staring at her, and Maria knew just what she was thinking.

"Is this what has happened," the woman said, "truly?"

"No." Maria had to smile. "Not truly." Her anger evaporated. "You invited me and I followed. And you didn't drag me. I came with you, because . . . I'm not sure why, actually."

"Because at the Billy Goat Tavern you were intrigued, because you had to go somewhere away from that man, and because you do not always act as a sensible young woman of wealth is expected to act."

"Wait a minute," Maria said. "How do you—"

"Now approaching Clybourn Station!" The intercom was way too loud. *"Clybourn!"*

"When we are off the train," Zorina said, "we will discuss."

"You don't know those things you just said. You're just assuming they're true. And assuming I'll get off the train and go with you."

"I know you will, my dear," she said. "And I know that my trust is not misplaced, and that you look for poor little Paulo only to help him."

They were the only people to get off at Clybourn. The train pulled away and left them alone in the warm sunlight on a long, deserted platform, on an embankment maybe twenty feet above street level.

"We must go quickly," Zorina said, and started toward the steps that led down to the street.

Maria followed, amazed that this strange woman somehow knew about Paulo. Knew his name, knew that Maria was looking for him. No one in the whole northern hemisphere knew that, except possibly Erica Donaldson, the woman at the detective agency.

Zorina eased down the steep steps as though her joints objected, clutching the rail with her thin hand, but never once stopping till they reached the bottom. There were two cabs waiting there, hoping for fares, and they got into the first one. It pulled away and Zorina gave the driver an address which meant nothing at all to Maria.

"Is that your home?" she asked. "Is it where Paulo—"

"You will see." Zorina gestured toward the driver, making it clear she didn't want to talk where someone could overhear them.

They rode in silence then, and Maria was aware that, if someone had challenged her, she could not have justified how absolutely confident she felt now with this woman, and how unafraid.

Barely five minutes later they stopped and got out, and again Zorina offered to pay, and then was obviously thankful that Maria paid. "I have little money," Zorina said, "and perhaps I will need what you have given me."

The cab drove away and they stood on the sidewalk in what seemed like a border zone between a residential area, with old homes and two-flats and trees, and open space where things had been torn down and new construction was going up— mainly town homes.

Across the street was a huge stone church that looked a

hundred years old. Twin bell towers rose at the front corners, and between them wide steps led up to three sets of tall wooden doors. The block was lined with brightly polished cars, most of them decorated with flowers, and the sidewalk and church steps teemed with people of all ages, in what had to be their brightest, fanciest outfits. The air was full of laughter and loud talk. People hugging and greeting and kissing each other like Hollywood stars. And children running everywhere.

You didn't have to be as fluent in Spanish as Maria was to know the people were there for a wedding.

NINETEEN

Maria followed Zorina across the street and up the church steps. No one in the happy crowd paid them any attention, and they went inside. The bride and her chattering entourage and family—at least the female side, the only males in here were little boys—filled the vestibule. Adjusting straps and necklines. Checking hair and mascara in handheld mirrors.

The young women flitted and fluttered like those colorful birds that drank from the cracked fountain in the patio at Porto de Deus. They spoke Spanish, not Portuguese, but still their excitement and enthusiasm made Maria think of Brazil, and of the children of the orphanage. She especially missed—

A sharp tug on her arm brought her back to reality. She followed Zorina through a second set of doors and into the huge, silent church. They went down a side aisle along the wall, and then through an absurdly modern set of plateglass doors and into a tiny side chapel. There was an altar, and a few pews, and the biggest, brightest, most grotesquely bloody statue of Jesus on the cross that Maria had ever seen. Zorina sat down in the last pew, off near the wall of the chapel.

Maria sat beside her and noticed for the first time how hard the old woman was breathing. "Are you okay?" she said. "Can I get you some—"

"It is nothing." The woman looked away and heaved several wheezing breaths, then said, "This is a good place. I will rest here a few moments." She turned back toward the crucifix, but

116

her eyes were closed.

They sat there, side by side, for maybe five minutes, but it seemed forever to Maria. The woman's breathing quieted down, and finally she put a hand on Maria's arm. "There are so many things to think about."

"What do you mean? What things?"

"I listened closely, and overheard things there, at the Billy Goat Tavern. And other things, things not spoken, I could see. About you, I mean."

"Like what? What could you see?"

"That the Russian man frightened you. That you seek a black man who had a boy with him at the restaurant, and know nothing of another man who took the boy. You came here from Brazil, and you are—this is not a criticism—you are not always what people call 'wise,' when they mean 'cautious.' " Zorina paused, then added, "These are things I have heard and seen."

"Maybe you could hear and see all that," Maria said, "but I know I didn't say the boy's *name*. No one said his name. And still you said it on the train. How do you know him? Where is he?"

"We will discuss these things. And I will help you." She looked straight at Maria as she spoke, and Maria had no doubt she meant what she said. "But first," Zorina added, "there is the question of the woman."

"What? The woman?" Then it hit her. "You mean the woman who missed the train?"

"Yes. You were surprised to see her. Who is she?"

"I don't know. I'm not sure I ever—Well, I'd swear she was someone I saw at the airport. I mean, I flew in yesterday from Rio de Janeiro—Brazil, like you said—and after I left customs this woman . . . well, she bumped into me. And then she was gone. It was just such a wild coincidence to see her twice in two days."

"She knows you."

"What?"

"She came into the Billy Goat right after you. She spoke into her phone and watched you. I saw this. Then, at the train station, when I went to make a phone call, I saw her again."

"My God! Who is she?"

"I wonder," Zorina said. "Did she see you looking at her?"

"What? Oh, from the train? I don't think so. She was concentrating on her cell phone just then."

"So perhaps she doesn't know you were running from her."

"But I wasn't run—Oh, of course. That's why we ran to the train."

"And Paulo, he is from Brazil?"

"What?" Maria suddenly felt like that guy her father sent to meet her at the airport, saying *What?* every other sentence.

"Paulo. Is he from—"

"Yes, from Rio de Janeiro. An orphanage. I work there. That is, I . . ." Maria paused. "But anyway, how do you know his name?"

"I learned it from him."

"You *talked* to him? Where is he?"

"The boy does not talk, but he is safe for now. He is with the man the cashier spoke of—the Italian man. He is a good man."

"Thank God."

"He believes he must take the boy to the police."

"But why? I mean, he shouldn't *do* that." Maria was suddenly frightened again for Paulo. "Sister Noonie . . . the nun in charge of the orphanage . . . she says that would be bad for Paulo."

"Oh? Then perhaps this Sister Noonie is correct. Because, although the boy does not talk, I see that he fears being taken to the police."

Zorina went on to tell her about the Italian man—Charlie Long, she said, which to Maria sure didn't sound Italian—and how he had unexpectedly appeared at her studio with Paulo.

She explained how Charlie had been going to take Paulo to the police, and how the boy's fear had convinced her that this was a bad idea, and she fled with him, and then couldn't go back home because someone—"the Russian men, I am sure"— had broken in her back door looking for them. So she and the boy had walked and walked, all the way to Charlie's.

"But how could you *do* that? You already said he wants to take Paulo to the police, and they'll—Well, I don't know what they'll do. I just know Sister Noonie doesn't like the idea."

"It was night, and cold, and I was afraid." It was a plain explanation, not an apology. "It is true that Charlie Long thinks he must take the child to the police. But he will find that a difficult thing. He will want to speak to me again before he can bring himself to do that."

"How do you know?"

"How?" The woman smiled gently, and said, "The same way I know that you too, Maria, wish deeply to do whatever is best for Paulo."

She stood up and left the chapel, and Maria followed.

The wedding group which had seemed so large outside was huddled together up near the altar with a priest now, in a circle of light and flowers, with the rest of the huge church looking empty and dark. The organ was playing and Maria was surprised she hadn't heard it from inside the chapel. She stopped to watch. The music crescendoed into the wedding march, and the bride started up the aisle, on her journey through the semidarkness toward the circle of her loved ones and her bright, hope-filled future.

"We must go." Zorina tugged at Maria's arm. "I called Charlie Long from the station and told him we were coming."

But Maria didn't move. Her eyes were on the bride, brown-skinned in white satin and lace, clinging to her proud father's arm, moving stiffly in time with the solemn music. Maria's heart beat fast and she said a little prayer for the bride. A surprise, because prayers so seldom came these days. She felt a wave of joy, but at once also felt afraid for poor Paulo, and then—*admit it,* she thought—she felt lonely.

Suddenly she was crying, a flood of tears running down her cheeks. Were they for this young *novia Mejicana?* Or for Paulo? Or for herself?

"Ssssst!" Zorina pulled at her arm harder this time. "Please. There is no time now for crying."

TWENTY

As they walked away from the church, Maria explained to Zorina that Paulo had been snatched off the street in Rio, while on a field trip with some of the other orphanage children.

"He could not merely have gotten lost?" Zorina asked.

"No. I was in charge. I didn't know Paulo very well, just that he never talked and didn't participate much. He didn't want to go that day and I talked him into it. Then I got involved with some of the kids and I . . . well . . . I let Paulo lag behind. I looked up and he was on the other side of a busy street. He went the wrong way and I saw a man grab him. I screamed and ran, but they were too far. They . . . they disappeared around a corner."

"Kidnapped? A boy from an orphanage?"

"Apparently the man was part of a gang that snatches up street kids, but I don't see how they could think Paulo was—" Maria stopped. "Anyway, awful things like that happen all too often in Rio. Street children kidnapped and sold in . . . in what they call the sex trade."

"Even young boys, I suppose," Zorina said, and shook her head. "But if that is what happened, why is he brought here, to Chicago? For . . . for prostitution? There are so many other cities in the world for that." She paused, as though analyzing what she'd heard. "And there are other children, so why are these men so anxious now, when he escapes, to get this particular boy back? Do they fear he will identify them to the authorities?

Surely he would be the worst of witnesses. Or is there some other profit to be made from him?"

"I . . . I don't know." Maria was amazed. Those must be the very questions Sister Noonie had asked herself. But she kept what Erica Donaldson said about Sister's speculation to herself. She didn't know how much to reveal to this woman—a person she instinctively trusted, but really knew nothing about.

"Perhaps if such men discover a child is not homeless," Zorina went on, "they might think of demanding ransom. But an orphanage child?" She stopped and touched Maria's arm. "Does Paulo have relatives who could pay?"

"What? Oh . . . no." Paulo's mother and father were both dead, she knew, and all he had was an uncle. A policeman, and they weren't wealthy. "No, all the orphanage children are poor." Again she didn't mention Sister Noonie's speculation, which Erica Donaldson took to mean a ransom demand.

Zorina looked up at her and waited, and Maria hoped the woman couldn't tell she was keeping something to herself. But finally Zorina just smiled and said, "Come, Charlie Long will be waiting for us."

They walked another block and then, as they started to cross the street, the older woman pulled on Maria's arm. "No," she said. "First we should go this way."

Maria followed her and they went to a huge Target store to buy new clothes for Paulo. They put it all on Maria's credit card, of course, and Maria was happy to do it. Her father had told her to make the most of her visit home, and to him that would naturally include running up lots of bills. He'd feel good about that, making his daughter happy in a way he was able to understand. Of course, he'd be surprised she'd shopped at Target. Or his secretary would, since she took care of paying his bills.

As they hurried through the store, Maria thought again of Alicia's party that night. It was her annual "End of Summer Bash," and she'd been thoughtful enough to include a number of Maria's friends on the guest list. People Maria had known for years. They might even go for a swim in the lake off their private beach. The air would be chilly, but the water wouldn't have cooled down much yet. Maria loved to swim, although she hadn't been to Ipanema or any of the other beaches of Rio in the whole time she'd been down at Porto de Deus. The other volunteers went a few times, but when Maria wasn't teaching she worked as a sort of unofficial executive assistant to Sister Noonie. She'd been flattered that Sister asked her so soon after her arrival, but it kept her very busy.

The party would be fun, but besides that she should be there because her father was leaving tomorrow for San Francisco, where he was lead counsel in a huge case involving patent violations and experimental asthma drugs. The trial would last the entire month of her home visit. He had said he'd try to come home weekends, but even if he did, she knew he'd have little time for his family.

"No way this could be put off," he'd explained last night. "Too many lawyers involved and the date's been set for a year. Sorry, sweetheart."

She told him not to worry, and didn't remind him that even back when she was living at home she rarely saw him. Nothing had changed.

Maria had time to think about all that, because Zorina wasn't one to chitchat while shopping. With her scarf down around her shoulders—revealing surprisingly black hair—and her coat unbuttoned, she was a woman on a mission. She bought her way methodically up Paulo's little body: shoes, socks, pants, underpants, shirts, jacket, and cap. She seemed quite sure of the sizes of everything. She even bought a toothbrush and toothpaste and a comb, and finally a little duffel bag to put everything in.

Maria had never been inside a Target store. It sure wasn't Bloomingdale's, but there were such cute things for kids everywhere that Maria—who'd been out of the consumer loop for a year—would have spent more time choosing, but Zorina said no, they had to hurry.

Zorina was sure the man named Charlie Long would be waiting with Paulo when they got to his place. "He will not wish to give the child over to the police so easily," she said. "Also he will receive my phone message. He will be there. This I know. I have seen him with the boy."

But the woman with "the gift of seeing" was wrong this time.

They took a cab to a run-down two-story house on a block where Maria thought it fit right in. Lots of kids on the street, mostly Mexican. There was an outside stairway in the back and they went past the second floor up to what had to be an attic apartment.

Zorina knocked on the door. There was no answer. She opened the screen door and knocked on the inside door. Still no answer.

"You're sure this is the right house?" Maria said.

Zorina turned to her. "Go downstairs and see if anyone is home and if they know where Charlie Long is."

It was a command, not a suggestion, and Maria didn't take to commands well. But she could see fear in the older woman's face, and she began to feel afraid, too. Not for herself, but for poor Paulo. So she did as she was told. There was no response at the second floor. None at the first, either. The whole place seemed deserted. She went back up.

The little porch was empty. The woman had vanished.

Then the door opened in front of her and Zorina told her to

come in. "He left it unlocked," she said, and Maria found herself relieved that the woman didn't have a magic key. "He did that," Zorina went on, "because he knew we were coming."

"Or maybe he's just careless and doesn't lock his door."

"I was here last night and it was locked." Zorina shook her head. "But why is he not here? Where is the boy?" She walked over and looked at the answering machine. "It shows no messages, so he has heard my message and erased it."

She's like a detective in a movie, Maria thought. "Should we just wait a little while?" she asked. "Or we could check with the police, I guess, just to find out if a man brought a boy in to them. Or maybe . . ." She let her voice trail off, though, because Zorina obviously wasn't paying attention. She was walking around the apartment.

There wasn't much to the place. One long room, and a bathroom that could have fit in Maria's walk-in closet at home several times. It reminded her of her room at Porto de Deus, only this one was larger and had sloping ceilings. She didn't have her own private bathroom at the orphanage, either. But she had a real bed, not just a mattress on the floor.

"Something is not right," Zorina said.

"Yes, well, the bed's not made—if you can call it a bed—and the sink's dirty, and there's a smell like urine. But otherwise—"

"No. I mean something is different from the way it was." Zorina looked around. "Ah," she said, "why would he move his dresser today, and put a rug there?" She went over and moved the shag rug with her foot. There was a trapdoor and she opened it.

By then Maria was beside her and the two of them looked down. It was a closet, pretty empty, just some winter coats on hangers. There was a ladder leading down. The closet door was open.

"You must go down," Zorina said. "My joints are too stiff."

"But that's someone's apartment. Their home."

"You knocked on their door and they did not answer. Go quickly!"

Another command.

Maria slipped her purse off her shoulder and set it on the floor beside the trapdoor. She climbed down and stepped out of the closet into a hallway. There was no one around. It was very quiet. In fact, it was definitely creepy.

"Is there anyone here?" she called, but not too loud. "Hello? Anyone?" No one answered and she went slowly down the hallway. "I'm not a burglar," she added, a little louder, in case anyone was listening. "I'm . . . I'm a friend of Mr. Long's, upstairs. My name is Maria McGrady. I'm looking—"

She heard something.

There! By that half-open door at the end of the hall. A bathroom door. And then it opened all the way.

"Oh my God, thank you!" she said. "Paulo! Oh, thank God!"

The boy stood there, wide-eyed, with one hand on the doorknob, and she swore he was starting to smile that shy little smile of his—but then his hand slipped off the knob and he crumpled to the floor.

Twenty-One

They took Charlie in one of those caged squad cars where the prisoner can't reach over and strangle the cops in the front seat. Lieutenant Swanson drove, with Harter—the Nazi—beside her, and the cop from the day before in the back beside Charlie. They stopped at a district station and the three of them got out and left him in the car. They walked a few yards away and then stopped and he could see Swanson giving some shit to Harter, and him just sort of blowing it off and walking away.

The other cop followed Harter into the station, and Swanson came back and got behind the wheel. She was obviously pissed off, but didn't say a word. They drove to a bigger station on Grand Avenue where the sign said "Area Five Headquarters."

Swanson turned out to be with the Youth Division, so Charlie realized she wouldn't be looking into a homicide—behind the Billy Goat or anywhere else. She said they'd gone back to Zorina's last night to follow up on what he'd told the two officers, but found no one there. She didn't say they found the place broken into. She said he wasn't a suspect in any crime, and she just had a few questions. He insisted on calling his lawyer and she said fine, but acted like that was a waste of time.

It was Saturday, so Sal was watching a football game when Charlie called and was pissed off and asked what kinda shit was going down. But before Charlie got very far Sal said, "Don't say anything more, not on the phone."

"So," Charlie said, "do you think you can—"

"I'll be there in a half hour."

"Hey, thanks. I was worried that maybe . . . you know . . ."

"Maybe what? You think I'd leave you there by yourself, asshole?"

Damn, he loved Sal.

He sat in a little room and waited for Sal. He got up once and tried the door and it wasn't locked, which made him feel better. Plus, it wasn't one of those rooms with a two-way mirror the cops could watch you through.

Still, he was nervous. Back in that little park, with no time to think and Paulo so scared again, he'd made a quick decision. Then, with cops unexpectedly knocking on his door, and knowing Zorina had "found someone" and was on her way, he'd stayed with that decision. Now, though, with time to think, he wanted to check with Sal. Sal always had good advice.

But Sal could be surprising as hell, too. Charlie remembered that Tuesday a few months ago when he and Sal got to the Billy Goat at the same time, which meant Sal was late. Their usual table had someone at it, a couple of beefy hard hats from the construction site around the corner. Charlie started toward a different table, but Sal walked right up and set his burger and Coke on the guys' table. "Excuse me," he said, but not apologetic at all. "You'll have to move." The two of them, big weather-beaten faces, looked up at Sal, not about to move, and one of them said, "Who the—" But Sal stopped him, held up his palm and leaned down and said something Charlie couldn't hear. The two guys blinked, looked at each other, then picked up what was left of their lunches and hauled ass outta there. What did he say, was what Charlie wanted to know. "It's not what," Sal had said, grinning. "It's fucking how."

★ ★ ★ ★ ★

So where the hell *was* Sal, anyway? He said half an hour, and it was past that. Of course he'd have to shower and get dressed up. Sal would wear a suit and tie because he was on lawyer business. Impress the cops. "Projecting the right image," Sal always said, "showing people who you are, that's important." Maybe Charlie should have put on something besides jeans and a T-shirt to come down here. But Christ, he'd been in a hurry, wanting to get the cops away from his—

The door opened. "Hey, mope." It was Sal, grinning. "How you doin'?"

"Okay, I guess. But . . ." He stared at Sal, amazed.

"What?"

"Nothing, I guess. It's just . . . I thought you'd be wearing a suit, man." But Sal was in tasseled loafers, tan slacks, and a blue golf shirt. Everything looking brand new and expensive as hell, but still . . . "I mean," Charlie said, "I told the cops you're my lawyer."

Sal grinned again. "They know I'm your lawyer. More important, they know me. Like, who I am, you know?"

"You mean, like, your family and all?"

"Some of them do, yeah. But that's not the thing. The thing is they know they got a lawyer here doesn't need to mess with a pinstripe suit on a Saturday to impress a bunch of low-level cops. I don't need that." He paused. "You gotta project an image, man. I musta told you that a thousand times. But not someone else's bullshit image. A real man, he's true to himself, follows his own mind. Then you just let your damn clothes express who you really are."

"Yeah, well, sit down." Charlie himself sat on one of the three chairs by a little table in the center of the room. "Thing is," he said, "I got a problem."

Sal sat across from him. "Nope," he said. "No problem. I

already talked to that youth investigator. She says you're fine. You stopped a beat car yesterday and told them how you saved a little kid from some thugs on Halsted Street. She says when you took the cops to where you left the kid with some old lady, the old lady and the kid were gone. The beat cops are the ones got a problem, 'cause they blew you off and the kid's a hot item. Anyway, she knows you don't have him."

"She say that?" Charlie asked.

"Yeah. They just wanna ask you some questions. You know, describe the kid and the guys bothering him and all. So you just answer the questions and then you go home." Sal leaned back and tipped his chair onto its back legs. "I'll be with you, man. It's not a problem."

"Yeah, right. Except . . ." He took a deep breath. "Except I *do* have the kid, y' know?"

Sal lurched forward and the front legs of his chair banged on the floor. "What're you talking about? Don't mess with me, Charlie."

"I'm not. I hid the kid back at my place when they came banging on my door. So you gotta help me with this problem."

"Jesus Christ! What? Tell me."

So Charlie told him. Most of it. The Billy Goat. A black guy with a kid. Some thugs chasing the kid and Charlie grabbing him and running, thinking he'd go to the cops once they got away. He didn't mention seeing the murder because if the cops weren't going to ask him about that, why bring it up . . . even to Sal? But he mentioned the thugs looked like Russians.

"Not good," Sal said. "If they were Russians, they're crazy." He shook his head. "You know my Uncle Rocco?"

"Yeah. He's, like, a made guy, right?"

"Anyway, he deals with Russians sometimes. He says they got no honor, no respect. It's like they're all related to each other, and one's crazier than the next."

"Yeah, well, thanks," Charlie said. "Makes me feel a lot better."

He told Sal about the ride in the truck. Hiding at Zorina's place. Her taking the kid when he went for the cops, then the two of them coming to his place and staying all night. And how he saw that morning how someone had been torturing the kid. And Zorina calling to say she found someone who could help. Which is why he couldn't just turn the kid in to the cops. Not yet.

When he finished Sal shook his head, then said, "It's very simple. You gotta tell them everything. I mean all of it. Like you just did me."

"Yeah, well, I was thinking you'd say that. But I can't. Not till I talk to Zorina. See what she's found out and—"

"Bullshit! You'll be charged with kidnapping or something."

"Yeah, but you didn't see Paulo's face, man."

"Paulo?"

"That's his name. You didn't see how scared he is. Someone took a pair of pliers to him, man. And the burn marks, y' know? Anyway, I can't tell 'em, not till I find out what's going on and shit."

"Listen to me, asshole. There's some big-time pressure on the cops about this kid, I think."

"Pressure like what?"

"How the hell do I know? I can feel it, though. You refuse to answer questions, they're gonna know something's up. They'll lock you down tight."

"I know I have to answer. But until I know he's not gonna get sent back to whoever it was pinched him and burned him in the first place . . . I guess I gotta just, you know, lie about it."

"Jesus! Are you shittin' me?"

"You haven't seen him. I couldn't handle living with that on my mind. Once I know that's not gonna happen, I'll tell everything. But for now . . ."

"Uh-uh, not with me sitting there, you're not gonna lie. Because they're gonna find out, and then I'm gonna lose my law license." Sal put his hand on Charlie's arm. "Look here. I understand how you feel sorry for this kid. But I got two ways I can go, Charlie. With my fucking life, I mean. I got a law license, and I can try to get somewhere with it. Or I can pitch that and go with my uncle and cousins and the rest of those *paisanos*. And you know what? I grew up with those guys, and they want me, man. And part of me wants—" He pulled his hand back. "But I'm trying something else, and no way I'm gonna sit there and have you lie your ass off right in front of me, and lose my license."

"So you're just gonna . . . walk out on me?"

"It's not *me* walking, Charlie. It's *you*. It's your choice. You wanna walk away from real life into some kinda dream of being a hero, that's up to you."

"Yeah." Charlie stared down at the floor and all he could see was Paulo standing in the shower, and all those red, puffy scars. He looked up at Sal. "Well, till the kid's in safe hands, that's my choice."

"Look here." Sal stood up. "If that was your decision all along, why the hell'd you call and drag me over here?"

"Because I wasn't sure what I was gonna do. Not really sure. Not till you got here. Then right away you made it clear, telling me again how a real man is . . . you know . . . true to himself, and follows his own mind and shit."

"Jesus." Sal turned away, then turned back to him. "Look, I'll tell them you just wanted to check with me first, but you didn't really need a lawyer after all. Then I'll leave and you . . . you say whatever the hell you're gonna say."

"Yeah, okay. But, you know, I was wondering . . ."

"I suppose you're broke." Sal stood up and pulled out his

billfold and laid two fifties on the table. "I'm outta here and you're on your own now, Charlie." He shook his head. "On your fucking own."

TWENTY-TWO

Maria had known right away that Paulo only fainted. Whether it was from fear, or surprise, or plain happiness at seeing her, she didn't know. But she'd gotten him revived and up the ladder into Charlie Long's apartment.

He hugged her tightly, and then hugged Zorina, too. And Zorina cried as hard as Maria did. It was a wonderful moment. Paulo was safe! It had been her fault he was kidnapped, and now he was safe again.

She asked him what happened, but knew that was no use, even in Portuguese. He just looked at her.

"He does not talk," Zorina said.

"I know. I can't believe you actually got his name out of him. He never talks. Not even to Sister Noonie."

"And what language do you use to speak to him?"

"Portuguese. But he knows a little English, too. That's obvious, even though he doesn't answer. The doctors say there's nothing wrong with his brain. He's just . . . well . . . given up on talking."

There was hardly any food, but Maria boiled water on a hot plate for a package of Ramen instant noodles she found in a cabinet above Charlie Long's sink. Paulo ate a whole bowl of the noodles and broth. Then he curled up on Charlie's bed and fell asleep.

Maria paced up and down the room. She wondered if she'd

even like this guy Charlie Long. For one thing his small, dark apartment was a mess, with piles of dirty clothes everywhere. Then it seemed weird that he kept all kinds of unrelated things—including noodles, aspirin, toothpaste, two light bulbs, soap, pencils and pens, a frying pan, even a box of condoms—mixed together in the same cabinet by the sink, in no order at all.

There was an old TV set, but no computer. It appeared Charlie Long was taking some college courses, though, because there were textbooks and a backpack on the floor near the door—sociology, economics, English literature. Otherwise, the only reading materials were that day's *Sun-Times* and a couple of old issues of *Sports Illustrated.* She wished there were a picture of him somewhere, but didn't see any photos at all. There wasn't much of anything personal except the dirty clothes.

She stopped walking. "How much longer are we going to wait for him?" she said. "We don't know if he's *ever* coming back."

"He is coming back," Zorina said. Maybe she was worried, too, but she just sat there, hardly moving.

"How do you know? You don't know *everything.*" She wondered why she suddenly felt so angry at this woman. "You're the one who said he'd be here when we got here. So much for your supernatural powers."

"The boy is here," Zorina said, ignoring the taunt. "Charlie Long will be back . . . once he is able."

"Once he's able? What do you mean?"

"He did not leave here because he wanted to. Someone took him. I believe it was the police, because his door was unlocked, not broken. Not really broken—only the hook on the screen door." Maria hadn't even noticed that. "If it had been the Russian men . . ." Zorina paused. "Whoever it was, he had time to hide the boy. He will be back."

"But we can't stay here forever. We already have Paulo, and that's what counts. He has to go back home, to the orphanage. We should go."

"You are not thinking!" Now it was Zorina who was angry. "Have you given even one thought to where you would go? Would you go to the airport and fly off with Paulo to Brazil? Does he have a passport? If the police are looking for him, would they not be notified at once, and stop you? And are the Russian men not watching?"

"Well," Maria said, "just to sit and wait for some guy who—"

"I have met him, spoken with him. Charlie Long is young, but he is one of those the grandmothers would have called 'old in his soul.' There is more to him than he admits . . . or understands. We will wait."

Zorina's words had stunned Maria, but the old woman was so sure of herself that she didn't know how to respond, so they sat in silence for a long time. Then she had an idea.

She went over to Charlie Long's bed, where the phone was, and sat on the floor because she didn't want to wake up Paulo. She dug her billfold out of her purse. She finally found the card she was looking for and tapped out a lengthy phone number.

"What are you doing?" Zorina asked.

"Calling Sister Noonie," she said. "At the orphanage. She'll know what to do. Only Sister Noonie really knows about Paulo. She's the one who dealt with Paulo's father when he brought him there."

She waited through a long series of clicks and beeps and various odd noises . . . and was cut off. She tried again. Phone service in Rio still wasn't as good as the government kept saying it was, and—

The connection was made and she heard the phone ringing. She was surprised, in fact, at how many times it rang. When

Maria was there she answered it herself most afternoons. She never took this long to answer.

"*Alo?*" Finally. A young woman's voice. Brazilian.

"Porto de Deus?" Maria asked.

"*Sim.*"

"*Bom dia.* Sister Noonie, *por favor.*" There was silence. "Please," Maria said, "may I speak—"

"Hello?" It was Sister Noonie, her voice clear enough, but faint.

"Sister? It's me. Maria."

"Oh, but why . . . Are you all right, Maria?"

"Oh yes, I—" Maria stopped. "But what about you, Sister? You sound so . . . weak."

"It's nothing serious." But the older woman didn't sound at all well. "The doctor says it's a touch of pneumonia. Please, though, why do you call?"

"It's about Paulo. He's with me, here, in Chicago. Safe, for now."

"Thanks be to God," Sister said. "Was it the detectives who—"

"I'm not sure what all happened. A man and a woman here helped him. But the kidnappers are still after him and . . . well . . . I think we'll have to go to the police, even though you said—"

"Oh Maria," Sister said, "is there no other way?"

"None that I can think of. And anyway, why would that be so bad?"

"I don't like to burden you with my worries, but . . ." Sister hesitated, then went on. "I'm sure the police there will contact the Brazilian police at once, and Paulo's uncle has influence here. He is . . . he wants custody of Paulo."

"His uncle?" Maria didn't understand.

"He is Paulo's only relative and Paulo lived with him when

137

his father was in jail. He is a captain in the police. Not the police department of Rio de Janeiro, but the federal police. After Paulo was kidnapped he warned me that he intended to find the boy, and that when he did he would get legal custody of him. He said he would prove that he can take better care of him than . . . than we did here."

"But I thought Paulo had no one to care for him," Maria said. "I thought that's why he was at Porto de Deus."

"Paulo's home is here because it was his father's wish."

"I'd heard that, but I thought that must be because his uncle couldn't take care of him . . . or didn't want to. Plus, you said it was God who sent Paulo to the orphanage."

"Yes. At least . . . that's what I have hoped and prayed for."

"I don't understand."

"It was a choice I had to make. Before Paulo came to—" Sister suddenly started coughing. She coughed deeply, over and over, and it took her some time to get her breath. "Before . . . before he came to us, our building was old and unsafe. The authorities had ordered us to move, threatened to close us immediately if I took in even one more child. In fact, I had already found a beautiful new place, but could not get the money to buy it. Then Paulo's father came to me at night, in secret. He had escaped from jail and was running from the police."

"And he brought Paulo?" Maria knew Paulo's father had been killed by the police, but had never heard just how Paulo got to the orphanage.

"Yes. He begged me to take the boy. I told him I could not, told him what the authorities threatened. But he said he had money, and he would provide a new home for us if I would take Paulo, and be his legal guardian." Sister paused to get her breath, then went on. "I didn't know what to do. The man was involved in violence and drug selling. I prayed over whether I could accept his offer, with so much evil and death behind his money. In the end, for the children, I accepted."

"I'm sure it was the right thing," Maria said.

"I must leave that to God." Sister struggled with another bout of coughing. "At any rate, Paulo's father contacted his lawyers, and the property I had been looking at—this place, the one you know—was purchased. And Paulo has had the home his father desired."

"And this uncle? What does he—"

"He says that I and Porto de Deus did not care for Paulo properly, and that Paulo's kidnapping is proof of negligence. He says the boy should be with him."

"But it wasn't your fault," Maria said, tears filling her eyes. "The negligence was mine. I'm the one who . . ." She was crying hard now, and not able to talk.

Zorina sat on the floor beside her and Maria didn't object as she took the phone and spoke into it. "Sister Noonie, I am Zorina. The man Charlie Long and I are helping Paulo. We wish to get him home. We—"

"You have to tell her," Maria managed, "that we need to go to the police." But Zorina was ignoring her, and was listening to Sister.

"Yes, Sister, a gentle, sweet boy," Zorina finally said. "And no, never a word, beyond revealing his name to me." She paused, then said, "Only because I was able to . . . to break into his sleep."

Maria stared at Zorina in amazement, her guilt forgotten for the moment, as she realized how little she knew about this woman.

". . . understand your fear," Zorina was saying, "and you have my solemn promise." She stopped and listened some more, then said, "Yes, but—Sister?" She held the phone out in front of her and stared at it.

"What happened?" Maria said. "Why did you stop talking?"

"I did not stop. Sister had to stop. Someone came to take her to . . . Santa Catarina." Zorina set the phone down. "Is that a hospital?"

"Yes. She has pneumonia. She said a 'touch' of pneumonia."

"Well then, she will get better."

"I don't know. She was very weak even before I left, and she must be worse now. People *die* of pneumonia, Zorina. Even in the hospital."

"She will get better." Zorina put one hand on Maria's shoulder and, with some difficulty, got back up on her feet. "You were right to remind me that I do not know everything, but—"

"I'm sorry," Maria said, looking up at her. "I shouldn't have spoken so harshly to you earlier. I'm just . . . Oh, I don't know."

"You spoke the truth. I have the gift of seeing. It is not the sight of the giver. It is only a gift." She paused, then added, "But your friend, Sister Noonie, she will recover."

"My *friend?* She's more like . . . almost a mother."

"I understand," Zorina said. "But tell me, what did Sister say of this uncle of Paulo's?"

"He claims the orphanage neglected Paulo, and that led to his kidnapping."

"And that is all she said?"

"Yes, and she's very worried about it. Why do you ask? Did she tell you something else?"

"No," Zorina said, "but she said she had been telling you about the uncle's reasons why Paulo should live with him, and not at the orphanage. As though there were more than one reason. But someone came, and she had to leave for the hospital." Zorina patted Maria's hand. "The important thing, my dear, is that Sister Noonie will recover." She spoke with such certainty that Maria felt more confident, too.

"But I wanted her advice," Maria said, "about the police, and what to do." She stood and looked down at Paulo. He was waking up, stretching his spindly arms and legs. "What in the world are we going to do?"

"We will continue to avoid the police. That is what Sister Noonie asks of us. That is the promise I made to her." She held out her hand and, with Maria's help, got to her feet. "So . . . now we will wait," she said. "And Charlie Long will come."

TWENTY-THREE

Paulo was awake now and Zorina showed him his new clothes and got him dressed in them. Meanwhile, Maria went around the apartment gathering coffee mugs, glasses, and plates. She washed and dried them, along with what was already piled beside the sink. She picked up all the beer and soda cans and food wrappers and other debris, and put them in a plastic bag from Target. By then, Zorina had found just one clean sheet in a dresser drawer—Maria herself would never have looked through someone else's dresser—and made the bed. They gathered the various piles of dirty clothes into one big pile near the door, and added the dirty sheets and Paulo's old clothes to the pile.

While they worked, Paulo sat silently and paged through that morning's *Sun-Times,* which Maria discovered had a child's coloring book stuck inside it. He was obviously playing "grown-up," as he turned each page of the paper and studied it.

There was plenty of additional scouring and scrubbing that could have been done, but that was a bit much to ask, especially when all they were doing was trying to fill up empty time until Charlie Long got there.

If he didn't arrive soon—and, in fact, even if he *did*—they'd have to take some action, and she couldn't see how they could avoid calling in the police, like it or not. Meanwhile, though, a few more minutes wouldn't hurt. Besides, she had a desire to learn more about this woman, Zorina.

"Let's sit and relax a bit," she said, "and talk."

While Zorina made two mugs of instant coffee, Maria got a glass of water for Paulo and sat him down in front of the TV. The reception was poor, but she found some silly cartoons and Paulo got interested. He didn't laugh, or even smile, just sat there solemnly—as though watching C-Span or something.

She joined Zorina at the table. "So," she said, "this 'gift of seeing.' Are you one of those . . . *readers?* Do you predict people's futures? Look into a crystal ball?"

Zorina sipped her coffee. "I do these things," she said.

"Really?" Maria had been onlyhalf serious.

"This surprises you. But do you not sometimes listen to a person and then read a different meaning than what their words say?" She paused. "Or at the orphanage, perhaps you warn a little girl, 'If you are always so mean, you will never be popular.' Is this not telling her of her future?"

"I suppose, but . . . that's different." *Or was it?* "I certainly don't look into a magic ball and see things."

"The crystal may help to focus the attention, which is so easily scattered. People come to me because they are searching. I try to help them find their way. This is what I do. And, my dear, what is magic?" She cupped her hands around her mug, as though warming them. "We have all, I think, seen wondrous things, changes in people which surprise us."

"Well, sure, but . . . Do people pay money to consult with you?"

"Certainly. Some come to me many times. Others do not feel helped, and do not return. Or if I see they are not being helped, I encourage them not to return."

"I guess," Maria said, "it's a sort of . . . therapy."

Zorina smiled. "There are many ways to help people in their searches."

"And then yesterday," Maria said, "out of nowhere, in comes

Charlie Long . . . with Paulo."

"Yes." The woman turned and looked at Paulo, and Maria did, too, but his eyes stayed fixed on the TV. "Yesterday was . . . a special day for me," Zorina added, turning back to face Maria.

"I'm sure it was. Paulo is a special boy. But—"

"Not only that. It was already a special day. It is the day . . ." She lowered her head, then looked up again at Maria, and there were tears in her eyes. "Yesterday was the anniversary of my son's death. My only child."

"Oh, I'm so sorry." Maria reached across the table and laid her hand on the woman's wrist.

"It was a long time ago," Zorina said, and gently withdrew her hand. "But still, I keep that day as a special day. Each year on that day I eat nothing. I schedule no appointments. But I leave my door unlocked for . . . for anyone who may need help. I have only one photograph of my son, and I set it out only on that day. Otherwise, no. It is too painful. It is . . ." She didn't finish. She was crying.

"Please," Maria said, "you don't have to talk about it. I didn't mean to pry."

"I am sorry." Zorina tried another smile. "But I wish to share this with you, to help you understand." She took a deep breath. "Each year is the same. No appointments. And the door unlocked. In all these years, no one ever came through my door on that day. Ever. And then . . . yesterday. He reminded me so much of my son." She sighed. "Do you believe in signs?"

"I . . . I don't know."

"I feel I could have helped my son if I had been a better mother, stronger."

"When someone close to us dies," Maria said, "we always feel we should have done more for them. I felt that way when my mom died." Tears were flooding her own eyes now. "But by then it's too late."

"Yes, but for me, yesterday, the sudden appearance of Charlie Long, with the boy, seemed a sign. Some men—the Russian men—came looking for them, and I tricked them . . . and they went away. I could not help my own son, but this time I helped." She lifted her mug, then set it down again without drinking. "I have not many years of life ahead of me, and I—"

"Oh, no. Don't say that. You probably have a long time."

"Perhaps. But one cannot be certain. So I decided. The moment I saw those Russian men go away, I decided. I would not stop at that. This time, before it was too late, I would use my wits, and my gift." She leaned forward. "This one I would save."

Maria didn't know what to say. She looked over at Paulo and was surprised to see him staring back at her—at the two of them—with that same serious expression as when he watched TV.

They sat in silence, and Maria's mind wandered. She thought of her mother, and of her father's new wife, Alicia, who was way younger than her father, but a very nice person, with a ton of money on her own. She was way too *thing*-oriented, but then, except for Sister Noonie and some of her staff, who did Maria know—including herself—who wasn't? And she didn't think of Alicia as stealing her father's affection, because he'd never paid much attention to her or her brother—or to her mother, for that matter. His whole life was his work, and—

She jumped a little when Zorina stood up and took their cold coffees to the sink. "You have been far away," Zorina said.

"Yes, I was thinking of Alicia. She's—" Then Maria remembered. "Oh my God!" She looked at her watch.

"What is it?" Zorina said.

"The party." She told Zorina about Alicia's party that night. "I promised I'd be there, but now I can't go. I can't leave you two here to wait alone." What she didn't say was that she wasn't going to let Paulo out of her sight, no matter how badly Zorina wanted to help. "I better call home and apologize."

"You should go," Zorina said. "The boy and I will come with you."

Maria was amazed, but Zorina said that even though she was certain Charlie Long would be back, they had no way of knowing when. It might not be until the next day, and the three of them couldn't just sit there hour after hour with nothing to do. They would leave a note.

"Why, of course," Maria said. "Paulo and you can sleep in the guest bedroom, next to mine." She was ready to do anything other than sit and wait. "I'll tell my father and . . . well . . . there'll be no chance tonight, but I can talk to him in the morning, before he leaves town. He'll help us figure out how to get Paulo home without involving the police."

"Paulo would be glad of that," Zorina said, "and I could keep my promise to Sister Noonie."

"I should have thought of asking my father before." But she knew why she *hadn't* thought of it. She hardly *ever* thought of her father, and tried never to ask for his help. And when she accepted it—like that morning with the red Mercedes—she usually resented it. Then she thought of something else. She looked at Zorina. "You know . . . we might run into some of the guests and . . . well . . ."

Zorina glanced down at her dress, with its stars and astrological signs. "Something to wear, yes. We will go first to the Target store again. But how are we to get to your home?"

"I have a car," Maria said. "We'll have to take a cab to get to it."

Zorina opened Paulo's new little duffel bag. She went and got his dirty clothes from where she'd thrown them with Charlie's pile and stuffed them in the bag, along with the coloring book. "It is best that we leave no child's things." She tore a sheet out of a tablet she found with Charlie's textbooks. "Write only your phone number," she said, "and sign it 'Maria.'"

"Shouldn't I say we have Paulo, and he's safe?" But as soon as she said that, she knew it was a dumb idea. They didn't know who might come in and look around. So she wrote only what Zorina suggested.

After adding "Z" below Maria's name, Zorina put the note on the trapdoor and covered it with the rug. "Even this much is dangerous. But we must trust." She took Paulo's hand. He was standing, obviously aware that they were on their way somewhere.

Maria looked around the room. "Anyone who knows this guy Charlie Long will know someone else has been here, and that it was probably a woman." She picked her billfold up off the floor by the phone and slid it down into her purse—and felt something. "That's odd," she said.

"Odd? What do you mean?"

Maria held up a penny. A US coin, so it must have been stuck down there in a fold of her purse the whole past year. She didn't remember it falling out at the customs counter. "I didn't know I had this."

"The old people used to say that finding a penny is good luck," Zorina said.

"I hope so." Maria smiled. "Here, Paulo, put this in your pocket."

The boy's eyes widened and he took the penny and wrapped it in his fist as though it were a gold piece.

Twenty-Four

"Thank you very much, Mr. Long." The youth investigator gave Charlie her business card. *Mr. Long* now. Did that mean she believed him? "Call me," she said, "if you think of anything you left out. Okay?"

"Oh, yeah," he said. "Anything." He wanted out of there, but he didn't want to look worried, so he just sat on the chair beside her desk and tried to look honest.

"Well," she said, "you can go home now."

"Oh, sorry. Okay."

"I'll get someone to take you."

"Uh . . . no . . . thanks." He stood up and stuffed the card into his pocket, down there with the money from Sal. "I sure hope the kid's okay, I mean . . . is he lost or something?" Like they'd tell him shit.

"It's a matter of police business," she said, "so . . ."

"Oh, yeah. I see. Well, so long."

He walked to the bus stop. He'd been scared at first, with Sal leaving him. But now he felt . . . well . . . proud. Not proud of lying, exactly, but proud that he made up his own mind. Proud of how he handled himself, too.

He had tried not to lie except by leaving things out. He was vague on the time and some of the details. "I'd guess I'd been drinking a little," he explained, "because I lost my job." He told how it all started at the Billy Goat, when he saw a little boy and some black guy headed toward the washroom. He didn't say

148

anything about looking out into the alley. The cops apparently didn't know about anyone getting shot, and how could he tell them now, and have to explain why he didn't report a murder right after he saw it happen?

So he told how suddenly he saw the kid again, scared, running away from a couple of foreign-looking guys, and how he picked him up and would have called 911, but had to escape in a truck, figuring he'd take him to the police as soon as he could. But the goons followed, so he hid the kid at Zorina's. When he came back with the police, she and the kid were gone. No, he didn't think the old woman would purposely do anything wrong. Maybe the foreign guys came back while he was out looking for a cop. Maybe they used the alley and went in by the back door and . . . well, he just didn't know.

It was almost five o'clock when he got home. Zorina wasn't there and Paulo'd be scared to death down in that apartment by himself. He started across the room and then he stopped cold. *What?* His brain must have been tired because it took him a few seconds to figure it out. Someone had been there. Jesus, they'd cleaned the place up.

He went and snatched up the shag rug to get to the trapdoor, and when he did a piece of paper underneath it went sliding across the floor. He picked it up. It had a phone number, the name "Maria," and the letter "Z." The "Z" had to stand for Zorina, and Maria must be the person she found to help. He figured the note wouldn't be where it was unless they'd found Paulo. He went down the ladder and checked, though, just to be sure. The boy was gone.

Back up in his place he got a can of Miller Lite from the fridge and set it on the table beside the note, and sat down. The whole business was out of his hands. This should end it, he thought.

Right here. Right now.

He'd done what Zorina asked, right? He'd kept Paulo away from the cops until she was able to find someone to help. She'd come back and taken Paulo and she had some new person now—"Maria" something—to lay her "chosen to help" routine on. It was somebody else's problem now, and he could take his nose out of it. He could listen to Sal and not "walk away from real life."

Of course he wondered who this Maria was. And what made Zorina so sure she could help keep Paulo out of the hands of whoever was—

The phone rang. He reached for it, then let the machine take it.

"Hey, Charlie, pick up." He knew the guy, but he didn't answer. "It's Terry, man," the guy said. "What happened? You forget we had a game? They whipped our asses. We needed you, man. You—" He stopped and Charlie could hear yelling, and he knew the call came from a bar. "Anyway," Terry went on, "there's a party tonight, a porch party, on Sedgwick somewhere. I'll get the address. Call me on my cell." Terry hung up.

Charlie couldn't believe he'd forgotten all about the basketball game. He reached for the Miller Lite. Thinking of basketball made him think of Paulo, wadding up the bag from his breakfast and tossing it toward the trash basket, and missing by ten feet. He popped open the beer and took a long pull. He looked to his right, into the tiny bathroom, and closed his eyes and saw again that skinny little brown body . . . and those sickening scars. He felt—

The phone rang, and again he let the machine answer.

"It's me again," Terry said. "Hey, remember those two hot chicks from Tuesday? They'll be at the party. Call me . . . before I'm too shitfaced to know who you are." He hung up.

Charlie grabbed his beer again and gulped down a couple

more swallows. He was cool with the cops, and Paulo was off somewhere safe. And any Russians who could find out what address he gave the cops would find out pretty quick that he'd kept his mouth shut. It was time to get back to real life. Life where there were basketball games, parties, and a couple of hot chicks he remembered . . . sort of . . . except he couldn't really picture their faces.

"Right," he said out loud, "my real fucking life." He knocked down the rest of the Miller Lite and flipped the can into the sink, then went to the phone and punched out the number.

A woman answered. "McGrady residence," she said.

* ★ ★ ★ ★ ★

PART III
PARTY NIGHT

★ ★ ★ ★ ★

All day Saturday the men talked of nothing but the "negotiations" Flavio Rabassa mentioned that morning. Bill Grayson tried to temper their optimism with reality. He knew they needed hope, but he also knew that negotiations could go on for a long, long time.

Grayson was a soldier, paid to carry out orders. But he liked to know what was going on, and he'd done his homework before taking on "Operation Catnap," the mission that landed the four of them here.

With the US dropping another billion or so into the war on drugs in "Plan Colombia," there were renewed concerns in Brazil that its neighbor's drug lords would dodge the additional helicopters and missile launchers by slipping across into Brazil. Grayson figured the border between the two countries as about a thousand miles long, much of it unpopulated jungle. Add another eight thousand miles of border shared with other neighbors, and no way did Brazil have the manpower to patrol its frontiers.

Yes, Brazil had "Sivam," its hot new billion-dollar, American-

153

financed radar system, but Grayson understood Sivam to be question- ably effective. Still, the official word was that Brazil itself would keep the Colombians and their cocaine and heroin factories out of the Brazilian jungle. Outside help was not wanted.

So that was the problem with Operation Catnap. It had meant go- ing into Brazil, and as a matter of law, treaty, policy, and God- knows-what, US forces were to stay the hell out of there. The mission was the brainchild of Howard Lockman, a rapidly rising star at DEA headquarters in Arlington. Grayson was wary of rising stars and the often reckless ambition that drove them, and as on-site CO of the military force supporting DEA operations in Lockman's sector, he could have vetoed this one. He knew the man hadn't had time to jump through all the hoops needed for approval of such a mission. But he also knew the drug war wasn't always played by the rules, and this was a rare chance to take down the infamous Raul Agosto, "El Gato," a major Colombian player. So Grayson gave his okay, and if they had to fudge a little about just which side of a remote border they found the bastard on . . . well . . .

Sources put El Gato's new base on Brazilian soil, some fifty miles east of Tabatinga, a sad little town where the frontiers of Colombia, Brazil, and Peru met. The Brazilians patrolling the border—both army forces and federal police—were spread thin and, as his squad crossed from Colombia into Brazil, Grayson knew that running into them was unlikely.

But run into them they did . . . in the dead of night.

Both capture and resistance were unacceptable, so Grayson ordered his men to disperse into the darkness, confident they'd make it to safety. He himself stayed with the far less experienced DEA guys . . . and into this stinking hut is where it got them.

Why they'd been held so long in this remote hellhole was the ques- tion, and he didn't like the only answer that made sense. The US presidential election was approaching, with the outcome too close to call. The incumbent wasn't anxious to announce an illegal US military incursion into Brazil, not when he'd recently signed an agreement with the area nations forbidding such activities, and was making a major campaign issue of how well he got along with America's allies. Also, given his claim about how on top of things he was, the president could hardly plead ignorance of the mission—true or not. So . . . the US had apparently chosen another option: clandestine negotiations.

Maybe to make up for her absence the night before, Nita came earlier that evening with supper, before nightfall. She saw the trouble Grayson's knee gave him as he moved to their usual corner, and asked about it.

"A gift from your capitão," *he said.*

"Ah." She turned and spat on the floor. "O diabo em pessoa!"

"I don't understand." As always, they spoke in near whispers.

"He is the devil in person."

"So why allow your granddaughter to work in his household?" They had never actually discussed the man before.

"One does not allow anything to girls like her. They do what they will. She is sixteen, a beautiful girl, but very foolish." She shook her head and he was stunned to see tears running down her cheeks.

"What is it?" he asked.

"My Rosa, she is . . . what is the word? She has sex with him."

"With Flavio Rabassa?"

"Sim." She looked down at the floor. "And . . . also with his wife."

"Both of them?"

"They have strange desires, those two. For the men and the women, and . . . Aiee, other things. Things I could not speak of." She looked up at him. "This is why I must take my baby away."

"Yeah, well, my men and I want out, too." This seemed an opening to see if Nita would help. "Rabassa says he's talking to my government. But if he thinks they'll buy us back, he's wrong. They won't pay anything."

"I know nothing of this." She shook her head. "My Rosa—"

There was shouting outside, then laughter and loud conversation.

"I must go," Nita said, and as she was gathering up the plates the door opened. It wasn't the usual night guard, but Gold Tooth. He grinned at Nita and said something in Portuguese.

She looked at Grayson. "This one, he is a fool. He asks if we are enjoying our party, and if my buceta *is sore from fucking all of you." She turned to Gold Tooth and the two of them talked and Grayson made out the word* capitão, *but nothing else. Then she turned back. "This fool says that the* capitão *will have you talk on the telephone tomorrow. He says the* capitão *asks that you do him the favor of not dying overnight."*

TWENTY-FIVE

"McGrady residence," the woman said, and by the area code Charlie knew it was somewhere in the northern suburbs.

"Is Maria there?" he asked.

"No, but she's on her way. I can take a message." A black woman.

"Uh . . . no." He tried to think. "You see, I was supposed to meet her there tonight but I lost the address, so . . ."

"Oh, she must have asked you to the party."

"Right," he said, "the party."

She gave him the address and he wrote it down. It was in Lake Forest, for chrissake, so maybe the black woman was a maid. You'd have thought she'd be more suspicious, but maybe up there people didn't worry about guys they didn't know busting into their parties.

"Are you from Brazil, too?" the woman asked.

"What? I mean . . . why?"

"Just that Maria called and said she was taking the train and bringing some friends—one of them a little boy—from Brazil, so—"

"Oh, yeah," he said. "Anyway, in case I decide to come, did you say there was a train? Because my . . . uh . . . my car's in the shop."

She said she took the train back and forth every day, so he'd guessed right and she just worked there. She even looked up in a schedule and told him when the next couple of trains left.

"When you get to Lake Forest," she said, "there'll be cabs at the station. Or you could call here and Mr. McGrady will send a driver to pick you up."

Jesus, a driver? Picking up people at the train?

"If you take that seven-thirty-five train from downtown, you'll still be okay. The orchestra won't even start up till eight thirty or so, after people are mostly through eating. I'll tell Maria you're on your way. What's the name?"

"I probably won't make it," he said, thinking maybe he'd sit outside until the party was over. "I suppose it's a real dress-up event?"

"Well, it's black tie optional, but you come along. Just wear what's comfortable, you know? You'll be fine."

"Yeah, thanks." She'd never seen his corduroy sport coat.

Zorina had warned Maria that anyone following her that morning would know where she parked her car, and might be watching it. So, instead of the car, they'd taken the train to Lake Forest and a cab from the station.

When they pulled up to the front door at Shorewood Point it wasn't yet seven o'clock, too early for guests to start arriving for the party. Alicia met them at the door and threw her arms around Maria. "Oh, and your new beau called," she said. "But he told Annie he probably wouldn't make it."

"My new beau?" Maria said. "Oh, that must have been . . ." She let it go.

Alicia was too wound up getting ready to be hostess to have much time to gush all over Zorina and Paulo, but she said, "Oh, what a beautiful little boy!" and kissed Paulo on the forehead. Zorina didn't say a word, and Alicia obviously thought she was Brazilian, too. "We'll have a nice long chat tomorrow. I want to learn all about Brazil. I've been to Rio, you know. But just Copacabana, not the *real* Brazil, where the *people* are." She kissed Paulo again. "You're so darling!"

"He doesn't speak English, Alicia," Maria reminded her.

"That's what's so interesting. You can translate. We'll talk tomorrow, dear. The Blue Room is ready." And Alicia was off to check with the caterers, while Maria took her two bewildered guests upstairs.

She had called from Charlie Long's to say they were coming and to ask if Annie could set up the Blue Room—a guest room next to Maria's room. She'd have to remember to thank Annie when she saw her on Monday.

The room was large, with twin beds at one end and a sitting area with a TV at the other, and a private bath. The windows looked down over the front of the house. Zorina and Paulo—both in their new outfits from Target—sat silently on the very edges of their respective beds. Maria didn't know which one looked more lost and uncomfortable,

"My room's next door," she said, pointing. "I'll get you some supper first. Then I have to change. The noise from the party will be out back and shouldn't keep you awake. Oh, you better lock the door from the inside." She showed them the turn bolt. "Someone might wander in looking for a bathroom or something. I have a key, and I'll check on you from time to time during the evening, okay?"

"And Charlie Long?" Zorina asked. "How will he know where we are?"

"I'll keep an eye out for him. But you heard Alicia. He probably won't be here."

"He will come," Zorina said. "The boy is his responsibility."

Maria flared up inside. *And what about me? I'm just the one with the credit card?*

Zorina smiled, and Maria realized she might as well have spoken her anger and jealousy out loud. "Paulo needs you also, Maria. Because he loves you."

What could she say to that? She closed the door softly behind her, and heard Zorina turn the lock.

Twenty-Six

Charlie didn't plan on actually going inside and joining the party at this Maria McGrady's house. But if he had to, jeans and a T-shirt weren't gonna do it for "black tie optional." Good thing Sal gave him some money. He ran to the cleaners and picked up his brown pants and a dark blue shirt. He only had two ties and they were both pretty ratty, so he went without. He shined his shoes and brushed off his sport coat, and figured he'd be on the low end of "optional."

He took a cab downtown to catch the seven-thirty-five. Once he got on the train he wished he'd bought a newspaper. It was an hour's ride and he couldn't see out the window because it was light inside the train and dark outside. He sat back and thought how strange it was that he'd forgotten all about the basketball game that afternoon. It didn't seem possible. None of this seemed possible. It was even weird how comfortable he'd been talking to Zorina yesterday. Without seeming nosy at all, she got him to talk about his growing up days, which he never did.

He remembered telling her about his ma, and about his ma's ma, his grandma, who lived with them until she died. And how even after his old man was dead, his grandma couldn't stop griping about the guy. And his ma just taking it, smoking her cigarettes and staring out the window. He told her how he and the other little boys ran around acting tough, raising hell in the park and at the pool. Nothing serious. Some of the kids' fathers were mobbed up and they'd have whipped the shit out of any son of theirs who got mixed up in real trouble.

The wine had made it a little vague in his mind, but he remembered telling Zorina how it was only football and basketball that kept him in high school, and how even then he spent a lot of his time with so-called friends who mostly didn't play sports. Guys more into drinking and smoking dope and bragging about all the snatch they got, when they couldn't even get a chick to talk to them, much less put out. He might not have told Zorina that part . . . at least not in those words.

He did tell her how he was always wishing he had a father, but if he ever brought it up his grandma would tell him his old man had been no good, anyway. Couldn't hold a decent job . . . yada, yada. Then she'd start in about her own husband. Another bum. None of the men around there were any good, Charlie included. "Look at you," she'd say. "Treat your mother like dirt."

No friends ever came over to his house, because of his grandma. Always up in your face and running her mouth, and his sister Loretta like in training to grow up and be grandma. Both of them picking at him, telling him what to do, twenty-four/seven.

He still had a lot of trouble with people telling him what to do—especially women. Even Zorina tried it. Except Zorina seemed to catch on that it pissed him off, and when she pushed she tried not to push too hard. Plus, she was pushing him for Paulo's sake . . . not her own.

He'd never met anyone like Zorina before. He wondered, though, why she didn't wait for him with Paulo at his place. Maybe she got scared when she discovered he wasn't there. Or maybe this Maria McGrady figured she was too good to wait at his crummy place and talked Zorina into taking the kid up to her house. He had an idea he wasn't going to like Maria

McGrady. From Lake Forest? She was probably stuck up and liked to dress up in one of those weird English riding suits and have her "driver" take her to ride horses around in fucking circles and—

"Hey, pal, it's Lake Forest. Wake up. Better hurry if you wanna get off."

So he did. There was a cab waiting and he got into it and gave the driver the address.

"Is good," the guy said. "Is difficult to find, but I think I know. Is in Lake Forest, right?"

Jesus! Everywhere you go—Russians.

"Is this a big party you go to?" the cab driver asked.

"I don't know," Charlie said. "Why?"

"Because so many cars."

There were cars parked along both sides of the road, and they drove in under a sort of arch thing. There were four or five guys in valet caps, waving flashlights around, directing traffic. Mostly for show, because the only way to go was down a long, curving drive to the front door of a mansion. People in tuxedos and long dresses were getting out of their Mercedes and Infinitis and Beemers, leaving them for the valets to park.

Not exactly Charlie's crowd. He leaned forward. "Hey, don't stop. Just circle around and go on back out."

The driver thought he was a nutcase, but dropped him off down the road a little and Charlie walked back. There were a few other people walking, too, ones who maybe parked their own cars so they wouldn't have to tip a valet. That's what he would have done. The sign on the arch said *SHOREWOOD POINT* and he had a feeling the property was right on the lake. In fact, he could smell the water. A clean smell, though, not fishy. Even the fish didn't stink up here in Lake Forest.

He went under the arch and walked alongside the curving

driveway, staying behind this tall guy with gray hair and his wife or girlfriend or whatever, who looked a lot younger and had a dress on with pretty much no back at all, and a great tan. He thought of going past them to check out what was holding up the goddamn dress, but he didn't.

There was music coming from behind the huge house and it was a warm night, so the orchestra was probably back there, outdoors. He realized he should have brought a tie, no matter how bad it looked. Everybody else was dressed like for the Emmy Awards or something. Well, fuck it. He'd tell everyone he was a TV guy from New York City. They'd think he was cool, no tie and all. As long as he didn't fucking run into someone who knew something about TV . . . or New York City.

But how was he supposed to find Zorina and Paulo? He'd have to ask around for Maria McGrady. People should know her. She lived here, for God's sake.

He was about to cut across the lawn and head for the back of the house when a car swept past from behind, too fast and too close to the edge of the drive. It pissed off the man walking ahead of Charlie and he yelled something. But the guys in the Beemer probably never even—

The Beemer? Jesus! A silver BMW, four-door sedan.

Twenty-Seven

The Beemer slowed down at the front of the house and then, like Charlie's cab had done, kept going and followed the drive around and went out under the arch. He didn't see their faces, but there were three people in it, all men, which seemed strange for a party like this. It had to be the Russians. Driving by to figure out a good approach, just like he did. But how did they know to show up here? At this address? Maybe they had his phone tapped? No, that was too weird. So . . . was Maria McGrady in with the Russians? Did she trick Zorina and lure Charlie up here? That was pretty weird, too, but how else to explain those damn Russians being here?

He stopped to think. Maybe he better take his chances with the cops. He could go inside and find a phone. But he'd never reach that Chicago youth officer, and no one else would know what the hell he was talking about. If he called 911 he'd get the Lake Forest police, and what would *they* do? Search the home of a local billionaire on Charlie's say-so, looking for a fortune-teller and a little boy who never talks? Even if they wanted to, they'd need a warrant. And they wouldn't want to. What they'd want was to bust the ass of the guy with the corduroy sport coat and no tie who talks about a car full of Russians and a kidnapped little boy like he's sailing on meth.

On the other hand, maybe he was being paranoid. Maybe it wasn't the same silver Beemer at all. He never did get the license plate. Not tonight, either. What a fucking genius!

165

He had to check out the Beemer and see if it was really the same guys. He turned and walked all the way back to the arch. There were still people arriving, but just a few. The street was one-way and cars going out the drive could only turn right, so that's where the Beemer must have gone. There were no sidewalks, or even curbs, here. You couldn't see any houses, either. Just trees and bushes alongside the road, maybe ten feet in. Cars were parked along both sides of the narrow street, half up on the grass, leaving one lane open down the middle.

From maybe thirty yards back he spotted it. The silver Beemer, the last car parked on the right shoulder. He hadn't seen the Russians walking back toward the house, so most likely they were inside the car—if it was really them.

Keeping down in a crouch, he made his way forward along the passenger sides of the cars, away from the road. It was pretty dark, but there was a streetlight a block or so up ahead, so if the guys in the Beemer were looking back this way, or watching through the side mirror, they'd see him pretty soon.

He got as close as three cars back, but couldn't see from there into the Beemer. A car came along from behind him and just after it passed he ran to his right into the bushes. Hidden in there he could get closer, and have a better angle.

So he pushed forward through the bushes, and he saw them, all right. The vein in the side of his head started pumping again, and then the back door of the Beemer, on the passenger side, opened up and a guy got out. His friend with the leather jacket. Charlie froze. But the guy turned and went across the road and walked back, and when he got even with the archway to the mansion he moved into some shadows, staying on the other side of the road.

The bastards were waiting till the party was over, and the guy was watching the entrance in the meanwhile. Which meant Charlie had to go back to the house. But he couldn't, not by the driveway under the arch, anyway.

It was very quiet. He could hear the noise from the party, sounding farther away than it was. And he heard something else, too. The waves on the lake washing up on the beach. He moved deeper into the trees and came to a rusty old chain-link fence and followed it. But the fence ran parallel to the road, taking him farther away from the house, when he wanted to move away from the road and get to the beach. It was a high fence, maybe eight feet, but it had no barbed wire and he was over it pretty easily.

Jesus, it was like a goddamn forest . . . and dark. It wasn't all that far back to the McGrady place and he couldn't see any lights or houses between here and there, but he moved through the trees straight toward the lake. Once he got to the beach he could follow it easily back to the party. Then he'd mingle with the guests in the backyard and look around for the maid. Couldn't be a whole lot of black people there. He'd ask where Zorina and the boy were. She'd probably tell him.

And if he ran into Maria McGrady first? He'd just have to play it by ear.

Twenty-Eight

Alicia had invited about a dozen of Maria's friends. People she'd gone to school with, partied with, hung out on the beach with. Most brought boyfriends or girlfriends, and two of them brought soon-to-be spouses.

Then there was Donald Fincher. She and Donald had been friends since second grade. He was always a cute, outgoing boy, very bright, and a gymnast who'd started training for the Olympics at about age ten. His father bought and sold hundred-million-dollar companies by the handful, mostly in Europe and the Far East, but Donald's plans—at least his plans for after his try for the gold—had always been closer to home. He wanted to teach school, coach gymnastics, and have a wife and children.

But by the end of high school his Olympics dream had collided with reality, and Donald went off to Harvard. And began to change. "I've discovered the real world," he said. Now the dream was to be a mergers and acquisitions consultant, cultivate the right contacts, become an Important Person.

He said he loved her, while her feelings about him were less certain. Even back in high school, though they went out together on and off, she'd always thought of him as just a friend. He agreed that that's how it was then, but insisted that friendship was the perfect foundation for love. Maybe that was true, she thought, but these days there was something else—something she couldn't ignore. She was starting to dislike the man he was becoming.

Oh, she knew he'd be able to provide the sort of comfortable life her father provided. But she had no real feelings of love for her father . . . in fact she didn't like him very well. And Donald was beginning to resemble him a little too closely. Did she want to relive her mother's life?

It wasn't fair to string Donald along, and she'd planned to tell him how she felt when she came for this home visit. That night, though, after not having seen him for nearly a year, she thought he looked more handsome than ever, and more mature—tall and square-jawed and confident, sporting a tux that fit him perfectly. She felt her resolve melting away.

The two of them went and sat side by side on a wooden bench a long way down the terrace from the house, overlooking the lake. He told her he'd flown in that afternoon from New York, just for the party. "You know how much I've missed you," he said, "so let's not put it off any longer. You could come to New York with me and we could—"

"Wait." He hadn't even asked her yet about her year in Brazil. "This isn't really the time or place for such a serious conversation."

"Why not? We love each other, and now we've wasted a whole year."

"I care for you, Donald," she said. "But I don't feel I've wasted a year. Not at all."

"You know what I—"

"And the kind of commitment you want? I haven't made up my mind about that yet."

"Is it that nonsense," he said, "about us being too close, for too long, to ever fall in love? Because if it—"

"That's part of it, but—" She didn't want to hurt him. "Yes, that's it."

"Part of it. What's the other part?"

"There is no other part."

"Tell me what it is, Mary." For a year now she'd been *Maria,* and had told him that in her occasional responses to his almost weekly cards. His calling her *Mary* made the distance between them seem even wider. "Is it some other guy? Someone you met in that goddamn third world—"

"No, there's no one else."

"Then tell me."

"I just . . ." She didn't want to tell him, but finally she said, "What ever happened to teaching school, coaching gymnastics?"

He stared at her. "For God's sake, Mary, you wanted to sell cosmetics at Bloomingdale's. You wanted to be a nun, once. Then a veterinarian. Before that you wanted to drive at Daytona. People change. They grow up. I suppose you think I should quit the consulting firm and—"

"No, I'm not saying that." She turned toward him. "As you said, people *do* change. You've changed. I've changed."

"My God! Are you telling me it's all—"

"No, I'm simply telling you I need more time. I'm saying you seem to be . . ." She couldn't stop herself. "You seem so much like my father now. Making money . . . getting ahead. Those things seem more important to you than . . ." She was crying now. "I'm sorry."

She wanted to look away, but couldn't. She saw his mouth open, then close. Saw the flaring anger, and saw anger replaced by hurt. "I'm sorry, too," he said, and stood up. "You like money, and what it can buy, but you don't want to face up to what it takes to get it. The problem's in you, Mary." He shook his head, then sat down beside her again. "I mean . . . would you at least consider that possibility?"

"I *do* consider it," she said, "quite often." She tried to smile. "And I didn't mean to insult you."

"I know you didn't." He took her hand. "I love you, Mary. I want us to be together."

At that moment she couldn't help feeling closer to him than she'd ever felt before. "I love you, too." She leaned in and kissed him on the cheek, then pulled away. "Let's leave it at that for now, okay?" She stood up. "People are waiting. Let's go join the party."

He stood, too, and she tugged on his hand, but he didn't move. "The thing is," he said, "one of the partners wants me to review a buyout deal over the weekend. He needs my input Monday morning."

"I understand," she said. "I have things I need to do over the next few days, too. But for now, let's just—"

"Actually, I have to leave right now." He looked at his watch. "I'm on a night flight to LaGuardia."

"Oh," she said, and dropped his hand.

"Sorry," he said. "I'll call you tomorrow."

She watched him walk away, then turned and stared out at the dark lake. Maybe she did love Donald. Because she missed him already. Like her mother must have missed her father.

There were lots of people to say hello to. Her father's friends, and Alicia's. She didn't get too involved in chitchat with the older people, though, because this was her chance to get caught up with her own crowd. She'd be taking Paulo back to Porto de Deus as soon as arrangements could be made, and wasn't sure how soon she'd return to finish her home visit.

The orchestra was great and played all kinds of music, and her friends all loved to dance. Some of them asked about Donald, and she said he had business in New York and tried to make nothing of it. She told them about Rio, but of course not about Paulo and what was happening now. No one brought up going for a dip in the lake, so maybe they were all getting old.

By nine thirty there'd been no sign of Charlie Long. He'd certainly ask for her if he came, but she doubted he'd come. It was a warm evening with just the hint of a breeze. No moon, but the clear sky full of stars. Alicia, in a strapless red gown, was in heaven. Even Maria's father seemed to be having a good time. At one point she reminded him that with everybody staying outside in the back the house was empty, and they should lock the front door.

"No need for that," he said. "We're not in Brazil or some other place where thugs barge in and kidnap your guests or walk off with your furniture." But then he said he'd get someone to watch the door.

"That's even better," she said, "because I've invited a . . . a friend who hasn't shown up yet. He won't know anyone here and I want him brought to me right away if he comes."

Her father winked, obviously thinking, like Alicia, that she had a new boyfriend. He got the man in charge of parking, a tall guy in a valet cap, to stay near the front door and keep an eye out.

Maria had surveyed her closet and rejected all the formal gowns. Shoes would have been a problem and her hair wasn't right for those. She decided on a long-sleeved black crocheted sweater—with a black camisole, or it would have been too see-through—and a black skirt that didn't hug her hips *too* tightly and ended, midcalf, with a flounce. Elegant enough, but comfortable. It was fun to dress up again, and chatter with friends and dance. She was having a good time, even though she couldn't help thinking about Donald's quick departure, and Sister Noonie's poor health.

Of course she didn't forget about Paulo and Zorina, either. Once, she went inside and got the key from the top shelf of the linen closet and looked in on them. They'd both been worn out by the time they got here—Zorina even more than Paulo, she thought—and both were asleep on their beds, still dressed in their clothes. They were safe here, thank God, and in the morning they'd all sit down and talk to her father about how to get Paulo out of the country and back to Porto de Deus. He probably knew someone who could pull some strings with the Immigration Service.

She locked the door and put the key back on the shelf. There was really no need to keep checking up on them.

Twenty-Nine

It was dark as hell, but when Charlie broke out of the woods there were lots of stars in the sky. He looked out at the lake, surprised to find himself up on a sandy bluff. He scrambled down to the beach, half running, half sliding on his rear end. Then he ran along the water's edge, able to see just well enough to keep from tripping over the rocks and chunks of wood or whatever that lay scattered along the sand.

He went south, back toward the house, with the lake on his left, hearing the music and laughter getting louder. The bluff on his right kept getting higher, dark and full of bushes and little trees growing out sideways. It got steeper than where he'd come down, too, almost like a cliff by the time he got to where the party noise told him the house was. He'd never have been able to climb up, except for the wooden stairway from the sand up to a high deck that stuck right out over the beach on stilts. From the deck he had to climb some stone steps before he could actually see the house, forty or fifty yards back from the top of the bluff.

Between him and the house was a stretch of grass, then a low stone wall, then another stretch of grass and another low wall, then more grass and finally a wall that must have been the edge of a large patio, because that's where the orchestra was. Off to the right was a big open-sided tent which he figured was where the food was, but there weren't many people under there now. Most people were dancing, or milling around, or sitting at smaller tables on the lawn. There were hanging lanterns and a few burning torches and about a million little white Christmas tree lights strung along wires, all up closer to the house. But it was pretty dark where he was, and even darker below the bluff down on the beach.

One thing that surprised him was that with all these people—maybe a hundred or more—and at least two bars set up that he could see, it wasn't really that noisy a party. If they were his friends and there'd been half that many, and free booze, they'd have had cops in from every town from here to Wisconsin to try to hold things down. Thing is, though, these people were mostly pretty old—at least forty or fifty, or older. There were some young ones, though, doing a lot of the dancing.

He'd seen a few people down on the beach, walking the other way, and even ran into a couple—late thirties, maybe, the guy in a tux—coming down the steps. They'd just nodded and smiled. Now he caught the familiar odor of pot in the air. Coming up from the beach, he thought. He'd have loved to go and join them, but . . .

Damn, it didn't sound like a wild party, but who knew what all might go on before the night was over? Millionaires were well known to be into coke, meth, ecstasy . . . whatever. And expensive exotic shit. It pissed him off to think they'd drag Paulo up here tonight and expose him to all that.

He stood in the shadows and watched. Luckily his clothes were dark. He could lie low, stay in the shadows until the party was over, then go up to the house and find Paulo and Zorina and get them out of here. Except the Russians weren't stupid. They'd wait till everyone was gone, too.

So he had to make his move before they did, at the first sign things were winding down. And because the Russians had the front covered, he'd go in the rear. Take Paulo and Zorina down to the beach and head south along there as far as they could

go—he had no idea what was along the lakefront around here—
and then go back to the road. Not much of a plan, but he hadn't
thought he'd need a plan. He hadn't thought Zorina—with her
seeing into people and all—would get mixed up with someone
who was tight with the goddamn Russians.

He was scared, but not about to run away. He really felt like
it was up to him, now, to keep Paulo away from those Russians.
The kid hadn't done anything to them. Not a goddamn thing.
They should leave him alone.

He stayed in the dark and waited, and the time dragged, and he
was getting antsy. He walked down the steps to the beach and
looked around, and then back up again. He ran into another
couple of people on the stairs, but they were old and he just
acted like he belonged there and they said hello and kept going.

Finally, about ten o'clock, he saw the guests start taking chairs
and putting them up near the orchestra. Must have been fifteen
people in that orchestra and from what he could hear they were
pretty good, mixing rock and roll, oldies, and slow dancing
music. There was one woman in a red dress, with a pretty hot
body for as old as she was, who seemed like she was in charge.
He figured her to be Maria McGrady, and wondered if maybe
she and her husband were mobbed up or something, and had
dealings with the Russians. Again, bizarre. But *someone* brought
the damn Russians here.

The woman in red was directing things, and it seemed like
there was going to be some sort of show. *Shit.* That might go on
an hour or something and he couldn't stand it anymore. He
hadn't seen Zorina and Paulo at all, so they must be inside.
This might be his best chance to go get them, since everybody'd
be outside and the goddamn Russians would still be waiting for
the end of the party. Unless they were as jumpy as he was.

He couldn't go in the back way, not past all those people, but if he snuck through the bushes he could get around to the front of the house without being seen. If one of those valets or whatever stopped him he'd just say he was one of the guests and tell the asshole to fuck off.

He waited a little longer, until the show actually started. They had loudspeakers but the sound didn't carry very well outdoors, or they had them aimed so it wouldn't spread all over the neighborhood and disturb the neighbors—if they had any neighbors. Anyway, the show started with a song by a guy in a tux and a chick in a tight white dress, and it must have been funny because they got the crowd laughing.

And while that was going on he made his move.

When he got to the front of the house—it was a big house, all right—Charlie almost ran right into not just one valet, but the whole damn crew. There were six of them in a group, Mexicans or something, except for one white guy who seemed like the boss, and was talking. Charlie crouched by the corner of the house and listened.

It didn't make sense. The boss was sending them home before the party was over. Collecting their caps and flashlights in a box, telling them the guy whose party it was said they had to go. All the time looking real nervous, or scared, glancing back toward the house like he was watching for somebody. The crew was all pissed off and saying they wouldn't get their tips from bringing people their cars back, and the boss said he couldn't help it. Then he said he'd see they all got a hundred bucks to more than cover the tips they didn't get. That satisfied them and they left, walking down the drive toward the archway.

Weird, but that was five guys he didn't have to worry about, anyway.

The white guy, the boss, went toward the front door of the house. Charlie leaned around the corner to look and the guy seemed to be talking to someone, but Charlie couldn't see the other person and couldn't hear what they were saying.

Then the guy, still with the box of caps and flashlights in his arms, started to back away from the door, and this other guy stepped out into the open and—

Jesus! The Russian, the one with the leather coat. With a fucking gun in his hand. The guy with the box turned and ran away, across the drive and onto the grass . . . and the Russian held up the gun and shot him in the back. A shot, but not real loud because the gun had a silencer, like the one the older Russian had behind the Billy Goat. The parking guy was on the ground then, squirming around, and the Russian stepped up and leaned over him and popped him again. In the head this time.

The Russian dragged the body behind some evergreen bushes, then went back and took one of the caps from the box the guy had dropped and put it on his head. It was too small, so he tried another and that one fit.

He hid the box by the body, tilted the cap to one side and, with a smile on his face, walked back to the house.

Thirty

Alicia told Maria she had the orchestra signed up until two a.m., but she knew that by eleven some people would already be wanting to go home. "So at ten," she said, "I'll have the band leader start the floor show, and we'll draw for the trip about eleven."

"The trip" was a week for two—airfare included—at Alicia's villa in Bermuda, and the "draw" was from tickets purchased by the guests from men in tuxedos seated at little tables beside each bar. It sounded odd, and should have been terribly tacky, Maria thought. But it wasn't. The invitations had tasteful inserts advising the guests of the raffle—which they all expected, anyway, because Alicia did this every fall. The tickets were five hundred dollars each and the proceeds went to a battered women's shelter which was her pet project. No one went around hawking tickets. People could buy or not. Most of them bought—many of them several tickets—and one year Alicia cleared nearly a hundred thousand dollars. People loved the idea, and everyone stayed to see who won.

At ten o'clock they all brought chairs up around the patio and settled in for the "floor show." But the opening, a comic medley of Cole Porter tunes, had barely started when Maria felt a sudden wave of anxiety—like a panic attack—something she'd never experienced before. She whispered an excuse to her friends and got up and went inside.

She wandered through the quiet, empty rooms toward the

front of the house, and the laughter and music outside seemed very far away. She tried to tell herself it was stress, or she was overtired, but it was more than that. A voice in her head was telling her something was wrong. She had to look in on Paulo. First, though, she went to check the front door.

The man was still there, thank goodness, standing and looking out the open doorway. Or no . . . not the same man. Another one, but also a large man with a valet cap. She turned to head for the stairway, then stopped and turned back toward the door.

"Oh, my God," she said, not meaning to speak out loud, but when she did the man turned around. And she knew her premonition was accurate.

"Ah, yes," the man said. "Is Judy. Or I should say 'Maria.'" It was the man from the Billy Goat. "'Maria' is better fitting you. Is more pretty than 'Judy.'" There was a gun in his hand, pointed straight at her, and even in her terror she saw that it had a very long barrel, with something she knew from the movies must be a silencer.

He closed the front door and stepped toward her. She shrank back, but couldn't run, couldn't scream, couldn't even breathe. She realized her hands were clamped over her mouth and she was finally able to pull them away, but still couldn't talk.

"Do not make noise," he said, wagging a finger at her, "if you wish boy to live."

"The boy . . ." she managed. Her breath was back, but coming in huge gasps now. She glanced over her shoulder toward the stairs and at once realized she shouldn't have done that, shouldn't have let on that she knew about any boy. "How do you know my name? What makes you think there's some boy here?"

"Your friend Joanie," he said. "She does not like to, but she says you talk about boy." He held up the match pack she'd written her name and number on and waved it at her, and the smile on his face sickened her. "And now you say boy is here."

"You're wrong. There's no boy here. And you better get out while you can," she said. "The valets, they're like security guards. They—"

"Not such good guards. Their boss, man by door here, he tell them to go home."

"What about him? He went home too?" She prayed he had.

"He is . . ." The Russian shrugged, acting mystified. "Who knows where these people go? Maybe—"

"*Sssst!*" The hiss came from the top of the stairs and Maria looked up. Another man—dark black hair and younger, barely beyond his teens—called down softly to the man with the gun, who answered back. All in Russian, and Maria couldn't understand any of it.

The man with the gun seemed disgusted, as though the one upstairs were incompetent, and then spoke to her in English. "There are many rooms in this house and boy is in one of them." He gestured with the gun. "We go up now and get him."

"And if I don't?"

"Then I kill you." It was simply a fact. "And I still find boy."

"You can't be serious. There are over a hundred people out back." There was laughter and applause from outside. "Someone's bound to come in and—"

"If someone comes I kill them." He moved so close that she could smell the beer and onions on his breath. "We go upstairs now," he said. "I have business with boy."

"I told you I don't know about any boy. Why don't you—"

"Bitch!" The slap across the face—his hand seeming to come from nowhere—sent her staggering backward. "Do not lie to me."

Her head and neck hurt, and she was shaking with fear. But he'd awoken her anger now, too. She would *not* let him hurt Paulo. When she regained her balance he grabbed her arm and yanked her toward the stairway. She started up and he followed, nudging her in the buttocks with the gun barrel.

How could she have been so stupid? No matter what Sister Noonie said, she should have taken Paulo to a police station right away. It was her fault he'd been kidnapped in the first place. And now, when she'd had the chance to save him, she'd betrayed him again.

The house had three stories and an attic, and front and back stairways. The younger man met them on the second-floor landing, where hallways led off in both directions. Paulo and Zorina—the man hadn't mentioned Zorina—were down to the left. So she turned and started toward the stairs to the third floor.

"Wait!" the man said. "Where you are going?"

She stopped. "You can hit me all you want, but the boy isn't here. I'll show you all the rooms, starting at the top."

"Start here!" He pushed her toward the hall where the Blue Room was. "Is one door that is locked. Open it!"

She went to her own room and threw open the door. "Not locked. See?" Across the hall she opened a door to an empty bedroom. "And not this one, either."

The younger man said something in Russian, and the man with the gun pushed her toward the Blue Room door. "Open that one."

"That's *never* locked." She tried the door and pretended to be surprised when it didn't open. "I don't have the key," she said. "See?" She stretched out the sides of her skirt. "No pockets. We never—"

"Tell boy to come out. Do not waste more time. I do not wish to kill boy. I have business with him. But if someone comes, I kill you and boy first, before someone can do anything."

They'd knock the door down if they needed to. It would be

another half hour, maybe longer, before Alicia even got to the drawing for the trip, and—

"Tell him!"

"Paulo?" she called, knocking on the door. "Are you in there? Some men are here." She paused, trying to think just what to say. "Don't worry," she added, sticking to English. "It's not that man Charlie Long. It's—"

"Shut up!" The Russian spoke in a whisper, and slapped her hard on the back of the head. "Why is this talk of Charlie Long?"

"He's someone Paulo's afraid of. He'll never come out if he thinks Charlie Long's here."

"You are lying. Tell him to open door."

"Paulo?" she said. "It's Maria." She put her ear to the door, but couldn't hear a sound. She wasn't telling him to open the door, and hoped Zorina was hearing her message about who was out here—and who wasn't. "Paulo?"

The younger man said something and tapped on his watch. The man with the gun answered. He seemed uncertain what to do.

"He must not be in there," Maria said. "Maybe—"

"We find out," the man said. He shoved her aside and, aiming the gun toward where the door latch caught, he fired several times. She jumped, even though the silencer kept the noise down. With the wood splintered away he pushed the door open and turned on the light. All three of them stepped inside.

At the far end of the room one of the two beds was made. On the other, sitting with his back up against the head of the bed, was Paulo. Zorina wasn't there. The boy was fully clothed, with even his cap and his jacket on, and one hand gripped the handle of his little suitcase. He stared at them, his eyes wide open, and Maria knew he was terrified. But he didn't move. He didn't make a sound.

The man with the gun said something and the younger man

went to get Paulo. He reached to pick him up, but Paulo lunged forward and sank his teeth into the man's hand . . . and didn't let go. The man yelped and tried to shake him off, but Paulo held his teeth clenched on the webbing between the thumb and forefinger of his right hand. The other man ran over and, when the boy still wouldn't let go, tapped the butt of his gun down on his head, hard enough to stun him . . . and to make him let go.

The younger man stared down at his hand, oozing blood now. He clamped it tight under his left armpit and rocked back and forth, clearly fighting not to cry out. The two men argued, and Maria could tell the younger man was so angry he would have killed Paulo right then.

But the man with the gun turned to her. "Pick up boy," he said, "and come." She hesitated and he nodded toward the younger man. "Or else he beats boy to death. And then I kill you. It is your choice."

She went to the bed and Paulo let her pick him up. He seemed to weigh almost nothing. She left his bag on the bed, and they all left the room. On the way down the hall to the stairs, she soothed Paulo and talked to him, but refused to lie. She told him in Portuguese that she didn't know where they were going, but that she'd try to stay with him. "These are bad men," she added, in English.

They didn't bother to contradict her.

THIRTY-ONE

Charlie still crouched in the dark at the corner of the house. He hadn't moved since he saw the gunman turn away from the body of the man he shot, select a valet's cap that fit, and walk back to the front door. The door didn't close right away, though, and light still spilled out, throwing the man's shadow across the yard. Charlie felt like he should at least check on the valet guy. But why? No question he was dead. Plus Charlie'd be seen, and he couldn't go up against three armed thugs.

But would all three of them be in the house? Probably not. They'd leave a guy in the car to—

The yard was suddenly darker. The front door had been closed. He looked around and saw, way off through the trees, a pair of headlights pull into the entrance and start up the long drive. Then right away the headlights went out. The Beemer, for sure. Who else would drive up with no lights? So probably two of them were inside, getting Paulo, and the third was coming to pick them up.

He still didn't move. If they got a chance they would kill him. Period. He heard laughter and music from out back, and felt the pulse in the side of his head pounding. He remembered what he'd said to Zorina, that whatever this was all about, dammit, Paulo was not his problem.

Anyway, what could he do? Charge into the house and take a bullet in the head? Run out to the backyard yelling about some Russian gangsters and a dead man and a boy? They'd all think

185

he was a maniac and not do a goddamn thing, at least not soon enough. By the time he even got someone to call 911, the bastards would have Paulo and be gone. That's if they didn't kill the kid in the meantime . . . although he didn't think they wanted him dead.

He still had time to do the one smart thing. He could sneak his ass back down to the lake and get the hell out of here. Take the next train back to the city. Jesus, who'd even know he'd been here?

You'd know, asshole.

He left his hiding place and ran across the asphalt drive that swung in close to the front door, and then across the grass to where the dead man lay on the ground behind the evergreen bushes. If the guy'd been in charge of the parking guys, wouldn't he have a cell phone?

He did, and Charlie punched out 911. The operator would think he was nuts, too, and ask for his name. So when she answered he told her there was this huge fire at the McGrady house, right here in Lake Forest.

"I said 'McGrady,' for chrissake. Right on the beach. Fucking flames are everywhere. Hurry!" She tried to get more but he turned off the phone and stuck it back in the guy's pocket.

Dim light glowed out from just a few of the windows and, from where he was crouched in the shadow of the evergreens, he peeked out to look for the Beemer. It was on the drive, still a long way off, just barely creeping forward. No lights, waiting for the other two to come out of the house with Paulo.

The getaway car was their weak link.

Charlie grabbed a valet's cap, then picked out the heaviest flashlight in the bunch from the box the dead guy dropped on the ground. Staying in the shadows and running as fast as he could, he circled around and came up a little behind and on the driver's side of the car. It was the silver Beemer, all right, standing still on the drive now, with a good view of the front of the house through the trees. And the driver all alone.

Charlie walked quickly toward the car and, maybe ten yards away, switched on the flashlight. "Excuse me, sir," he said. "May I help you?"

The driver turned and looked his way through the open window, squinting against the light. It was the older man, the one who'd shot the black guy in the alley behind the Billy Goat. "Is okay," he said. "No help."

But Charlie, never stopping, was right at the window now. "I'll park it. It's my job." Keeping the light in the asshole's eyes the whole time.

"I told you," the guy said, his hand reaching inside his jacket, "no—"

Charlie snapped the head of the flashlight, backhanding it as hard as he could through the open window, smack into the guy's face. Then he hit him again, straight on this time, smashing the flashlight straight into his cheekbone hard enough to break the lens. Then he had the door yanked open and the guy was tumbling out, cursing in Russian or whatever, but dazed. Charlie wasn't thinking too well, either. All he knew was the guy must have been reaching for a gun, so he kept pounding the flashlight onto his head. The guy struggled to stay on his feet and get his balance, but then stumbled and bent over and Charlie slammed his knee up into his face.

The son of a bitch still wouldn't give up, his face streaming with blood and him growling like some kind of wounded animal. But if he'd had a gun under his jacket he'd lost it—or forgotten it. He came at Charlie with just his hands, fingers spread wide like he'd tear out his throat. But Charlie'd grown up on the streets, and was a good thirty years younger.

He stepped to the side as the guy charged, and swung out his leg and swept him off his feet and flat on his face onto the ground. But then, and Charlie couldn't fucking believe it, the asshole got up. This time Charlie crouched and when the guy charged him Charlie lowered his head and drove it full force into the motherfucker's chest. He was sure he felt some ribs give way, and the man sagged on top of him and stopped struggling.

He straightened up, lifting the thug off his feet up into the air. He staggered forward a few steps and then dumped the bastard on his back in front of the car. There was no resistance left in the man's body and his head flopped against the asphalt with a thud.

Still breathing . . . but at least this time he didn't get up.

Charlie stood listening, but heard no sirens yet. He turned back toward the Beemer, and stepped on something hard lying off the pavement in the grass. He knew what it was—the asshole's gun. He picked it up and stared down at it, weighing it in his hand. *Shit.* He threw the gun deep into a thick clump of bushes and slid behind the wheel of the Beemer. The motor was still running. He yanked the lever into reverse.

Maybe they'd get Paulo out of the house, but they wouldn't get far without a fucking car. He drove like hell backward down the curving drive, and was so pumped up he kept steering off the road onto the grass. But he finally turned around and made it to the entrance.

He slowed almost to a stop to turn onto the road, and that's when he first heard, finally, the faint, distant wailing of sirens.

THIRTY-TWO

At the end of the hall Maria set Paulo on his feet and they walked down the stairway hand in hand, the two Russian men behind them. When they got outside, she knew at once that something wasn't happening the way the men expected. They argued again, and it became clear they'd thought a car would be waiting. She held tight to Paulo's hand. She was scared, but she wouldn't be separated from him again without a struggle.

"This way," the man with the gun said, and started down the drive toward the entrance gate.

But they hadn't gone ten feet when he stopped. Maria stopped, too. She'd heard the same thing he had. Sirens.

The man turned to her. "I have business with boy," he said. "If you help us get away with him, he lives. But if we are caught he is worth nothing to me. I kill him before cops or anyone stops me. Also you. Do you understand?"

"Yes." She didn't doubt him for an instant, but the sirens were getting louder and maybe she could stall. "I have no car, though, and—"

"Show us a way." He aimed the gun at Paulo's head.

"We could . . . we could go that way." She pointed. "Through the woods down to the lake and then north and . . . and then I could show you a road. From there you could get to downtown, and the train station. It's a long walk, but there might be a cab there, or—"

"Show us," he said.

189

So, still holding on to Paulo, she led the way across the yard.

Long ago there'd been another house on their property, to the north of theirs. It was torn down before she was born, but had its own set of stone steps—long abandoned—down the bluff to the lake. Her father had never had the property cleared, so underbrush and scrub trees grew thick and wild under tall old oaks. As kids, she and her brother and their friends had played there in "the woods," a seemingly immense world of castles and caves, excitement and adventure. Then they grew up and the property was left to the squirrels and blue jays, and the raccoons at night, and the deer who'd roam along the beach sometimes and bound up the bluff for breakfast.

Away from the house and in the woods it was much darker. Although she knew her way, she led them through the undergrowth toward the bluff as slowly as she dared. Farther north there was a somewhat gentler slope down to the water, but here the way down was very treacherous.

The bluff was steep, over thirty feet down to the beach, and overgrown with brush and small trees that clung to the loose, sandy soil. If you didn't find the abandoned steps it was a difficult and dangerous descent, impossible in the dark. Over the years the bluff would be built up here, washed away there, leaving exposed roots and a thousand tiny crevices to catch a person's feet and twist their ankles.

With all the new growth she almost went right past the old steps to the beach, but she spotted the rusty iron pipe that served as a railing. "This way," she said.

By now the sirens were close to Shorewood Point. The roar of the engines sounded more like fire trucks than police cars.

The abandoned stairway had been built in the nineteen thirties, maybe, with stone and timbers and that pipe railing along the right-hand side. The first few steps were wide and shallow and faced toward the lake. Then there was a ninety-degree turn to the left, and on the rest of the way down there was a drop-off on the right and the descent was steeper. The final steps at the bottom had been wood and they'd rotted away years ago, leaving a three-foot jump down to the sand.

Maria started down, feeling her way in the dark with her feet, holding onto Paulo with her left hand and gripping the railing with her right. The man with the wounded hand was moaning to himself close behind, almost touching her, and the man with the gun came last. They could all hear fire engines roaring up the drive toward the house, and now some shouting. Both men crowded forward, anxious to go faster.

"Careful, Paulo," she said. "It's steep and dangerous in the dark." She doubted that he understood, and her words were for the men behind her. She could see the lake now, but couldn't even make out where it was lapping up on the sand. The sky was darker than it had been, with no stars anymore.

She was convinced that as soon as she'd gotten these men to where they thought they could get away with Paulo, they would kill her. Maybe as soon as they got to the beach . . . and maybe she should let that happen, so Paulo didn't get killed, too. Except she wasn't ready to die. Besides, with her or without her, if they thought they had to, they'd kill Paulo.

They were past the sharp left turn now, and a section of the pipe railing was missing. She stopped. "Be careful," she said. "There's another turn here some—"

"Move, damn you!" The man with the gun reached past his partner and slapped the side of her head. "Move!"

"I'm sorry," she said. "It's so dark, and—Here, Paulo." She got him in front of her. "You go first and I'll hold you from behind."

She pushed him forward a little—then spun around and threw

herself into the man behind her, grabbing his injured hand and tearing at it, knocking him backward into the man with the gun. "Run, Paulo!" she yelled. *Corra! Corra!* Her own voice gave her strength and she never stopped shoving and pushing until both men went off the edge of the steps where the railing was missing.

It was a drop of only four or five feet onto the steep side of the bluff, and the dense bushes and growth kept them from rolling and sliding down to the beach, but at least they both went flying onto their backs in the brush, thrashing their arms and legs. It was the gun she was most worried about. She turned and raced down after Paulo. The quickest way to the house was back along the beach, not up and through the woods. Besides, she couldn't abandon the boy now.

As she caught up to him, he turned to see who it was, and stumbled and fell in the darkness. She pulled him to his feet and hurried him down the steps ahead of her. At the bottom she lifted him down the last high step to the sand. She heard at least one of the men back on the steps behind her. *"Corra, Paulo! Corra!"* She shoved him to the right, toward the house, but pushed too hard and he fell face down on the sand. Then, as she jumped down after him she felt a sharp pain across her forearm, as though someone had slit it with the edge of a knife.

She yelled out in pain and fear, knowing she'd been shot, and fell and landed on her side on the sand. Terrified of being hit again, she rolled and crawled and scrambled to her right and made it to the bushes that grew out of the bluff down to beach level. She lay motionless in the brush and heard the two men reach the bottom of the steps, arguing in Russian. She was facing away from them and hoped in the darkness they wouldn't see her. She was scared and hurt, but afraid to cry, afraid even to—

But where was Paulo? It was very dark, but she'd have been

able to see him running on the beach back toward Shorewood Point. He must have gotten up and run the wrong way.

The men kept arguing in hushed voices. Then *"Dah!"* one of them said. *"Dah!"* and she could tell they were leaving, headed down the beach in the direction Paulo must have gone.

Her arm was on fire, but she got up to her knees and looked out. She could barely see the men as they hurried away. She hadn't noticed before that they were both dressed in black. Then again, Paulo would be hard to spot, too. His skin was brown, his jeans and jacket and cap all dark. Even his new sneakers were blue, not white. That had been Zorina's idea, and Maria suddenly wondered if . . . No, not possible. The woman couldn't see into the future.

She should go back and get help. The police would be there, too, along with the fire trucks. But by the time she got there and brought them back the men would have caught up to Paulo and been long gone. She was shaking and short of breath, but she had to go after them. At least she could see where they went, see if they stole a car, or what.

She stood up and started after them. She'd lost her shoes somewhere and—

"Hold it! Right there!" A man's voice, deep and strong, from behind her. "Down on your knees. Hands on your head."

She dropped to her knees, but somehow in her terror she couldn't get her hands to go to her head. They just waved around in the air by themselves, helplessly. She heard other voices. But then the voices, and even the fear, slid away from her.

Everything slid away.

THIRTY-THREE

Charlie had left the Beemer maybe a quarter mile down the road and taken the keys. He'd fumbled with the hood to get at the engine and yank out some wires, but couldn't get the damn thing open. There was no time to fool with it, so now he was over the fence and racing back to the beach again. He had to get back to the house. The fire and police departments would be there, milling around. He'd mix in with the crowd and find out what the hell was going on—and get to Paulo.

He was running in the dark, and going way too fast when he started down the steep hill to the beach. He lost his balance and spilled head over ass, rolling and ending up on his hands and knees on the sand. When he picked himself up it took a second to figure out which way was which. The beach, and even the sky out over the lake, seemed darker than they were before. Where'd the goddamn stars go?

He headed back along the beach and figured he was halfway to the house when he spotted someone running toward him in the dark. He stepped off to the side. It was *Paulo,* for God's sake, pumping his little legs and wind milling his arms like he was out of breath. Then he stumbled and lost his balance and fell on his face in the sand. Charlie ran and scooped him up in his arms, and took off in the direction Paulo had been running, with the kid kicking and punching and trying to get loose.

"It's me, dammit," Charlie said. "I'm saving your fucking life."

Paulo stopped struggling then, and when Charlie thought he was about where he'd fallen down the hill to the beach, he stopped and looked back. It was too dark to see anyone, but he could tell the kid thought someone was coming after him. It was time to get away from the beach, so he started up the hill, still carrying Paulo.

Thick, tall grass grew out of the sand here and it seemed even darker. It was tough going, and in the loose sand he couldn't keep his footing. He needed his hands, too, so he put Paulo down and tried to get him to climb on his back. "Here, take hold of my jacket."

But the kid grabbed on with only one hand. He wouldn't open his other fist.

"Come on," Charlie said, and pried Paulo's hand open.

It was a penny, and the kid tried to close his fingers again. Charlie was pissed off and got it away from him, and tossed the damn thing down the beach as far as he could.

"I'll get you another one, dammit. Get up on my back and hold on."

They made it to the top and he untangled himself from Paulo and they lay on their stomachs on the ground and looked back, and he saw two men—like shadows in the darkness—coming along the beach.

He knew goddamn well it was the Russians. Not coming very fast, obviously searching around for Paulo. They got close and he was hoping they'd go on by. But they stopped, for chrissake. It was dark as hell, but maybe they could see where he and the kid had turned and scrambled up. He didn't wait to find out. He got up and picked up Paulo and ran like hell.

Maria was still on the beach in the dark when she came to, and she didn't know how long she'd been out. Someone helped her get up and sit on the last of the stone steps down to the sand.

Her head felt very light, her nostrils cold and clear. There was a woman leaning over her and maybe the woman had made her breathe something that woke her up.

There were two men standing there, too. Both were dressed in dark clothes, and she couldn't see their—

". . . answer me, dammit," the woman was saying. She seemed angry at Maria, and in a big hurry. "I said tell me your name."

"Oh, I'm sorry. Maria McGrady."

"Is that 'Mary,' or 'Maria'?"

"I go by 'Maria,' " she said, and pointed down the beach to the right. "I live in that house back—"

"I know who you are."

"Then why—"

"To be sure you know." She grabbed Maria's hand and pulled it toward her. "What happened here?"

Maria looked down. The sleeve of her sweater had been pushed up to show the wound on her arm. No more than a scratch, really. "I . . . I think I was shot. There were two men who—" She stopped and stared up at the woman. "My God, you're the one from the airport, the woman who missed the train." She shuddered. "Where's Paulo? Where is he?" She tried to stand, but the woman clamped her hands down on her shoulders, and Maria didn't have the strength to struggle. Besides, both men had stepped closer. "Where's Paulo?" she repeated.

"A penny," the woman said, "did you give the boy a penny today?"

"As a matter of fact, I—" But wait. Who was this woman? "No," she said. "Why would I give someone a penny?"

The woman flipped open a cell phone and spoke into it. "You're on the money, Jack. The boy has it." She paused to listen, then spoke again into the phone. "Right. They're on their way." She closed the phone and spoke to the two men. "Two subjects in view," she said, "but the reading has the boy somewhere ahead of them on the beach, stationary." She paused. "We need that boy. Whatever it takes."

The two men took off.

"I'm going home." Maria's voice came out shaky. "I'm calling the police. There's a little boy out there and—"

"The boy will be fine," the woman said. "They'll bring him back."

" 'They'? Who's 'they'? Who *are* you?" She started to stand again, but the woman stepped close to her and she sat back down.

"Special Agent Lynn Brasher. United States Drug Enforcement Administration." She was taller than Maria, mid-thirties. Short dark hair. She showed a card which Maria could hardly read because it was too dark. "And 'they' are my people. Everything's okay. You've been—"

Explosions, like firecrackers, sounded from up the beach and the woman's head jerked in that direction. The look on her face made Maria want to scream, but by then she couldn't even breathe. There were several more shots, then silence . . . and finally the woman's cell phone beeped.

She answered and listened in silence. "Thank God for that, anyway," she finally said, and listened some more. "If you're still getting a clear signal and he's not there, he must have dropped it in the sand. He's on his own. Scared, probably hiding. You have to find him—now." She ended the call and turned to Maria. "They'll find him," she said. "They have to."

Charlie and Paulo had made it to the chain-link fence when they heard the gun shots. Three, then two more—and then he stopped keeping track. He hoisted the boy up and over the fence in front of him.

When they got to the car they climbed in and he started the

engine. But he didn't drive off yet. Christ, he had to decide. There'd be police back at the house. He could take Paulo and hand him over now. Except Zorina, wherever she was, had begged him not to do that until he talked to her. So unless the fucking Russians came bursting out of those trees—which he didn't think they would—it couldn't hurt to take a few seconds to think it over.

"Well, kid," he said, "you wanna go back and let the cops figure out what's best? The police?"

Paulo stared at him, breathing too hard to say anything even if he wanted to. But he was shaking again. That was his answer.

"No? Well . . ." Charlie reached for the lever to yank it into drive. "Sometimes we—"

A fist pounded on the window, right beside his head.

THIRTY-FOUR

Charlie had the Beemer already on the move when he turned to see who was pounding on the window.

"Christ!" He hit the brake and sent Paulo flying into the dashboard. It was Zorina. She got into the backseat and he drove off. "Jesus, where'd you come from?"

"I saw you," she said, "but . . ." She was gasping for breath, like she'd been running or something. "We must . . . go somewhere."

"Yeah, but where? I mean, we—"

"Somewhere," she said. "Hurry!"

He drove, and they hadn't gone far before Paulo climbed over the seat and sat in the back with Zorina, which pissed Charlie off for some reason. They came to downtown Lake Forest. It was dark and deserted, and he pulled over and stopped. They were across the street from the train station.

He cut the ignition and turned around toward the backseat. "You have new clothes on," he said, "both of you."

"Maria bought them for us. We slept in them because I feared something bad would happen, and we should be prepared."

"And something bad *did* happen."

"Yes, two men came and took Paulo and Maria," she said. "I hid, thinking the men might not know to look for me, and I would do something. But what could I do? I went outside and heard sirens and decided not to stay there." She seemed to be getting her breath back. "I went down the road and . . . and

199

now I find Paulo somehow safe with you. But I am worried about Maria."

"You should be. I think she's part of the problem."

"Maria? You think—" She stopped. "There is not time to discuss this. What will you do now?"

"You mean what will *we* do. You're the one who . . ." He let it go. "We don't have a whole lot of choices. Go back and give the kid to the cops, that's what makes sense."

"And another choice?" she asked. "You implied there were more."

"Yeah . . . well . . . I figured you'd try to talk me into something else."

"I have no plan."

"Really. So I guess we'll go back."

"Paulo is trembling. He and I both fear the police will send him where he will be hurt again. Maria knows about him, where he has been living, and she also fears—"

"I just told you. I don't trust Maria."

"Yes, you must judge for yourself. But first you need time, to find out what has happened this night. If nothing bad has happened to her, you can meet her. I trust her, but the boy is your responsibility, not mine, and—"

"Would you stop *saying* that? I was just in the wrong place at the wrong time."

"But you have done much since the Billy Goat. You cannot believe—" She stopped. "What is that sound?" she said.

"What?"

She opened the car door beside her. "A train is coming." She grabbed Paulo and pulled him closer to her. "See?"

Charlie heard it then, too. He turned to look out the windshield and saw the bright headlight of the train as it approached the station. Still a few blocks away. "So what?" he said, but when he turned back she had the kid out of the car.

They were running toward the platform.

He got out, but Zorina and Paulo were already headed across the tracks to the boarding platform on the other side. There was still time to run and catch them before the train came between him and them. But if he did, he'd either have to stop them from getting on, or get on with them. He sure couldn't leave the Beemer here, not with his fucking prints all over it. He'd stolen the damn thing, even if . . . *well, shit.*

And he wasn't going to grab them and hang on, just to keep his own ass outta trouble. Fuck that. Maybe he wasn't exactly responsible for Paulo, now that he was safe again from the Russians, but dragging the scared little guy to the cops wasn't his job, either.

He stood and watched the two of them hurry along the platform on the other side of the tracks. They stopped and both of them stared across at him, looking lonely and small. Then the engine roared past and the train stopped between him and them.

When the train was gone, so were they. He felt his fingernails digging into his palms, and he realized then how bad he wished he'd gone with them.

THIRTY-FIVE

By eleven o'clock Lynn Brasher and her people still hadn't found Paulo, and Maria felt as if all her energy had drained away. Brasher was obviously in charge of whatever was going on, and she and Maria were sitting in two of four captain's chairs in the back of a van, a block from Shorewood Point. One of the men from the beach was up front in the driver's seat.

They'd already been to the hospital. In the emergency room there'd been none of that giving your insurance information and then sitting and waiting. They'd passed right on through to the restricted area. A nurse pulled the curtains around an examining table, and a doctor appeared at once.

He took her blood pressure and pulse and peered into her eyes, ears, and throat. He listened, tapped, poked, checked reflexes, and asked questions—including about her fall and whether she'd hit her head, which she hadn't. He looked at the wound on her arm, which was really just a scratch. He cleaned it, smoothed some antiseptic ointment on it, and covered it with a bandage. Finally he turned to Brasher. "Scrapes and bruises, but nothing to be concerned about. Take a tube of this oint—"

"Excuse me," Maria said, "but I'm the patient here."

"Sorry," he said, turning back and smiling. "Anyway, you're fine."

So now they sat there in the van, with Brasher taking constant phone calls and occasionally talking to Maria. She was polite, but the bottom line was she wouldn't let Maria go back to the house. "I could arrest you and hold you as a material witness to a crime, but I'd rather not."

"Because you know my father has money," Maria said, "and he's a lawyer and he'd raise a big—"

"Actually," Brasher said, "that's not my concern at all." She seemed so definite that Maria didn't doubt her. "What I care about is not drawing attention to the boy. Right now your parents' guests have gone home and the place is crawling with homicide investigators. And possibly media."

"Homicide?" Maria said. "Someone was murdered?"

"There was a man in charge of parking cars. He's dead."

"Oh no! He can't be! I mean, I'm the one who insisted my father put him by the front door." Her eyes filled with tears. "It was those men, wasn't it. The ones who took . . . who tried to take Paulo."

"The local police are handling the homicide, and I have to deal with them. It's a touchy situation."

"But why?" Maria couldn't understand at all. "Those monsters tried to kidnap Paulo. You came along and . . . well, you scared me to death, but at least Paulo got away. So what's so 'touchy' about dealing with the police? There's a little boy out there in the dark somewhere, and . . . And what are you *doing* here, anyway? What was that 'penny' business?"

"I can't answer all your questions, but . . ." The woman hesitated, as though figuring out what to say. "I'm here to find Paulo and get him away from . . . from whoever kidnapped him. That's why I put this penny," she held it up, "a tracking device, in your purse at the airport."

"You thought I kidnapped him? That's ridic—"

"You were a possible lead," Brasher said.

Then it hit Maria. "That was *you*, wasn't it. Walking with that man on the beach yesterday."

"Just keeping an eye on you . . . and checking out the surroundings."

"Then, when you saw me talking to that Russian man in the restaurant, you followed me. God, why didn't you follow *him* instead?"

Brasher's answer was a slight smile that Maria could tell meant someone else had followed the man—and had lost him.

"And you lost track of me, too," she said, "when I got on the train."

"You *did* surprise me, taking the train . . . when you had such a nice car."

"So you came up here and waited for me to show up. But when I got here, and you saw that Paulo was safe, why didn't you just step up and identify yourselves? Then none of this would have—"

"There were . . . too many people around."

"What do you mean, 'too many people around'? You should have—"

"Let's wait," Brasher said. "There'll be time to talk after we've found the boy. And don't worry, we've spoken to your father and your . . . stepmother is it?"

"She's my father's wife," Maria said.

"Anyway, they know you're safe, and with me."

Maria couldn't even go get a change of clothes. She knew she should stand up for herself and insist, but she just didn't have the strength. Besides, these were federal agents, and maybe they knew best. Brasher was getting reports on her cell phone, and was obviously anxious to find Paulo. That's all that counted. At least the Russian men hadn't taken him. Which reminded her . . .

"Those two men," she said, "they didn't get away, did they?"

"No."

"And they'll be charged with trying to kill me, too? As well as—"

"Let's talk later, okay?"

Maria leaned closer to her. "I want to know where they are. They would have killed me. They might try again."

"You won't be hearing from them. Count on it."

"How can you be so sure?" Maria stared at her. "Wait. Do you mean . . ."

"I mean exactly what I said."

The world seemed suddenly unreal. "And where is—" She stopped. No one had mentioned Zorina so far, and if Brasher could hold back, so could she.

"Where is who?"

"I mean," Maria said, "there must have been another man. I know those two thought there'd be a car waiting out—"

Brasher's phone beeped again. She answered, listened, then turned to Maria. "I believe," she said, "that we have that car."

THIRTY-SIX

Maria and Lynn Brasher sat in the van and waited and finally Brasher's phone beeped again. She answered and listened, then signed off.

"Well," she said, leaning close to the window to look out into the dark, "here he is."

The side door opened and one of Brasher's men poked his head in. "We have—" He stopped when he saw Maria. "We have him," he said.

"Good. I'll talk to him here."

"Where should I take the woman?"

"Miss McGrady is staying."

"Is that a good idea? The procedure would—"

"Get Mr. Long in here," Brasher said, in a hard-edged tone Maria hadn't heard from her before, and the man withdrew.

Finally another man—the man who had to be Charlie Long—climbed into the van. His sport coat was torn and his face was bruised and scratched. He'd obviously been in a fight—maybe with Brasher's men. He was about her own age, and big, like a football player or a boxer. Regardless of his name, that cashier at the Billy Goat, Joanie, had been right. He looked Italian. He could even have been Brazilian, for that matter.

Joanie was right, too, that he looked like a gangster. Good-looking, for sure, but in a more rough-edged, street-tough sort of way than any of the guys Maria knew. Zorina obviously had confidence in him, but Maria had to wonder. Was this someone you'd trust with a little boy?

All this went through Maria's mind while Charlie Long climbed into the van and got settled into one of the captain's chairs. They all swiveled to face each other, and he glanced first at Lynn Brasher and then looked at Maria—a guy look—but right away he turned back to the DEA agent. "You're in charge?"

"Yes." She handed him her ID in a leather folder. He took it and spent such a long time reading it that Maria decided he was trying to figure out what to say next. When he finally gave the folder back he nodded toward Maria without even looking at her. "She got any ID?"

"Her name's Maria McGrady," Lynn Brasher said, "You've never met?"

"Nope." He shook his head. "But hey, am I under arrest?"

"No," she said.

"Is *she?*" Pointing at Maria.

"No."

"Maybe she should be. Someone brought those fuck . . . I mean, sorry . . . brought those Russian gangsters here. Maybe . . . In fact, it had to be her. How else did they know the kid was here? She must have—"

"Mr. Long," Lynn Brasher interrupted, "relax."

"He's crazy," Maria said.

"Not crazy," Brasher said, "just mistaken." She turned to Charlie Long. "Those men—and I'm not commenting on their identities—were not invited here by Miss McGrady . . . any more than I was."

"If you say so," he said. He didn't look convinced, though. He looked exhausted, more than anything else. Like he was about to pass out.

Maria felt that way, too, now more than ever. "What counts is finding Paulo," she said, "and getting him back to Porto de Deus."

"Back to *where?*" Charlie Long turned to Brasher. "What's she talking about?"

"It's late and we're all tired," Brasher said. "I've arranged for some rooms in a hotel not far from here. In the morning we'll take statements from both of you."

"Statements?" Charlie Long asked.

"Yes." Brasher stared at him. "And I trust you'll be more forthcoming with us than you were with the Chicago police."

"Forthcoming?" he said, and Maria knew he'd been caught off guard.

"They'd have put me on to you a lot faster if you'd been open and honest with them," Brasher shook her head. "Anyway, their problems aren't my problem. Mine's the boy. By morning I hope we'll have found him and—"

"*You're* looking for him, too?" Charlie Long asked, and Maria could tell he was as confused as she was.

"Yes," Brasher said, "and we'll have a Portuguese interpreter, so we can talk to him."

"Lotsa luck," he said.

"What do you mean?" Now it was Brasher who looked confused.

"I think he's discovered that Paulo doesn't talk," Maria said. "Not to anyone."

"So anyway," Charlie said, "if I'm not under arrest, am I in some kind of custody, or what?"

"Let's just say you—and Maria, too—you're both cooperating with a federal investigation." Brasher leaned and told the driver to get going. As the van started to move, she turned to Charlie. "There's something I need to know right away, though. About that car you were in . . ."

"Right," he said. "Like I told the guy who brought me here, it was those Russian creeps' car."

"How do you know that?"

"I saw 'em in it."

"And was there a driver?" Brasher asked. "That is, how many men were there?"

"There were three in the car at first. Two must have gone inside the house. And then I seen . . . I mean I saw . . . the third one coming to pick them up."

"See?" Maria said. "I told you they were expecting someone else."

"You mean you don't have the driver?" Charlie Long looked surprised. "When I left him on the road there—the drive up to the house—he sure wasn't going anywhere."

"He did, though," Brasher said. "That's not really my problem, either. But one of them's still out there."

THIRTY-SEVEN

Although still frightened for Paulo, Maria felt safe in Lynn Brasher's hands. The hotel, a Lytham Inn, looked brand new. Brasher seemed to have arranged for a whole corridor on the fifth floor just for them, and she herself took Maria to a room and gave her a tube of antiseptic ointment and some bandaging from the hospital. She also lent her a sweatshirt and a pair of jeans. "You'll have to turn up the cuffs," she said, and left.

Charlie Long seemed especially taken with Brasher. She was tall and slim and athletic-looking, and he had spent the whole ride to the hotel staring at her, as though Maria weren't even there. Not that she cared, of course.

There was a knock on the door and Brasher came back in. "It's for you." She handed a cell phone to Maria. "I'll wait outside while you talk."

It was her father on the phone, frustrated and angry because he hadn't been able to get the government agents to bring her home. He'd already spoken to several DEA people, including the man in charge of the Chicago office. "I made them give me his home number and I woke him up, dammit. I've met him before." That didn't surprise Maria. Her father knew lots of people. "Typical bureaucrat," he went on. "He says that female agent . . . Bradley is it? . . . or—"

"Her name's Brasher," Maria said.

"That's it," he said. "Lynn Brasher. Anyway, he says she's not from the Chicago office. She's here on special assignment.

Frankly, I don't think he himself knows what it's about. But they have no right to hold you." His voice was getting louder. "Those bastards don't—"

"No one's *holding* me." Her father was making her angry. His problem was that he wasn't getting his way. She was tired and didn't want to go home. She wanted to be here when they found Paulo, and—

"Hey," he said. "Are you *listening?* A man was murdered here. Alicia's hysterical." He paused. "Do you need anything? I could bring it right over."

"No, I'm going to bed now. You could bring me some clothes tomorrow, though. Come before you leave for California. You can give me a number to reach you there, and we'll stay in close touch."

"California?" She heard him sigh. "I'm not going. I'll get the trial date continued."

"No, please, there's no need to do that." She really hoped he'd go, and take Alicia with him. "You . . . let's talk about it tomorrow, okay?"

"Well . . . okay. Tomorrow then." Was she only imagining relief in his voice, about maybe not having to postpone his trial? " 'Bye, sugar."

She opened the door to the corridor and gave the phone back to Lynn Brasher. "Try to get some sleep," Brasher said. "If there's any news about the boy I'll wake you."

Maria took a soothing hot shower and slipped into the sweat-shirt and jeans. With the lights in the room turned off, she sank into a chair and stared out the window into the night. She was exhausted, but the events of the day raced through her mind. All of them—she, Paulo, Charlie Long, and even Zorina—could have been killed.

Would the DEA agents find Paulo? And what about Zorina? Why hadn't Brasher or her father once motioned her? She must have been hiding in the closet when Maria and the two men went into the guest room and got Paulo. She decided to call her father back and ask about Zorina.

But there was no phone. Phone jacks, but no phones. Panic surged up inside her and she ran to the door to the corridor. It wasn't locked from outside, thank God, and she looked out. One of the agents was sitting on a chair down where the corridor turned to go toward the elevators. He was looking up from a newspaper and talking to another man. Just then a door opened a few rooms down from her and Charlie Long stuck his head out and looked both ways.

"Hey," he called out, "there's no phone in my room."

"Special Agent Brasher's orders," the standing man said. "And right now she wants to talk to you—both of you."

Maria wasn't feeling so safe anymore.

Charlie followed the DEA guy and Maria McGrady—wearing a sweatshirt now, and jeans with the cuffs turned up—down the hall. He was tired as hell, and confused, and his muscles ached, and Paulo and Zorina were out there somewhere. There were just too many things to think about. Like this Maria. She was really pretty and he'd had to struggle not to stare at her on the ride to the hotel, but he still wasn't sure Zorina should have trusted her. And then Special Agent Lynn Brasher—not as pretty as Maria McGrady, maybe, but damn close. She seemed like a decent person, too, not someone who'd mess with you just to prove she was law enforcement and you weren't shit.

Maybe he should have told Brasher about finding Paulo on the beach, and about Zorina and the train. At first, though, he hadn't said anything because he didn't think she even knew about Paulo. Then, by the time he found out she was actually *looking* for the kid, she seemed to take for granted he didn't know where he was. So he'd kept quiet.

The sign on the last door at the end of the hall said "VIP Room." Inside it was nothing special, just a room like his, but set up like a living room, with a TV and couches and chairs, and no bed. Brasher was sitting at a round table, and on another table were a coffeepot and a Dunkin' Donuts box. The coffee smelled great, and he realized he hadn't eaten in a long, long time.

Brasher stood and held up a white mug. "It's real coffee," she said, "not decaf, so maybe you want to skip it. And there are bagels there. So . . . feel free."

She sat back down and Maria McGrady sat, too, but Charlie went over and got himself a mug of coffee and a bagel. And that's when he made up his mind.

He joined the two women at the table. "So," looking at Brasher, "you want my statement now?"

"That can wait," she said. "Right now I—"

"No, it can't," he said. "I can tell you where Paulo is."

"What?" Maria McGrady said. "How do you—"

"Let him talk," Brasher said, and he didn't understand the look on her face . . . like she was pleased about something.

"I don't know *exactly* where," he said, "but he's with a woman named Zorina. They got on a train in Lake Forest, and—"

There was a beep and Brasher took a phone from her jacket pocket. "Yes?" She listened, then said, "Fine. Thank you." She looked at Charlie. "It's good you told me that. Good for you, I mean."

"For me? I don't under—"

"Wait." Brasher stood up and looked toward the door to the corridor. Then the door opened.

It was Zorina. She looked very old, and very tired. "Some policemen came on the train and found us," she said, "Paulo and me. They brought us here."

Charlie was so surprised he just stood there while Maria ran over and helped Zorina to a chair. "Paulo is here? That's wonderful!" She turned back toward Brasher. "Is he okay? I want to see him."

"There's a nurse with him," Brasher said. "I'm sure he's asleep by now."

Charlie still couldn't believe it. "How did you know they were on the train?"

"We were looking lots of places," she said. "Trains were a possibility."

"How soon can I take him back to the orphanage?" Maria asked.

"Wait a minute," Charlie said. "Who says he should go—"

"We'll talk about that tomorrow," Brasher said. "Right now, though, let's go look in on him." She led them back down the hall to a door and opened it. "Don't wake him up," she whispered.

They squeezed into a short entrance hall, past the door to the bathroom, and peered in. The light was dim, but Paulo was there, flat on his back in bed and peacefully asleep. There was an IV hooked up to his arm, and a black woman in a white coat sat in a chair beside the bed.

Brasher led them back out into the hall and Maria asked again, "When can I take him back?"

"As I said, we'll talk more tomorrow. It's late. We should all go to our rooms and get some rest."

That was fine with Charlie. He was still confused, but—coffee or not—with Paulo and Zorina both safe, he knew he could sleep.

THIRTY-EIGHT

Someone kept banging on the door and Charlie finally remembered it was Sunday and he was in a hotel room. The clock radio showed ten thirty. He pulled on his pants and answered the door. The guy there gave him a bag that said *Lytham Courtesy Kit*, with a plastic razor and a toothbrush and other stuff in it. "Breakfast in a half hour," he said. "VIP Room."

Charlie could hardly believe everything that had happened, except he had pain in every muscle and joint in his body, for proof. Maybe it was a good thing the federal government was involved. They might be more careful than ordinary cops would, and not just send Paulo back to where he'd been abused in the first place.

But what about this Maria McGrady? If she had so damn much money and cared about the boy, why did she want him stuck away in some orphanage off in Brazil? He didn't like that. Torture and child abuse probably happened all the time down there. Paulo was better off in the United States. Any kid would be.

Then it suddenly came to him. He could take care of Paulo himself, seeing as the kid was an orphan. Of course his own place was too small, and they'd have to go live at his ma's. But not for long. Paulo wouldn't like it there. All Charlie needed was a job and enough money to get a decent place. He knew what it was like to grow up with no father. He could be a father to Paulo. How hard could it be?

He stood for a long time under the hot shower, trying to ease the pain in his muscles. Then he shaved and smoothed the wrinkles out of his clothes and put them back on. The sleeve of his sport coat was ripped where it was attached to the shoulder. That must have happened during the fight with that maniac who wouldn't give up until Charlie almost beat him to death. And then the guy gets up and walks away? Tough fuckers, these Russians.

He found some safety pins in a match pack sewing kit in the bag the guy brought, and fixed the tear in his coat as well as he could. Then there was more banging on the door. "Let's go. You're late."

The guy led him to the VIP Room, but stayed outside when Charlie went in.

Brasher looked up. "Morning, Charlie." She and Maria McGrady were sitting at the round table. It had a tablecloth on it this morning, and was set for four people. On the other table were serving dishes full of eggs, sausage, hash browns, and oatmeal—everything steaming. And sweet rolls, too.

"Uh . . . hi."

"Have some breakfast," she said. She looked great, in a white turtleneck and a sharp blue blazer that reminded him how shabby his coat was. "We started without you. Sorry."

"No problem," he said. He didn't know which smelled better, the warm food or the perfume . . . or cologne or whatever.

Maria was leaning with her elbows on the table, holding her coffee mug in two hands. She wore the sweatshirt and jeans she'd changed into last night, and he realized she must have gotten them from Brasher. Even without makeup she looked good. Worried, though, and not as businesslike as Brasher. "Good morning," she said.

"Morning . . . uh . . . Maria." Between her and Brasher he

didn't know which one made him more nervous. "Where's Paulo?"

"Still sleeping. Get some breakfast," Brasher said. "You can sit here." She pointed to the chair to her right, across from Maria. She poured coffee into a mug for him.

"Oh, yeah. Thanks."

He took a plate and filled it, happy to have something to do. He ate some of everything, then went back for more. As far as he could tell, neither of the women had eaten anything but toast. They didn't seem interested in talking, either. Brasher had the Sunday *Trib* in two piles on the floor beside her and was reading parts from one pile and dropping them on the other. Maria just sat and sipped at her coffee and looked worried.

Finally, after he'd downed one half of a delicious sweet roll and was buttering the other half, Charlie couldn't stand the silence. "When we gonna go see Paulo again?"

"Let's just wait," Brasher said. "When Zorina gets here we'll talk. Then you can make your decisions. After that . . . well . . . one thing at a time."

"Fine." He didn't know what else to say. What the hell did she mean by *make your decisions?* He was thinking maybe Paulo'd be better off with local cops after all.

Thirty-Nine

Zorina arrived and Maria fixed her a bowl of oatmeal, which was all she wanted.

Lynn Brasher said it was time to talk. "Paulo," she said, "is suffering from stress and exhaustion. He needs rest and quiet. He is, and for the time being will remain, in the care and custody of the US government. As for the three of you, you're free to go, or stay. But if you leave you will *not* be allowed back in. It's your call."

All three voted to stay, which must have been no surprise to Brasher, Maria thought, since this was where Paulo was.

"Okay," Brasher said. "There'll be a senior DEA official here to talk to you this afternoon, from Washington. Meanwhile, you have your own rooms to go to, and you can use the VIP Room. But you will not leave this floor on your own. Period. And now, if you like, we can go visit Paulo."

Paulo was awake and not very energetic. Still, Maria could tell he was happy to see them. She hugged him tight and he smelled like bath soap. The nurse looking after him was from Mozambique and spoke Portuguese as well as English. She said he was doing fine, although he wouldn't talk to her.

When they left his room it was past noon and Brasher and one of the male agents took Maria down to the hotel lobby. Maria's father was there with fresh clothes for her, and with Paulo's bag and his clothes. She wished he hadn't come, with his acting overprotective and trying to push people around—including her.

He tried to interrogate Brasher, but got nowhere. She just led them to a small meeting room, and said she'd have the bags taken upstairs and she'd wait in the lobby while they talked.

"I'm thankful you're safe," her father said, once Brasher was gone. "Alicia's almost hysterical and it bothers the hell out of me that I can't get a straight answer as to why federal agents were snooping around our house in the first place . . . or why they have you in custody. They haven't heard the last of me."

"I told you, I'm not 'in custody.' Paulo's here, and I want to stay close to him." She knew it was no use asking him to give up his complaints, or the calls he'd probably be making to politicians. It had become for him a matter of personal outrage . . . at being treated like an ordinary citizen.

"I intend to get some answers," he said.

"Fine, but you should go to California, and take Alicia. You can fight with the DEA from out there as well as from here. You've spent a year preparing for this trial, and putting it off would be a huge expense and inconvenience to everyone."

"Well . . ."

"Besides, if you don't get away Alicia will have to deal with all sorts of curious friends . . . not to mention the media."

"All right," he said. "We'll go. Only for Alicia's sake."

She knew that wasn't *entirely* true. But it *did* seem true—and this came as a pleasant surprise—that his concern for Alicia, and for herself, was genuine.

"I left a cell phone in the bag with your clothes," he said. "Call me every day."

She agreed, and when he left she couldn't believe she was actually feeling good about him keeping an eye out for her.

★　★　★　★　★

Making sure everything went okay for Paulo was the big thing, but Charlie had another reason to stay when Brasher said they could leave. He'd seen a murder and not reported it. And then keeping Paulo and lying to that youth officer? Hell, there might be Chicago cops out there right now, waiting for him. So the best thing was to sit tight and see what the feds wanted, and make sure the kid got the best deal for his future.

When Maria came back to the VIP Room there was nothing to do but wait for the man from Washington, and Zorina said they should tell each other what happened to each of them since Friday afternoon.

Maria started, and told about the orphanage and the nun called "Sister Noonie," and about Paulo getting kidnapped. She described Brasher bumping into her at O'Hare. And the "penny." She explained about Intertec, and them quitting the case. "But at least they led me as far as that tavern," she said, "and to Zorina." She told how they got to his place and found Paulo and took him to Lake Forest, and finally about the two Russians and how she knocked them off the steps down to the beach, and Paulo running away.

Charlie told about getting fired and going to the Billy Goat to meet Sal. Then about picking up Paulo, and the bread truck, and going into Zorina's place. He left out seeing the black guy—Intertec's detective, for sure—get shot. He wasn't certain if he'd told that to Zorina when he was drinking her wine, but decided not to bring it up now. He told about his fight with the third Russian and taking the Beemer, and finding Paulo on the beach. "Which was only possible," he told Maria, "because of what *you* did."

She seemed impressed by what *he'd* done, too, and that made him feel good.

He was getting a whole new picture of Maria. A girl like

her—great looking and all the money in the world—and she volunteers to go and live in an orphanage in Rio and take care of poor kids off the streets? She seemed to really like working there, and she admired that nun there so much that somehow he got the idea that she might even want to be a nun herself. Jesus, what a waste *that* would be! He understood better, now, about her wanting to take Paulo back there. But the kid could have gotten abused there, by some older kids, or even by staff, and she might not even know about it.

Zorina didn't say much herself, mostly asked questions. She looked pretty tired, and finally she said she was going to her room for awhile. She left and they sat there, not saying anything. Charlie knew the Bears game was on TV, and it surprised him that he had zero interest in watching. Except he didn't know what to say to Maria, either. So they just sat.

"Brasher say when that DEA guy's getting here?" he finally asked.

"Just 'later this afternoon,' is all."

"Right," he said, and that was it for a few minutes.

He could feel himself sweating a little and he almost *did* turn the Bears game on, just to make some noise. Luckily, though, Maria came up with a question—not exactly a topic he'd have picked, but something to talk about, at least.

"Why did you get fired?" she asked.

He told her about the supervisor who bullied people. "So one day the guy's hassling this girl about how she had big . . . you know . . . about her figure. When she started to cry I guess he thought that was cool, and he laughed. So . . . well . . . I told him to stop." He shook his head. "I was pissed off, and I said a few things, and I guess I went a little too far."

"He's the one who should be fired," Maria said.

"Yeah, well, things don't work that way. My mouth's always

getting in the way. That's the reason I didn't even last a year in college."

"Really? What happened? What college?"

"Michigan State. To play football. Not a full grant, but a special program for guys who were . . . possibilities. Anyway, we had this one assistant coach who was a real asshole. Oh, sorry, I—"

"Forget about it, Charlie. Just go ahead." She seemed actually interested, which amazed him.

"Okay," he said. "So this one day it's near the end of a long practice. We're all like dead on our feet. I'm playing defense and this big blocking back just kinda collapses and lets me run right over him. I go back to see if he's all right, and he's lying on the ground trying to get his breath back, and this coach comes over. 'Up off your lazy ass!' he screams. 'You're not worth shit, you pussy!' Stuff like that. His way of motivating, I guess. But it wasn't fair and . . . well . . . I kinda lost it."

"Really? What did you do?"

"I yelled, 'Shut up, asshole!' and I even took a step forward, but luckily some guys stepped between us. Then later, when I'm thinking it's all over, the coach takes me aside and gets up in my face and says, 'You'll play for this team over my dead body.' So I say, 'Yeah? Well, I fucking *hope* so.' "

"And you got thrown off the team?" she asked.

"Not exactly. I'd suit up for practice, but I never got a chance to show what I could do. He just pretended I wasn't there. Pretty soon I got discouraged and . . . well . . . I partied myself right out of school after that." He shrugged.

Maria didn't say anything to that, and he tried to think of how to get the conversation away from his past stupid mistakes. Finally he stood up and said, "I should go make sure Zorina's okay."

Maria had seemed like she actually liked him, and he'd been

making a good impression for awhile, but he'd probably fucked that up big time.

Maria could tell Charlie was embarrassed by his story. He was unpolished, for sure, and his world seemed about as far removed from hers as Paulo's was. Still, she was beginning to see why Zorina thought so highly of him. He cared about other people, especially when they were being picked on, and he had certainly moved decisively when Paulo needed help. Despite his rough edges, she found him . . . well . . . intriguing.

FORTY

Charlie went to his own room first and then went and knocked on Zorina's door. When she didn't answer he decided to ask Maria to check on her, but when he got to the VIP Room Zorina was there. He was glad. With her around it was easier to talk, and he was hopeful he could convince Maria he wasn't a complete mope.

"Join us," Zorina said. "I am asking Maria to tell us again how Paulo was kidnapped."

Charlie sat with them at the round table and Maria explained how she'd talked Paulo into going on a field trip she was taking a group of the kids on, and how he lagged behind and was snatched. She obviously blamed herself, but Charlie's opinion was she should stop beating herself up about it. She'd had a whole group to look out for. Some damn Russian kidnapper puts the eye on Paulo, how's she to know?

"I still wonder, though," Zorina said, "why do these men bring Paulo to Chicago?"

"Sister Noonie thought that was odd, too," Maria said. "But the police said they were probably sex traffickers, and I thought maybe they had a . . . a customer here."

"Damn." Charlie shook his head. "What kind of person would—"

"Then the Intertec woman told me they have a headquarters here," Maria said. "So, who knows?"

"Yesterday," Zorina said, "it seemed you thought it surprising that such kidnappers would believe Paulo to be a street child."

"That was something Sister Noonie told the police, but they ignored her. She said kids kidnapped for the sex trade are usually girls. But whether girls or boys, they're street urchins, running around in rags. Paulo, though, was wearing neat, clean clothing. He even had an ID tag pinned to his shirt."

"His *name* wouldn't mean anything to them," Charlie said.

"But they'd know he had a home, and Sister said they *might* even have recognized his name, because of his father, actually, and his uncle. His father was a well-known gangster, involved in drugs and violent crime, while his uncle was a policeman."

"You spoke of this uncle on the phone with Sister Noonie," Zorina asked. "After you had already told *me* that Paulo *had* no relatives."

"You asked if he had relatives to pay *ransom*. His father's dead and the uncle's a captain in the Brazilian federal police. I'm sure even captains aren't wealthy, not enough for kidnappers to bother with."

"Some cops get pretty rich," Charlie said, "if they make friends with the right crooks, or sell dope on the side or something."

"Anyway," Maria said, "his father was a criminal and his uncle's a policeman. Strange, isn't it?"

"Not that strange," Charlie said. "I know two families like that from my old neighborhood. Cops and crooks aren't that diff—"

"Yes," Zorina interrupted. "And what of the boy's mother?"

"His mother's dead," Maria said. "One night some policemen—not federal police like his uncle, but city police, from Rio—they broke into the house where Paulo and his mother lived, looking for Paulo's father. He didn't even live there, but he kept men there as guards. There was a gunfight, and Paulo's mother was killed. It stirred up a lot of bad will with the public, because Paulo's father was famous for helping out poor people. Sister said they still tell stories about him in the *favela*."

"Probably made up the stories himself," Charlie said. "The old 'Robin Hood' bullsh . . . baloney."

"Anyway, shortly after that Paulo's father was arrested, and for awhile Paulo lived with his uncle. But then his father broke out of jail. He got away in broad daylight, in a helicopter, and a guard was killed. While he was free he got Paulo from his brother and took him to Porto de Deus and begged Sister to take him in. She told him the authorities wouldn't let her take any more children, because the facility was overcrowded and in bad condition."

"But I bet he paid her off," Charlie said. "Right?"

"Actually . . . yes. Paulo's father said if Sister took the boy in he'd buy some property for them, and he did, and that's where the orphanage is now. Later on, the police found his father again, and this time they shot him . . . killed him."

"Jesus," Charlie said, "first his mother, then his father. Killed by cops."

"The child must have been taught from infancy that police were to be feared," Zorina said. "And the teachings came true."

"Policemen *do* frighten Paulo," Maria said. "That day when he lagged behind, he ended up on the other side of a busy street and a traffic policeman started to go help him. But Paulo got scared and . . . and ran the other way." She stood up and took a few steps toward the window. "Traffic was backing up and drivers started honking and yelling, and the policeman turned and yelled back. By then Paulo was half a block away and that's when I saw a man grab him and . . . and . . ."

"Hey, c'mon," Charlie said, afraid she'd started to cry. "It wasn't your fault. Besides, he's safe now."

"I know." Maria turned back toward them. "But still, it *was* my fault. Sister Noonie says Paulo's uncle accuses her and the orphanage of neglect. He told her he'd find Paulo, and when he did, he'd make sure he never went back there again."

"Yeah, well, his uncle *didn't* find him," Charlie said. "I did. And if he was so worried about the kid, why'd he let him be stuck in an orphanage in the first place, and get abused and—"

"*What?*" Maria's voice was so loud it made Charlie jump. "Paulo was *not* abused at Porto de Deus." She leaned forward and looked like she might come over and slap him. "How could you *say* such a thing? You don't know what you're—"

"Hey, take it easy, will you? I just . . . you know . . . I saw the scars, and—"

"I never saw his scars. But Sister told me about them, and said he had them when he came. And Sister does not lie."

"Yeah, well . . . some orphanages . . . I mean . . . you hear things."

"Whatever you *hear,* you shouldn't say things when you don't know what you're—"

"Please, Maria," Zorina said, her voice very gentle. "It still seems an odd thing that a child is placed in an orphanage, yet has an uncle who says he would take care of him."

"Well, obviously what his father *wanted* was Porto de Deus." Maria came and sat down, but didn't even look at Zorina. She was still glaring at Charlie. "And he was not abused there. In a year I've never seen one *hint* of—"

"Hey, relax," Charlie said. "I guess I shouldn't jump to conclusions." He knew he'd been stupid to say it, even though he still thought it was at least possible. "I'm sorry."

"Right," Maria said, "you *should* be." She seemed to be cooling down, though . . . a little. "Sister Noonie told me once that *God* sent Paulo to the orphanage. I didn't understand, not until I heard about his father buying the property. And something else she said about God I didn't understand was—"

"Nuns are always talking about God doing stuff," Charlie

said. "Something happens and they drag in—"

"Please!" Zorina gave him a dirty look, then nodded to Maria. "What else did you not understand?"

"Sister said if Paulo didn't come back and live at Porto de Deus, God would have to provide a new home for the orphanage."

"And she didn't explain?" Zorina asked.

"No. But now he *can* go back, so I guess it doesn't matter."

"No, perhaps not." Zorina stood up. She breathed hard, like it was a struggle for her. "I must walk again, to loosen my joints."

Charlie watched her go, then turned to Maria. "I guess your mind is made up, huh? I mean, that the orphanage is the best place for Paulo? Even if he has an uncle who wants to take care of him?"

"It's what his father wanted."

"Yeah, I guess." He picked at his thumbnail. "Except . . . I've been thinking. He might be better off staying *here,* y' know? I mean . . . in the United States."

"That makes no sense at all." She was shaking her head. "He has no one here. He needs to go home."

"Uh-huh." Charlie was thinking Paulo *did* have someone here . . . himself. But he could tell she still wasn't happy with him. To change the subject, he said, "I wish that Washington guy would get here. I'd like to find out why the DEA's involved. *That's* what makes no sense."

"I think it makes *perfect* sense," she said. Like she was the fucking expert. "Kidnapping's a federal crime, so naturally the federal government steps in."

"Yeah, okay. Feds maybe." He got to his feet, knowing he should just shut up and get out of there. But he couldn't resist adding, "The FBI, though. *Not* the DEA."

He left before she had a chance to answer that one.

So much for making himself look good.

FORTY-ONE

That evening they were back in the VIP Room, this time with Brasher and the guy from Washington. He was maybe fifty, and his cold eyes and the cocky way he carried himself tagged him as a cop. Still, Charlie was willing to give him a chance to prove he was a decent guy.

"There's coffee if anyone wants it," Brasher said.

No one took her up on it but Charlie. He felt jumpy and what he'd have really liked was a Bud Light, but he got up and poured himself some coffee because it was something to do. He came back and sat down and put the mug on a little table beside his chair.

When he finally looked up, it was very quiet in the room and he was surprised to find everyone staring at him. "What?" he said. "I'm supposed to say something?"

The DEA guy stood up. "I'm Howard Lockman," he said, "a deputy administrator with the United States Drug Enforcement Administration. I'm aware of all your names, so—"

"What's going on with Paulo?" Charlie figured let's get to the point. "Why all the secrecy?"

"The boy is fine," Lockman said. "But this will move more quickly without interruptions. Later, you'll all get a chance to ask questions." He paused. "But I must tell you, because of the nature of this matter there is certain information I'm not at liberty to share."

"Right," Charlie said. "But you're 'at liberty' to come in and push people around, and when someone tries to find out what the hell—"

"Y' know what, Charlie?" Brasher's voice had a sharp edge to it. "A couple of days ago you weren't as honest with the police as you might have been. Frankly, that could be a problem for you. So my suggestion?" Leaning forward now, staring hard at him. "Shut up!" Then she sat back and smiled like she'd just asked him to pop open the wine and dim the lights. "How about it?" she asked.

"Yeah," he said. "Okay."

"I share your concern about the boy," Lockman said. "Now, though, I must warn you. It's in the national interest that this matter not become public, and you may be guilty of a serious crime if you speak of it to anyone outside this room. I'm assuming, for now, that yours has been an innocent involvement."

Lockman waited a few seconds, and Charlie figured that was to let the *for now* part sink in.

"What's important," Lockman went on, "is that the boy is safe and in our custody. I can't say—"

"Excuse me." It was Zorina interrupting this time, and no one tried to stop her. "You are asking that we keep silent about your taking custody of Paulo?"

"Not asking," Lockman said. "Requiring."

"And your plan for him? Is this also not to be revealed?"

"Plan?" Lockman stared at her. "I can't—"

"Those Russian men, they kidnapped Paulo and brought him to Chicago."

"Please, Zorina," Brasher said, "you should—"

"Let her talk," Lockman said. "I want everyone feeling comfortable, knowing we're all together on doing what's best." He smiled at Zorina. "You may go ahead." Like to a kid needing permission.

"So," she said, "after we have saved the boy from the Russian men, you have taken him."

"We've taken him, yes. And he's safe."

"And you have plans for him, would use him for—"

"Hold on a minute." Lockman stood up, and Charlie figured that was it for *everyone feeling comfortable.* "Why is it, ma'am, that you think you know things that haven't been said?"

"She's Zorina," Charlie said, enjoying the guy's discomfort. "She has a gift."

"Really. A gift." Lockman stuck his hands into his suit coat pockets. One of those on-top-of-things gestures that Charlie's college professors thought was so cool. "Okay, ma'am, what else do—"

A cell phone beeped. Lockman looked startled, then pulled the phone from his pocket. He answered and listened, then leaned down and whispered to Brasher. She stood up and, as the two of them headed for the door, she turned to them. "That's it for now. I'll be back to see what you want for supper."

Lockman had failed the *decent guy* test. Which didn't make Charlie feel any better.

FORTY-TWO

Charlie's pepperoni pizza wasn't half bad. Maria ate most of her chicken salad, but Zorina pretty much ignored her spaghetti, so Charlie ate most of that, too. Finally Zorina stood up and said they should come to her room in half an hour, obviously taking for granted they would.

When she was gone Maria said, "She's . . . an unusual person, isn't she?"

"Yeah." He felt nervous again, it being just the two of them. "Right . . . she's unusual."

"I think she went overboard, though, challenging Mr. Lockman," Maria said. "He was about to tell us what—"

"He's a cop, for chrissake. They don't tell anyone shit. Besides, Zorina's . . . you know . . . a smart person."

"Well, she admitted to me that she doesn't know *everything*."

"I didn't say she did."

"She seems to think the government might do something to *hurt* Paulo. Why would she think that?"

He shrugged. "I don't know. She doesn't miss a thing, though. Maybe she heard someone say something."

"I think it's ridiculous," Maria said.

"What," he said, "the fucking government's perfect?" The tone of his own voice surprised him. "They'd never do anything to hurt anyone? Jesus, what planet do you live on, anyway? Did you ever—"

"Don't *yell* at me. I'm not stupid, and I'm not naive. I know more about the 'planet' than you ever will. You've never lived in a foreign country. You don't even have a college—" She stopped. Her face was red and he could tell that at first it was from being mad at him, but that now she was embarrassed about putting him down. "I'm sorry," she said. "I didn't mean anything."

"Yeah, well, no problem." For something to do, he took a sip of cold coffee. "I'm just talking in general . . . you know . . . about the government not being perfect."

"I understand, but I think we have to give Mr. Lockman the benefit of the doubt." She stood up. "Anyway, I'll see you at Zorina's."

He watched her as she left. She had a really nice way of walking. He'd have to keep his cool—and clean up his mouth—when she was around.

Charlie stood outside Zorina's door, trying to decide what to think about Lockman and the DEA. He wasn't sure. He knocked and the door was opened right away . . . by Maria. She'd changed into a tan sweater and some brown pants. He felt his heart speed up. Damn, she looked good, and—

"Charlie?" she said. "Aren't you coming in?"

"Oh . . . yeah." He stepped inside. "Why's it so dark in here?"

"Zorina's . . . well . . . she's thinking, I guess."

He followed Maria past the open bathroom door—which is where the only light was coming from—and into a room just like his. King-sized bed, TV cabinet, desk, and the same sort of easy chair that rocked and swiveled around. Two desk chairs, though, instead of one. And this room had a view out onto the dark night. With the drapes pulled wide open and so little light in the room you could see out the window and across the tops of the trees toward the expressway.

At first he didn't spot Zorina, but then realized she was sitting in the easy chair. She had it turned so she was facing the window.

No one said a word. He stood in the dark with Maria close beside him, her perfume driving him nuts. Jesus, it felt like a hundred years since he gave away his last fucking cigarette to that chick in the mail room. How the hell did he get from there to here in two and a half days?

Zorina swiveled her chair around. "We must be careful," she said, "to do what is best for Paulo."

Right, he thought. *That's* how I got here.

He and Maria joined Zorina by the window and, for what seemed to Charlie a long time, they all just looked out in silence. Finally Zorina said, "Perhaps you would tell Charlie about your phone, Maria."

"What phone?" Charlie said. "I didn't hear about—"

"My father said he put a cell phone in with the clothes he brought me," Maria said. "But Brasher took the bag while I talked to him, and a few minutes ago I discovered she must have searched it and taken the phone. I asked her about it and she said it was a 'national security' issue."

"What the hell's a little kid got to do with national security?" Charlie said. "The feds get involved, and they throw a blanket over everyone who helped find him: you, me, Zorina. All of us."

"And do not forget Maria's detective agency," Zorina said. "They, too, were looking for Paulo. And then on Saturday, although they were paid, they suddenly withdrew."

"What are you saying?" Maria asked. "That the government *made* them quit the case? That's—"

"I am saying," Zorina interrupted, "that Paulo and his rescue are important, and must be secret, and that no one tells us why."

"Well," Maria said, "Charlie says law enforcement people never tell civilians what they're thinking." Damn, that made

Charlie feel good, Maria quoting him. "And my father said the same thing. I see no reason to suspect federal agents of some evil conspiracy."

Zorina stood up and faced out the window. When she turned back she looked straight at Charlie. "So," she said, "what is your thought about this?"

"In my world you wouldn't trust a fed to hold a door open for you. And Lockman? I'm thinking he made his own phone ring, to break up the meeting, 'cause there's something he can't talk about. But still, they know we got our eyes open, and Maria's father does, too. They won't do anything to hurt Paulo. Not with us all watching." He wasn't trying to ease anyone's mind, either. That's how he looked at it.

"Yes," Zorina said, "perhaps you are right."

★ ★ ★ ★ ★

PART IV
FLY AWAY, LITTLE BIRD

★ ★ ★ ★ ★

On Sunday Bill Grayson and the three DEA guys didn't really talk on the phone with anyone. One of Rabassa's men held up the receiver and they all said enough to identify themselves. That was it. They couldn't even be sure anyone was listening on the other end.

That night, though, Nita brought a surprise. A pot of stew, with little chunks of what looked like real meat mixed with vegetables. And for the first time, spoons! The stew smelled good, but Nita moved very slowly. She seemed upset, sadder than ever. Finally she set the bowls and spoons out on the floor and stepped back, and the men snatched them up.

Grayson retreated with her to their corner in the shadows. Those little chunks were meat, all right. Tough meat, with a gamy flavor—a little like possum. "What is this?" he whispered.

"If the capitão *knows I bring this I will be beaten. But you need such meat, especially now. The men of the old way eat this meat."*

"The men of the old way?" He kept chewing. It wasn't bad.

"The ones you call indios," *she said. "The ones who live the old*

way, in the forests. They eat this meat. It makes them strong and brave."

"Jesus!" He spat a chunk of meat out into his palm. His stomach was churning. There were still tribes in the interior who lived as they had for a thousand years. He stared at the half-chewed piece of meat in his hand. Across the hut the DEA guys were wolfing the stuff down. He looked at Nita. "You're not talking about—"

"Do not worry what it is."

"But those natives," he said. "Some of them are cannibals."

"Can'bals?" She stared at him. "What is can'bals?"

"They believe that eating the flesh of their enemies makes them strong and brave."

"Aiee, foder! Are you so stupid? You think—"

"Then why not tell me what it is?"

"Ignorante! Such a fool!" She shook her head. "The indios fish on the river, and at the end of the day they drag their boats onto land. Then the big rats that have entered the boats to eat the fish jump out and run back to the river. This is the way it is, because the river rats must also eat. But on certain days the women catch and cook these rats, and the meat makes the men strong and—"

"Okay, I got it. I suppose it's as good as—"

"Hey, Grayson," one of the men called. "Ask her what this shit is."

"She says it's jungle beef," Grayson said, chewing the piece he'd put back in his mouth. "Says it'll make you strong and brave."

Grayson ate his stew, but Nita didn't go into her usual recital of her family's tragedies. She crouched in silence, her back against the wall. Once she looked up at him as though about to speak. But she didn't.

When he finished he pushed the bowl aside. "What's the matter, Nita?" he asked. "There's something wrong, isn't there?"

"It is Rosa. Minha filha. Rosa . . ." She stopped, and in the dim light he saw her eyes filling with tears.

"I'm sorry," he said, "but you yourself told me, you can't control *what these young people do."*

"But now is much worse. This afternoon they begin a celebration and they . . . they hurt my beautiful child."

He had no doubt who "they" were. "What have they done?"

"I cannot tell of it," she said, then suddenly she tugged on his arm. He leaned toward her and she whispered. "To say it fills me with shame, yet I cannot keep it inside." He waited until she went on. "They hurt minha filha. But first they . . . What is the word? To remove the hair."

"Remove? You mean . . . shave?"

"Aiee, yes. Shave . . . around her private parts. Then they use her. And hurt her, and when the sores rise up they laugh and call them 'love marks.' " Nita was crying now. "She was foolish and thought they would be good to her. Now she hurts so bad—in her flesh and in her heart. She wishes to die." Nita grabbed his spoon and bowl and stood up. "I wish to die, also."

"Wait," he said.

"I must go. Rosa needs me."

But when he pulled her down she didn't resist. "I'm sorry," he said. "I need to know something. I need to know why you said 'especially now.' "

"What?"

"Earlier you said we need this meat 'especially now.' Why is that?"

Her eyes widened. "You do not know this?"

"Know what?" He leaned toward her. "Dammit, woman, tell me."

"If you do not know, then no one must know I tell you." Her eyes flicked toward the DEA guys. "Do you swear to this?"

"On my mother's grave," he said.

"Aiee!" Nita crossed herself as though to ward off the dead. Then she said, "Your people, the American people, are coming."

"What?" He fought to keep his voice down. "We're getting out?"

"Your people are coming soon. Rosa has told me this. This is why they celebrate. But whether the capitão *lets you go I do not know."*

"*They'll pick us up and fly us away. They must have made a deal.*"

"*You should not trust the* capitão *with a 'deal.'* O diabo na pessoa." *She spat on the floor.* "*He says one thing and does another.*"

"*They'll do it in a way he can't cheat,*" *he said.* "*He's not stupid.*"

"*But he drinks very much, and takes the drugs. His mind is rotten. Who knows what he thinks?*"

"*Yeah? Well, he's—*"

"*I must go.*" *She glanced around. Then, in one quick motion, she reached down the front of her dress and came out with a folded piece of cloth and set it on the floor.* "*If the* capitão *does not keep this deal, maybe this helps you.*"

She took the lantern with her when she went.

It was very dark and Grayson had to feel around for the cloth on the floor. He'd just laid his hand on it when one of the DEA guys spoke. "*She seemed upset tonight. What was that all about?*"

"*It's her granddaughter,*" *Grayson said.* "*Apparently the kid's a pretty girl, and Rabassa's . . . you know . . . going after her.*"

"*That's the way it is in these third world countries,*" *the guy said.* "*They fuck anything that moves.*"

There was general agreement on that principle, and the men settled down. In the dark Grayson picked up the gift from Nita. The cloth was damp and warm, as though fresh from the oven. It must have been nestled between her breasts. There was something wrapped inside and he knew, without unfolding the cloth, what it was.

Grayson was certain Nita had been telling the truth about everything, and equally certain that she'd had an agenda, from the moment she came in until she pulled that little bundle from her bosom. She'd brought them the most substantial meal they'd had so far, at the risk of being discovered and beaten. She'd told him in some detail how Rosa had been abused, though it obviously shamed her. And why? Because when the time came for him to act, Nita wanted him strong enough . . . and motivated.

He unfolded the warm cloth and ran his fingers over her gift in the darkness. She'd stolen it from the kitchen. The handle was wood. The blade was metal and no more than four inches long, but he could feel that it was very strong . . . and very sharp.

FORTY-THREE

Maria felt her faith in the government vindicated on Monday morning when Lynn Brasher announced that the DEA was flying Paulo home to the orphanage in Rio. Mr. Lockman would accompany him on a government plane, leaving that evening from a small airport northwest of Chicago called Palwaukee.

"We can't send the boy on a commercial flight because there'd be complications, including his not having a passport," she said. "And our orders are still to maintain strict secrecy."

Paulo had started eating that morning, but only a little, and only if Maria or Charlie or Zorina were with him. If he was awake for very long without one or another of them stopping in to see him, he became agitated. It was because of that, Brasher said, that they wanted Maria to go along when they took him home. Of course Maria was anxious to do that, anyway.

Charlie and Zorina could go, too, if they wanted to. The plane would return to Chicago right away and bring the two of them back, and Maria could either stay down at the orphanage or come back with them.

Of course Charlie was thrilled to go, but not Zorina. "It is enough that you go," she said, speaking directly to Charlie. "You are the one chosen to help Paulo."

Although a little offended by that remark, Maria was very glad Charlie would be coming along. He was excited about it, full of questions for Brasher, such as how far it was to Rio and would it be nonstop.

"From here to Rio it's over five thousand miles," she said, "and we *do* make a stop. In Colombia. We go past Bogotá, and continue on south to a military airstrip north of the border towns of Leticia and Tabatinga, where the tip of Colombia touches Brazil. It's a long-range plane for its size, but that's about thirty-two hundred miles, and we'll have to lay over there to refuel and service it."

Maria had no interest in such details, but Charlie persisted and Brasher told him more about the two border towns, and how she'd seen them when she'd taken a cruise once down the Amazon River from Peru. The cruise—and, in fact, everything Lynn Brasher said—seemed to impress Charlie. He kept pestering her with questions until finally she told him she had lots of other things to do, and turned to go.

"Wait," Maria said, and Brasher turned back. "I need to call Sister Noonie and tell her Paulo is safe."

"I don't think . . ." Brasher started, then seemed to change her mind. "Let me check on that." She went to the far end of the room and spoke into her cell phone.

While they waited Charlie leaned close to Maria. "A cruise on the Amazon from Peru to Brazil?" he whispered. "Damn, she's really something, isn't she?"

"I guess." Maria felt a twinge of jealous anger, which surprised and annoyed her. "Of course, she told me she worked for years for Interpol. I mean, she must be ten years older than you and I."

"That much, you think?" He seemed surprised. "Anyway, she doesn't seem happy about flying Paulo to Brazil."

"She just got tired of all your questions, that's all, and—"

"Okay," Brasher said, coming back to join them. "It's a 'go' on the phone call to the nun. You can tell her he's safe, but you can't mention the DEA, or that we're were bringing him back. Do you have the number?"

"She's probably still in the hospital," Maria said. "Santa Catarina is the name, but I don't know the number."

"That's all right. Special Agent Ferris will get it," Brasher said. "He'll set up the call, and—"

"That bothers the hell out of me," Charlie said.

Brasher stared at him. "*What* bothers you?"

"All this bullshit secrecy. Why not just let Maria go to a phone and make the call?"

Brasher flared up. "It's a government operation, my friend. We don't have to lay everything out for you. If you don't want to cooperate you can forget about—"

"Okay, okay," Charlie said. "But there's one other thing. I need to go out and buy some clothes."

This time Brasher sighed. "I told you yesterday . . . if you leave, you can't come back."

"Jesus, the same underwear Friday, Saturday, Sunday, and now Monday?" He ticked the days off on his fingers. "It's not just for *my* sake, y' know?"

"Okay." She nodded. "Give me your size. I'll send someone."

"It's not only shorts." He stood up and spread his arms out. "I need pants and a shirt, too. And some kind of jacket. I gotta go myself."

"He obviously needs clothes," Maria said. She was surprised he hadn't mentioned it earlier.

"Sorry." Brasher shrugged. "If he leaves, he can't—"

"Perhaps," Zorina said, "if you sent someone with him?"

Brasher seemed to think that was a possibility. "I'll talk to Lockman."

When she was gone Charlie said, "She'll convince him. She's tough, but I like her." Then he turned to Maria. "So . . . if I *do* go shopping, you got any cash you could lend me?"

Maria almost asked if he didn't have a credit card, but instead she pulled her billfold from her purse and handed him two of the fifties her father had given her Saturday morning . . . so long ago.

"Uh . . . you got two more of those?" he asked.

She gave them to him.

"Thanks," he said. "And don't worry. You'll get it back."

They sat around for ten minutes until the agent named Ferris showed up. He'd arrived with Lockman the previous day and was apparently his chief aide. "I'm ready to set up your call to the nun," he said. "But first," turning to Charlie, "there's an agent down the hall who'll take you shopping."

"I told you Brasher'd do it," Charlie said, and hurried out.

Maria stared after him. Brasher's *really something,* she thought, and I'm good for clothes money.

Maria and Zorina went to Zorina's room and plugged in the phone Ferris had given her. When it rang she answered and there was a click, and Sister Noonie came on the line. "Maria?"

"Oh, Sister, I'm so happy to hear your voice. How *are* you?"

"Do not worry about *me,*" Sister said, and Maria's heart sank just to hear the weakness and strain in her voice. "What is the news about Paulo? Did you go to the police?"

"No, we didn't have to. And Paulo is safe. We just don't know yet when—" She recalled Brasher's instructions. "Well, say a prayer for him."

"Of course, Maria. I always—" Sister started coughing so hard that it frightened Maria. When it subsided and Sister finally got her breath back, she said, "I'm sorry. I haven't improved as quickly as . . . as I thought I would." And then the coughing started all over again.

With Sister Noonie sounding so weak, and then coughing like that, Maria burst into tears, just as she'd done the last time they'd spoken. Zorina took the phone and Maria walked to the window and looked out, feeling the tears slide down her cheeks.

"Hello?" she heard Zorina say, and then, "Oh no, it is just that she is so happy to hear your voice that it makes her cry. But I have a question, Sister. It is about Paulo's uncle. I wonder . . . Hello? Sister? Hello? Are you—" Zorina stopped talking, and Maria heard her set the phone down very hard.

Thinking the poor woman must be as upset as she was, Maria turned around, and was shocked at what she saw.

Zorina sat completely motionless, clinging tightly to the arms of her chair with both hands, her knuckles gone white with the effort. Maria was terrified. She went and leaned close to the older woman. "Are you . . . all right?"

But Zorina didn't answer. The muscles in her face seemed drawn and tense. She was struggling to breathe, like she'd been running and couldn't get her breath back. Then, as abruptly as it had come, whatever it was seemed to pass and Zorina began to breathe more easily. "It is only the shortness of breath," she finally said. She managed a smile. "It comes and it goes."

"But you should see a doctor. It could—"

"Sister Noonie," Zorina said, "wants you to know that they tell her she will have a complete recovery."

"I said you should see a doctor," Maria repeated. "It could be serious."

"Everything is serious, Maria. And so nothing is. You must not speak of this incident to Charlie Long. Do you promise?" Maria nodded and Zorina said, "I do not wish him to worry." Then she smiled. "And, my dear, nothing 'serious' will happen to me now. I still have my great responsibility."

Maria didn't dare ask what she meant by that, and instead asked, "Why did you hang up?"

"I did not hang up until the line went quiet. But please, now I must rest."

Maria escorted her to her room and left her there. She was frightened for Zorina, but she would keep her promise not to tell Charlie about the "incident," whatever it was. Then she remembered that she better call her father and keep that promise, too, so he wouldn't think the DEA had kidnapped her, and try to come charging in on a white horse to save her.

She ran into Ferris in the hall and told him about the call to Sister Noonie being cut off. He shrugged and reminded her how unreliable Brazil's phone system was. He said he'd put a call through to her father, but again, she must say nothing over the phone about taking Paulo back to Porto de Deus.

She went back to her room, and when the call came through all she got was her father's voice mail. She left a message that she'd call back the next day. That was fine with her. She hadn't been looking forward to talking to him and hiding the fact that she was leaving in a few hours on a flight to Rio.

She should have been excited and happy. They were taking Paulo home! But it was difficult to feel joy when Sister Noonie—and now Zorina, too—seemed quite ill. And when she had to keep secrets from both Charlie and her father. And when the government she believed in was acting so strangely about what should have been so simple.

FORTY-FOUR

The guy was tall and thin and stiff-backed, with smooth pale skin, short black hair, a gray suit, and a blue tie. "Special Agent Jerome Goodyear," he said. "I'm to drive you to the mall." His tone made it clear that he thought special agents had far more important things to do.

"Cool," Charlie said. "Okay if I call you 'Jerry'?"

"I'm to ensure that you contact no one, and that we return as quickly as possible."

Charlie gave a little salute. "Aye, aye, Agent Goodyear."

The man didn't even blink, and that was it for conversation. All the way to Prairie Oaks.

It was a huge enclosed mall, and just before noon on a Monday there weren't a lot of teenagers roaming around. Not many men, either. Lots of well-dressed women, though, about half of them pushing strollers or dragging little kids around.

He had two hundred eighty-five dollars and change, way more than he needed for clothes. But now that he was here he realized he'd been kidding himself. It wouldn't be easy to make that other purchase he'd thought of. Not with Goodyear sticking as close as he was. They walked along, with Charlie thinking hard, studying all the stores. Then he stopped at a place called *Jeans et al.*

"This'll do it," he said. But he was mostly interested in the store next door.

"Just hurry up," Goodyear said.

"Okay, but finding my size is always a problem, so this could take a *little* while. You could get coffee over there." He pointed to a Starbucks kiosk in the middle of the wide walkway, about twenty yards away. "And you could still see that I don't try to make any calls or anything. Which I won't."

"I'll stay right here by the door."

There were just a few customers browsing around, and four clerks—two male, two female. They all looked younger than he was. The two guys stood at the back of the store, talking to each other. He made a choice, then moved forward with his eyes fixed on the smiling, husky one with lots of thick black hair. It worked, and the other one drifted off to straighten stacks of jeans.

"Need some help, sir?" the husky guy said.

"Yeah, thanks." Charlie had a feeling, for reasons he couldn't have explained, that this guy was a quick study, and also someone he could relate to. "I need a shirt, a pair of pants, and," he pointed, "maybe one of those light jackets over there. Oh . . . and some underwear."

"Okay, sir," the guy said, "let's start with—"

"Jeez, don't call me 'sir.' Makes me feel old," Charlie said. He steered the guy toward some tables loaded with shirts on sale. When they got there Charlie said, "Do me a favor?"

"Sure."

"Don't be obvious when you look." Charlie kept his back to where the DEA agent waited. "But is there a man by the entrance? Tall, skinny, short hair? Dressed like . . . I don't know . . . an accountant?"

The clerk looked around the store casually, and then said, "Yeah. Why? Is there some problem?"

"That's my girlfriend's older brother, is all. He doesn't like me, thinks I'm cheating on his sister. Which of course," Charlie said, and winked, "I would *never* do."

The clerk smiled back at him, like they were co-conspirators already.

"I thought I ditched him." Charlie pawed through a pile of shirts. "I'm meeting someone, and I don't want him seeing who it is. And telling his sister."

"Right. I get it."

"I need to call and tell . . . this person . . . I'll be late."

"Hey, no problem. You can use my cell—"

"Nah, he'll see me and know I'm up to something." He kept sorting through shirts. "Gotta get my own phone and sneak in a call . . . like maybe from the men's room or something." He pulled out his wallet, keeping his back to Goodyear, and took out the four fifties. "See these?" he asked.

"Sure."

"These two . . ." Charlie stuck two of the bills in his own shirt pocket. "They're *yours,* if you can buy me a cell phone from next door without Jerome catching on. That's her brother's name, Jerome. A real prick, too. Know what I mean?"

"Yeah, he looks like it."

With their backs still to the entrance Charlie selected a blue-and-white striped shirt, at the same time giving the guy the other two fifties. "Take these and get the one they're advertising for fifty-nine bucks, and put as much time on it as you can with whatever's left over. Got it?"

"Yeah, but how do I bring it back and get it to you without him seeing?"

"Hey, you'll think of something." Charlie took the shirt and they headed to a rack of nylon jackets on sale. "If you do it, and fast, you get the hundred bucks. If you don't, well I'm fucked, I guess."

Charlie started trying on jackets. The clerk walked away, then turned back to him. "I have to run, sir," he called, "but you let somebody know if you need any help." Charlie didn't look at him, just waved his hand as though to say okay. The clerk called out again, this time to his buddy. "Hey, Andy. I just noticed what time it is. Be back in ten minutes."

Charlie turned and made eye contact with Goodyear, then grinned and held up the shirt he'd chosen so far. Goodyear lifted his wrist and tapped his finger on his watch, and the husky clerk—with a shirt box under his arm now—nodded to him as he went past him out the door.

Charlie looked at every jacket and pair of pants possible, but by fifteen minutes later the husky clerk still wasn't back. Goodyear was obviously anxious to go, and Charlie had to take his choices to the cash register. He left them on the counter and went to Goodyear. "Won't be long," he said. "Just a few more things." He went to the revolving underwear racks.

After studying all the various types and sizes and colors of shorts he made his selection. He waved at Goodyear. Then it was socks. And then, finally, the husky clerk came back and went to the register and Charlie hurried over. The clerk rang up the purchases, took his two fifties, and put Charlie's new clothes in a shopping bag—on top of Charlie's new cell phone.

On the way out, Charlie was able to breathe again.

FORTY-FIVE

Back at the hotel, Charlie had lunch with Maria, Zorina, and—for the first time—Paulo. Maria said he knew he was going home. Charlie watched him and in his own silent way the boy seemed really content. Was he actually *happy* down there? In an orphanage? Happier than he'd be with, say, Charlie?

After lunch the nurse took Paulo, and when they were gone Charlie said, "This stuff about us being free to leave if we want to? I think it's a bunch of crap."

"Are you saying if I tried to leave," Maria said, "they wouldn't let me?"

"Once you got out the door, they'd lock you up somewhere, at least till Paulo gets home. They don't want us talking to anyone. At the mall I couldn't go anywhere without that DEA guy holding my hand."

"Well," Maria said, "as long as Paulo gets back to Porto de Deus, I don't—"

"Which reminds me," Charlie interrupted. "What about the nun?"

"She's still in the hospital with pneumonia. She's not well at all."

"But," Zorina said, "the doctors say she will recover. She told me that." She turned to Charlie. "I started to ask her a question, but the connection was broken."

"Yes," Maria said, "Brazil has a pretty bad phone system."

"Right." Charlie looked at Zorina. "What was your question about?"

"About Paulo's uncle, the uncle who wants to take care of Paulo himself."

"Yeah," Charlie said. "The same guy who didn't care enough about him before to keep him from having to go to some orphanage and—"

"Don't go there, Charlie," Maria said, with an edge to her voice.

"No, I just . . . Don't you think it's strange that now the guy wants to take care of Paulo?" He turned to Zorina. "You started to ask, and got cut off?"

"Yes."

"And this nun," Charlie said, looking at Maria, "she speaks English, right?"

"Of course. She's been in Brazil for, like, forty years, but she's originally from Iowa. Why?"

"Just wondering." Charlie finished off his Pepsi. "Let's all go to *my* room for once, and talk."

Charlie could tell Maria was nervous about it, but she agreed to call Sister Noonie again, this time on his new phone.

"Will that small thing connect you all the way to Brazil?" Zorina asked.

"I don't know why not," he said. Even though they were in his room with the door closed, he noticed how they all sat huddled together—he and Maria on the edge of the bed and Zorina on a chair pulled up close in front—whispering, like school kids getting away with something.

Maria took the phone and went to work to get the hospital number from international directory assistance. Charlie was nervous. He'd been having a hard time not staring at her for two days, and now they were sitting almost thigh to thigh, and her with that same perfume. She stiffened and pulled away the first time they made contact, but then she got busy on the phone and must have forgotten, because her leg fell back against his. He glanced up to see Zorina staring at him. *Jesus, was she reading his thoughts?*

". . . right, Sister, it's me," Maria was saying, and Charlie realized she'd gotten through. "Yes, you sound better," Maria went on. "Not coughing so much." She paused to listen, then said, "Well, remember earlier, when Zorina was asking about Paulo's uncle?" She listened, then looked at Zorina and whispered, "She wants to know what you were asking, and I'm not sure I—"

"Let Charlie talk," Zorina said, surprising him. "He knows what to ask."

Maria nodded. "Sister? I'm going to let you talk to Charlie Long."

He took the phone from her and realized his hand was damp. "Hello?"

"Mr. Long?"

"It's 'Charlie'," he said. "Anyway, what we can't understand is why this uncle's so interested in getting Paulo now, when he could have kept him a long time ago and Paulo wouldn't have had to live in an orphanage. I mean, I'm sure your place is . . . you know . . . a great place for kids, but—"

"I understand," Sister said. "We do our best, but a home and loving parents . . . that's the ideal."

He was shocked to hear her say that. "That's exactly what I think, and—"

"But Paulo's father took a great risk to bring him here. This is the home he wanted for Paulo." The nun coughed a few times, hard, and then went on. "At any rate, you have asked a good question. This uncle . . . his name is Flavio Rabassa . . . and I believe I know why he wants Paulo now."

"Really?" Charlie looked at Maria and Zorina and nodded. "Why?"

"Because of the property."

"The property? I don't—"

"What property?" Maria interrupted. "Ask her what—"

"Please." Zorina patted Maria's knee. "Allow Charlie Long to talk."

". . . in a trust," the nun was saying. "And he—"

"Wait," Charlie said, "I lost track. Start over."

"Did you know Paulo's father bought the land where the orphanage is?"

"Yeah, Maria told us he bought some land and gave it to you."

"It was a great gift, yes. A blessing from God. But Paulo's father was a careful man. He contacted his lawyers and had the property purchased and given to Porto de Deus, but in a trust."

"A trust?"

"By the terms of the trust this is our home as long as Paulo is with us. If Paulo no longer lives here, the trust stops and the property belongs to him. It was a large old estate, needing repairs, but with trees, and space for the children to play. Now, though, it is suddenly worth many times what it cost then. The equivalent of millions of American dollars. Expensive housing is moving this way, and—"

"Hold on." A chill went through Charlie. "What if Paulo . . . you know . . . *died?* He's got no other relatives, so . . . would the property go to his uncle?"

"At this point I am Paulo's legal guardian. According to the trust, if Paulo were to die while I am guardian, the property goes to Porto de Deus."

"Okay. So what good would it do this uncle to get hold of Paulo?"

"If he has Paulo with him it will help him if he goes to court and seeks to transfer guardianship away from me and to himself. I believe this is his plan."

"And if that happened, what then?"

"Then he would control Paulo's property," the nun said. "Also, if Paulo died then, the property would be his."

"Jesus!"

"If he gets hold of Paulo, he could then argue to a judge not only that our neglect caused the kidnapping, but that he was able to save the boy."

"Yeah, but it wasn't your fault. And he didn't save Paulo. We did. So those reasons won't—"

"Charlie Long." This time it was Zorina interrupting. "Ask if there are other things the uncle might use to keep Paulo away from the orphanage."

"Are there any other things this guy could argue," Charlie asked.

"Yes," she said. "He claims Paulo was . . . was sexually abused, even tortured, while here. The boy has scars, which—"

"I've seen them." Charlie felt his stomach churning. "But Maria says he didn't get them there."

"She is right. He did not. But . . . but if . . ."

"But what? Why should it worry you?"

"The man is a captain in the federal police. And if he claims—" She started coughing. Deep hacking coughs that sounded painful.

"Relax," he said. "Take your time." He waited until she got control of the coughing, but even when she did she was panting like she'd just run a mile. "Are you okay?" he asked.

"Yes," she said. "If Flavio points to Paulo's scars as proof, I will explain that the poor boy had them when he came here. I had a doctor document them, but . . ."

"But what?"

"Our lawyer says even a doctor's testimony is open to attack, and Flavio is a police captain, a man of some influence. Still the lawyer is hopeful he may not succeed in getting guardianship transferred to him on the questionable abuse charge alone. But together with his claim of our neglect leading to a kidnapping, and his own diligence in finding the boy and saving him . . ." She didn't finish.

"You really think—" He stopped, because he heard the nun having serious trouble breathing. Then she started coughing again, and this time she couldn't stop.

Maria could obviously tell something was wrong, because she grabbed the phone from him. "Sister Noonie?" she said. "Sister? Are you—" She paused, then said, "Um . . . *sim, sim.*" She looked up at them. "It's a nurse. She says Sister can't talk on the phone just—"

Someone banged on the door, and Charlie snatched the phone back and stuck it under a pillow. "Yeah?" he called.

Goodyear stuck his head in. "Special Agent Brasher wants to see you all. Says it's important."

All Brasher wanted was for Charlie and Maria to sign releases saying they were voluntarily flying down to Brazil and wouldn't hold the government liable for any damages. "Damages like what?" Charlie asked, signing where she wanted him to. "You think the plane might go down?"

"I hope not," she said. "Because I'll be on it, too." She left with the releases.

"Y' know," Charlie said, "I still think she's upset about something."

Maria shook her head. "I didn't notice any—"

"I have seen this also," Zorina said. "As though she has a worry she does not speak of." She touched Charlie's arm. "It is good that you will be at Paulo's side, until he is finally home."

FORTY-SIX

The night air was cool and crisp, and filled with the smell of jet fuel. Seven of them walked across the concrete and up the steps and boarded the plane: Charlie and Maria and Paulo, Lockman and Brasher, plus two soldiers. "Special Forces," Brasher said. Mean-looking black guys who Charlie thought seemed just one step up from street thugs. No one explained why they came along.

It was a small jet, with comfortable seats for twenty or thirty people, and lots of room to move around. Brasher said it was a new design and it had what she called "long-range capabilities." When he asked, she said it cost probably twenty million dollars or something, but she wasn't certain. Charlie knew one thing, though: the feds had gone to a lot of expense to get them all down to Brazil, and in a hurry.

Big expense . . . big hurry . . . and total secrecy. What did that add up to? It didn't help that when he'd gone back to his room to get his things for the flight, he'd discovered that his cell phone wasn't there. He ran out into the hall and saw Brasher. "I don't know what the hell's going on," he said, "but I want my damn phone back."

"Come here." She stepped into his room with him, closed the door, and stood with her back against it. "I told you," she said, surprising him by whispering, "no phones. Special Agent Good-year got suspicious and searched your room."

"Listen," he said. "I don't work for the goddamn government, and I'm—"

"I have the phone and I haven't told Lockman. But go ahead, run down the hall shouting. Raise a stink." She kept on whispering, like she thought someone might be outside the door. "Tell him about your damn phone . . . as long as you don't mind that plane leaving without you."

"You can't—" He stopped, finally realizing that she was trying to *help* him.

"Right," she said. "I can't do a damn thing. Lockman *can*."

"Jesus." Charlie whispered now, too. "What's all the secrecy about? Is it that guy Rabassa? Because he's after Paulo? You need to get the boy home without Rabassa hearing about it, is that it?"

"All I've been told," she had said, "is what I'm telling you. We're taking the boy to Rio. And no one's to know."

Now they were on their way, Charlie sitting across a wide aisle from Maria, with Paulo in the window seat beside him on his right. They took off and nobody did much talking. Eventually the pilot made an announcement about how they'd be flying over Tennessee, and then toward Florida and the Gulf of Mexico. He and Maria looked out, but couldn't see anything but darkness.

Paulo didn't look. He was already asleep, which surprised Charlie because the kid had been jumpy and nervous all day. Once he got on the plane, though, he'd eaten a few bites of a cheese sandwich and was drinking juice out of one of those little cardboard boxes when he fell asleep—more like went into a coma, Charlie thought—with the straw still in his mouth.

Charlie took a piece of hotel notepaper out of his shirt pocket and unfolded it. He'd written down the names of the places Brasher mentioned. The town at the end of Colombia, south of where they'd be stopping to refuel, was Leticia. It butted up against Tabatinga, which was across the border in Brazil and right on the Amazon River. They were isolated places, and not many outsiders had ever been there. "Except people in the drug trade," Brasher had said, "or tourists on an Amazon cruise."

He checked his notes. Brasher had said her cruise started in a town called Iquitos, in Peru. They went down the Amazon for a few days, as far as Leticia and Tabatinga, where passengers could get off and visit a little zoo and buy trinkets and stuff from native people who Brasher said lived a lot like they did a thousand years ago. Charlie figured they wouldn't be living that way much longer, not if tourists kept dropping by on cruises.

Brasher's taking a boat trip on the Amazon impressed the hell out of Charlie. Definitely not a traveler, he was lucky to put together cash for a goddamn monthly bus pass. He'd flown only once before in his life, to Cancun during that first spring break after he'd washed out of college but was still hanging around East Lansing. He'd been pretty drunk most of the time and—

Wham!

Paulo's fist backhanded Charlie smack in the chest, hard. Lucky the kid was strapped in, because he was suddenly awake and out of control. Screaming things Charlie didn't think were words in any language, in a high pitched, angry voice. And it didn't stop. Thrashing around with his arms and his feet. Whipping his head from side to side.

Maria was out of her seat at once, but Charlie got up, too, and blocked her from Paulo because he didn't want her getting hurt. The boy was small, but he was throwing some hard punches and kicks. Brasher came running down the aisle. Lockman was up on his feet, too, but he stayed where he was. The two soldiers started forward, but Brasher told them to keep their distance.

"Don't touch him!" She had to yell to be heard over Paulo's screams. "It's just a nightmare. It'll pass."

261

"Jesus!" Charlie yelled. "His eyes."

He watched as Paulo's eyes rolled way back up under his lids. Like a doll's eyes, Charlie thought—except the lids didn't come down, and the whites stayed showing. And he kept yelling and throwing himself around. Charlie had seen kids get mad and lash out, but he'd never seen anyone so small act this angry and violent. It was like the goddamn *Exorcist*, for chrissake.

And then came the belching and the vomit to go with it. Not green vomit, though. Just cheese sandwich and juice. Slimy and red and sour-smelling.

Then Paulo was screaming again, still thrashing around, and Charlie thought the kid might break a bone by banging on the hard window beside him, or pull a muscle in his back or neck with all that twisting and flailing around. The hell with not touching him, he thought, and he moved over Paulo and held his arms down. The boy kept kicking and Charlie stopped that with his own legs.

Finally, finding he couldn't move, Paulo stopped screaming. His eyes rolled down and he stared at Charlie . . . and Jesus! . . . he spit in Charlie's face and would have bitten him if he could. But by then Brasher was behind his seat with her hands clamped on his forehead, holding his head tight to the seatback. He started moaning like he was in pain.

"Just hold him down," Brasher said. "It'll pass."

So Charlie kept Paulo's body from moving and Brasher kept his head from thrashing around. And it did pass. He gradually eased up until his struggling stopped altogether and his moans died down to silence. His eyes were back to normal again, too. Except now they were filled with terror—like he'd seen some unspeakable horror—and he was shaking visibly.

"I need to hold him," Maria said. "He's afraid."

"Yeah," Charlie said, "but what if—"

"That's a good idea," Brasher cut in. "Take his seat belt off. It's over."

"How the hell do you know?"

"It was just . . . I mean, look at him. He has no more strength. He had a nightmare, and now it's over."

So Maria took Paulo and held him close to her and he calmed down and stopped shaking. Pretty soon he was looking around, wide-eyed, as though wondering how he'd come to be sitting with Maria. She settled him into the seat by the window beside her, and Brasher brought him a plastic cup of water with a straw. She brought some towels, too, to clean up the vomit.

The whole seizure thing—or whatever it was—didn't last five minutes, and Charlie was positive Paulo didn't even remember what happened.

Charlie settled in and must have dozed a little, because he jumped when the pilot came over the intercom, telling them in hushed tones that the Caribbean was down below them. Across the aisle Paulo was asleep beside Maria. She was sleeping, too, with a blanket pulled up to her chin. God, she was cute. He turned around and saw the two soldiers in the back, both of them asleep. Up ahead Lockman and Brasher sat motionless on opposite sides of the aisle.

The pilot came on again with more talk about the Caribbean. Jesus, all this was *real*. Him in a government plane. Flying through the middle of the night to a place he'd never even thought about before. Rio de Janeiro, for God's sake. With a girl too pretty to imagine. And a little boy named Paulo, a boy who needed him.

Earlier that day, when Zorina said again that he was the one chosen to help Paulo, Charlie hadn't objected. He saw now that he was responsible for the boy, had been from the moment he scooped him up and ran from the Russians. And now they were flying him back down to an orphanage in Brazil, where his own uncle claimed he'd been tortured and abused. Charlie wanted to believe that wasn't true. Not just because he was part of taking Paulo back there, but also because he didn't want to believe Maria could be so badly mistaken. But he'd heard about orphanages, dammit, and things in a country like Brazil might be worse, even, than the system kids go through in the United States.

He'd check the place out, though. He was responsible for Paulo. Zorina said "chosen," which he wasn't so sure of. But responsible, yes. And with that came a scary sort of feeling. Not because people around Paulo got shot at—all that was over now—but because what he did now, or didn't do, seemed more important. He'd never had the sense before that anything he did made much of a difference to anyone.

FORTY-SEVEN

Charlie woke up with Brasher telling Maria to tighten Paulo's seat belt because they'd be landing soon. She said it was Tuesday morning, a couple of hours before dawn. A few minutes later they touched down in a landing so smooth Charlie couldn't tell when they hit the ground.

Maria looked wiped out. She stepped aside while he gathered Paulo up in his arms and followed Lockman and Brasher to the exit door. Maria came behind him. One of the two army guys had gone first, before anyone, and the other one came behind Maria. They'd been in fatigues before, but now they were in full battle gear. Helmets and flak jackets, and gear hanging from their belts: things like flashlights and phones . . . and huge pistols. The one in the lead had an automatic rifle.

Charlie, still carrying Paulo, went down the steps from the plane and stepped off onto a paved runway that was still giving off heat in the middle of the night. There was a circle of light right where they stood, but everything dropped off into blackness beyond that. Then, past the darkness, maybe fifty yards out from each side of the runway and much farther away at the ends, was a tall chain-link fence, topped with coiled razor wire.

The fence and a flat open space as wide as a superhighway running along the outside of it were lit up with an orange glow—like the lights in the alleys back home—and ran around the whole area. Beyond that, the way Brasher had explained it, was God knows how many miles of hot, swampy, deadly jungle in every direction.

He didn't see any other airplanes. But there could have been a dozen of the damn things lined up out there in the dark somewhere. The pavement they stood on looked like freshly poured concrete. No skid marks or oil lanes like on a highway once it's been used. This was a new base, Brasher had said, built for the war on Colombian drug traffickers.

The seven of them stayed in a group about ten feet out from the end of the boarding steps. Waiting for someone, he thought. If anyone said anything, he didn't hear it over the noise coming from the jet's engines. He still had Paulo in his arms, with the kid's chin resting on Charlie's shoulder and his skinny legs wrapped tight around him. The poor little guy was shaking again.

Maria stroked the boy's hair and said something to him in Portuguese.

"Yeah, it's okay, kid," Charlie said. "Everything's gonna be okay." He found himself sort of bouncing Paulo up and down, like you see mothers doing with their babies. He caught Brasher watching him, and for an instant he felt embarrassed. But fuck that. He kept bouncing the kid.

All at once the plane's engines died out and there was a new roaring sound, and a couple of Jeeps raced into the circle of light. They skidded to a stop and everyone piled in, with Lockman and Brasher and one soldier in one, and Charlie and Maria and Paulo and the soldier with the fucking M-15 or whatever in the other. Charlie put Paulo on the backseat between him and Maria, and the soldier sat up high behind them. The whole time, no one said anything—except for Maria and Charlie whispering to Paulo.

The Jeep took off so fast Charlie was surprised the soldier didn't fly off the back. He wondered how the driver could see where he was going, with his headlights off and it being so dark.

In the morning a blazing sun came up. They were in a barracks, but they might as well have been in fucking jail, as far as Charlie was concerned. Paulo and he were in the same room with two cots, a small desk, and a couple of metal chairs. Maria had her own room, but Charlie didn't know where it was. There was a uniformed soldier—an armed guard, for chrissake—out in the hall. Like they might run away or something. When they first got there Brasher said it would take some time to refuel and service the plane, and they should get some sleep. Charlie dozed a little, but no way he could actually sleep.

The room was air-conditioned. It had one window, which didn't open. There was a ceiling light, and a lamp on the desk, and also a little TV with a built-in DVD player, but none of the channels got anything and there were no DVDs to watch. Charlie went out in the hall once and the guard told him he had to stay in the room. "I don't know why, sir," he said. "It's just orders." Charlie asked where Maria was and the guard said he didn't even know *who* Maria was, but maybe when they went to the mess hall she'd be there.

"When will that be?" Charlie asked.

"I don't know, sir. I guess when they come and tell you." He was a tall, beefy guy, younger than Charlie. Chubby red cheeks like fresh off some farm in Wisconsin. But tough-looking, too. The helmet and the uniform and the .45 automatic helped in that department.

So Charlie and Paulo sat around with nothing to do, and he tried to get the kid to talk. Which he wouldn't do. Nothing. Maria had said no one found anything wrong with him physically that kept him from talking. He was smart enough, and obviously understood a lot of what was said to him—even in English. She said Sister Noonie took him to a psychologist in Rio, who said he had an emotional block, and if he stayed at Porto de Deus long enough and felt really safe, he might start talking on his own . . . maybe.

Charlie was really hungry by ten o'clock, when Brasher finally came to their room. "What the hell's going on?" he asked. "Where's Maria? When are we gonna get something to eat? When are we—"

"Follow me," she said, like she was pissed off at something—not at him or Paulo, but something. She led the way to the mess hall, which looked like a high school cafeteria, but smaller. "I'll get Maria," she said, and left.

There were only two guys in there, sitting apart at separate tables, eating and reading paperback books. Both wore dark blue pants and shirts that looked like mechanic's uniforms. Both glanced up when they came in, but quickly went back to their meals and their reading.

Charlie was hungry as hell, and decided not to wait for Maria. He took Paulo to the food counter and Paulo pointed at a carton of milk, then an orange, then at the oatmeal in the steam table. Charlie put the stuff on the kid's tray. For himself he had the guy behind the counter make three grilled cheese sandwiches and took a Pepsi and two bags of Fritos. "Jesus," he said, "they fly all this shit in from the States?"

"I don't know," the guy said. "From somewhere, I guess."

"Hey, pretty good guess," Charlie said, but the guy didn't get it.

They took their trays to a table and sat down. Charlie wondered if the two guys reading books thought it was weird how Paulo made the sign of the cross on himself and bowed his head, or how he and the kid started eating and didn't say a word to each other the whole time.

Brasher came back with Maria, and he stood up, and then Paulo did, too. Brasher left again, and Maria ran over and lifted

Paulo up and hugged him and kissed him. She put him down and said something to him in Portuguese. He sat down and picked up his spoon and she pulled Charlie over to the food counter with her.

"What the hell's going on?" he whispered.

"We should have left by now." She was staring at the food, but he could tell she wasn't even seeing it. "We were to stop here just to refuel and service the plane," she said. "Now Lynn Brasher says there'll be a longer delay, and Mr. Lockman's coming to talk to us, and explain things. Something's wrong. I can see it in her eyes . . . and it frightens me."

FORTY-EIGHT

Charlie and Maria sat down. All she'd taken from the food counter was a Diet Sprite and some soda crackers. She spoke to Paulo in Portuguese again and he dug into his oatmeal. Charlie was nervous, but he didn't want Paulo to know, so he finished his second grilled cheese and just then Brasher came in, with Lockman. She stayed by the door and Lockman came their way.

Before he even got there, Charlie was on his feet. "What's going on?"

"I understand why you're worried," Lockman said. "The delay is due to . . . to a situation. One that has to be dealt with before we go on to Rio."

"Bullshit!" Charlie said. "You—"

"I can have you removed from this room, Mr. Long, or you can sit down and listen." Over by the door, Brasher was gone, replaced by the rosy-cheeked soldier with the .45. The two guys who'd been reading books stood beside him.

"Fine," Charlie said, "I'll listen."

Lockman nodded, "I've told you from the start," he said, "that we're dealing here with a matter of national interest. I've been trying to resolve it for some time now, and . . . well . . . conditions have taken an unexpected turn."

"But what does it have to do with us?" Maria asked. "Or with Paulo?"

"You may know," Lockman said, "that the boy's only living

270

relative is an uncle, Flavio Rabassa."

At the mention of the name, Paulo gasped and Charlie turned to him. His eyes were wide and he started to tremble, and Charlie thought he might throw up. Maria slid her chair close to his and whispered in his ear.

"Paulo doesn't seem to like his uncle," Charlie said.

"The boy's attitude toward his uncle is not at all relevant."

"The hell it's not. If you're gonna—" Charlie stopped when Lockman turned toward the men at the door. "Okay, okay," Charlie said. "Go ahead."

Lockman turned back. "Rabassa is a captain in the Brazilian federal police, assigned to border patrol. He's also a man of . . . well . . . questionable repute. But most importantly, right now he's holding four Americans hostage in a remote part of the Amazon jungle. He threatens to kill them if we make the situation public. For their own safety, the United States can't go in on an armed mission to extricate them. But the United States also doesn't intend to leave them in this man's hands. Whatever *any* of you, including the boy, thinks about Rabassa, or me—or your government, for that matter—is irrelevant. Do you understand?"

"I . . . I guess so," Maria said. She had her arms wrapped around Paulo.

Charlie just sat there.

"I'm the one negotiating with Rabassa," Lockman said. "We've been at it for days, and I need not go into the nature of his original demands. Suffice it to say that he's finally convinced that it's the policy of the US government not to pay ransom money. So he's reduced his demand to two remaining conditions. One, a promise that we won't reveal his crime or take any punitive action against him. I gave him that assurance, even though I—"

"Okay," Charlie said. "So what's the other thing?"

"From the start the man has expressed a great concern for

his nephew, whom he knows to have been kidnapped. One of his original demands was that the US government retrieve the boy safely from the kidnappers. As you know, we've done that, and—"

"It was done," Charlie said, "but not by you."

"I have the boy," Lockman went on, "and I've so informed Rabassa. When I did, however, he modified his demand as to the boy. And I've agreed."

"No!" Maria said. "You can't give Paulo to him."

"Of course not." Lockman shook his head, as though amazed she'd said such a thing. "His demand is to *see* the boy. Face to face. He wants to see for himself that his nephew is safe in our custody and unharmed. I intend to do that. I intend to fly the boy to Rabassa's compound, which is not far over the border, inside Brazil. I'll show him, pick up the hostages, and leave."

"But why can't you show Paulo to him by . . . I don't know . . . closed circuit TV?" Maria asked. "Or by teleconferencing or something?"

"The man doesn't trust us not to manipulate the technology," Lockman said. "And frankly, I don't trust him to deliver my men. It will be done all at once. In and out. When that's over, we'll all continue with Paulo on to Rio."

"But we already know that what this guy really wants is custody of Paulo," Charlie said. "You'll be on his turf, and who's to say you don't fly in and he grabs Paulo? Shoots down your plane, whatever?"

"Helicopter, actually. And we'll have backup. He may be . . . unbalanced . . . but he won't do that. It would be suicide. The boy will be safe. I personally will be on the helicopter with him, and I'll see to that."

"Christ." Charlie looked at Paulo. Maria still had an arm around him and he looked scared, although he probably hadn't understood much of what was said. "So let's say the guy finds out he can't grab Paulo. What if he doesn't give up the hostages?

I mean, he's obviously a wacko, so . . ."

"That won't happen. But if it did, the army would send in a Special Forces unit. They'd take out Rabassa, for sure. But I have no confidence the hostages would survive."

"I don't know," Charlie said. "It seems . . ." He stopped and looked at Maria. "What do you think?"

"Well," she said, "I guess if it means saving four lives, and if Paulo stays right with Mr. Lockman, maybe we should—"

"You misunderstand." Lockman stood up. "I'm not asking for anyone's permission."

When Lockman was gone Brasher came back. "I don't know yet just when the helicopter is leaving," she said. "This afternoon, though."

Charlie told her he wanted to talk to her alone and the two of them went out in the hall. "I'm going along," he said, "in the helicopter."

She stared at him. "Not a chance."

"The kid's scared to death. He'll freak out. And no more of that shit you gave him before we left Chicago. You saw what it did. His heart pounding like a fucking jackhammer."

"What 'shit' are you talking about?" She was trying to act mystified, but he could tell he'd gotten it right, and that Paulo's episode on the plane was a reaction to something they gave him to keep him calm. ". . . and anyway," she was saying, "Lockman won't—"

"Fuck Lockman. Tell him if I don't go, Paulo doesn't go. Or he's gonna have to fucking lock me up, or blow my brains out."

"Don't be—" She stopped, though, and he could tell she was thinking something through. "All right," she said, "I'll see what I can do."

Back inside the mess hall Maria told Brasher she had to call her father or he'd be calling government agencies to find out what happened to her. Brasher told Maria to come with her and she'd set up the call. She told the soldier to take Charlie and Paulo back to their room.

On the way out, Charlie stopped to study a couple of dozen DVDs lined up on a shelf by the door. Action flicks, war flicks, and music videos—mostly country and western. Nothing for a kid.

"You can take two at a time," the counter guy called. "You gotta sign for 'em, but no rental fee, y' know?"

Charlie turned. "Yeah, well, I don't see any . . . like . . . *Winnie the Pooh*, or anything, right?"

"Uh-uh. Christ, we never . . ." He stopped. "Say, man, there's a checkers game. On that table over there." He pointed.

Charlie got the box back and showed it to Paulo. "You know how to play checkers?" When Paulo seemed to understand, and nodded, Charlie asked, "Think you can whip my butt?"

The kid looked at him, like trying to figure out what he'd said, then nodded again.

"Okay, big guy," Charlie said. "Let's go see if you're as good as you say."

FORTY-NINE

Paulo turned out to be pretty good at checkers, so Charlie didn't have to work all that hard to let him win a few games. It was fun, teaching the kid how to do two-handed high-fives. Paulo even clapped his hands when he won a game.

They were interrupted once by soldier Rosy Cheeks. "Special Agent Brasher said to give you a message, sir. She said your request has been granted." He spun and left the room before Charlie could say anything.

They played a few more games, and then Charlie decided he had to level with Paulo. Brasher might be along any minute, and he didn't think the boy understood what was coming. He put the checkers back in their box and sat Paulo on one chair and himself on the other. "Okay, kid," he said, "let's talk."

Paulo stared at him. Maybe he didn't know the words, but he sure as hell knew something was up.

"I mean, you got a right to know what's going on, okay?" He paused, but knew the kid wouldn't answer. "Pretty soon you and me," pointing to indicate first the boy, then himself, "we're gonna get back on the plane, and we're gonna fly into Brazil." He pronounced it *Bra-seal*, like he did that day in the park when the cops drove up. "Porto de Deus," Charlie said.

He was sure the boy knew what that meant, from the way he nodded his head.

"But first," Charlie said, "we have to stop off to see your uncle." He paused. "Flavio Rabassa."

That set Paulo off. His eyes went wide and his shoulders jerked, and he swung his head around, like looking for somewhere to run away to. But there was nowhere to go. His body went into that shaking routine, like he might fall apart. It scared Charlie and—hell, he didn't know what else to do—he stood and picked Paulo up and hugged him and swiveled around, back and forth.

"It's gonna be okay," he said. "I'll stay right with you. Me, Charlie Long. You can trust me, goddamn it. I'll stay right with you."

He set Paulo down and, holding his palms out like the kid should stay there, he backed away and went around to the other side of his own cot. First he pointed at the boy and said, "Paulo. To *Bra-seal*. To the orphanage, Porto de Deus." Then he pointed his two thumbs backward toward his own chest and said, "Charlie. To *Bra-seal*. To the orphanage, Porto de Deus."

He spread his arms out like an airplane and circled around his cot and then back across the room until he was right over Paulo. He lifted him and swooped him up over his head and "flew" him—like he'd flown him to make the cops think they were father and son. He flew Paulo across the room to behind the boy's cot. He flew him to Bra-seal and Porto de Deus.

He set the kid standing up on his cot, and held him out in front of him by the shoulders. "Okay?" he said. "You got that?"

Paulo stared at him with those huge eyes of his. He still looked scared, but he wasn't shaking any more, and he wasn't crying. He was nodding his head up and down very slowly.

Charlie nodded, too. "And you know what? If you don't like it in that damn orphanage, I'll take you home with me. To America. I'll take care of you, for the rest of your fuck—your whole life, I mean. Me and you, kid. We'll—"

"Excuse me." Brasher had come in without even knocking, and Charlie was glad his face was turned away from the door because she might have seen he had tears in his eyes, for God's sake.

He lifted Paulo up off the cot and set him standing on the floor, then turned to Brasher. "He's . . . afraid, y' know?"

"I know." She had a small duffel bag with her. "I brought you some clothes suitable for the jungle," she said. "Couldn't find anything to fit Paulo."

"What, the clothes are in case the helicopter crashes?"

"That's not gonna happen. But . . . better safe than sorry." She tossed the bag on one of the cots. "Oh, and I brought those videos you asked for."

"I didn't—"

"That's about it," she said. "So . . . see you later."

That's what she said, but she didn't go out. Instead, she held a finger to her lips to keep him quiet, and pulled the door closed with a bang. Then she went across to the little TV and turned it on.

"Hey," he said, "that thing—"

She waved him quiet and slipped a disk in the slot, and finally a music video started up, with some country and western singer in the middle of a song. Charlie had no idea who it was, but the guy had a loud band behind him, and Brasher set the volume up pretty high. Then she came back and sat on a chair on the other side of the cot near the door, as far from the TV as possible in that small room.

Charlie took Paulo and sat with him on the cot, facing her. He leaned toward her and whispered, "Is this place bugged?"

She nodded. "The lamp," she whispered back. "And back in the hotel? All the rooms. Lockman had it done. I only found out when we were leaving."

"Jesus, what—"

"Please." She held up her hand to quiet him. "I've been thinking and . . . and what I have to say is just between you and me. Agreed?"

"Okay, I guess."

" 'I guess' won't do it. My whole goddamn future's on the line here. So it's either 'yes,' or 'no.' "

"Okay. I mean . . . yes. Jesus, yes. Between you and me."

"Those hostages," she said, still whispering, "four Americans held for . . . I don't know . . . a week anyway. Have you seen anything in the media?" He shook his head and she went on. "Why not? Why no round-the-clock TV coverage?"

"How the hell do I—"

"My job was to find the boy. Otherwise I've been kept out of the loop. But there are hostages. I was able to verify that. Three DEA agents and a Special Forces officer. Other army personnel got away."

"Yeah, but what's that—"

"I think whatever that crew was doing—probably a drug raid—crossing over into Brazil was illegal. There've been some recent agreements signed, specifically forbidding that. So it could be a major embarrassment for the US. Which would be bad news for a president in a tight race for reelection, and that makes it a huge problem for Lockman. He's in charge of DEA operations in this sector, and it was his decision that put those men there."

"So," Charlie said, matching her whisper, "he feels responsible, and—"

"I'm not talking about *feeling* anything. I think he made a hasty decision he had no authority to make. Now he either gets them out, and quietly, or his career is over. And he may have more to lose than that. These are tough days—scary days—around Washington. CIA agents get outed. Mistakes turn into something worse. People get accused of things . . . indicted . . . whatever."

"Are you saying . . . ? What are you saying? Is Lockman—"

"Just listen. Before I came to the DEA I was with Interpol, a child trafficking unit. So I get this special assignment—to find a boy kidnapped in Rio—and it's not surprising, because the Russians who snatched him were part of a group I'm familiar with. They move around a lot, and right now they're headquartered in Chicago. So it made some sense that they'd take him there." She paused. "But for the sex trade? That didn't fit."

"For what, then?"

"I figured it was something to do with drugs. So I find the boy. But then . . . flying him back to Rio? All of us? That seemed weird. That's when Lockman says there's this guy holding hostages who said he'd let them go if we saved his nephew, got him home safe. Strange demand, but possible. And the hostages are real. Now he says the guy suddenly demands to see the boy, in person, to know he's safe. That . . . well . . . again, it could be true, and there are four lives at stake. But . . ." She didn't finish.

"What?" But then Charlie realized she was waiting for a new song to start on the video. He found himself rubbing the top of Paulo's head, while the boy just sat there, not moving.

"But then *you* insist on going along," she said when the music got loud again, "and first I think 'no,' but now I'm thinking it might be a good idea."

"Yeah, well, Lockman knows the kid'll freak out if one of us doesn't go. Unless you dope him up and almost kill him again, which I won't—"

"That won't happen. The ketamine was . . . lost. I'm already in deep shit about that." She shrugged. "Anyway, you're going. And in a deal like this you always have to assume something will go wrong. If it doesn't, fine."

"And if it does?"

"If it does, then whatever happens," she nodded at Charlie,

"you need to be smart."

"What," Charlie said, "you think I'm not—"

"Hey, if I didn't think you were smart, and could be trusted, would I be talking to you? I'm just saying you have to be on your toes out there, not do anything that might keep you from getting back. Understand?"

"No," he said. "What the hell might—"

Her cell phone rang. She answered it and as she listened she mouthed, "Gotta go." She stood up and left the room . . . and closed the door without a sound.

Charlie waited a few seconds and then went over to the TV and turned it off. "See, Paulo," he said, probably louder than he needed to, "I knew you wouldn't like that country and western shit . . . no matter how long you wait for it to get better."

FIFTY

It was late afternoon when Charlie and Paulo and Brasher got into a Jeep to ride out to the helicopter. A soldier rode beside the driver. Maria wasn't there and Brasher said she was still trying to get through to her father.

"The chopper you'll be taking," Brasher said, "is called a 'Little Bird.' The army uses it a lot as a companion to the Blackhawk—that's the chopper everyone's heard of—which is way bigger and can carry ten or twelve soldiers with full combat gear."

When they arrived Lockman was already there, along with a pilot and a copilot—who turned out to be the two black soldiers who flew down on the plane with them. Charlie realized why they called it a *Little* Bird. He, Paulo, and Lockman would fit inside the thing only because Paulo was so small.

"Coming back with the four hostages," Brasher said, "you obviously won't all fit inside. But the Little Bird carries six men externally."

Charlie thought he misunderstood her, until she pointed out what she called two "benches," really just fat pipes, each long enough to seat three men, one on each side of the chopper. "Jesus," he said. "we ride outside? How fast does this thing go?"

"You'll be outside only on the way back. I did it once, just to see what it was like. It was fun, but . . . that was a short ride. Anyway, they list this thing at one-seventy-five an hour, but I don't know if they run that fast fully loaded, with external passengers." She reached inside the aircraft and brought out a sort of sling, or a harness, made of belts—like seat belts—and rope. "You use one of these," she said. "It's a rappel seat."

"Rappel seat?" Charlie asked.

"Like rock climbers use when they rappel down a cliff."

"Looks like a sling for a window washer on a high-rise building."

"Probably the same," she said. "Anyway, you step into it and tighten the straps. Then you sit on the bench and take this," she showed him a longer strap extending from the rappel seat, "and attach this clip on the end to that D-ring on the chopper." She demonstrated attaching the clip. "You hold onto the safety strap to keep your balance, but even if you slip off the bench you can't really fall."

"Right, real safe," he said. "And you're sure this thing can carry all the weight it'll have?"

"That's what they're built for. With four more men coming back you'll just about top out your weight allowance, but you won't go over."

When Brasher was gone Charlie stood there with Paulo, waiting while Lockman and one of the pilots talked quietly together. Charlie suddenly remembered Sal telling him once that one of Sal's uncles on his mother's side was a helicopter pilot in 'Nam. "The guy never came back, not even his body," Sal had said. "Anyone flies one of those things in a war must be crazy. If they don't get shot down, they fall down. Maybe their first time out. Maybe their twenty-first. Just a matter of time."

This wasn't exactly a war, but Charlie didn't like it already. Then the engine started up, and the blades were whirling around and whipping up the wind. And that *whop, whop, whop,* pounding over and over, was so loud it felt like it came from inside his own head—making an announcement. *Stop! Stop!*

Stop! it said. *Dumb! Fucking! Mistake!*

It looked like they were the only ones taking off and Charlie, yelling to be heard, asked about the backup Lockman said there'd be. "They're already deployed," Lockman yelled back. "They'll be there."

One of the pilots handed out earplugs and helmets. Charlie helped Paulo with his earplugs, but the helmet was way too big for him and he wouldn't wear it. When Charlie saw that Lockman, besides his helmet, had a headset with a microphone, he yelled, "Where's my headset?"

The pilot looked at him and shook his head.

"Then we don't fucking go!" Charlie said, and took Paulo's hand. "I wanna hear what's going on."

Lockman and the pilot talked and the pilot brought out another headset and Charlie put it on, and then his helmet. Then Charlie and Lockman each stepped into a rappel seat. Paulo was too small for one of those, too, so Charlie just hoisted him up and inside—and then climbed in himself. He and Lockman sat on metal fold-down seats and attached their safety straps to rings that hung down from the ceiling—the kind of "D-ring" Brasher had shown him they'd use sitting on the outside benches. Their use inside was a good idea, too, because the Little Bird had wide openings on both sides where there should have been doors.

Charlie held Paulo on his lap, the two of them facing the direction they'd be flying. Lockman would ride backward, facing Charlie and Paulo but closer to the pilot and copilot behind him. Charlie had to pretend it was all a piece of cake, so Paulo wouldn't be even more scared than he already was.

When the pilot and copilot climbed on board they cracked some quiet joke between themselves and then laughed so hard Charlie thought they must be nervous about something. Getting ready to take off, though, they sure seemed to know what they were doing, reaching around to push buttons and flick switches, hardly having to look at them.

In a sense, Charlie thought, you could understand a regular airplane. Thing gets a big head start on a runway and then sort of glides up into the air . . . and the wings hold it up there. But this damn thing just sat on the ground, getting louder and louder, shaking and shuddering more and more, and then lurched pretty much straight up.

They'd been underway about ten minutes when the pilot's voice came over the earphones. It wasn't easy to hear over the roar of the wind and the engine. "Thirty minutes to the border, then about fifteen minutes farther. And that storm's movin' in from the south. A little ahead of schedule." Charlie saw the pilot point when he said that. "But with luck we'll be in and out before it's a problem. We'll hug the treetops all the way, stayin' under the radar."

"Jesus!" Charlie yelled. "He think someone's gonna try to shoot us down?"

"Not a chance." Like Charlie, Lockman shouted into his mike. "But we'll be inside Brazil. If they picked us up on radar they'd want to know who we are, what we're doing. We could be drug couriers, arms runners, whatever."

Charlie stared out at a thin line of black clouds on the horizon, wondering how much luck they'd need to beat the storm. Then he leaned toward Lockman again. "How come you're coming with?" he yelled. "You're, like, pretty high up, aren't you? You could send someone else to do shit like this."

"Those hostages are my men," Lockman shouted back. "And I'm bringing them home myself."

That sounded heroic enough, but Charlie noticed he didn't mention what Brasher had said, that he had fucked up somehow, and that if he didn't get those men back his career was down the toilet . . . and he might even end up in jail.

FIFTY-ONE

Charlie held on to Paulo and watched the ground below them sweep by. If they'd had a different reason for being there, he thought, the ride might have been exciting. Roaring along in the slanting sunlight, a couple of hundred yards above what looked like a carpet made out of fifty different shades of green. Out the two open sides he could see half a dozen brown rivers, twisting and circling through the trees—or maybe just one river, winding around like a road built by a drunk who got lost.

Then he got a glimpse of a real road, too, because the pilot came over the earphones again. "Off to the right," he said. "Three o'clock. Tabatinga Turnpike." But the narrow road was out of sight before Charlie could tell if there were any cars or people on it. After that there were just more trees, and—

"Mr. Long!" Charlie jumped and looked across at Lockman. "I'm glad I brought you along," the guy said. Like it had been his idea. "It's our first chance to talk, away from Ms. McGrady and . . . that other woman."

"Yeah? Talk about what?"

"About the boy."

"He's got a name, you know?" Charlie said. "Paulo. And 'that other woman' has a name, too. Zorina."

"Yes. Well, about the boy. As you know, he's been living in that orphanage . . . in Rio de Janeiro."

"Right. And we're taking him back there," Charlie said. "So . . . what's your point?"

"No point. It's just . . . he's obviously been traumatized. Sexually abused, and in terrible ways. You've seen his scars?" When Charlie nodded, Lockman went on. "I've never had much faith in orphanages. They're—"

"It didn't happen there. Maria's sure of that. She said so."

"Well, she would, wouldn't she? And I'm sure she believes that. But, you know, priests and nuns aren't the holy people we thought they were. Right?"

"Some of them, yeah. But—"

"Just read the newspapers. Priests . . . and altar boys. Nuns . . . and kids in their care twenty-four hours a day. Why, you yourself must have wondered if an orphanage is the best place to raise a child."

"I've thought about it." If the hotel was bugged like Brasher said, Lockman might have heard him say that to Maria.

"An orphanage . . . it's hardly the ideal environment for raising a child."

"Yeah, well, how many kids get 'ideal'? Paulo's got no relatives, and—"

"Not true," Lockman said. "He's got his uncle. I mean, the man's holding hostages, and that's a criminal act, but he's obviously deeply concerned about his nephew."

"He's a fucking cop gone wrong." Charlie studied the black clouds looming in the south. "By now your people have checked him out."

"He's a man with . . . a bothersome reputation," Lockman said. "But the boy's father was a criminal himself. Also, the boy lived with the uncle for a time, before he was taken to the orphanage."

"I heard that," Charlie said. "When his old man was in jail."

"And his uncle says the boy had no scars, showed no sign of sexual abuse, or any abuse at all, not when he left his custody. So it had to have happened in the orphanage."

"It might have," Charlie admitted. He wondered where Lockman was going with this. "But hell, it might have been his uncle, too. Family members do terrible things like that."

"So do priests and nuns. And if Rabassa did it, why would he make my saving the boy from kidnappers a condition for the release of my men? And now that I've done it, why—"

"First, you didn't save Paulo. I did. I mean . . . Maria and Zorina and I. Second, even if Paulo's abuse *might* have happened at the orphanage, it *might* have been his uncle, too. Hell, it could have been his *father*, for chrissake. We don't know."

"That's true. We don't know," Lockman said. "And that's my point. Who's to decide what's best for—"

A roar rose from the engine and the Little Bird shuddered, then suddenly lurched into an upward arc, leaving Charlie's stomach behind. He knew they were out of control and they'd stop going up any second, and then drop like a rock into the jungle. He hoped he'd be dead by the time the snakes got to him.

But they stopped climbing and didn't fall, and the pilot's voice came over the headset. "That's it," he said. "Nine o'clock."

The three of them leaned and looked, and Charlie spotted a clearing cut out of the jungle. The helicopter didn't draw any closer, just made a wide circle at a distance of—he couldn't tell—maybe a mile or a little less. The cleared area was the shape of a football field. Maybe not much bigger than that, either, but again Charlie couldn't tell. Close to one end were a long narrow building and a big square one with a flag flying in front, and off by itself at the other end was what looked like a house. They all had red roofs. Then there were some metal buildings, storage sheds or garages maybe, scattered around.

"The police compound," Lockman shouted. It didn't look like anywhere Charlie'd like to live.

He figured the big square building for the headquarters, and the long narrow one for a barracks. The one by itself at the other end had a lawn of green grass around it. That was maybe where Paulo's uncle lived, since he was in charge. The circle they were flying in brought them closer to that end, with the low afternoon sun behind them, and they dropped closer to the ground. He could see now that the clearing was way bigger than a football field, but he still couldn't tell how big. And there were trucks and jeeps; some standing still, some moving.

"Where's the fucking backup?" Charlie yelled.

"Don't worry," Lockman yelled back. "They're available. Out of sight unless they're needed."

Charlie was getting a bad feeling. Out of sight where, for chrissake? He saw Lockman staring across at Paulo, and he suddenly realized the boy was shaking, and squeezed him tighter. Paulo's head was down, like he was studying his own tiny fists, clenched tight and resting on top of his knees. He sure wasn't seeing anything outside the chopper.

"It's okay, kid." Charlie leaned close to Paulo's ear. "Relax. It's only—"

"Bingo!" the pilot yelled. "Eleven o'clock. Destination Nineteenth Hole."

Charlie didn't know what the man was talking about, but he looked out. Just past the end of the large clearing where the house was, there was a smaller area hacked out of the jungle, more of a circle.

Lockman twisted around and leaned close to the pilot, and pointed out the right side of the helicopter. Charlie looked that way, too. Those heavy black clouds were coming up pretty fast. Then there was a sudden change in the sound of the engine again, and they started forward and down. The smaller, circular clearing grew larger and larger as they approached. There were people down there. He clenched his teeth and held his body as stiff as he could, because he didn't want to start shaking as hard as Paulo was.

It suddenly struck him. If this helicopter trip was a change of plans, why had the pilot and copilot been along on the plane ride from Chicago?

FIFTY-TWO

The Little Bird tilted to one side and moved down toward the clearing, where three men in dirty khaki uniforms sat on chairs lined up in a row. With their bearded faces turned up and their mouths open, they were obviously happy to see the chopper. But they didn't wave or stand up, and Charlie finally saw that they were tied to their chairs with their hands behind their backs. There were two other chairs, too. Both were empty, one at each end of the row.

Four hostages. One chair too many.

Across the tiny cabin, Lockman had unhitched his safety strap and was on his feet, leaning close to the pilot, with his back to Charlie and Paulo. He was talking but he'd removed his helmet and headset, and Charlie couldn't hear what he said. The pilot heard, though, because the chopper stopped moving closer. It just hovered in the air, then turned a little, giving the copilot a clear view from his side. He held an automatic rifle, pointed down at the clearing.

They hung there in midair, maybe fifty feet up. Charlie could see the stumps where trees had been cut down to make the clearing, and the ragged grass and brush that remained, blowing in the chopper's down draft. The tops of the tall trees around the clearing were bending and waving, too, but blown by a different wind. He looked to the south and saw the black clouds racing their way, filling almost half the sky.

"Hey," he said into his mike. But he got no response, so he

leaned across toward Lockman. "Hey!" he yelled.

"What is it?" Lockman yelled back over his shoulder.

"That storm, for chrissake. It's like a goddamn hurricane! We gotta get outta here. Now!"

Lockman turned to face him. "When we see the fourth hostage," he shouted, "we land. We show the boy. We pick up my men. Then we get out. And not before."

"Are you fucking crazy? We'll be blown out of the air."

"No way. These guys fly in this stuff all the—"

"That storm!" the pilot yelled over the earphones. "It's worse than you'd expect this time of year. We got maybe ten, fifteen minutes. Then we gotta run like—"

"There!" Lockman yelled. "Let's go!"

Charlie looked where Lockman was pointing. The fourth hostage, a black man, was limping across the clearing between two men in blue uniforms and blue caps. One of them tied him to a chair, while the other stood looking up at them, holding what Charlie thought must be an AK-47.

The chopper had barely touched down when the pilot jumped out onto the ground. By then Paulo was standing beside Charlie, who had his arm around the boy's shoulders. The noise from the rotor blades and the engine was deafening, and Charlie could barely think.

Lockman was facing them and suddenly grabbed Paulo away from Charlie. The boy started screaming—not words, just long, howling screams, but before Charlie could get his safety strap unhitched, Lockman turned with Paulo and threw him right out the open side of the chopper. The pilot was waiting and caught him in his arms.

The fifth chair was for Paulo.

The boy never stopped screaming. He fought hard, too. Punching, slapping, kicking, biting at the pilot's gloved hands.

But it was no use. The man heaved him up with ease and carried him over his shoulder. Paulo's outstretched arms reached back toward Charlie over the pilot's shoulder, his mouth open, his eyes wide with terror.

Charlie got himself unhitched and jumped down to the ground to go after them, but heard Lockman jump down behind him. He spun around and Lockman stood just three feet away, the pistol in his hand pointed down at the ground beside his leg.

"You gonna interfere with the US government?" Lockman yelled.

"You lied," Charlie said. "Your plan all along was to hand him over."

Lockman lifted the gun waist high, pointed at Charlie, and reached with his free hand and snatched Charlie's headset off. "My plan all along was to do whatever it takes to get my people back. And remember, the man is the boy's uncle." He stepped back and tossed the headset into the chopper behind him.

"So what's the gun for?" Charlie asked. "To shoot me, for chrissake?"

"I will . . . if that's what it takes."

"In front of the pilot and copilot? The four hostages? You won't."

"You're the hero." Lockman shrugged. "You decide."

Charlie didn't move. In all this noise and confusion what would the others see? Only that he tried to keep Lockman from saving the hostages, tried to keep a little boy from being reunited with his uncle.

"If I hadn't come along you'd have made up some bullshit story of how things went wrong out here . . . and Rabassa managed to grab Paulo."

"Like I say, whatever it takes. But you *are* along, and guess what? Turns out you're too damn scared to lift a finger. What's the kid think now?" Lockman had a weird smile on his face.

"Where's the big brother who promised he'd stay by his side?"

Charlie was stunned. "Jesus," he said, and shook his head. "What you want is an excuse. You'd love to keep me from getting back and telling what happened."

"Like I said, hero, it's up to you."

Charlie recalled Brasher's advice. Had she guessed something like this? Or had she known? Whatever, there was nothing he could do. Nothing he *should* do. Not now. When he got home he'd raise enough shit to make the government get Paulo back. And if they didn't, Charlie would come back himself and get him. So he would not die now.

Paulo was still screaming as Charlie backed away and lifted his rear up onto the bench. The terrible threatening chug of the engine and the roar of the wind never let up, either, and now he felt rain hit his face. Their time was running out. He was still wearing the safety harness—or the rappel seat or whatever—and he felt around, trying to untangle the safety strap. He fumbled with the damn thing. It would have been easy if there'd been no guns, no storm, no little boy letting out long, high howls . . . cries of fear beyond words.

Charlie finally got the strap clipped to the external D-ring. "You don't get rid of me that easy," he yelled. "And you won't keep me quiet."

Lockman stepped closer to him. "Right," he said. "You'll have great credibility. A guy who drank himself out of college? Lost his city job for insubordination and dishonesty?"

"What the hell? Have you been—"

"A guy with ties to low-grade Outfit mopes? Oh . . . and a guy who left his prints on a gun used to murder a former FBI agent in an alley? Lotsa luck, Charlie." He smiled and turned away.

Speechless, Charlie looked around. Paulo was already tied to the fifth chair. But he was quiet now, staring right at Charlie and looking hopeless . . . abandoned. I'll be back! Charlie wanted to yell. But he'd already made too many promises.

FIFTY-THREE

The clearing was a circle fifty to a hundred yards across, and four more guards in blue uniforms had shown up—two from the trees off to the right and two from the left. Thuggish-looking, like Chicago gang-bangers. Latin Kings or something. The copilot was still in his seat in the Little Bird, his weapon lowered now, out of sight. And the pilot was back, yelling something to Lockman about the storm, when suddenly a Jeep burst out from an opening in the trees at the far end of the circle and bounced over the uneven ground toward them. Two passengers sat in the back. One was a large man in a blue poncho and a cowboy hat held in place by a cord tied under his chin. The man beside him struggled to hold an umbrella over the big man's head. Even with the wind whipping up like it was, the rain wasn't that strong yet, so maybe the big man—who had to be Flavio Rabassa—had a thing about protecting his hat.

The Jeep bounced over the rough ground and stopped near Paulo, who appeared to be howling again. Rabassa called out to him. Charlie couldn't hear much over the wind and the *whop* . . . *whop* . . . *whop* of the Little Bird, and it was probably Portuguese, anyway. Whatever the guy said, though, the only answer he got was that Paulo closed his mouth and dropped his head till his chin hung down to his chest. After that, he might have been dead.

Rabassa turned away from Paulo and, as his driver pulled the Jeep closer to the Little Bird, the chopper's engine was cut way back and the noise dropped. Charlie suddenly noticed how hot it was. Ninety degrees, easy.

"You are the man Lockman?" The big man had a harsh, loud voice.

"Yes. And you're Flavio Rabassa."

"You must come here." Rabassa stretched out a bare arm from under his poncho. Not just big, he was fat. And despite the wide-brimmed hat and umbrella his brown face was shiny wet. "You must show me your ID."

"You're crazy. You've got the boy. Cut loose my men."

"But you have come into my country illegally. Just as these men did." Rabassa waved toward the hostages. "You must produce your identification when asked by police authorities. You—"

"Hey, motherfucker!" The booming voice was the copilot's. "Look at me!" Everyone did. He had his weapon trained on Rabassa. "If you don't wanna deal, then let's all dic . . . starting with you."

Rabassa broke into a grin, then shook with laughter like he couldn't care less who died. "I make the joke, my friend, about the illegal entry. But now," and he was serious again, "our agreement was that the man Lockman makes the delivery in person. Mr. Big Shot American Drug Man, the man who threatened me—the weak, stupid policeman from Brazil—over the telephone."

Another reason Lockman had to come himself, Charlie thought.

Rabassa waved a paper in the direction of the copilot. "I have a picture, from the Internet. This man is like him, but I will see the ID. After that, these sorry dogs of yours will be untied and you may take them." He shrugged. "Otherwise, as you say, maybe we all die."

Lockman stepped forward and handed a little leather folder

to the jeep's driver, who passed it to Rabassa. He looked at it, then tossed it on the ground near Lockman's feet. "So," he said, "what threats do you make now, Mr. Big Shot?"

Lockman picked up his ID and walked back to the chopper.

"Okay, motherfucker," the copilot roared, "cut 'em loose."

Rabassa laughed again and then said something in Portuguese. A guard stepped behind the first hostage next to Paulo. He reached down with a knife and cut the rope holding the man to his chair. When the man realized he was free he stood up, then stumbled over and would have climbed up into the chopper, but the pilot grabbed him and helped him deal with the rappel seat and hoist himself onto the bench on the other side from Charlie. When the second guy was cut loose he got to his feet and made it over to where the pilot helped him on beside his buddy.

"As you see," Rabassa said, "your men still have their health—and even their clothes and their boots. Here we do not strip prisoners naked and put them in cages, as you Americans do." He seemed to be enjoying himself.

The next guy came over and got up on the bench, too, to make three on that side. All of them had slouched through the rain, heads hanging down. If Rabassa's guys looked like fucking Latin Kings, the hostages looked like those shabby, unshaven men who bummed quarters on the street in the Loop.

The rain was heavier now, the wind stronger. It was getting dark, too, and the vein on the side of Charlie's head was pumping away like crazy. Finally the last hostage was cut loose—the black guy. His beard was as ragged and his shirt as filthy as the others. One leg of his uniform pants had been cut or torn off, and his knee—the left knee—was wrapped in a bandage obviously made from the cloth. He walked without bending that knee, but still looked less whipped than the others. This had to be the army guy. "Special Services," Brasher had said. Or was it

"Special Forces"? Something like that.

But the guy was cool, all right. As he passed between Paulo slumped in his chair and Flavio Rabassa perched under his umbrella, he stopped to look at each of them. He shook his head as though not liking this trade any more than Charlie did. But he couldn't do shit about it, either.

Lockman was already up on the bench on Charlie's side, and the pilot led the army guy to the spot in the middle, between Lockman and Charlie. Meanwhile, Charlie was trying to relax a little, slow down his breathing—when there was a sudden blinding flash of lightning, followed at once by one enormous clap of thunder. No rumbles before or after, just one huge explosion that sounded like the end of the whole damn world. Then came some other, smaller explosions, like a short burst of gunfire in the distance. He realized his eyes were squeezed shut and he opened them and looked around. The wind rose even higher and rain burst over them now like a dam had broken, and—

What the hell?

Two women burst out of the trees and into the clearing. They were obviously running for their lives. Running straight toward the chopper.

FIFTY-FOUR

Maria sat in her tiny barracks room and watched the evening sun send gold light slanting through the window. Charlie and Paulo were long gone on the helicopter, and all she could do was wait. She'd turned the air conditioning down and the room was warm, but she was cold with a chill that came from deep inside her. She'd been to blame for Paulo's kidnapping in the first place. And she was to blame for what she feared must be happening now.

Her most recent mistake had been letting Lynn Brasher take so long to set up the call to her father. She'd sat there in her room with a phone on the little table because Brasher told her how hard it was to get through from this remote base to a phone in the United States. "Don't you have a satellite phone?" Maria had asked. "Or something?"

Brasher said to be patient, so she had foolishly sat there and waited. Charlie had talked Lockman into letting him ride with Paulo on the trip to show him to his uncle, which had made her feel better about it. While she waited by the phone she'd worried that she'd miss seeing the helicopter take off, but Brasher said when they reached her father she should be there to pick up right away, because no one knew when the connection might be broken.

Finally the phone had rung and yes, it was her father. "I got your message yesterday," he said. "I tried to call you back, and

I've been trying again today, but they keep saying you're out. I don't like whatever's going on, and I want you to leave that hotel right now, and go home."

"I'm not at the hotel anymore."

"What are you . . . Where *are* you?"

"We're taking Paulo home." She'd been warned all along not to mention Paulo on the phone, but she was tired of doing what she was told. "We're taking him home, flying him to Rio."

"I don't understand. Where are you? Are you on a plane?"

"No. We had to lay over," she said, "somewhere in Colombia, to refuel and service the plane."

"Jesus Christ! Have you completely lost your mind? You—"

"Stop it! I didn't call to have you bully me over the phone."

"Okay, okay," he said. "I'm sorry. It's just . . . well . . ."

"What is it?" She didn't like his tone.

"I don't know. There's . . . something going on, and I don't understand it." He sounded confused, worried. Which was unlike him. "I got a call earlier, from a man who said he was Special Agent Ferris, from the DEA."

"Ferris? He's one of the ones I've met. But why would he call you?"

"He said he wanted to chat. Said he hoped he could count on me to keep recent events confidential. Then he mentioned an audit the IRS is doing of my recent tax returns. Which is true, and . . . well . . . it *is* a bit of a problem. This guy Ferris said enough to show me he knew the gist of it, too, and then said it probably wouldn't amount to anything. Then he mentioned some stocks I sold last year, and how the SEC is getting very aggressive these days and . . . well, I got the picture. This guy was threatening me."

"Threatening? But why—"

"I've had my staff making calls. To senators, people like that. Looking for straight answers about this DEA business. And I must have struck a nerve. This agent, Ferris, was telling me to back off. I was so goddamn mad . . . but I figured he was recording the call so I just hung up. I would have called my own lawyer right then, but . . . but I thought about you."

"I'm . . . I'm not sure I understand," Maria said, but that's when the chill came over her.

"Whatever these people are up to, they don't want it out in the open." She listened, trembling now with fear for Paulo—and maybe even more, she realized, for Charlie. ". . . you I'm most worried about," her father was saying, "but if the feds want to find dirt on a person, they'll dig until—"

"I have to go," she said. "Please, I have to go." She hung up and ran out into the hall.

There'd been a soldier there and he blocked her way. But just then Lynn Brasher came along and hurried her outside to a Jeep. The driver raced down a runway . . . but they had been too late. By the time the Jeep got there, the helicopter was in the air and far off.

So now it was over an hour later and Maria knew something terrible was happening. She had watched the helicopter disappear in the distance, and she was back in her room. The phone was gone and the soldier was still out in the hall. She sat, hardly moving. Blaming herself.

Maybe they couldn't scare her father into silence . . . and maybe they could. They'd been able to mislead her all too easily, to keep her quiet and cooperative. Charlie and Zorina had both been suspicious of Lockman, had both seen something wrong about Brasher's attitude before the flight. But she'd been too wrapped up in being grateful that the boy was safe. And the others went along with her, as though *wanting* Paulo to be safe would make it so. But it didn't. Something was very wrong. And she was afraid she knew what it was.

There was a knock on Maria's door and Brasher came in and set a tray on the desk. A little loaf of French bread, a salad, a glass of water, and a small pot of coffee with two mugs. "You should eat something," Brasher said. Then she unplugged the little lamp on the desk and took it out in the hall and set it on the floor. She came back in and closed the door.

Maria stared at her. "You—" She stopped. "Is this room . . . wired?"

"It was."

"My God, I—" Maria drank some water. "You knew we wouldn't get there before the helicopter took off," she said.

"There's a lot I *don't* know." Brasher sat on the edge of the bed. "I don't—"

"You knew all along what Lockman was up to."

"You're wrong about that," Brasher said. "He's way higher up on the chain of command than I, and he's told me nothing at all, beyond what he orders me to do. Yes, I started having suspicions about what he might do, but I couldn't act on mere suspicion."

"So you did nothing."

"Those hostages' lives are important, too. I can't forget that. I did what I could. You wanted to call your father, but Lockman nixed that. So after he'd left for the helicopter I put you through myself. In addition, I refused to give the boy more ketamine, and—"

"Ketamine?"

"It's a sedative. Charlie knew that the . . . the episode Paulo had on the plane was a bad reaction to it."

"Charlie knows what ketamine is?"

"No, but he knew the boy's behavior was a drug reaction. He's a bright guy." Brasher nodded, as though to herself, and poured out a mug of coffee. "Anyway, Lockman planned another dose for Paulo before today's trip. I told him it was dangerous and I wouldn't be involved. He went to get someone else to administer it, but the drug . . . well . . . let's just say it couldn't be found. I'll face charges in connection with that, but . . ." She drank some coffee. "Charlie was demanding to go, and . . . I think it's a good thing Lockman took him. There'll be a witness to whatever happens."

"He's going to leave Paulo there, isn't he? With his uncle."

"I think . . . I think that's possible. But like I said, that's a suspicion, and there are four lives at stake. And even if he does, that boy's a survivor. He's proven that. And between you and Charlie and Zorina, you'll get him back. And your father, too. He'll raise a stink and—"

"My father? While you people threaten him, scare him off with tax audits and SEC investigations?"

"I don't know anything about that. Honestly."

She sounded sincere, but Maria was tired of being fooled. "I don't believe you," she said. "And Charlie . . . you know about him too."

"What do you mean?"

"Stop pretending. A man like Lockman, who'd use a little boy as a pawn in some secret game he's playing? He won't want to come back with a witness he can't control."

"It's not a 'game', Maria. The lives of four men are on the line. That much I've been able to verify. They're out there."

"Then why doesn't the government drop all this secrecy business and demand their return?" Maria was on her feet now. "Anyway, don't deny it. You know Lockman will never bring a problem like Charlie Long back with him."

"Please," Brasher said, "listen to me." Again she sounded like someone who really wanted to help, and Maria sat down. "Lockman's on a tight deadline. It's his fault that those men are out there, and people higher up than he obviously want them brought home. Right away. And without anyone knowing they were ever gone. He's taking a lot of heat . . . and I don't think he's up to it. He's not thinking straight."

"So why didn't you tell—"

"I was in a bind. If I'd told Charlie I suspected Lockman might be planning to leave Paulo with his uncle, he'd have gone ballistic. Lockman would have locked both of you up, taken the boy in restraints, and worried about how to deal with you later. Apparently he's already started dealing with your father."

"But this way Charlie—"

"If leaving Paulo was Lockman's plan he was going to do it either way. None of us could stop him. Maybe he plans to claim something went wrong out there, that Rabassa pulled something." She poked at the food tray, lining it up along the edge of the desk. "This way, at least you have a witness."

"But Charlie's at risk out there."

"Yes, dammit, he is. But I warned him it was dangerous, warned him to watch out for surprises. He insisted on going. And whatever Lockman's thinking, he won't harm Charlie. At least . . . not if Charlie uses his head."

"And if he doesn't?" Maria was sliding the water glass around in circles on the desktop.

"Don't underestimate him, Maria. I know guys like him. He's . . . well . . . maybe so far he hasn't been able to get his life quite on track, but Charlie Long is tough . . . deep-down tough. And he's smart. He—"

Brasher stopped talking and Maria looked up. The woman was staring at her . . . and smiling a little. Something Maria couldn't remember her doing before. "How can you smile at a time like this?" she asked. "When somewhere out there—"

"You know, Maria, I *do* understand."

"What? Understand what?"

"You like Charlie, don't you." It wasn't a question.

"Well . . . sure. He's gone to a lot of trouble, taken a lot of risk to save Paulo. He—"

"No," Brasher said. "I mean you *like* him. I'm not blind, you know. There's an attraction there that I saw even yesterday. Just a couple of short days and you've found something in him." She nodded. "Of course he's a handsome guy, for sure. But there's more."

"Don't be silly. He's not—" She sipped her water. "We're from two different worlds. And he sure hasn't shown any 'attraction' for me."

Brasher's eyes widened. "You've got to be kidding. You mean you haven't—" She stopped and just shook her head.

"I just don't want him to get hurt," Maria said.

"Right. Well, don't underestimate him." Brasher was all business again. "Whatever Lockman's plan for Paulo is, Charlie Long will be on that chopper when it gets back."

Maria wished she could be so sure. She wished it with all her heart.

Fifty-Five

One of the runners was a black-skinned woman in a baggy dress. A big woman, tall and broad, and Charlie thought she looked too old to be running that fast. Her large breasts bounced wildly under her rain-soaked dress, and her bulk made the suitcase she carried look tiny. Her other hand held tight to the hand of the woman she pulled along beside her. This one's skin was lighter, and she was much younger—just a girl, he saw, as they got closer. She wasn't as tall, either, but she was more overweight and clumsier as she ran. She wore a bright-colored blouse and a wide skirt that billowed in the wind, and she had a dull, flat look on her face.

Everyone else must have been as stunned as Charlie, because the two made it all the way to the chopper with no one stopping them. Not even the two armed policemen who ran out of the trees behind them.

"Forget them!" Lockman shouted, leaning forward from his seat on the bench. "On board, Grayson. Let's go!"

Rabassa was yelling now, too, in Portuguese, and all his policemen were running toward his Jeep. The big woman threw her suitcase up into the chopper, and tried to get her heavy young companion over the bench beside Charlie and up in there, too.

The pilot started toward them, but Grayson stepped in front of him, and just then a short, sharp burst of gunfire rang out. It was Rabassa, standing up in the Jeep, holding an AK-47 pointed in the air. "Take the stinking dogs that belong to you," he shouted. "But the women stay." His men had all joined him, eight of them standing near the Jeep, weapons pointed up.

"What are they to you, Rabassa?" Grayson yelled, and at the same time he grabbed the older woman's arm. "Nita," he said. "What are you—"

"*O diabo,*" the woman called Nita cried, "he hurts my baby!" She yanked her arm away. "You will take us." She helped the girl step up on the bench, where she tried to stand but fell forward, half into the Little Bird. Then, as Nita grabbed her ankles to push her farther in, the wind caught the girl's skirt and it ballooned wide, burying Charlie's face in the rough, wet cloth. "See?" Nita screamed. "See what *o diabo* does?"

Charlie couldn't see anything at all, not with the girl's skirt in his face, until Nita managed to push her up and inside. Then Nita started to climb up, too. And that's when Charlie first saw the red stain spreading out on the side of Nita's dress.

"She's wounded!" Grayson shouted. "They're coming with us."

"No way!" The pilot was just as loud. "I'll never get this—"

Another burst of gunfire sounded from the Jeep. "The women stay!" Rabassa yelled, his weapon still aimed high over their heads.

"Stop and think about it, Rabassa!" Grayson answered. He stood with his back to the women, shielding Nita as she hauled herself into the chopper. "You got the boy. A downed US helicopter can only fuck up your whole life."

The chopper was rocking now in the wind that roared through the clearing, and Charlie thought about Brasher's statement that they'd top out the Little Bird's weight limit with six adult passengers. Now they had eight, with the last two adding close to four hundred pounds.

Rabassa held his weapon high and looked over at Paulo. Then he turned back. "Take them," he finally called. "Take the fat cows and go."

"Okay!" Grayson shouted. "We're outta here." He was up and onto the bench.

But the pilot just stood there. "Can't do it!" he yelled. "I'll never get this motherfucker off the ground. And if I do, I can't control it overloaded in this storm. We get rid of the women, sir, or we all go down."

Grayson stared at him, then unhitched his safety strap and jumped to the ground. "Fine," he said. "I'll stay. Cover me into the trees and—"

"No way. And that wouldn't do it, anyway." He pointed into the chopper. "Those women equal two men, easy. They gotta go, dammit."

Grayson looked in at the women, then leaned and got right up in the pilot's face. "Look here, soldier," he said. "You wanna physically throw two women—one of 'em wounded—out of your goddamn aircraft, you're gonna have to climb over me to do it."

There were a few seconds of silence, and finally the pilot said, "Get on board, sir. We'll make it."

Grayson hoisted himself onto the bench again, between Charlie and Lockman, and the pilot ran around and climbed up and in. There was lightning and thunder constantly now, and rain like Niagara Falls. Charlie twisted around and saw one of Rabassa's men already untying Paulo. For five days he'd been telling the boy everything was going to be okay. That very afternoon he'd held him close. "You can trust me," he promised. "I'll stay right with you."

And now?

Now Paulo, ignoring the man who was untying him from the chair, kept his face turned straight toward Charlie. The Little Bird's engine roared to full throttle and there was a jolt, as though something had clicked into gear, and the chopper lifted off the ground. Through the driving rain, he saw the boy watching the Little Bird rise, watching it fly away with the man who promised to stay with him.

★ ★ ★ ★ ★

PART V
PAYBACK

★ ★ ★ ★ ★

As the Little Bird struggled to get off the ground, Bill Grayson knew they were leaving a little boy behind as the price for their freedom, and it tore out his guts. But there was nothing he could do about it. Nita, though . . . she was a different story. She'd been decent, and tried to be helpful. He owed her for that. No way he'd have flown out of there and left her and her granddaughter behind.

The aircraft, badly over its flying weight, bounced around in the gusting wind. He'd always been lucky, though, and something told him his luck would hold once more. Despite the roaring storm, he knew they were going to make it up and over those goddamn trees. No question. They had to.

This young guy beside him, though, one hand stretched up and holding the safety strap where it clipped onto the D-ring, had to be scared shitless. Grayson turned to shout encouragement.

The look on the guy's face surprised him. Fear, yes, but more than that. A look he'd seen before, on too many soldiers' faces. The look of a guy who was getting away . . . and leaving a buddy behind. He

311

saw sadness, and rage, and helplessness. And on this face—maybe more than on any he'd ever seen—he saw a toughness that couldn't stand giving up.

FIFTY-SIX

Charlie held tight to his safety strap. The Little Bird rose maybe ten feet off the ground, then suddenly lurched sideways and down, slammed by another gust of wind. The pilot regained control and they started moving, but horizontally, just a few feet above the ground, heading toward the tall trees that ringed the clearing. The chopper rocked wildly in the wind, but picked up speed across the clearing and then they were rising again . . . a little.

He turned and saw the soldier, Grayson, staring right at him. "Just hang on!" the man yelled. "We're gonna make it!" And they were. The wall of trees raced toward them, but they were definitely on the rise.

"Well, shit!" Charlie yelled back—and unhooked his strap and pushed himself off the bench.

He had meant to hit the ground running, like a paratrooper in a movie. Of course the chopper hadn't been all that high up . . . but he had no parachute, either. With no control of his arms and legs he'd slammed into the ground, rolling and bouncing off stumps, sliding across grass and brush as sharp as knives. He finally managed to scramble to his feet and run for cover into the trees only because he was too scared to care about how much he hurt.

Now he ran blindly, crashing into branches and tripping on vines, getting up again and running some more. It was dark in here and everything was wet and slippery, and Rabassa's cops were right behind him, firing their automatic weapons on the run and—

Except he heard no gunfire, no men calling to each other as they closed in on him. Even so, he kept running, fighting and clawing his way through the dense undergrowth. Eventually, when his lungs were about to burst, he slowed to a walk, then finally stopped and dropped onto his hands and knees on the ground, exhausted. He'd heard no helicopter crash, either. No screech of metal tearing apart, no screaming, no exploding fuel tanks. None of that. He was sure of it. The Little Bird must have made it up and over the trees.

He sat back on his haunches, gasping for breath, and looked around. Rabassa's men probably knew this fucking jungle like he knew the dingy alleys and dark rooftops of his childhood. But there was no sign or sound of them. Only the storm. Rain pounding on the branches of a million wide-leafed trees—like palm trees or something—a lot of it somehow getting through and soaking him and everything around him. The wind high above roared like the world's longest L train rushing past, but didn't even move things close to the ground.

He struggled to his feet and tested his joints and muscles. He had a hundred aches and pains, plenty of scrapes and cuts; but no broken bones, no serious bleeding. He looked around. It was pretty dark, and every time the lightning flashed—which seemed like every five seconds—it turned the dense, weird-looking branches and huge leaves around him to wet shining silver. The pounding thunder shook the earth so hard he could feel it through the soles of his boots.

He looked down at the boots. It was Brasher who'd brought him the heavy damn things. Thank God for that. And for the long pants and the long-sleeved shirt with a built-in hood, too. The hood had a drawstring and he tightened it around his face with those little spring things. The mosquitoes sure weren't staying in out of the rain. It was hot as hell and he was as wet inside his clothes as he was outside, but the fucking bugs swirling around his head weren't able to bite through the cloth.

He had jumped because he couldn't leave Paulo behind, because the idea that he could leave, and somehow ever make his way back here again, was bullshit. Then, when he thought Rabassa's guards might shoot him, he got scared and ran. Now he couldn't even tell which way he'd come from. He had to go back, though, because Paulo needed him, needed to know he wasn't abandoned. Besides, he couldn't just sit and wait for night to come, when it would be darker than it was already. He didn't want to even think about that.

"The boots are for snakes," Brasher had said when they were driving out to the helicopter. When he told her he wasn't going on any hikes, she repeated her "better safe than sorry" line, sounding like someone's mother.

Thinking of Brasher made him think of Maria, and that got him nowhere except sad that he might never see her again. Instead of that, he tried to figure how much time had passed since he jumped from the Little Bird. Fifteen minutes maybe. How could a storm keep pounding so hard for so long? Which reminded him. The pilot said the storm was coming from the south, so the wind must be blowing from south to north. Unless storms change directions. Which they might, but . . . Anyway, he could tell which way it was blowing now, so he knew which way was north. Right. Probably.

It seemed to him the Little Bird had been headed into the wind when it was trying to get off the ground, and when he jumped he'd rolled in the direction it was going. South. So he probably ran mostly south, too. He could have run in circles, but . . . Shit, that was like worrying about storms changing directions.

So if he was south of the clearing where they'd left Paulo, and if he went north—the way the wind was blowing—he should get back to the clearing. And even if he missed that, he might run into the compound itself, which was way bigger and was . . . what? . . . northwest of the little clearing? His watch was still working. He'd go twenty minutes or so north, with the wind.

Not much, but at least it was a plan. And he'd rather take his chances with Flavio Rabassa than spend a night alone in this jungle. Boots, hell. They might be good for little snakes that bite you on the ankle, but they had giant snakes around here, for chrissake. Boas or anacondas or something. Half a block long. He'd seen a picture of one that fell asleep after it swallowed an animal, with the animal's shape bulging out in the middle of the damn thing's body. He saw himself as that bulge, getting smaller and smaller until pretty soon he was gone and the fucking snake woke up and went out for dinner again.

He checked his watch and headed north, struggling through the undergrowth. He could hardly walk through this shit. These weren't ordinary trees and bushes like in the forest preserves around Chicago. Here, the leaves were stiff and wide, or long and pointy like on palm trees, and they grew right up out of the ground in clumps and grabbed at his legs. Actually, there were so many goddamn plants growing everywhere he couldn't even see the ground. Plus, he didn't want to look around down there because that's where the snakes would be . . . and fucking tarantulas and God knows what else. There were vines hanging everywhere and climbing all over everything, too, with weird-looking flowers. And millions of those fern things like his ma used to have in the backyard, except a lot of these were taller than he was.

He pushed his way through, waving the mosquitoes off his face with one hand and sweeping the other hand around in front of him to wipe away the sticky spider webs he kept walking into. The storm wasn't letting up, either. The thunder and lightning kept coming and the wind roared louder than ever. Every so often he heard some huge tree go crashing to the ground through the brush.

Twenty minutes later he stopped at the edge of a little area that was free of undergrowth, just knee-high grass. It was maybe fifteen feet across, and high above him the trees formed a canopy over the space. He took a step forward and the ground was spongy, like he was moving into a swamp. He stepped back, not wanting to cross it.

This wasn't the big clearing where they'd left Paulo. For all he knew he'd missed that one already. He looked around. Every tree looked like every other fucking tree. And how did all the rest of this leafy shit grow down here, anyway, underneath all these trees?

One lucky thing. He hadn't stepped on any snakes or run into any wild animals so far—except for the mosquitoes that swarmed around his head. He suddenly remembered the little tube Brasher had left in his pants pocket, and pulled it out. Insect repellant. He squeezed some out and rubbed it into his hands and face, and put the tube back in—

Someone coughed. Or muffled a sneeze.

Charlie dove forward into the clearing and hit the soft ground. He lay face down in the tall grass and felt the muscles in his chest squeeze tight around his heart. He twisted his head, very slowly, just enough so he could breathe, and right away heard the mosquitoes buzzing around the side of his face. They didn't bite, though. And even if they had, he'd have been afraid to move his hand to brush them away.

There was silence. And then a rustling, behind him and to his right. Someone was coming through the undergrowth.

FIFTY-SEVEN

Charlie lay motionless, feeling that familiar pulse pumping away in his temple. He heard nothing now but the wind and the rain and the whine of mosquitoes around his head. He didn't know if the person was gone, or had just stopped moving. As his heart slowed and he breathed easier, he was suddenly aware of a weight bearing down on his legs that he hadn't even felt before. Like a branch had fallen across the backs of his knees. Then the branch moved, hardly an inch. Just enough to tell him it was alive.

The rustling in the brush started up again, coming his way, then stopped. "Don't move." A man's voice, just a few feet away. "Don't move," he ordered, "or you're dead."

Charlie didn't move, didn't make any response. He couldn't.

"Stay still," the man said. "Don't move a muscle." The man was out of the undergrowth, almost on top of him now, near his feet. "Ohhh . . . *kay!*" he yelled, and the weight was lifted off Charlie's legs.

He was still afraid to move.

"You can sit up now." The man sounded out of breath.

Charlie sat up and saw that it was the fourth hostage, the soldier. He was holding a snake by the tail, twirling it in the air like you'd twirl a rope over your head. The snake was fat, green, and a good five feet long, and by twirling it the soldier kept its head out away from him. As Charlie watched, the man swung the snake harder and then let go and sent it sailing out across the open area, toward the trees on the other side.

"Jesus!" was all Charlie could say.

"Name's Bill Grayson," the man said. "Guess my boyhood spent flippin' snakes in the woods and swamps wasn't wasted, after all."

"You said if I moved I was dead. So that thing was poisonous?"

"Actually, odds are it wasn't. But did you wanna play the odds?"

Charlie stood up and swiped at the mosquitoes buzzing around his face and eyes. And then, for the second time since he could remember—the first time being just the day before, when he flew Paulo across their barracks room from cot-Colombia to cot-Brazil—he discovered there were tears running down his cheeks.

Charlie hadn't seen Grayson jump from the chopper before it rose and cleared the trees. And according to Grayson, it didn't entirely clear.

"I heard it break through some high branches after I jumped."

"But they made it, right?" Charlie asked.

"Yeah, well, the chopper kept going, but I'm glad I wasn't hanging out there to get my head taken off by a tree limb at that speed."

"You told me we were gonna make it. Then you jumped. What? You changed your mind? Figured the chopper wasn't gonna clear after all?"

"Hell no." Grayson seemed a little pissed off at Charlie's suggestion. "I jumped to stay with you."

He'd run after Charlie, but with his bad knee he couldn't keep up. Plus, he realized sooner than Charlie that Rabassa's men weren't coming after them. "The Jeep was already turning away when we took off," he said, "and in that rain and lightning,

I don't think they even saw us jump. Or they decided it wasn't worth chasing us. Electrical storms are deadly in the jungle. Figured they'd find us soon enough, or our bones, anyway." He paused. "People who don't know the jungle get lost easy . . . and die."

"Yeah," Charlie said, "I kinda thought that."

They were sitting with their backs up against a huge tree, under a sort of roof that Grayson had already built out of branches and leaves. It wasn't perfect, and some water still dripped through, but the storm was easing up now. Charlie had shared the insect repellant, and now Grayson was eating the roots of some plants he'd pulled up.

"How'd you cut the branches for this roof?" Charlie asked.

"With this." Grayson held up a knife about the size of one Charlie had in a drawer by the sink back at his place. He'd bought his at Walgreen's and broke the tip off right away trying to tighten the hinge on his bathroom door. This one looked a lot stronger, and sharper.

"You found that out here somewhere?"

"Nita gave it to me. I had it hidden here." Grayson patted the lumpy cloth around his knee. "Nita's the big woman who—"

"Yeah, I heard you call her that. So you knew they were coming? Her and that other woman? Or . . . girl, I guess."

"All I knew was Nita had a granddaughter she was desperate to take to the US. Nita said the girl was real pretty, though."

"To me," Charlie said, "she looks like she's . . . mentally handicapped or something."

"Her name's Rosa and in Nita's eyes she's a beautiful, foolish girl who got mixed up with Rabassa." He shook his head. "And his wife."

"Jesus, the wife, too?"

"That's what Nita says. They were . . . you know . . . not just fucking the girl. They're into perversions and shit."

"No wonder she wanted to get the girl out."

"Even if that Little Bird makes it back to base in Colombia," Grayson said, "I don't suppose Nita and the girl will ever get to America."

"If they didn't crash, they might be back already." Charlie looked at his watch. "Jesus, I'm hungry."

"Tell me about it." Grayson was rubbing the dirt off another root. It looked like a small potato, but Charlie waved aside the offer to share.

"Tired, too," Charlie said. He leaned back against the tree. But whenever he closed his eyes he saw Paulo, with his arms stretched back over the pilot's shoulders, begging Charlie to save him. Or Paulo, looking up and watching the helicopter lift off the ground.

He sat up. "Hey, you think we're gonna get out of here?"

"Hell, yes. I'm not dying in this shithole. I guarantee it."

Charlie had his doubts. "How do you know?"

"I know because I'm not ready to die." Grayson stared straight ahead. "I'm not saying it'll be easy."

"Right," Charlie said. "So what I'm thinking is . . . it'll be sort of a miracle, right? I mean, we don't have much of a chance, right?"

"Fuck that negative shit! You can't give up. You gotta—"

"Hey, I'm with you on not giving up." Charlie thought for a minute. "I'm just saying . . . that boy . . . his name's Paulo. He's Rabassa's nephew."

"Bad news for him. Rabassa's a sick fucking creep."

"Yeah," Charlie said. "So . . . I mean . . . since our chances are slim anyway, why not—"

"Hold on." Grayson stared at him. "I jumped because I thought you didn't clip on properly, and fell off. But you didn't fall, did you?"

"Nope."

"You wanna get the goddamn kid."

"I'm just saying . . . if we don't get him out, he's dead."

"You mean 'as good as dead,' right? Because Rabassa's no good?"

"I mean *dead* dead. He owns some valuable property in Rio. Me and my . . . my team . . . we think Rabassa will kill him to get the property."

"Your team? Who are you anyway? I mean, your name's Charlie Long, but you're not army, and you're sure as hell not the fucking DEA. So . . . who's your team?"

"I'm just . . . you know . . . trying to help the kid. And it's . . . it's not really a 'team.' Just this chick, this old lady, and me. We been working together. But Paulo's . . . you know . . . my responsibility. It's kind of a long story."

"Yeah, well, team or not, you got a lotta balls, Charlie Long, thinking you can get that kid."

"Balls, hell. Just sitting here scares the shit outta me. But you know? My life was headed down the toilet all on its own before I ever ran into Paulo. So now, if I leave him and I do get away, what do I get away to?" Charlie slapped at a mosquito. "I mean, there's gotta be a reason I ran the right way . . . and found you. Was it so you could help me save just my own ass? I don't think so. I think it was so the two of us could go after Paulo."

"A lotta balls," Grayson said again. "First, even if we got to the kid and got him out—which is impossible—I'd still have the two of you to drag through this stinking jungle. But . . . well . . ."

Grayson fiddled with the knife and Charlie kept quiet, letting him think things over.

"Rabassa kept the four of us locked in a hut," Grayson finally said, "near that clearing where you left Paulo. There's some kind of Jeep trail from the hut to the police compound. And there's gotta be a supply road from the compound to . . . to God knows where. I heard trucks coming and going sometimes.

So, if we follow that road . . .”

"See?" Charlie said. "You already got us a plan to get away."

"Getting past Rabassa's people to Paulo, that's the hard part."

"I don't know. They don't look too smart to me," Charlie said. "Except for the uniforms and the dumb little caps, they look like a bunch of fucking Imperial Latin Kings from north of my old neighborhood—cocky, vicious . . . and dumb as bricks. Of course they got AK-47s coming out the ass."

"And all we got's this." Grayson held up the knife. "And the element of surprise. Maybe we'll get us our own automatic weapon or two."

"I never even touched one of those things."

"I have," Grayson said. "Trust me, I have."

"So, you think you can find the compound?"

"Sure. It's not that far from the clearing."

"Yeah, but can you find the fucking clearing?"

Grayson pointed. "It's right over there, Charlie. Maybe fifteen yards." He laughed. "You were headed right for it."

"Damn," Charlie said, and felt pretty good about himself. "When do we look for the kid?"

"We'll rest first, make our move after midnight. Your watch work?"

"Yeah, but it's still on Chicago time."

"Doesn't matter," Grayson said. "You relax. Let me think on this."

Charlie leaned his back against the tree again and looked around. The only rain now was what dripped off the trees. The storm had moved on, but the sun must have been going down, because it wasn't getting any lighter. Without the wind and thunder, it was quiet. Except . . . not actually quiet at all. The whole place was alive. Leaves and grass rustled, branches creaked and groaned, and the birds and animals were starting to screech and yell things at each other. It was like living inside a fucking jungle movie. Who knew what the hell was out there?

He sat up. "Maybe you should sleep first," he said. "I'll watch."

"What, sleep here?"

"Yeah, well, you're the one with the jungle training. I thought you—"

"Rule number one is to find a place that's safe from whatever the fuck's roaming around out here. And I know a place no one's expecting us to hide. You're not afraid of scorpions, are you?"

"Any insect bigger than my thumbnail, I'm scared. But aren't scorpions just, like, in the desert?"

"First, scorpions aren't insects. They're more a kind of big spider."

"Jesus!"

"And the desert ones have jungle cousins. But we were in that hut for quite a few days and no one got stung, so maybe the scorpions were too busy with the giant centipedes and cockroaches."

FIFTY-EIGHT

While it was still light they had to get to the clearing where they'd handed Paulo over, then follow along the edge of it to find the hut. They'd rest a few hours there—Charlie knew he wouldn't sleep—before making their way along the Jeep trail to the compound. The storm was gone and if they were lucky the moon would be out to help them see.

"Right," Charlie said. "And when we find Paulo we'll get us a Jeep or a truck. I don't need a key to—"

"Don't get so far ahead," Grayson said. "In covert operations, you have to be ready to meet each contingency as it comes."

Which Charlie figured was soldier talk for they didn't know what the hell they were doing. But shit, what was the downside? If they didn't try for Paulo, they'd probably die out here, anyway, and Rabassa would kill the kid. Or if they tried and got caught, maybe Rabassa would go for another trade. Or maybe not.

Grayson was right. Best to take one step at a time.

When they reached the clearing there was just enough light to see that it was empty. Even so, they stayed in the trees, keeping the clearing on their left, circling it to find the hut.

"How do you know there won't be someone there?" Charlie asked.

"Why would there be? Rabassa's got no prisoners now, and

no one in his right mind would spend a night in that stinking shithouse if they weren't locked in."

"Yeah . . . well . . . maybe they're waiting for us. Like expecting us to come back and hide."

"If they even know we jumped off the chopper," Grayson said, "what they're expecting is for us to be thrashing around in the dark with the snakes and the jaguars and the hidden sinkholes that—"

"Jaguars?"

"Come on. It's getting dark."

Charlie followed. It was hot as hell—and humid—and his clothes would have been soaked through even if there'd been no storm. The mosquitoes weren't buzzing around his face, though, and he wondered if they slept at night. Then, out of nowhere, he got an idea.

He moved close up behind Grayson and said, "They do have one prisoner, y' know?"

"What?" Grayson stopped and turned toward him. "Oh, you mean the kid?"

"Yeah. Do you think they'd lock Paulo in there? I mean, he'd run away if he—"

"Actually," Grayson said, "that would be the best thing for us."

"Except there'd be fifteen fucking policemen there, guarding him."

"There'll be a guard, yeah," Grayson said. "But at the hut, even for the four of us, there was just one guard, except when someone was actually coming inside. I don't think Rabassa would want his whole unit to know everything he's up to. Otherwise, he'd have kept us in a regular jail cell. Nita used to bring our night meals, and I'm positive once she left there was only one guard. I heard a radio sometimes, but no talking. And one would be enough. There's just one door and no windows."

He held up the knife. "Christ, I hope the boy is in there." He turned. "Let's go, man. Guards . . . whatever. Fuck it!"

Charlie followed. Grayson was obviously getting himself psyched up. Like a boxer before a fight. Except this was a guy with a kitchen knife about to take on maybe two or three AK-47s.

Yeah, well it's not just Grayson, asshole.

It was slow going as it got darker, even though they stayed along the edge of the clearing. "Hold it!" Grayson whispered. He gestured Charlie up beside him and held a branch aside.

There was light showing up ahead through the brush, off to their right a little. But Charlie couldn't tell how far away. "What is it?" he asked.

"It might be the police compound," Grayson said, "but that's farther away. So it's the hut. Has to be. And one of those shitass lanterns the guards use."

They angled away from the clearing and headed straight toward the light. Grayson, a few steps in the lead, stopped suddenly and held up his hand. He leaned forward, then turned around. "My man," he whispered, "you're a goddamn genius."

Charlie stepped up beside him and peered through the leaves. It was pretty dark now, but up ahead in a cleared area was a squat wooden hut, lit up by a lantern on a stump—like one of those lanterns they sell at Sport-Mart for camping trips. The genius remark was because there was a guard there—another Latin King-type. So Paulo had to be inside. The door was barred with a wide board dropped into braces on either side. The guard sat on a chair tilted back against the wall of the hut beside the door. He was a big man, and had his arms crossed over a massive chest. The only weapon Charlie could see was a pistol in a holster at his belt.

The man might have been sleeping, except for the cigarette

sticking out of his mouth. Not moving his hands, he took a drag, and the glow lit up his dark, sullen face under the brim of his dumb little cap. For the first time Charlie noticed soft, tinny Latin music, like salsa or something, from a radio he couldn't see.

Grayson tugged on his arm and they moved backward a few yards. "Here's the deal," Grayson whispered. "You go to the rear of the hut and make some noise. Not words, just noise. Cough, snort, whatever. Loud enough for the guy to wonder what he heard, and just once. Then wait, say, ten seconds. If nothing happens, do it again. Keep it up as long as you need to, each time a little louder."

"What do you mean, 'if nothing happens'? What's supposed to happen?"

"I need to get his ass off his chair and his back away from the wall." Grayson still had the knife in his hand.

"Jesus, I didn't know they grew 'em so big down here. What—"

"Not a problem. When it's over, you'll know." He put his free hand on Charlie's arm. "Someone else might come along anytime, so hurry up. But be quiet."

Charlie moved away from Grayson, and in the dark and the vegetation he immediately felt very alone. He had to be quiet, which meant go slow. But he had to hurry up. Jesus! The damn vein in the side of his head was driving him crazy. He circled around to the back of the hut.

The lantern light didn't reach back here. But there must have been a moon or stars or something, because there was just enough glow from the sky to barely see about six feet of cleared ground between the trees and the hut. Two quick steps took him close to the little building and he pressed his back against the wall, to keep from shaking. He'd count to ten, then cough; then count to ten, then cough.

He took one step out from the hut—and put his foot flat down on something alive. He jumped and his heart stopped and he fell back against the wall. And then the something smacked the side of his right ankle. It hit his boot, hard, once . . . then again . . . and a third time. He kicked at the goddamn thing and maybe he hit it and maybe he didn't, but he heard it slither away in the dark.

"Damn sna—" He caught himself and fought for control, squeezing his fists tight. His whole body poured out sweat, and at the same time he felt cold and shaky.

Then he heard something. Like scuffling, from the front of the hut. Then some soft groaning, and after that nothing. He waited, his back pressed against the wall, and when nothing more happened he slid close to the corner. But still there was no sound and he waited, holding his breath.

"Charlie?" It was Grayson, calling just loud enough to be heard. "Charlie . . . you there?"

"Yeah," he called back.

"I . . . I need help."

Charlie looked around the corner and saw Grayson on the ground near the front of the hut. He was sitting with one leg stretched out straight and the other bent at the knee. His body was hunched over the bent leg and his hands were pressed, palms down, to the ground beside his hips. He looked up as Charlie approached. "You . . . you did great," he said. "I told you not to use words, but . . . but that's okay." He tried to smile, but Charlie could tell he was hurting.

"Where's the guard?" Charlie asked. "What's wrong with you?"

"My knee. We . . ." He stopped, breathing hard. "He put up a fight and we both fell . . . backward. My leg bent the wrong way and he landed on me." He stopped to catch his breath again, then shook his head. "I can't stand up."

"Where's the guard?" Charlie asked again.

Grayson gestured with his head, and Charlie went to the front of the hut. The guard lay face down on the ground. His police cap lay beside him, and the knife handle stuck up from the back of his neck.

"You better get him outta sight," Grayson said.

Charlie bent over and took the man's legs and dragged the body, face down, back around the corner. As he passed Grayson the soldier said, "Hold it." He reached and took the pistol from the guard's holster, and pulled the knife from his neck. By the rear of the hut Charlie let the guy's legs fall back to the ground. He was shaking. He'd never touched a dead man before.

"What you waiting for?" Grayson said. "See if the kid's inside."

"Oh . . . yeah."

He went to the door of the hut and lifted the board, a five-foot-long two-by-six, out of its braces and leaned it against the wall. He pulled the door open and the smell of shit slapped him in the face and almost knocked him down. He peered in and Paulo was there, sitting in the dark on the wood floor. He had his forehead pressed down on his knees, his arms wrapped around his shins.

"Hey, kid," Charlie said, stepping inside, "didn't I *say* I'd be back?"

Paulo jerked his head up, his eyes wide and shining in the dim light from the lantern outside. Charlie lifted him to his feet, and the boy threw his arms around his middle. And right then—with Charlie trying to make Paulo let go and stop hugging him—that's when he heard some sort of motor vehicle, still pretty far off, but coming their way.

FIFTY-NINE

Charlie was prying Paulo's arms from his waist when the boy suddenly gasped and let go on his own. Charlie spun around.

"It's me." Grayson was sitting in the open doorway. He must have heard the engine noise too, and dragged himself that far. "That's a Jeep," he said. "I guarantee it."

"Just one, though, right?"

"Right, which is one more than we can deal with. Take the kid and run." He handed Charlie the guard's weapon. "Find the compound, and then the supply road, and follow it out. You got no other chance."

Charlie didn't answer, but handed the gun back. He took Paulo and sat him back on the floor of the hut. "You stay here," he said, rubbing the top of the boy's head. "I'll be around."

Whether Paulo understood or believed him, he didn't know. He went outside and closed the door, and dropped the board back in place. The engine noise was getting louder.

"What the hell are you doing?" Grayson asked.

"Well, I'm not leaving *you,* that's for sure. You're the only damn soldier we got. I've never fired a gun in my life."

"Shit." Grayson held the knife up toward him. "Then take this."

Charlie took the knife and stuck it under his belt. He looked around, and in the pale light of the lantern he saw a break in the trees and brush. "You're sure you can't stand up?"

"No way, unless you stand me."

Grayson's left leg was useless and he moaned with pain as Charlie struggled to drag him up to a standing position and half carried him to the opening, which was where the trail entered the clearing. He leaned him, standing on one leg, against a large tree, out of sight from the trail. "When they drive into the clearing," he said, "you'll be behind them and have the drop on them. I hope you don't have to shoot, though, because that'll bring fifty more on the run."

"Shoot, hell," Grayson said. "When they see no guard sitting over there, they won't even drive in." The Jeep was getting closer, and Charlie caught the occasional flash of headlight beams through the trees, bouncing along what must have been a winding trail.

"Just don't faint on me or something, dammit." Charlie ran to the side of the hut and got the shirt off the guard's body and put it on over the jungle shirt Brasher gave him. He picked up the cap and put that on, too. His pants were dark, and they'd have to do.

He set the lantern on the ground beside the stump it had been on, so the shadow from the stump fell across the guard's chair, and ran over and sat on the chair himself. He tilted it back on two legs until he was leaning against the wall of the hut. With arms folded across his chest, chin down, and the cap pulled low on his forehead, he tried to look like a guard asleep on the job. The radio was still playing, but was soon drowned out by the approaching Jeep.

Headlights burst into view and the Jeep paused at the edge of the clearing—not far enough in for Grayson to challenge its occupants from behind—but then roared forward and stopped maybe fifteen feet from where Charlie sat. The driver cut the engine, but not the lights, which were pointed into the jungle off to the right. Charlie didn't move, but watched through eyes barely open beneath the bill of the cap.

He wondered why Grayson didn't shout something. What was he waiting for?

The Jeep was outside the circle of light from the lantern, but Charlie could see the outline of the driver. He was big, and wore a wide-brimmed cowboy hat, and it had to be Rabassa. The seat beside him was empty, but in the backseat, deeper in shadows, the tip of a lighted cigarette glowed. Rabassa turned and spoke in what must have been Portuguese. There was no response, but he kept on talking. Charlie couldn't understand a word, but it was Rabassa, all right, and he sounded drunk—or high on something.

Meanwhile, not a sound from Grayson. Then Rabassa rose from his seat and faced the hut and called out. It was obviously an order, and it could only be for Charlie. Like, *Wake up, asshole!*

He didn't respond. He just kept breathing, chest rising and falling, as though deep in sleep. Through the slits of his eyes he watched Rabassa get out from behind the wheel and step down from the Jeep. Meanwhile, the smoker in the backseat lifted the cigarette and took a deep drag, and the glow lit up a face. A woman's face. A girlfriend? A wife? Jesus!

The big man came toward Charlie. He wore a pistol in a holster hanging at his right hip, but his right hand was up and poised to reach out and slap his lazy officer awake. In better light, and with a brain less impaired, he might have seen before he did that the sleeper on the chair wasn't an officer at all. But he caught on too late—and too close.

He pulled his hand back toward his holster, but it never got there. Charlie was already up and stepping in on him, sweeping his own right arm around so that his forearm and elbow smashed into the left side of Rabassa's head. He followed through and then swung the same arm back again, slamming the back of his clenched fist into the man's head from the other side. Rabassa crumpled to the ground as though he had no bones inside his skin.

The woman didn't move as Charlie crouched down and took Rabassa's pistol and stuck it in his belt. Then he turned and removed the board across the door and pulled it open. When he turned back the woman was out of the Jeep, on the side away from him. She started to run.

"Grayson!" he yelled, but there was no answer.

The woman was headed for the trail back to the compound. Charlie followed, and at the trail opening he passed Grayson lying on the ground. Christ! He *had* fainted.

In the dim light Charlie saw the woman ahead of him, holding a long dress up by her waist so she could lengthen her stride. She had a big head start and ran surprisingly well, but the trail wound this way and that, and it was dark and the ground was rough. She'd have been better off to stand still and scream her lungs out. But maybe she thought the men in the compound had heard screaming in the night too often before . . . or maybe she just didn't think.

Whatever. All she did was run. And he followed. The pistol stuck in his belt was heavy and bulky, and he yanked it out—and the knife, too—and dropped them and kept on running. He was gaining on her, but he was also getting winded. She'd be back with a truckload of Latin Kings if she got away. She was the ball carrier, headed for the end zone . . . and he was his team's last hope. He put on a final burst . . . and tackled her. Hit her from behind, hit her hard, and went down on top of her. She was half his weight—and he didn't care if he fucking killed her.

Except, when he lifted himself off her and she didn't move, he found out he did care. He stood over her, gasping and heaving, and she just lay there . . . and it scared the hell out of him to think he'd killed someone.

Then Paulo ran up with the lantern in one hand, and Rabassa's pistol in the other. The knife was stuck in his own belt. Jesus, the kid was smart. But he wouldn't come any closer than about ten feet. Finally Charlie realized the woman was breathing. She struggled up to her hands and knees, and he crouched beside her. He'd knocked the wind out of her. Maybe broken a rib or two, but at least he hadn't snapped her spine.

He pulled her up onto her feet. Her dress was a dark color and low cut—a party dress, maybe to celebrate capturing Paulo. She was dark-skinned and slim, but way older than he'd thought. So maybe a wife, not a hooker or something. Pretty, too, except she had a lot of hard miles on her. She stood there, trying to focus her eyes on him, then opened her mouth and would have screamed, but he slapped her. Just once, but hard . . . and she didn't try to yell again.

Paulo stayed where he was with the lantern held high while Charlie spun her around. Hardly room under that dress even for underwear, much less a weapon. He hefted her up and over his shoulder and she hung there, limp, her breasts bouncing against his back as he hurried to the clearing to make sure Rabassa was still out.

Charlie knew he should hate her. She was Rabassa's woman. An accomplice, for chrissake. But he couldn't help feeling pity for her. She'd been young and cute as hell once, and now here she was. Feeling her body draped over his shoulder as he walked, feeling how helpless and human she was, he knew he had no fucking idea what bad experiences had led her to a guy like Rabassa. He pitied her.

When they got close to the clearing he could hear someone talking.

SIXTY

It was Grayson's voice he heard. The guy had dragged himself close to Rabassa and was keeping him face down on the ground with the threat of shooting him. "I guarantee," he told Charlie, "I won't go under again. The kid shook me and brought me around. He had the lantern, and he kept pointing till I saw this asshole. Then he went after you."

At Grayson's direction, Charlie put the woman in the hut with her hands and feet tied with strips of cloth cut from the dead guard's pants. He gagged her, too, tightly enough to muffle any screaming she might try, but still letting her breathe. He wiped the knife clean and tossed it down the stinking toilet hole in the corner, closed the hut door, and dropped the bar across it.

By then Grayson had Rabassa sitting up with his back against the front wheel of the Jeep. The guy managed to come up with one half-ass threat. "You do not know the way out of here," he said, "and my police are so many. They will shoot you like dogs."

"That's exactly true," Grayson said. "You bust us and we're dead. But only after I pump your sorry carcass full of .45 slugs." He held up Rabassa's automatic, which he'd taken from Paulo. "Your own fucking hollow-points. Got it?"

The guy got it.

They rode in the Jeep, Charlie driving, with Rabassa in the backseat and Grayson beside him. Grayson wore the dead guard's cap and shirt now, leaving Charlie to pull his hood up over his head and hope for the best. Grayson rode with his arm up on the back of Rabassa's seat, as though casually, but held the barrel of the .45 pressed against his neck.

Paulo was under a piece of canvas on the floor in the front beside Charlie. He'd been so scared to be that close to Rabassa that he could hardly move, and Charlie had to lift him in. That was after he helped Grayson up and into the backseat. The guy was obviously in a lot of pain and Charlie was afraid he'd faint again. "Bullshit," Grayson said, "I'm having too much fun."

They drove along the winding trail until finally they could see light up ahead. Charlie cut the headlights as they rounded one last curve and they were suddenly into a clearing. "Shit," Charlie said, and stopped the Jeep.

The compound was clearly shut down for the night, dimly lit by a few tall security lights. A chain-link fence ran around the perimeter, bathed in soft orange light, just like at that airfield in Colombia. Outside the fence the land was cleared for maybe fifty yards out to the trees, but the dirt road that led to the gate was lined along both sides with huge winding coils of razor wire. No way they could drive around the place. If there was a supply road leading out from the other end, and Grayson was sure there had to be, they'd have to go in and right on through.

"Okay, fat man," Grayson said, "you're taking us in this end, and out the other. I get one hint you're saying something I don't like in Portuguese to anyone and I will blow your fucking windpipe from here to Rio. My finger's on the trigger and even if a sniper picks me off, my guess is the spasm will tighten that finger and you'll have to hold your head on with your hands."

"And if I help you," Rabassa said, "what is there then for me?"

"We get caught, you die. But take us to somewhere safe, and we'll let you go and you can haul your ass back here. Right, Charlie?"

Charlie nodded, wondering if the guy was dumb enough to believe they'd ever let him walk.

Rabassa thought for a long moment, but must have realized—believe them or not—that he had no choice. Finally he said, "I will see that you are taken to the town of Tabatinga, on the border, from which you can walk across to the Colombian side."

"Fine, but you're not seeing to anything, fat man, you're coming with us. Once we're there, you can leave."

Rabassa shrugged. "I will take you."

Charlie drove up to the gate. Rabassa yelled something to a guard high up in a booth on stilts, and the gate slid sideways on a pulley system. If the guard noticed anything unusual, he didn't let on. They passed through the gate. There was nobody out walking around, and they drove forward through the eerie semidarkness without incident.

The compound was three or four times the size of a football field, with a lot of open space. They passed what Charlie had guessed from the chopper was Rabassa's house, and farther on he recognized the long, low building—showing a few lights on inside—which had to be the barracks. Past that was a square brick building with bars on the windows, the police headquarters. The only other buildings—five or six of them—were like metal storage sheds or garages. They were all way bigger than they'd looked from the air. There were a dozen Jeeps and as many trucks lined up in a row near the barracks.

As they drew near the far end of the compound Charlie saw another gate with a guard tower, and a road leading off from there into the trees. But before they got there, Rabassa told him to stop. "This Jeep is slow," he said. "There is a faster ride." He pointed toward a large metal building with a tall, wide overhead door that stood open. "Drive in there. The pilot will be sleeping by his aircraft."

SIXTY-ONE

Rabassa obviously had no doubt Grayson would shoot him without blinking an eye. Charlie felt the same, so he made sure that, with his help, the soldier never left Rabassa's side the whole time, from his waking up the pilot until they took off.

This helicopter was three or four times the size of the Little Bird, almost as uncomfortable . . . and even louder. But at least it had sliding doors that closed. They flew with just one pilot, and an empty copilot's seat. The passenger cabin was set up to carry eight people on straight-back sling seats made of pipe and some kind of cloth, like nylon. Again, they all had safety straps attached to D-Rings that hung down from the ceiling.

Neither Rabassa nor the pilot—who was young, and looked scared as hell—showed any resistance. Grayson had Charlie tie Rabassa's hands behind his back, and by the time they were in the air the guy seemed entirely sober. In fact, he seemed pretty damn cheerful . . . and certainly proud of his helicopter. "Much like your army's Blackhawks," he said. He had to raise his voice to be heard, even though they all—except for Paulo, who had earplugs in—wore headsets with microphones, like what Charlie wore in the Little Bird. "With our radar system and aircraft such as this, we—the federal police of Brazil—protect our borders. I myself am an expert pilot, and I fly this helicopter often."

"Yeah, right," Grayson said.

"We have the latest night vision goggles," Rabassa went on,

"and this pilot is an expert at flying in the darkness." When no one answered, he went on. "Also, we have enough fuel so that when we leave you at Tabatinga we will not need to refuel. My pilot and I will be free to fly home. *Sim?*"

"That's what I said," Grayson answered. "But I've got a new idea."

"And what is this new idea?" Rabassa didn't seem surprised.

"There's another town next to Tabatinga, but on the Colombian side of the border. I can't think of the name of—"

"Leticia," Charlie said. "It's a sort of a twin town with Tabatinga."

"That's it." Grayson swung around toward him. "Except . . . how the hell do you know?"

Charlie grinned. "What? You think I don't get around a little?"

"Anyway," Grayson turned back to Rabassa. "Have your pilot set down on the Leticia side."

"*Sim.*" The man seemed unconcerned with the change of orders.

"And I've seen those two towns from the air before," Grayson said, "so if we end up anywhere else I'll blow your fucking head off before we touch ground."

"I am not so foolish." Rabassa nodded, as though to himself. "And I am also not so foolish to believe that you plan to keep your promise to let me go home."

"Think whatever you want, partner."

"You will find the Colombian soldiers at Leticia to be children, poorly disciplined. But I know you are experienced, and you will talk to your own superior officers. They will tell you what must be done about me."

Grayson didn't answer, and Charlie figured he knew exactly what his "superior officers" would say . . . and it wouldn't be to set free someone who threatened four American hostages with death.

"It is sad." Rabassa apparently couldn't keep from talking. "If it were not for human greed we would not be wasting this time."

"Seeing as your price for our freedom was a little boy," Grayson said, "and from the things I've heard . . . and seen . . . I wouldn't call you 'greedy.' I'd say fucking 'perverted.' "

Rabassa stiffened, as though shocked, offended. "This boy is my nephew, an orphan. He has been shut away in an institution." He leaned forward across the cabin and spoke softly in Portuguese to Paulo. The boy kept his head down, staring at the floor. "I do not speak of my own greed," the man said, looking now at Charlie, "but of the greed of other men, Russian men, which brings us here."

"Forget it," Grayson said. "I'm tired of—"

"No, wait." Charlie was interested now. "Tell me about the Russians. They kidnapped Paulo, I know, but how come they took him to Chicago?"

"This boy was not kidnapped." Rabassa looked at Charlie. "He was *rescued,* liberated."

"What are you talking about?"

"As this boy's only living relative, I have struggled for years to get custody of him, to save him from a life in which he was being misused. But in Brazil one does not easily win a battle with the power of the Church. So . . . I was forced to turn to criminals to save the boy from his sad and evil situation."

"You mean you hired those Russians to grab him?"

"To save him. Porto de Deus has a history, my friend, a long, sad history of taking in helpless children and subjecting them to unspeakable treatment." He paused. "You have seen this boy's scars?"

"Yeah, I saw the damn scars."

"Then you know why I chose to act as I did. You would have done the same. We agreed on a fair price, but the Russians became greedy and demanded more money. Then they took the boy away, because they knew that I would hunt them down if they stayed in Brazil. They are clumsy men, and I was able to learn that they took him in a private plane, one they use in their evil business, to Chicago."

"Why Chicago?" Charlie said.

"Such men, they have no real home, but Chicago is their base at this time. They contacted me by telephone. Of course the amount they demanded was impossible for me, but I feared they would kill the boy, and I told them I needed only time, and I would gather the money. Then God blessed me with good fortune. I captured four Americans who were part of an illegal military invasion of my country. I contacted the US government, and we reached an agreement . . . that man Lockman and I. I would release the captives if the United States would seize my poor nephew and return him to me. I am a captain of the police and this was not legal, no. But . . . to save a child? What would *you* have done?"

"I don't know," Charlie said. He looked at Grayson, but he was sitting with his head hanging down and Charlie knew the pain was getting to him. "That you hired Russian thugs to grab Paulo . . . and that they tried to screw you out of extra money . . . that could be true, I guess. But the part about 'liberating' Paulo? I don't know. I've seen him with a teacher from the orphanage. He's not afraid of her, the way he is of you."

"Perhaps because she herself does not abuse the boy. It is the nuns who do these things, acting as they have for centuries, hiding behind their false piety. They threaten the children with hell if they tell anyone."

"Yeah, well . . ." Charlie shook his head. He knew that could be true. He'd read about some nuns in orphanages in Canada, but still . . .

"I am not a man without faults," Rabassa said, "but I do not abuse children, and I would never torture any—"

"You're a liar," Grayson said. He lifted his head and Charlie saw in his eyes the pain he felt. "I saw that girl, Rosa," he said, his breath coming in short gasps. "Her ass was bare under her skirt. Nita showed me what you did."

"What are you talking about?" Charlie said. "What did you see?"

"Fucking puffed-up blisters . . . from cigarette burns. All over her rear end. Other sores and scars, too."

"Jesus!" Charlie turned to Rabassa. "Just like Paulo. You did the same thing to him. You burned him with cigarettes."

"It was the nuns," Rabassa said. "They are so—"

"You son of a bitch." Charlie leaned toward Rabassa. "You lying son of a bitch."

Rabassa smiled, didn't even blink. "If you do not believe me, that is your choice," he said. "But your government will tell you what to do with me. They will say nothing, of course, of the men who invaded my country." He nodded toward Charlie. "And this you should believe, my young friend. Your government will not treat you well, if you try to make this story public." He sat back. "But for me? I expect to sleep in my own bed when this day is over."

"You think so?" Charlie said. He leaned forward. This was the animal who tortured a little boy—Charlie's little boy—and buried him in a silence he couldn't dig out of. "Not if I can help it."

"Ah, but you cannot." Rabassa smiled again. "You will see. They will send me home. And I will renew my struggle to save this boy. One day you will have forgotten about him. But I promise you . . . until I have this boy," nodding toward Paulo, "I will never stop."

Charlie had no answer for that. He felt a shudder pass through him. He knew the man was a liar. But he also knew the promise he was making now was one he fully intended to keep: *Until I have this boy, I will never stop.*

Sixty-Two

As they approached the twin towns of Tabatinga and Leticia, Grayson leaned across Charlie and pointed out the border crossing. The area was brightly lit, with both sides clearly marked with large flags. They landed in Leticia, on the Colombian side, where they were met by a dozen fully armed—and very hyped-up—Colombian soldiers.

Grayson managed to stand up in the chopper's doorway, and made a big show of handing over the two handguns right away. The soldiers' English was even worse than Charlie's or Grayson's Spanish. Like Rabassa had predicted, they looked like teenagers, and they had no clue what to do. Finally somebody made a phone call and they must have been told to wait for their boss to arrive.

Rabassa kept yelling at the soldiers the whole time, in Spanish, about how important he was and how they should arrest the *gringos*. They might have done it, too, except once they realized who he was, their attitude toward him turned hostile. They'd obviously heard of him—and hated him. They shoved him around like cops shove a street punk, and locked him and his pilot in a room while they waited.

The young Columbian soldiers had a different attitude toward Grayson. They took great care carrying him off the helicopter and inside. The way he presented himself and talked to them—injured as he was, and in his broken Spanish—impressed the hell out of them. Charlie thought at first they were afraid of him, then decided it was respect, not fear.

The soldiers brought them water, and some Hershey bars—which Paulo wouldn't eat until Charlie said it was okay. They came up with a wheelchair for Grayson, and a bottle of aspirins that he took a handful of. Ten minutes later their boss arrived. His name was Cordero and he was a sergeant. Not much older than Charlie, he had slick hair and a mustache like Clark Gable in *Gone with the Wind*. But he seemed smart, and he spoke English.

Grayson apologized to Cordero, but said he couldn't really explain everything. He said Rabassa had been holding the three of them illegally and that if Cordero would let him use a phone he knew he could reach someone who'd straighten the whole thing out. The guy let him make the call. It took awhile, and when he finally got through Charlie could tell it was Brasher he was transferred to. He gave a summary of what had happened and told her where they were. "I have Flavio Rabassa," he said, "and I want my orders."

Grayson listened for awhile, and then it was clear he was waiting for someone else to come on the line. Finally he identified himself again and listened some more. "Yes, sir," he said. "I . . . uh . . . I understand, sir." He didn't look happy as he handed the phone to Cordero. "Someone wants to talk to you, sergeant."

Cordero took the phone. When he spoke it was in Spanish, and too fast for Charlie to understand. Mostly, though, Cordero listened, like Grayson had, and he seemed even more pissed off about what he was told than Grayson had been. Finally he slammed the phone down on the table in front of him, and left the room without saying a word to anyone.

"What was that all about?" Charlie asked, at the same time pulling Paulo's chair closer and patting the boy on the shoulder.

"He doesn't like what he heard," Grayson said. "They're saying he's to send Rabassa back to Brazil at once."

"But Jesus, the guy's a monster. He oughta be—"

"You think I like it? But I'm not surprised. That mission my men and I were on? Top-secret . . . and fucking illegal as hell. Although you never heard me say it." Grayson shook his head. "Forget what 'oughta be.' This is the fucking army." He shrugged. "Anyway, for the three of *us,* everything's fine."

Grayson went on to explain that in the morning a helicopter would be there to pick them up and take them back to the base where Charlie and Paulo had played checkers. "The DEA guys and I will be staying on there a few days for medical treatment and debriefing. I don't *know* what's next for you and the little guy."

Eventually Cordero returned, and he still looked mad as hell. "I have confirmed my orders," he said. "I am to send Flavio Rabassa and his pilot back to Brazil, and to send you on your way. I am not to inquire of you what has brought you here."

"Okay," Grayson said.

"No." Cordero shook his head. "Not okay. I do not desire to let this man go free. I believe he has committed some crime worse than detaining you, and that you know what it is. This captain of the Brazilian federal police, he is known among the people along both sides of the border here. It is said he takes money from the drug traffickers to look the other way."

"Maybe," Grayson said, "but he's not under your jurisdiction."

"Not my jurisdiction?" Cordero shook his head. "I will tell you a story. A year ago the elders of a tiny village not far from Rabassa's police compound stepped forward and accused Flavio Rabassa of seizing their young men and women, forcing them to work to help build his personal residence. They spoke of torture, and sexual abuse. Shortly after that the bodies of two of those elders were found beside the road. Their skulls were crushed, as though in a vise. The charges were withdrawn." He looked at Grayson. "This too was in Brazil, close to the border, 'not my jurisdiction.' "

"I understand," Grayson said, "but—"

"The man is worse than an animal. He abuses even small children. My men, they know this." Cordero nodded toward Paulo. "Children such as this silent one." He turned then and pointed a finger straight at Charlie. "You, *señor?* I think you know Rabassa abused this boy who clings to you. But I am to let him go."

"Jesus Christ," Charlie said. "You think I don't wanna—"

"Hold it!" Grayson leaned toward Cordero. "You give Charlie here his way and he'd launch a rocket up Rabassa's ass and blow his fucked-up brain to the moon. But you and me, sergeant, we're soldiers. We got orders." He leaned back in his wheelchair then, and grimaced in pain. "But you know what?" he said. "Like everyone else, this man's time will come. Some day he'll step in front of a truck, or have a bolt shake loose and drop an engine or something off his aircraft, or maybe some villagers will catch him alone. Whatever." He stared at Cordero. "And when that happens, my friend, will anybody cry one goddamn tear about it? I don't think so."

Cordero stared back at Grayson. "I will see that you are taken for medical care," he finally said, and then he stood up and left the room.

Five minutes later a soldier came in. He gave some more chocolate bars to Paulo, and then wheeled Grayson away. "To doctor," he said, "to doctor."

Charlie couldn't believe what was happening. When they were in the Little Bird, Lockman admitted the US government had checked out Flavio Rabassa, and knew of his "bothersome reputation." But they traded a little boy to him. Now they were letting the monster walk—just to keep their own damn illegal mission a secret. Rabassa's promise echoed in Charlie's head: *Until I have this boy, I will never stop.*

Finally Cordero came back. "My superiors would not change their orders," he said. "They are under pressure from your government. I can do nothing with—"

"Hold on a minute, dammit," Charlie said. "I need to talk to you."

A couple of hours later, on their way out to watch Rabassa leave, Cordero took Charlie and Paulo first to see Grayson in the infirmary. He was sleeping, with an IV bag dripping morphine into his system. There were two beds in the room, and the other patient—no IV bag for him—was twisting around and moaning in pain. His face was bruised and battered, and restraining belts kept him fixed to the bed.

Charlie stared at the man, then turned to Cordero. "That's Rabassa's pilot, for chrissake."

Cordero shrugged. "My orders are to send Flavio Rabassa back. But of the pilot, nothing was said. My men sought to interrogate him and he was . . . uncooperative. They are not experienced soldiers and should have called me, but . . . now the pilot is in no condition to fly."

"Right," Charlie said. "And Rabassa?"

"He is a pilot himself. He does not wish to wait for a nobody such as this."

Charlie and Paulo stood in the dim predawn light in an open field and watched Capitão Flavio Rabassa climb into the helicopter he was so proud of. He cranked up the engine and the noise was deafening, and Paulo took hold of Charlie's hand. Cordero stood apart, about ten feet ahead of them.

Now, with a big grin on his face, Rabassa leaned from the

chopper door and waved good-bye. No one waved back. The engine roared even louder and the aircraft lifted off. It rose and grew smaller in the sky, and the noise diminished with it.

Finally Cordero did raise his hand and wave, just slightly. *"Adíos, Capitán Rabassa,"* he called.

The chopper was above the tree line, headed east, toward where the sky was turning a reddish blue. Charlie stared at it and wondered—

Paulo squeezed his hand tight . . . and Charlie saw what Paulo saw.

The helicopter had two propellers—what Brasher called "rotors"—and the smaller of the two, the one in the back, flew right off and hung in the sky a second before it fell out of sight. The chopper itself kept going at first, then tilted over on its side, and finally the whole damn thing started spinning around and around, like in slow motion, as it dropped. Charlie lost sight of it when it got below the tree line, but he heard the crash as it hit the ground . . . and then heard the explosion. A ball of red and orange flame shot up above the trees, then died down right away and finally there was only a flickering glow— and huge billows of black smoke rising up.

Paulo had his arms around Charlie's waist and his face pressed into his side. No one moved, until Cordero turned and walked back to them "The *capitán's* pilot should be grateful for his injuries, *sí?*"

"I know *I'm* grateful," Charlie said. "That part was bothering me."

Cordero nodded. "It is well known that the Brazilian police do not maintain their equipment carefully. Perhaps a bolt shook loose."

"Uh-huh," Charlie said. "And I guess Rabassa's time must have come."

"Claro que sí." Cordero nodded again. "And I guess nobody will cry one goddamn tear about it."

SIXTY-THREE

By Wednesday morning Maria had heard nothing. She was convinced that Paulo had been left with his uncle, and she was frightened to death for him . . . and Charlie. She was alone in the mess hall at the air base, sipping on a cup of cold coffee, when she heard someone by the door and looked up. It was Charlie, his shoulders slumped, a sad, tired look on his face. She jumped up, but he just turned and went out the door.

Then he came right back in again, grinning, and this time he had Paulo with him.

Charlie laughed and laughed and she made a mental note to kill him. But she couldn't really be angry. In fact, she was so happy she burst into tears. She hugged Paulo until the boy finally pulled away and grabbed Charlie by the hand and dragged him to the food counter.

She herself was suddenly aware of the smell of bacon frying, and she realized how hungry she was. They all picked out their breakfasts, and while they were eating Brasher came in and explained that Lockman had suffered a severe head injury when the Little Bird, taking off in the storm, brushed through the top branches of a tree. He'd been airlifted somewhere for medical attention. Then, that morning, Flavio Rabassa himself had died when his own helicopter malfunctioned and crashed. As for what to do next, she was waiting for word from Washington.

As it turned out, Charlie and Paulo were too tired to eat much, and they both went off to bed.

At six that evening, without Paulo, Maria and Charlie were back in the mess hall for supper. And, at Maria's request, Brasher joined them.

As far as Maria was concerned the next step was simple: get Paulo home to Porto de Deus. The problem was Charlie. He'd somehow gotten it into his head that *he* should keep Paulo. Maria really cared for Charlie, but his trying to raise the boy wouldn't work, and she couldn't believe he didn't realize that.

"He needs a father," Charlie said, "and I'm gonna be it."

"My God, Charlie," she said, "you can't just keep him because you *feel* like it. At the very least, Sister Noonie would have to consent. Which I'm sure she won't."

"Also," Lynn Brasher said, "the government . . . the Immigration Service among others . . . would have to be involved. It's probably impossible."

"Is that so?" Charlie said, and Maria's heart sank at the tone of his voice. "Well, if the government doesn't want to help me on this, maybe what's 'impossible' is for me to keep my mouth shut about where I've been the last few days."

Brasher leaned toward him. "I'd think hard about that, Charlie." She was serious, but not unfriendly. "You'd be way over your head."

Maria felt nervous, even afraid. That morning she'd been so happy and excited, and now . . .

"Look," Brasher said, "we can't take Paulo straight on to Rio now, anyway. My orders are to get you three on that plane and back to the United States. To Chicago. The plan is to return Paulo to Maria's custody there, and then choose the best way to get him back to Rio."

"Hold it," Charlie said. "What about helping me get—"

Brasher held up her palm to stop him. "I'll take it to my people. Who knows? Maybe, if the orphanage agrees, something can be worked out. Meanwhile, we leave tonight. Zorina must be anxious to see you. Maybe she can help you reach an agreement about the boy."

Sixty-Four

The plane didn't leave until past midnight and it was late Thursday afternoon, back at the Lytham Inn, before they had a chance to talk things over with Zorina. Charlie was sure she'd know how much Paulo needed a father.

"Porto de Deus may be a great place," he said, "for a kid with no one to take care of him. But Paulo *does* have someone. I know what it's like to grow up without a father. I'll adopt him. He won't have to go back to that—"

"Do you *still* think Paulo was abused at Porto de Deus?" Maria asked.

"No, I know better now. And I think I know why Paulo's old man didn't just skip the country after his jailbreak. He must have known his brother was abusing Paulo, and went and got him."

"Yes," Maria said, "and then trusted the orphanage to raise him."

"Okay. But damn, why didn't that nun *report* what Rabassa did? Another cover-up by—"

"Perhaps Sister wondered," Zorina said, "how she would prove it. Paulo would say nothing. His father was a violent criminal and was soon dead. The police would listen to one of their own, and—"

"Yeah, well, whatever." Charlie stared out the window. "Look, I saved him. He likes me. I can take care of him."

"We know you risked your life." Maria laid her hand on his

arm, and her touch and the tone of her voice made it hard to be mad at her. "Paulo's very fond of you. And I am, too. I mean . . ." Her voice trailed off. "That is, Zorina and I are *both* fond of you."

She seemed embarrassed, and he didn't dare look at her.

"But Paulo is from an entirely different culture." Charlie pulled his arm away, then, but she kept talking. "He'd have to learn a new language, and—"

"He understands some English," he said.

"Yes, some," she said. "But it's not just language. He'd have to adapt to a whole new world, and Paulo has so many problems already. Losing both his parents. Abused by the very people who were supposed to be protecting him. These things have left terrible scars, and not just the physical ones. Beyond his loss of speech, we don't even know yet what effect there's been."

"What are you, an expert on kids?"

"No, Charlie, I'm not, but—"

"So what do *you* think?" he said, turning to Zorina. "You're the one who said I was chosen, that Paulo was my responsibility. Tell *Maria*. I mean, I risked my life to save him . . . so I should get to take care of him. What's wrong with me as a father?"

Zorina finally spoke up. "I do not have the answer, but I have listened to your words, Charlie Long. You should pay attention to them."

"What words?" Charlie said. "What are you talking about?"

"You say you have taken a great risk for Paulo, which no one denies. And then you say, 'so I should get to take care of him.' You speak as though you have won a contest."

He couldn't believe she was saying that. "You know what I meant. I didn't mean what you're saying."

"These are not *my* words, but *your* words," she said. "That you should 'get to take care of him.' But, even at such a price as you have paid, a boy is not something to be won, or even earned, by another."

"I didn't say that, dammit. You just don't want me to—"

"Please." Zorina spoke very softly. "You love this boy, and he clings to you. These things I see, but not everything. And therefore I do not tell you what you should do." She paused. "You must ask yourself what is best for the boy. That is all I will say."

It wasn't what he wanted to hear. "What's best for Paulo," he said, "is to have a father. A man, you know? To teach him stuff . . . like how to throw a football . . . or whatever. And put a roof over his head, and buy food, and see he goes to school and stays out of trouble."

"You're right, Charlie," Maria said. "But right now you can't do that. You haven't finished your education. You don't have a job. You can't afford a decent roof over your *own* head. Paulo needs care and attention that you simply are not able to give him."

"Yeah, right," he said. " 'Care and attention.' Like taking him on a field trip and letting him—" He stopped. "Sorry," he said.

"Yes," Maria said. "I have to live with that. But don't you see that—"

"Wait, please," Zorina said. "Such a decision needs more time, and thought. We should ask the woman, Lynn Brasher, how much time we have to decide."

"Yeah, well, okay," Charlie said, but really, it was such a simple decision.

"First let me tell you what I've been told," Brasher said. "So far, no one's backed up Charlie's allegations. If Lockman did what Charlie says he did, he was acting outside his authority." She sounded like a lawyer. "He was not authorized to trade Paulo for any hostages, if there *were* any hostages."

"Jesus!" Charlie couldn't believe what he was hearing. "You—"

"I'm also to tell you Paulo is to stay here in the hotel overnight, to be sure he has no residual medical problems. I assume you all want to stay, too?" When they nodded, she went on. "Then tomorrow, Friday, assuming he's fine, he's to be turned over to Maria, as the representative of Porto de Deus. If you like, we'll be able to fly Maria and Paulo—again in a government plane—directly to Rio de Janeiro. The boy won't need papers."

"Hold on a minute," Charlie said. "What about—"

"Or the flight can be delayed until Saturday. The government has no position regarding who eventually has custody of Paulo. If the orphanage agrees to an adoption, and if you keep your allegations to yourself, the proper agencies here will work with their counterparts in Brazil to expedite the process."

"Allegations?" Charlie said. "That's bullshit. You—"

"Beyond nine a.m. Saturday the plane won't be available, and you'll have to make other arrangements. Of course, I'll expedite whatever paperwork Paulo would need in that event."

"Just 'expedite whatever paperwork' will help me keep Paulo here," Charlie said, "and I'll shut up."

"That can happen if the orphanage agrees. But whatever's decided as to the boy, the Justice Department insists that you all keep silent about any alleged trade for hostages. That's their word: 'alleged.' I'm to emphasize that your continued silence is vital to the national interest."

"Yeah, I bet it is," Charlie said.

"Make up your own mind about going public, Charlie," Brasher said, "but like it or not, I can't help. I wasn't along on the Little Bird. Other than what you say, what I know about this operation is what Lockman told me. Or, as *they* put it, what I might *allege* he told me. People way higher up than I want a lid on this, and if Lockman recovers—and that's questionable right now—God knows what he'll say. But believe me, it won't be designed to help you, or me."

"What about that guy Ferris? And Grayson and the other three? They were right there."

"I wouldn't count on anyone backing up your story. Some cans are better left unopened."

"Yeah? Well, I'm not—"

"We're all tired," Maria said. "Tomorrow's Friday and we can go to my house. My father and Alicia are in California, and I'll call and tell the housekeeper she doesn't have to come in. We'll have all day alone to—"

The door opened and a DEA agent came in and handed Brasher a phone. "For Charlie Long," he said. "A Chicago police investigator."

"Damn, are they still interested in me?"

"They found traces of blood in the alley behind the Billy Goat Tavern," Brasher said. "No DNA results yet, but it's the same blood type as that private investigator, Riggins. They found his body in a garbage dumpster. You were a suspect."

"What the hell," Charlie said. *"Me?"*

"Don't forget, you lied to them."

"Yeah, but—"

"Special Agent Ferris was in possession of a .45 semi-automatic, the type of weapon thought to be used in Riggins's murder, and he ran the prints taken from it—on Lockman's orders. Only two were identifiable—both of them yours. What Lockman intended to do with that is . . . well . . . it's unclear."

"He was gonna frame me, for God's—"

"At any rate, I've had the weapon delivered to the Chicago investigators and informed them it was found right where you told us you threw that Russian's pistol. That's taken off the heat, but you witnessed a homicide and they want a statement.

You have to cooperate."

Charlie felt like a Ping-Pong ball. "First you say you *might* help me if I keep my mouth shut, but then you say I have to tell the cops what happened."

"Just be open," Brasher said, "about what you saw in the alley, and what happened at Maria's. As long as you don't mention hostages, or Flavio Rabassa, then the DEA will cover you. You won't have to worry about an obstruction charge, and we'll give you what help we can with the boy. But you have to go. There's only so much interference any locals will take from a bunch of federal agents."

"Yeah, well . . ."

"It's important." She gave him the phone. "There's a killer still out there."

SIXTY-FIVE

Charlie took the train downtown in the morning. He'd meet the others later at Maria's.

Sal was waiting for him, wearing a suit this time, looking like a real lawyer and giving Charlie shit about how it was Friday and he'd scheduled a day off to sleep in and then go to his mother-in-law's that afternoon for her birthday, and now he had to spend his morning saving Charlie's ass. Same old Sal.

As they drove to Area Five Headquarters, Charlie told Sal what happened after Sal had left him at the police station. About finding the note and going up to Maria's house, and the Russians coming and grabbing Paulo again. About the DEA showing up, too. But not why. Nothing from Sunday morning on. Nothing about hostages, or flying to Colombia, or Brazil.

"They'll bust your ass for hiding the kid and not reporting the murder. And they'll wanna know where you been all week."

"As long as I shut up about anything from Sunday on, the feds say they'll cover me."

"Maybe," Sal said. "I'm your lawyer, though. You gotta tell *me.*"

"I can't." He felt bad, but the feds might find out if he told Sal, and he needed their help.

Sal pulled over and stopped the car. "Okay, asshole. You're on your own again."

"Hold on, I told you . . . it's confidential. Vital to the national interest."

"Forget the 'confidential' bullshit," Sal said. "Attorney-client privilege. I can't tell anyone."

"Yeah, but—"

"But nothing. I'm leaving you here, right now, unless you tell me."

So Charlie told him. About Lockman, and the hostages, and Rabassa, and trading Paulo. He felt better when he finished. "But keep it to yourself," he said. "If none of it gets out the feds are gonna help fix it so Paulo doesn't have to go back to that orphanage in Brazil."

"Yeah? Where's he going?"

"He's gonna stay with me. I'm gonna adopt him."

Sal stared at him. "You're shittin' me," he finally said.

"What?" Charlie said. "You don't think I can take care of—"

"You can hardly take care of *yourself*. Jesus, you can't even keep a job."

"That bullshit job? That job was too . . . I don't know . . . boring."

"That was the idea. Boring. So you could use your damn brain to study and graduate and go on to law school, for God's sake." He shook his head. "No way that kid should stay with you."

Charlie was stunned. Was he the only one who knew how much a kid, especially a boy, needed a father? But by then they were pulling into the lot at Area Five. Sal parked where it said Police Vehicles Only and they went inside.

Maria woke up Friday morning and opened the drapes on a dark world where a slow, steady rain was falling. She had the sense she'd been dreaming about someone she loved going away, or dying, but the dream had dissolved, and left her with only the sorrow.

She'd called Shorewood Point the day before to tell the

housekeeper, Annie, that she needn't come in. Then, out of nowhere, Annie told her Donald Fincher had been calling. "I told him I didn't know where you was," Annie said. "But I don't think he believed me. He got mad. 'Tell her to call me or else,' he said. His number is—"

"Just write it down for me, okay? I'll get to it." But she knew she would get to it only to say good-bye. She'd come to clarity about Donald, but that didn't make her feel any better about hurting him.

She didn't want Charlie hurt, either. And she didn't want him mad at her. Brasher's promise to facilitate Paulo's staying with him in the United States had gotten his hopes up for nothing, and they'd kept arguing even after they'd agreed to wait till today. She'd warned him. "I don't think Sister Noonie will agree."

"She will," Charlie answered, "if you recommend it. There are doctors here, and schools and decent jobs and good food and everything. Don't you think he'll have a better chance of a good life here?"

"Actually, no. And don't forget, without Paulo being there, Porto de Deus would have to find a new home."

Charlie had brushed that aside. "Who could object to the orphanage staying on his property, other than his legal guardian? And if that's me, they stay."

Nor had Zorina been much help. "It is not my place," she said, "to tell Charlie Long what to do." Which seemed odd, since Zorina's telling Charlie what to do is what had kept him so deeply involved with saving Paulo in the first place.

She met Zorina and Paulo in the VIP Room for breakfast. Paulo kept looking around, and she knew exactly whom he was looking for. She explained that Charlie would join them later at her house.

Zorina didn't say much more than Paulo did—which was

nothing, of course—and that didn't help lift Maria's spirits.

After a breakfast Maria didn't even taste, Lynn Brasher came and said a quick good-bye. A DEA agent was waiting to take them to Shorewood Point.

"Well," Maria said, as they pulled away from the hotel, "we're on our way." She was anxious to sound cheerful despite the rain and her own dismal mood. "There's food in the refrigerator and the key will be under the mat. There won't be a car for us to use, but if we want to go anywhere we can call a cab. Okay?" Getting no answer, she leaned toward Zorina, who was in the front seat. "Is that okay?"

"Yes," Zorina said, but as though she hadn't really been listening.

Maria leaned forward. "Are you feeling ill?"

"Just tired, my dear. That's all."

With Zorina obviously not feeling well, and Paulo staring out the window wishing Charlie was there, it would be a cheerless ride. But when they got there she'd turn on lots of lights and put on some music. There was a box of kids' games and puzzles in one of the upstairs closets and she'd dig that out. While Zorina rested, she and Paulo would play and she'd throw off this shroud of gloom and anxiety.

She'd call Sister Noonie, too, and tell her about Charlie wanting to keep Paulo. Sister would be able to help him understand.

It would all work out.

SIXTY-SIX

Charlie felt things went pretty well with the cops. It was obvious Brasher had talked to them. They stuck to what he saw in the alley, how he snatched Paulo and ran, how he ended up in Lake Forest, and how he beat up the third Russian. They didn't ask why the feds showed up, or go beyond that.

He went through two books of mug shots and picked out one guy—the thug he saw chasing Paulo inside the Billy Goat, the same one who shot the parking valet at Maria's house. He'd never even seen the other guy, the one Paulo bit in the hand. But those two were both dead, anyway.

Then he picked out the older guy, the one who pulled the trigger in the alley and drove the Beemer at Maria's. "That's him," he said. "I thought I killed him, at first."

"Too bad you didn't," one of the cops said. "He's not an enemy you want still walking around."

They told him to keep himself available because they'd want him to view a lineup if they pulled in a suspect. "It could be any time, day or night. You be here, understand?"

"Hold on," Sal said. "I don't want you communicating with my client. You call me. I'll call him."

The cops weren't real happy about that, but Sal wasn't all that easy to contradict. "Besides," he told Charlie on the way out, "they're just pissed because they been tied down by the feds, so they're jerking you around. They don't usually make someone come in at two in the morning to view some mope in a lineup, no matter if the mope's got Clarence Darrow for a lawyer."

"But if they call, get me right away. I don't need cop trouble. I got a *kid* to take care of."

"Yeah, right," Sal said. "Anyway, I got an extra cell phone in the car. Keep it with you wherever you go. And keep the damn thing turned on."

Heading up the drive to the front door at Shorewood Point, Maria felt better. The rain had stopped. She and Paulo and Zorina got out of the car, and the only drops still falling were from the trees and the eaves of the house. The sky, still overcast, seemed a lighter shade of gray. It was good to be home again.

The key was where Annie said it would be, and the DEA agent waited while she unlocked the door. Then he waved and drove off. Inside, she led Zorina and Paulo through the house, turning on lights as she went. "This way," she said. "The kitchen's the coziest place on the whole first floor."

She tossed her purse on the kitchen counter and had Zorina and Paulo sit down at the table. The kettle was where it had always been, and she put water on to boil. She found tea bags and a lovely little flowered pot Alicia must have gotten, probably in France.

"I know it's only eleven thirty and not that long since breakfast," she said, "but we deserve a snack. We'll have a big meal later, after Charlie's here. And Charlie *will* be here, Paulo. Don't worry. He misses you, I know, as much as you miss him." Paulo stared at her and she said it again in Portuguese, as well as she could, and he seemed to understand. "Now," she said, "let's call Sister Noonie."

The same wall phone was still there, in the same spot above the counter to the left of the sink. The keypad was in the receiver and there was a long, coiled cord, so she grabbed the receiver with one hand and opened the cabinet with the other. She found a package of oatmeal cookies and tossed it on the table.

"Oh, the number," she said, and turned back to the counter, tucking the phone under her arm so she'd have two hands to dig into her purse and—

She stopped. She'd felt something odd. No, *heard* something. Or *didn't*. She took the phone from under her arm and listened. No dial tone. She shook it, then hung it up. "You guys stay here," she said, and ran out, through the brightly lit dining room, down the hall, past the stairway. When she finally got to the phone on the little table near the front door she snatched up the receiver.

No dial tone.

There'd been rain, yes. But no lightning, no thunder. And the phone had been working fine when she spoke to Annie yesterday.

"Zorina! Paulo!" she screamed. "We have to get out of here!"

No one answered.

SIXTY-SEVEN

"That guy," Sal said, "I know who he is."

"Huh? What guy?" They were driving away from Area Five.

"That ugly thug whose picture you IDed. The one you beat the shit outta. Dimitri Chechov."

"Bullshit," Charlie said. "The cops didn't say his name. How would *you* know him?"

"I don't *know* him, asshole. I know who he *is*. And since when are the cops gonna say shit to you or me? Anyway, this guy Dimitri's been around here maybe a year or two. From Russia by way of New Jersey. I saw the fucker in broad daylight, at my Uncle Rocco's body shop."

"I thought you never went over there anymore," Charlie said, "what with Rocco being in the business and . . . you know . . . being a made guy and all. You said—"

"Rocco's got the idea I owe him, and sometimes he has things he wants me to do. Calls it paying installments, and . . ." Sal shook his head. "Anyway, the Russian I saw is the one you fingered."

"And he's hooked up with your uncle? Jesus, I'm gonna have *Rocco* on my ass now?"

"Just the opposite. Whatever him and Rocco had going, he screwed Rocco on it big time. Rocco's pissed at this man like you can't believe."

"If it's really the same guy."

"I'd bet my right nut on it," Sal said. "It's him. He was, like, big time in Russia. A paid assassin. Plus, snatching street kids and selling 'em for prostitutes was one of his things over there. Girls, boys, whatever there's a market for." He paused, then said, "That guy in the alley, how'd he shoot him?"

"How?" Charlie said. "I mean, the guy was, like, sitting up against the wall and—"

"And did he shoot down through the top of his head?" Sal asked. "Was he, like, aiming down so the slug would go through his neck and down into his body?"

"Jesus, right."

"That's him. Dimitri Chechov. I tell Rocco you fingered the guy, the only reason he'd be pissed at you is he'd rather settle up with the asshole personally."

"Yeah, well, don't mention my name, okay? Anyway, by now this Dimitri guy's holed up back in New Jersey somewhere. Maybe Russia. And, not to change the subject, what're you doing for a couple of hours?"

Talking Sal into driving him to Lake Forest was easier than he thought it would be. They stopped for sausage and pepper sandwiches, and while they sat in the car and ate, Sal called his wife. "It's me," he said. "I'm gonna be late." He paused and listened. "Yeah, I know it's her birthday. But something's come up. It's for Charlie, you know?" He listened some more, then, "Yeah . . . for sure." He signed off and rolled his eyes at Charlie. "I gotta be there by four o'clock—no way out."

Maria held tight to the dead phone, terrified, scarcely able to breathe. They had to get out of the house. There might be a cell phone lying around somewhere, but—

But why didn't Paulo or Zorina *answer?* She dropped the phone and raced back down the hall, through the dining room, into the kitchen. And stopped.

"You sit," the man said. He stood behind Paulo, pointing a

gun at the boy's head.

She heard what he said, but suddenly couldn't get her legs to move. Like her body was shut down, except she could hear how the water on the stove was just about ready to boil.

He was a broad, muscular man in a rumpled gray business suit, no tie. Maybe sixty years old. She'd never seen him before, but she knew who he must be, with his Russian accent. His battered, bruised face must have been too painful to shave after Charlie left him half dead on the driveway, and gray stubble covered his cheeks and chin. His eyes shone too brightly, as though he had a fever.

"You sit," he said again, "or I kill boy."

She moved very carefully and sat beside Zorina at the table, across from Paulo and the man standing behind him. Paulo sat perfectly still, his eyes wide open, but his little body scrunched up as though shrinking into itself. Even if he survived, how would his psyche ever be healed?

"What is it you want?" she asked. "You must know you can't—"

The screech of the teakettle stopped her. The man jumped visibly, but then put his free arm around Paulo's neck. He dragged the boy up from his chair and onto his feet and pulled him backward, away from the table and the stove.

"Tea," he said. "Only for me. Not you." He waved the gun at her. "Make tea, bitch!"

She got up and, with hands trembling wildly, managed to put a tea bag in a mug and pour in boiling water. He told her to leave it there on the counter and go sit down again. He was being careful, and she did what he said.

As soon as she sat down the man made Paulo sit again, too. "If any trouble," he said, "I shoot boy first." He took the mug and drank the near-boiling tea with tiny sips. "Now I wait, for this man Charlie Long."

"Charlie?" Maria said. "He . . . he's not coming here. He—"

"You were lying to boy, then, when you say how much Charlie Long misses him?" The man shook his head. "I wait."

"But you don't have to wait," she said. "I'll give you whatever you want. I have money."

"No money. I wait for Charlie Long, to kill him."

"No!" She half stood, but he leaned toward her and she sat back down. "Why?" she asked. "What has he—"

"Is payback." It wasn't fever shining in his eyes; it was madness. "Payback," he repeated, "for my brother and my son."

"You mean . . . those two men who came in after Paulo? That was your brother? And your son?"

He nodded. "My one son."

"But Charlie didn't kill them. It was the drug agents . . . on the beach. Not Charlie."

"He interferes with my business. He makes my brother and my son die." He glanced down at Paulo. "Now I take two lives. Is payback. Then I get away. And if no?" He shrugged. "I have nothing now, no life."

"But you can't—"

"Wait, Maria," Zorina interrupted. She tore open the package of cookies and slid it across the table, closer to where the man stood. "You are hungry."

To Maria's surprise the man set down his tea and took the package. He dumped the cookies out on the counter and started wolfing them down, but never lowered the gun.

Zorina said, "Only one person is responsible for all that has happened. That person is me. Take my life alone. And then go, while there is still time. You will recover from your loss. Everyone recovers who wishes to recover."

"But I do not wish." He swept the remaining cookies off the counter, sending them flying across the room. "And you, your life is of nothing to me."

"It is the boy you would kill, then?" Zorina said. "But he has done nothing."

"I kill boy for what he is . . . to Charlie Long." His voice was calm again, but cold and mean. "I watch Charlie Long lose child, like me. Then I kill him." He paused and smiled, as though enjoying the thought. "Maybe I kill you, too. Both of you. But most important is boy." He nodded. "Is payback."

SIXTY-EIGHT

Sal wanted to sleep, so Charlie drove. If he could convince Maria that he was up to taking care of a little boy, then the nun would go along, for sure. He rehearsed his arguments, and before he knew it they were at Lake Forest. He found the business district and the train station, and from there he found Maria's house.

The sky had brightened for awhile, but now dark clouds had moved in again and the wind was picking up. He slowed to a stop by the Shorewood Point sign, but didn't turn in.

"Well?" Sal had woken up, and was in a hurry. "This it or not?"

"Yeah. I'm just . . . nervous, I guess."

"About the girl, right? What's her name? Maria? Chick's got to you, I can tell."

"Yeah . . . maybe a little. But the thing is, I gotta convince her I can take care of Paulo, and—"

"To buy that she'd have to be as dumb as you. Anyway, hurry up. I got a birthday I can't miss."

Charlie turned into the drive. The wind was whipping up, bending the trees and lifting dead leaves and blowing them around in little whirlwinds. It was surprisingly dark for the middle of the afternoon and, Christ, the place was gloomy looking. He drove slow, leaning and looking through the trees. He finally made out a light shining in one of the first floor windows. Him, he'd have turned on every damn light in the house . . . on a dark windy day like this . . . as soon as he walked in the door. Just to celebrate being home, and safe, and all the bad stuff being over.

He stopped and they both got out. "You coming in?" Charlie asked.

"Hell, no. I gotta get back." Sal hustled around and got in the driver's seat.

When Charlie rang the bell the door swung inward. He turned and waved, but Sal was already gone. When he turned back, no one was there in the doorway.

"Paulo?" he called. "You're hiding behind the door, aren't you buddy. You can't fool me."

He stepped inside, and the door slammed shut behind him and there was Paulo. And beside him the same goddamn Russian thug—Dimitri something—pointing a gun at Paulo's head.

He was so fucking mad at seeing one more person trying to hurt Paulo that he lost it. Which was good, because if he'd been thinking he wouldn't have thrown himself straight into the son of a bitch and knocked Paulo away before the guy could get off a shot.

The two of them landed on a little table and it gave way and they hit the wall and the gun did go off then, with a deafening blast, and they both crashed to the floor. The Russian roared like a bull, like he'd been shot, but he didn't let up at all. They wrestled and thrashed around, Charlie grabbing and twisting the man's wrist and hand, fighting for the weapon, a stubby revolver. Christ, this guy was strong! Then, suddenly, Charlie had the gun, but holding it by the short barrel and only for an instant before the guy slammed his wrist and hand against the wall and the gun went flying.

Charlie screamed at Paulo, "Run! Run!" Over and over. And at the same time fighting like a maniac. Clawing, scratching, kicking, punching. Except his right hand hurt like hell and was useless. It felt like his wrist was broken, and maybe some bones in his hand.

He made it up to his feet somehow, standing over the fucker and kicking at him wildly. The guy ignored him, though, and scrambled around on all fours, looking for the gun. Charlie looked, too, but couldn't see it anywhere. He kicked hard at the guy's head. The asshole moved and the kick didn't quite hit dead on, but it sure must have shaken his brain. He stopped crawling and sank flat-out on the floor.

Charlie stood there holding his injured hand up to his chest and breathing hard. His ears were still ringing from the gunshot, but he heard a noise behind him—and spun around.

It was Zorina, and she had Dimitri's gun in her hand. "Hurry!" she said. "Maria and Paulo." She was out of breath, her chest and shoulders heaving like she'd been running hard. "That way." She pointed. "Through the kitchen. To the beach. Go help them."

"Not without you!"

"I cannot run. You must go," she said, still gasping for breath. "The phones do not work. What if there are other men, chasing them? Why do you wait?"

"Give me the goddamn gun," Charlie said. Dimitri lay facedown. He'd caught that bullet, and blood seeped through his pants leg onto the floor. But he was still breathing. "I'll kill him right now."

"No!" She stepped back against the wall. "He is helpless." Her eyes were bright with anger . . . or fear. "Please," she said. "My breath, I cannot run. But I can stay and watch him. And I can use this weapon." She raised the gun with two hands and fired a shot into the wall above Dimitri. "Please trust me to do this." She pointed the gun at the man, who still hadn't moved. "Maybe this one came alone, but we do not know that. I am afraid for them. Go and bring them back and we will get help. Please!"

She was begging, and he couldn't bring himself to fight her for the gun so he could shoot a wounded man in front of her. Besides, maybe Dimitri *did* have help, and Paulo and Maria were out there somewhere. "If he tries to get up," he said, "you'll shoot him?"

"Yes, I promise. Hurry!"

He raced through the house the way she pointed, into the kitchen and outside. The wind was stronger than ever and it was raining hard. He ran across the patio and down onto the grass. The lawn sloped in terraces toward the lake and the grass was wet, and he kept sliding and slipping as he ran. Jesus, it was a long way. He finally got to the steps and started down to the beach, then saw Paulo and Maria. Halfway down, looking up at him through the rain and the whistling wind.

"Have you seen anyone else?" he screamed.

"What?" Maria called back.

"Any other men?"

"No! Just the one who—"

He turned and ran back up the steps. How did he let Zorina talk him into leaving her alone with that maniac? Just as he reached the deck at the top he heard something, barely audible above the wind.

What he heard was a gunshot.

SIXTY-NINE

Charlie stood on the deck above the beach, frozen for an instant, then saw Zorina step backward out onto the patio, pointing the gun back through the door, using both hands. Her shoulders jerked and there was another shot, and she turned away from the door and ran, stumbling in the driving rain, fighting to keep her balance. At the edge of the patio she stopped, obviously to catch her breath. Then Dimitri appeared in the doorway and came out after her. He dragged his wounded leg along, and held his hand up to his left shoulder as though he'd been shot there, too. But he was coming, and Zorina was old and winded, and he was going to catch her.

She went down the patio steps to the grass, the gun in one hand, holding her skirt up and away from her legs with the other. By then Charlie was running again up the sloping lawn, but she turned and headed toward the trees. She was going away from him, and on the slippery grass he'd never get to her before the Russian did.

He yelled, but in the wind and rain she couldn't hear. She kept looking back at the wounded animal coming after her and then . . . she stopped! She couldn't go any farther. Shoulders heaving up and down, she turned to face Dimitri and lifted the gun again with both hands. The guy stopped and ducked to the side. Zorina fired. Once, then again.

Her shoulders and arms jerked up each time she fired. And then they didn't, because she was squeezing on an empty cylinder. Her arms dropped to her sides, and the gun fell to the ground.

She sagged to her knees, hunching her shoulders and gasping for breath. Charlie kept running, and the Russian finally turned and saw him coming, and veered away and headed into the trees. He'd been shot—at least twice—and he had no weapon. But Charlie ran after him anyway, anger and adrenaline both driving him. He only had one good hand, but he'd catch the son of a bitch and make sure this time that he'd never be able to come after Paulo again, or—

"Charlie!" Maria screamed.

He stopped and turned, and saw Maria and Paulo running— not toward him, though. Toward Zorina. She was still upright on her knees, still gasping for breath, but her body swaying forward and backward now. Charlie let the Russian go and ran to her, and Maria and Paulo arrived beside him. He crouched in front of the kneeling Zorina and caught her with his one good hand just as she fell toward him.

He held her upright and her head came up slowly and she saw him, and seemed surprised. "Charlie Long," she whispered, and smiled, and said something else . . . something about "see-ing." That's all he could make out. Then she closed her eyes and he could tell she was struggling to take a breath, but somehow couldn't seem to pull it inside of her. Her body stiffened for a few seconds, like she was using every bit of her strength—and then she went totally limp.

Maria screamed and pushed him out of the way and he let her do it. He knelt in the wet grass, with Paulo beside him, and they watched as Maria struggled to do whatever she could to revive Zorina. Rolling her onto her back. Pulling, pounding, breathing into her mouth. Crying. He thought he should be helping her, but he had no idea what to do. Besides, his wrist and hand were useless.

He knew it wasn't going to work, anyway. Zorina lay there with her eyes closed, not responding at all as Maria pushed and pulled at her, and Charlie knew she wasn't going to be there, not anymore, to tell him what his responsibility was, to remind him to face up to it.

Maria finally gave up. She sat back on her heels, breathing hard. When she turned to face him, there were tears streaming down her cheeks. "Charlie," she said, "I'm so sorry." Jesus, she was worried about *him*. He didn't know what to say. She lowered her head and covered her face with her hands.

The rain poured down over them. Charlie's hand hurt like hell, and he pulled it to his chest. He looked at Maria, then at Zorina on the ground, and then at Paulo. The boy—his boy— was crying. Charlie closed his eyes. And then he cried, too, and he didn't try to stop himself or hide it. He just knelt there on his knees in the rain, and sobbed.

Finally his crying slowed down. His breath came in short, sharp gasps, and he opened his eyes. Paulo was staring at him. The boy leaned forward and reached out one small hand. He ran it down Charlie's face, wiping his cheek, then pulled his hand back. He looked down at his fingers, studying them, as though trying to pick out the tears from the rain. Then he looked up again.

"Charlie Long," Paulo said. "Charlie Long."

Five minutes later Charlie was running down the driveway toward the road. He'd finally come to his senses and thought about the Russian. The guy was wounded and wouldn't be back, not now, but he might get away again. Maria said the phone lines were cut—which is when Charlie realized he'd left the damn cell phone in Sal's car.

He had to find a phone. The wind had died down, but it was still raining. When he got to the road he hadn't gone far when he saw a car coming. He waved his arms and knew whoever it was would think he was a maniac and wouldn't stop.

The car did stop, though. It was Sal, for chrissake, and he lowered his window and held out the cell phone. But when Charlie grabbed for it he pulled it back. "First you gotta hear what happened," Sal said.

"No, there's a guy out—"

"I get maybe half a mile away from here and I see this Ford Taurus parked way up on the grass along the road and I wonder who the hell parks like that. And just then I notice, shit, you left the damn cell phone in the car."

"Call nine-one-one, dammit! There's a guy out there who—"

"Shut up and listen," Sal said, "for once in your fucking life. I turn around and I'm bringing the phone back and I see this guy come limping out of the trees, headed for the Taurus. I slow down and . . . Jesus Christ, it's goddamn Dimitri. So . . ." He didn't finish.

"So?" Charlie said. "So what? You let him drive away? What?"

"The guy can hardly walk, and still he puts up a helluva fight. Turns out he's been shot, twice. And I'm thinking, Jesus Christ, Charlie shot the son of a—"

"Cut the bullshit! Where is he?"

"If I told you, you'd have to tell the cops. Right?" Sal nodded, answering his own question for Charlie. "But this way you're gonna wait a couple minutes to let me—and whatever might somehow be stuffed into my trunk—get the hell outta here. Then you're gonna call the cops. You're gonna say I dropped you off and you haven't seen me since." He handed Charlie the cell phone and started to pull away.

"Hey! Wait. Where you going?"

Sal stopped and looked back. "To my uncle Rocco's," he said, "to pay the last installment on my debt."

SEVENTY

The rain was down to just a drizzle, and after he called the cops Charlie went and sat with Maria and Paulo, out beside Zorina's body. "We were locked in the pantry," Maria said, "just Zorina and I, and we heard the fight. Then Paulo came back and let us out. He had the gun and Zorina took it. She convinced me to take Paulo down to the beach and hide, while she went back to help you."

"If she wouldn't have done that," Charlie said, "she'd still be alive."

"Maybe, but maybe not. She had trouble with her breathing and . . . and I think a bad heart."

"She had a son once, y' know?" Charlie said. "But he's dead."

"Yes, she told me—in the pantry. We were in there a long time and we were both really scared and she told me. He was just a little older than you are when he died."

"No way," Charlie said. "He was like Paulo's age. I saw his picture. 'He was taken from me,' she said, 'right after that photograph was made.' "

" 'Taken,' yes. As a child." Maria nodded. "But it was her son's *father* who took him then . . . and ran off with him. She said she should have gone after them, but she gave up, thought it was hopeless. She never saw her son again, not till he was twenty-five years old. Then he just showed up one day, walked through her door. He was . . . well . . . she said he was a lot like you, Charlie." Maria stroked Paulo's hair as she spoke. "She said he was young and smart, but . . . you know . . . no job, not such great friends, going downhill. Drinking a lot. She tried to help him, but he . . . one night he was drunk and stumbled into the street in front of a car, and was killed."

"Jesus, she . . ." He could hardly talk. "Still, though, trying to save me today killed her."

"In a way," Maria said, "but that's the way she wanted it."

"What? Why do you say that?"

"I told her she should take Paulo and run, and I'd go help you. But she got angry. She said you were *her* responsibility. Then I *got* it. Trying to save *you* was what she was doing all along."

"Me? You mean, like . . . because she couldn't save her son, so she had to save me?"

"I think so. That was part of it. But more than that, too. Once she got you to change your mind, and not take Paulo to the police, she felt responsible. 'You can't step into someone's life,' she said, 'and take him in a new direction, and not be responsible for him.' She said you understood that."

That's exactly what Zorina had told him on the day he showed up at her place with Paulo. So she saved both of them. Saved him by getting him to save Paulo. "She told me I was an angel," he said, "chosen to save Paulo."

"She was right." Maria reached over and took his hand.

He jumped a little when she did that, and then he reached and took Paulo's hand. The three of them sat on the wet grass and looked at Zorina. They hadn't covered her face because her eyes were closed and she looked so peaceful and . . . well . . . beautiful. He stared at her, this woman who'd had the gift of seeing, and wondered who it was who'd chosen *her* . . . to be *his* angel.

He was still wondering that when he heard the cop cars come roaring through the gate and up the long stone drive.

SEVENTY-ONE

The big woman, Nita, went to work in the kitchen at Porto de Deus—and her granddaughter, too. Grayson had warned Charlie it would be a hard sell getting them into the United States, and Brasher agreed. And Jesus, what would they do if they got here? So Charlie talked to Maria, and she talked to Sister Noonie.

And Paulo? After saying Charlie's name that day in the rain, he clammed up again, and the psychologist said it might take a long time. Years, maybe. "But some day he will talk," she promised.

The psychologist was in Rio, and so was Paulo. Because when Charlie put his mind to it again, it seemed so clear. "Damn," he said, "what was I thinking, anyway? This kid needs care and attention I can't give him. He needs other kids around. He needs his own country, and Porto de Deus, his home, where people love him—even if he doesn't talk." Of course Charlie loved him more than any of them, which made it tough.

Maria took Paulo back to Rio on the government plane, and Charlie was surprised at how badly she wanted him to come with them. "You've *got* to see the orphanage, and meet Sister Noonie." But he didn't go. He couldn't stay there forever, and it wouldn't get any easier when he had to leave.

He'd stay in touch with Maria, and maybe they'd all get together again. Maybe. Which meant maybe not, too. Things had to shake out. They'd saved Paulo's life and now the kid had lots of work to do. He needed help, sure—who didn't?—but it was work no one could do but Paulo. Charlie could see Maria had work to do, too, a life to figure out. She might become a nun, even. He should stay out of the way.

Zorina had first seen Charlie, and then she'd turned him around. Saved his life, for chrissake. Now Zorina was gone, and he had to find his own damn way. School . . . job . . . friends. Whatever. Maybe he'd see something in her crystal ball—which he kept in a box now, on top of his dresser—but he didn't think so. Anyway, if he was going to be any use to anyone, Charlie had to get busy saving Charlie. Like Maria had to get busy saving Maria. Like Paulo had to get busy saving Paulo.

ABOUT THE AUTHOR

David J. Walker is the author of eight previous crime novels, four in his "Mal Foley" series, and four in his "Wild Onion, Ltd." series. *Saving Paulo* is his first stand-alone novel.

Walker has been an Edgar® nominee, and is a past president of the Midwest Chapter of Mystery Writers of America. He is a full-time writer and lives just north of Chicago.